Advance praise for *East Coast Girls*

"Kerry Kletter's *East Coast Girls* is a mix of gorgeous writing and page-turning suspense as four friends enjoy summer pleasures that lead to terrible mistakes, desperate choices, and, as we all hope from the ones we love, the grace of forgiveness."
—Nancy Thayer, *New York Times* bestselling author of *Surfside Sisters*

"With lush prose and poignant reflections on fate, forks in the road, and the power of female friendships, *East Coast Girls* is a book whose pages demand to be both snuck in under the covers late into the night and savored. I've already made a permanent place for it right beside Judy Blume's *Summer Sisters* in the bookshelf of my heart."
—Chandler Baker, *New York Times* bestselling author of *Whisper Network*

"*East Coast Girls* is a dazzling and thoughtful beach read that brings to life the unique friendship of four unforgettable characters, a gorgeous Montauk setting, and a driving mystery that touches on timely feminist themes. Readers of Elin Hilderbrand and J. Courtney Sullivan will devour this book."
—Brenda Novak, *New York Times* bestselling author of *One Perfect Summer*

"A powerful and compassionate story where young lives are forever altered in the aftermath of tragedy. Beautifully layered with hope, sorrow, and keen observations into the complexities of the heart."
—Beth Hoffman, *New York Times* bestselling author of *Saving CeeCee Honeycutt*

"A brilliant firecracker of a book. *East Coast Girls* perfectly captures that time in a girl's life when friendship and the summer sun is enough to make you feel invincible—and the fallout when you realize that you're not. A beautiful, heartfelt, and life-affirming story about the things worth holding onto and those moments when you just have to let go."
—Emily Henry, author of *Beach Read*

"With equal parts true grit and big heart, *East Coast Girls* is an unputdownable exploration of the enduring bonds— and unexpected tests—of friendship, love, and who we are deep down."
—Mia March, author of *The Meryl Streep Movie Club*

Also by Kerry Kletter

The First Time She Drowned

EAST COAST GIRLS

KERRY KLETTER

mira

Recycling programs
for this product may
not exist in your area.

ISBN-13: 978-0-7783-0949-9

East Coast Girls

This edition published by arrangement with Harlequin Books S.A.

For questions and comments about the quality of this book, please contact us at
CustomerService@Harlequin.com.

Mira
22 Adelaide St. West, 40th Floor
Toronto, Ontario M5H 4E3, Canada
BookClubbish.com

Printed in U.S.A.

For my hometown friends of Ridgewood NJ
especially my own crew of first responders
Amanda Fredericks
Marti Daniel Moats, Ruth Brown and John Tashjian
because you are home to me.

EAST

COAST

GIRLS

PROLOGUE

It was mid-July, when the sun shined the memory of every good summer before it, and the days wandered like beach walkers, hot and indolent, catching chance breezes off the ocean. They'd stopped at the fair on a whim on their way back from Montauk, were supposed to be home hours before, but the vibrancy of live music and crowds and the feeling of a party not yet over beckoned them, so they lingered, wanting to stay inside this future memory a little longer.

The photo booth was Hannah's idea, and now they erupted out of it into the flash and shimmer of daylight, giddy with the theater of posing. The image spat out like a lottery ticket and Hannah reached for it. But Maya, ever impatient, yanked it out of her hand. Maya squinted at it, covered the other three girls' faces with her thumbs. "With a little cropping I think we might just have a masterpiece!"

"Oh, give me that," Blue said, rolling her eyes.

They passed the photo around, each looking down at their leaping white smiles, their faces full with youth and colored by the sun. There was a looseness in their eyes from the peach wine coolers purchased at a local deli with the worst fake ID ten bucks could buy and a heavy dose of Maya's winning charm.

As usual Maya was in the center of the picture, hugging the others like dolls to her chest, her three best friends who had never asked her to be anything but who she was, who never hinted that she should contain her big spilling personality in order to be loved. Beside her, Blue was wearing the sweatshirt of a boy she met earlier that weekend, the sleeves carefully rolled to the elbows, the memory of his kiss, her first, alive in her stomach as if it had been caught there, netted like a butterfly. Renee was squeezed in practically on Blue's lap, half cut out of the photo, her head on Blue's shoulder as it so often was, as natural as sunlight on trees. And finally, Hannah was on the other side of Maya, her arms outstretched in raucous exuberance, her red hair a wild burst, salted and wind dried after a day in the ocean, her face blurred with laughter at something Maya had said just before the camera clicked.

They'd been captured in perfect summation—four best friends celebrating their recent graduation from high school.

"I love us," Hannah said. "Best vacation ever!"

Maya placed the photo in her purse. "Promise we'll come back every year, no matter where we are, for the rest of our lives."

"Yes!" everyone agreed.

"Should we make that pact in blood?" Hannah asked.

"I think we're good with just…ya know…saying it," Maya said.

"So…" Blue said, nodding toward the parking lot where they'd hidden the booze in the car trunk. "I feel like I'm starting to regain my balance. Round twelve, anyone?"

Hannah hit speed dial on her phone as they walked. A moment later Henry's voice came on the line. She pictured him, hair probably slicked from a post-tennis shower, a wry smile at the corners of his mouth. He was not handsome in the classic sense, but there was a benevolence in his eyes, a kind of soft patience, that made him so. He said something Hannah couldn't make out over the staticky sound of a local band playing through bad amps, the tinny merry-go-round music, the meandering crowd full of parents and children. But she heard the tender tone of his voice. He missed her.

She put him on speaker and held her phone out to the girls.

"Hi, Henry!" the other three shouted, sticking their faces into the phone, making kissing noises.

"Loons," he said, and they laughed. Though he belonged to Hannah, he was theirs, too, the extra limb.

Hannah took the phone off speaker, put one finger in her ear to block out the noise.

"Are you having fun?" Henry asked.

"Yes, but I miss you." She missed him every summer when the girls took their annual trip to stay at Blue's nana's beach house. But the longing itself was part of the fun, a romantic ache that reminded her how lucky she was.

He said something she couldn't hear.

"What?" she said.

"Come home."

Her heart whooshed. "We're leaving soon. Can't wait to see you!"

"Bring me a souvenir!" he said. And then, "Never mind. All I need is you."

"Cheeseball," Hannah teased, but her face hurt from smiling so big. "Love you so much." She ended the call, already daydreaming of their future. She imagined the two of them renting a small summer cottage that sat watch over the ocean, a hammock lolling in the breeze, a picnic table where she could sit on pink-lit summer evenings and write. As much as she was excited to attend college together, she was more eager for what followed, for the realizing of all their plans and dreams. Henry would take over his parents' newspaper, and Hannah would teach college classes while she worked on her book. They would have a house on an intimate East Coast campus outside Boston or perhaps in Maine, hosting potluck dinners with bright-eyed students and fellow teachers, talking poetry and literature and current events. She would catch Henry watching her from across the table—he loved when she got passionate about things—and she would smile back at him. How safe she would feel being a family with him, living in a warm, loving house just like his parents' home, and nothing like her own, so depressive and quiet.

"Hurry, Hannah," Maya called.

Hannah moved to catch up with the others, pausing just a moment to consider a psychic at a booth, a young woman with white-blond hair, a sharp, narrow chin and big, loopy earrings that hung like small nooses. She made a mental note to tell the girls about her. It would be fun to get their palms read before they left.

At the car, Blue dug into the trunk and retrieved the wine

coolers and a water for Hannah, who was their designated driver, and passed them around.

"A toast," Maya said. "To you three lucky bitches who get to be friends with me!"

Maya waited, arm in the air, while they stared at her. Blue coughed.

"Okay, fine," she said. "You're shy. I get it. To us, then."

The girls raised their arms high and clinked, faces glowing with hope, the sun igniting in the glass bottles as if they had caught it there.

"To us," they all said in unison, four forever friends on the cusp of their lives.

TWELVE YEARS LATER

HANNAH

Another July. Hannah sat by Henry's bedside, her wild red hair pulled into a tight bun, her pale face underlaid with gray like winter light. She stared out the window as she so often did these days, the view familiar as a painting, inciting surprise and a sense of unreality anytime life appeared inside it, a person passing by, for instance, or a bird fluttering past.

The day was in slow retreat, the night sky drawing its navy blue blind upon it. Soon a nurse would be in to give Henry a sponge bath. Hannah closed the book of crossword puzzles she'd brought, as if they could actually do one together. On the nightstand, a picture of the two of them at senior prom, their smiles almost too big for their faces, Maya, Blue and Renee goofing in the background. She'd planned to put it in the frame she'd brought back for him from the summer fair all those years before, but then as soon as the girls got home from their trip, tragedy had struck, and she couldn't bring herself to even look at the gift he'd been unable to receive.

Now she squeezed Henry's pale hand, soft and round as sorrow, and watched his face, hoping for his eyes to register the touch or the sigh or the puzzle book or her leaving.

Once in a while, out of nowhere, he would be suddenly present, wide-eyed and able to recognize her, as if his mind had simply wandered off somewhere, gotten lost in a wooded dream and then unexpectedly emerged through a clearing. At these times, she, too, would feel instantly awake, her heart lit up as if on a wick. Each day she sat waiting for it. A tight prayer in her chest that this time he would stay. *Maybe tomorrow*, she thought when it didn't come.

She leaned in and kissed his untroubled forehead just below the cowlick. The faint bready smell on his neck—that scent of home, of the breathing soul inside—always gave her comfort. Then she walked out into the hallway, passing rooms inhabited by people so much older than both her and Henry. In the last was Mrs. Miller, all cotton-ball hair and lived-in eyes tucked inside a shriveled brown face.

"High five, Mrs. Miller," she said when she spotted her sitting in her wheelchair, hunched but alert, in the doorway of her room.

The old woman raised her delicate, tremoring hand for Hannah to slap. Hannah couldn't remember when or how they'd developed this ritual, but it always buoyed her to see her youth reflected in the wistful gaze of Mrs. Miller. It was as if the old woman could see the expanse and promise of Hannah's life, and for that moment Hannah, too, could imagine it, could almost believe in something beyond her small routine.

"Are those new slippers?" she asked, pointing to the old woman's leopard-print footwear. "I'm telling you, Mrs. Miller, you're bringing sexy back."

"Ninety is the new eighty-five," Mrs. Miller said with a wink, and Hannah watched with something like envy as the full history of her laughter crinkled across her face.

Mrs. Miller reached up and Hannah bent to her hand, which caressed Hannah's cheek. "You seem tired," Mrs. Miller said. "You come every day. I don't know how you do it. But you're not going to do him any good if you don't take care of yourself too."

"I do," Hannah lied. "I'm fine. Really. Thanks though."

She said her goodbyes and hurried out the door into the breezeless, sticky summer evening.

Moments later she was on the Metro, watching the tunnel walls flash past, wondering as she always did how all that graffiti got there. The train shrieked and rumbled, and she imagined the crash of steel on steel as the car coming from the opposite direction bore down on them. She turned to the businessman beside her and envisioned a bomb going off from inside his briefcase. She looked up at the three teenagers looming over her, pictured one pulling out a gun. Finally, she caught her own reflection in the window, her red hair too bright and conspicuous, her body tucked into the smallest package she could be. She doused her hands in Purell, closed her eyes to the world.

The Metro chimed at her stop and the doors opened. She was jostled with the crowd, pushed toward the steep stairway, climbing up to the small square of sky at the top. Her apartment was a short block away.

Her cell phone rang. She glanced at it, saw that it was Maya.

She hit Ignore. She loved Maya, but right now the world felt like too much, and she would have to call her back on a day when it was less so.

Once in the safety of her small apartment, she took off her clothes and put them in a plastic bag, zipping it tight so that whatever Metro germs were on them wouldn't leak out. Maya often told her how neurotic this was, as if she didn't know it. Sometimes she watched those television shows about extreme obsessive-compulsives, and a gnawing worry would hatch in her chest that someday she might be one of them. She could see how it could happen, how each day you needed to do just a little bit more to make yourself feel secure, until one day you woke up to find your entire apartment wrapped in plastic, no hole to breathe through.

"Why don't you just get a hazmat suit and call it a day?" Maya had said recently.

Maya had limited tolerance for Hannah's anxieties, which Hannah actually appreciated. Something about the way Maya trivialized her concerns helped to shrink them, took some of the terror out. Hannah had laughed the comment off, not admitting that she thought it was a great idea. Nothing gets in. Nothing gets out. She'd even priced them on Amazon.

Her cell rang again. She sat down on the couch, pressed herself against the pillows and waited for it to stop. A moment later, a text from Maya appeared on the screen.

Pick up the phone, loser.

Hannah rolled her eyes and smiled. But still she didn't answer. She was just too tired today. Every day, really.

I know you're sitting in your apt. ignoring me.

She sighed.

Unless you're dead.

Are you dead?

Hannah considered the question.

The phone rang again.

This time she picked up, realizing that the calls wouldn't stop until she did. "I do go out, you know," she said.

But Maya, who never listened, wasn't listening. "Hold, please."

There was a series of clicking noises, Maya muttering to herself and then silence.

"Okay," Maya said finally, "I've got Blue on the line too."

Hannah frowned. They never did three-way calls. Something must be up. "Hi, Blue," she said.

"Hey, you," Blue said.

"Okay, ready, Hannah?" Maya asked.

"For...?" Hannah braced.

"My great idea!"

Ever since they were kids, Maya was always having "great ideas" that not only weren't great but, in fact, were epically terrible.

"No really, this time it's a good one!" Maya said into Hannah's pointed silence. "Nothing like that time we got locked out of my house and I said that you could fit through my doggy door."

"That was me, actually," Blue said. "I still have the scar."

"No, Hannah has the scar."

"Different doggy door," Hannah said.

Though they talked often on the phone and through varying forms of social media, it had been a while since Hannah had seen either of them in person. Adult concerns had slowly eclipsed superfluous things like fun, and the seductive promise of technology had rendered in-person visits seemingly unnecessary. The last time they'd been together was for Blue's father's funeral a few years back. Hannah had taken the train from DC and Maya drove in from New Jersey, and the three of them had gotten so bombed in Brooklyn after the wake that they almost missed the service the following morning. Hannah and Maya knew it was what Blue needed, how she honored the man who had never been present for her—through dark-humored toasts and temporary obliteration. In retrospect, Hannah's life had been slightly more expansive back then—each year it seemed to shrink a little further, the way people's bones do as they age. Occasionally Blue would come to DC on a work trip and they'd have lunch, and those visits were always the highlight of Hannah's small life. But it had been twelve years since all four of them, including Renee, had been together in one place. Twelve years since the summer that would both haunt and link them and Henry together for the rest of their lives. Shortly after that, Blue had taken off to some small school in Vermont with a name Hannah always forgot, Maya to Ramapo College in New Jersey before dropping out entirely, and Renee, their long lost fourth, to Duke. Only Hannah had stayed in DC, her plans to attend UCLA with Henry shredded. She went to community college instead, unable to leave him behind. It was never even a question. It was what he would have done for her.

"Anyway," Maya said. "The reason I'm calling is because we're going back to Montauk."

"What?" Hannah said.

"Long weekend. You, me, Blue and a twelve-pack of wine coolers—just like old times."

Old times. If only. Old times seemed like someone else's life—that's how far removed she felt from her carefree youth or their summers together in Montauk. They'd spent two weeks every year there at Blue's nana's beach house, staying up late and laughing until they'd cried, playing drunk truth or dare in the kitchen and watching the sun climb out of the ocean by the lighthouse. She thought of them soaking in light over long, luxurious days at the beach, chasing the umbrella they'd failed to secure as it skidded like a leaf in wind across the sand, Maya pretending to drown to get the attention of a cute lifeguard, ice cream and souvenir T-shirts and more laughter. The last time life had been perfect, the last time Hannah had ever believed it could be.

Now she looked out the window. The evening had turned cloudy with the promise of rain.

"Before you even *think* about saying no, we made a vow. Remember? We said we'd go back every year, and now we're almost thirty. We *have* to go back before we turn thirty."

"I'm already thirty," Hannah said. "Thanks for the card by the way."

There was a pause.

"Let me tell you something," Maya said. "I am sick and tired of the postal service. Rain, sleet and snow my ass."

"Mmm-hmm."

"Come on, it's gonna be great! We'll rent a convertible and

wear our old bikinis, maybe even accidentally run over an-other fruit stand. Seriously, this is nonnegotiable."

Hannah remembered Maya plowing through the fruit stand, bright oranges bouncing like giant hail off the wind-shield, Nana's Volvo coming to a stop in the potato field be-hind it. That was the summer Nana was teaching them to drive, and there had been a moment of shocked silence before Maya said, "Well, I guess that wasn't the brake," and Nana said, "It appears not," and then they all burst into hysterics. Later Nana said the price of paying for all those oranges was worth it just for that one good laugh.

Now Hannah smiled at the memory. It seemed impossible that the girls were ever that innocent. When they didn't know what life could do.

"Where is this all coming from?" she said. There seemed an unusual urgency in Maya's voice.

"Stop overanalyzing and say yes," Maya said.

"Maybe next year," she said.

"We can't go next year," Blue said. "We put Nana's house on the market."

"Oh no." Hannah could hear the sadness in Blue's voice. It made her sad too. They all loved Nana so much, the one adult in their world whom they'd trusted. But Blue was forced to move her into a home last year when Nana lost the last of her memory. Already, Nana's apartment in Manhattan had been sold; the Montauk house would probably go just as quickly.

"Now or never," Maya said. "It will be so fun!"

Hannah tried to picture herself on an actual vacation, re-laxed, driving with the top down, sea salt and the smell of cut grass on the wind, the rosy sunset blushing across the Atlantic, her lifelong friends beside her. She felt a pressure lift. Then she envisioned all the terrible things that could happen. Their car swerving off the road. Careening into the ocean. All of them going under. What would Henry do without her? "I can't."

"You need to," Maya said.

"I have things to do, Maya. I have a life."

"What things? You don't have things. And you definitely don't have a life."

Hannah tried to come up with examples, but the truth was she worked from home and was beholden to nothing. Well, nothing except Henry. She wanted to tell them about how well he was doing lately, how just a few days before she could see his eyes tracking her with understanding as she talked, and then as if to prove it, he had smiled at her. Smiled! At her! And, my God, didn't they know there was no more important place to be, no more important thing to do than to witness that? But she knew it would be a mistake to talk about Henry. It was the unspoken condition of their friendship that she speak of him as little as possible and definitely never of the night that changed them all. Anytime she'd tried, she'd felt her friends' walls go up. Maya didn't like to talk about hard things. She put them away like china in a cupboard, stored them somewhere just out of reach. Blue simply didn't know *how* to talk about them, grew uncomfortable and shifty.

"Really, I want to, but…"

"Sorry." Blue made crackling noises into the phone. "I think you cut out there. Did you hear her, Maya?"

"Sounded like she said yes."

"I said—"

"Hold, please," Blue said and began humming Celine Dion's "My Heart Will Go On" into the phone.

Hannah tried to speak over her. Blue hummed louder.

Hannah sighed and leaned against the wall and wished she was still the kind of person who could do, who would dare. She wanted to ask them how they went about saying yes, or at least saying it ever again.

"Listen to me. Are you listening to me?" Maya shouted over Blue's singing. "You're coming. Do you understand me? Ask yourself this—when was the last time you were truly happy? You know the answer. Now go pack your bags. We leave the day after tomorrow. Blue and I will even pick you up."

"We will?" Blue said.

"Yes—road trip!" Maya said. "It'll be great."

Hannah chewed her lip. "I'll think about it," she lied and hung up the phone before they could argue.

But the thought was like an earworm the way it kept wiggling its way back into her consciousness. She missed her friends. She missed *fun*. She missed herself—the girl she'd once been with them, the one who would've already had a suitcase packed. She thought of the fortune-teller at the Bridgehampton fair all those years ago with that fountain of white hair and that pointy jaw that jutted out like an accusation, whose face had startled when Hannah sat down before her and let her palm be read. She still wondered what would've happened if only she had listened to her warning, how different her life, all of their lives, might have turned out.

Pointless to think about, she told herself. *Besides, I can't leave Henry*. She climbed into bed, convinced, and fell asleep with the TV light flickering across her closed eyes.

Even in her sleep Hannah could sense the storm when it came, beating at her windows, thundering around the building, making the city its drum. She was restless inside all that rain, inside Maya's question about happiness, and in her dreams the storm got inside her apartment, the water rising higher and higher. She woke at one point with the sheets so drenched that she decided she had leukemia and spent an hour online both confirming her diagnosis and discovering several other deadly afflictions she had, as well. She could practically hear Maya's voice in her head saying, "I'll give you a diagnosis. Batshit crazy."

In the morning the sky was the color of loneliness, and in the jaundiced light of her bedside lamp, the walls seemed to close in on her like a migraine. The phone call from Maya and Blue had latched like an infant to a breast at the back of her mind, a small incessant tug, a hunger. She made instant coffee in the microwave, turned on her laptop and sat on her couch with both, hoping to distract herself with work. There were so many letters to answer. It was something that Hannah both loved and hated about her job. So many people sought out her counsel, and most of the time it amused her to be perceived as someone who knew things, and perhaps in moments, she believed that she really did. Other times the sense of being something she wasn't made her solar plexus ache like someone had hurled a baseball through it.

Henry's mother, Vivian, had given her the job at the paper. Even before disaster had struck, Vivian had always been kind to Hannah, intuiting, Hannah suspected, that her parents were...not very loving. Now that the two of them shared the bond of pain, Vivian was even kinder.

"It doesn't pay much, I'm afraid," Vivian had said, "but nothing is easier and less taxing than dishing out advice— which is why everyone feels the need to give it so freely."

Hannah had secretly wanted to write obituaries instead. She'd thought there might be something in the reviewing of a life that might reveal the secret of how one went about having one. Or at least on her better days that was why she had wanted the job. On her not-so-better days, Hannah wanted to know all the ways a person could die so she could know what to avoid.

Now Hannah opened the first letter of the morning and sighed. *Dear Miss Know-It-All: My neighbor's dog barks incessantly. I'm going crazy! What should I do?* Not for the first time, Hannah wondered what kind of people took the time to write in to an advice columnist. She decided that most of them were probably like her, reclusive and frightened, hoping that seeing their words in print might offer proof of their existence, something they could cut out and tape to their fridge the way an Everest climber marks their place in history with a flag. They often signed their letters "Anonymous," which Hannah suspected was more an attempt at accuracy than privacy.

Most of the letters answered themselves, the writers already knowing what they wanted to do but looking for permission to do it. People were always looking for permission to be who they were, to feel what they felt, which was, of course, always the thing that scared them. She tore through a few more letters, trying to pick out the most interesting ones—but they all seemed like the same problems, the same answers. Why didn't people ever change? Always stuck in ruts that made them unhappy but unwilling to give them up. She caught her reflection in the mirror beside her bed, frowned, looked away. The clock said 10:00 a.m.—it was time to go see Henry. She got up, got dressed, buttoned her raincoat against the day.

It was cold for summer, and the rain was dirty, splashing from its puddles up into her shoes. On the way to the Metro, she saw a group of girls, four of them, laughing as they raced down the street, reminding her so much of Maya and Blue and Renee, of those times when even rainy days felt sunny. Hannah watched them live inside the hug of friendship, her longing like talons inside her.

By the time she reached the care facility, her pants were plastered to her skin. An image of the beach popped into her mind, its warm sand, the rupture of ocean spray, a vibrant sun spoked with shiny beams. She buried the thought, or tried to. The long-term care facility, usually strangely comforting in its familiarity, today seemed as cold and sterile as an autopsy suite. The sound of her footsteps down the empty hall echoed in the aching hollow of her chest.

Henry was in his wheelchair, eyes glazed and fixed on the wall. She'd fallen for those eyes back when they were fourteen and she'd walked into her favorite bagel shop one morning and there was a new person behind the counter—Henry. She recognized him from school, though they never talked and rarely crossed paths. He'd taken the part-time gig to pitch in for his college tuition, though his parents were against it, said he didn't need to. He was so responsible like that, so determined.

She started going every day, and when the tinkling doorbell announced her, he would glance up from beneath a flop of bangs with this shy, delighted grin, almost like he'd been waiting for her. Each time he looked at her like that, she'd get this acrobatic tickle in her stomach, a kind of intense internal smile. Soon, she noticed he was tucking in his shirts, his hair began to have comb streaks in it and he was taking more time to select her bagel—always choosing the biggest ones. Then an extra packet of cream cheese began appearing in her to-go bag.

He had a boss that ordered him around with mumbling, indecipherable words, and one day Henry did a perfect imitation of him just loud enough for Hannah to hear. She'd erupted in giggles, the sound surprising even her, and he had beamed at her with such unabashed glee—as if making her laugh was the best thing he'd ever done. A week later he wrote a note on a napkin and tucked it into her bag with her order. *Do you want to go to a movie with me?* He'd supplied check boxes with preset answers: *(1) Yes. (2) I'll think about it. (3) Ha ha not in a million years, and even then still no.* The following day when she bought her bagel, she handed him the note back with her cash. She'd checked yes.

That first date she was so nervous, but when he tripped over his own shoelace and crashed into a cardboard cutout of Tom Cruise and sent their popcorn flying, she realized he was way more anxious than she was. "Meant to do that," he'd said and proceeded to bump into multiple objects, including her, until they reached their seats. She'd loved his desire to make her laugh and his efforts to win her—his cologne and scrubbed face and ironed shirt. She'd relaxed until the lights dimmed and her breath caught being next to him in the dark. They'd sat with their arms slightly touching and her skin tingled every time he shifted, his crisp shirt brushing against her bare arm. Her hyperawareness of his nearness was something new to her, so magical and distracting. The movie was some stylish indie that was clearly meant to impress her, but she had such trouble concentrating on anything other than him that she couldn't have named a single character or plot point. Afterward he walked her home. The rain had just let up and the bright glow of streetlights echoed off wet roads, the sky washed clean and glossy. He put his jacket around her shoulders, and they bumped teasingly into each other the whole way home just to have that contact. He told her about his dreams and plans for the future and she told him about hers, and already it seemed like they were talking about theirs. They reached her building and he lingered in her doorway, working up his courage. She was so excited at the possibility he might kiss her that she shook with adrenaline. Finally, he leaned in, his pupils dilated and shiny with what looked like love. The moment their lips touched felt like a match against a striking surface, friction and heat turning her whole body into a spark. She'd never been so purely alive or so happy to be so.

They were nearly inseparable after that. Everyone said they were too young to be so serious. That it was puppy love. That it wouldn't last. She was so glad she didn't listen. It was almost as if they sensed that their time together would be interrupted. Even when they were apart each night, they Skyped until they fell asleep and then kept their laptops on so they could wake to each other in the morning. She always woke up earlier than he did so she could see his soft expression when he blinked awake and realized she was there. How seen she had felt in his gaze, how beautiful. He couldn't have known what that meant to her, just to be looked at, just to see in someone else's face that she affected him. Just a reaction, any reaction at all.

To lose that expression in his eyes was a raw, unending grief. But she'd get it back someday. She would.

Now she adjusted the blanket around his shoulders, wiped his mouth, smoothed back his hair. Her fingers grazed the scar. Even after all this time, she could still see the memory of the smile in his face, still hear his voice, hear the laugh now locked away. She sat down beside him.

"I talked to Maya and Blue yesterday," she said, shivering in the air conditioning. "They're going back to Montauk. They want me to go with them. Some sort of turning-thirty-even-though-I-already-am trip. So stupid, right?" She searched his empty eyes. Not that she thought he'd actually respond. But sometimes it seemed like she could see the answer there. Or maybe it was in his eyes that she got permission to see the answer she already knew. "Obviously I'm not going." She could hear her voice sounding strange, sped up. "I would never leave you for that long." She waited. "I'm just saying that I know you need me." She scanned his face again, looking for a reaction, one clue, anything. The rain outside was coming down harder, sounding like a constant blast of radio static. "You do need me. Right?"

His mouth was slack, his glassy eyes staring into some world she could not see.

"I just need a sign."

Some stupid machine behind her in the hall would not stop its monotonous beeping.

"For God's sake, just *say* something!"

Hannah sat back, startled. She looked behind her, terrified that her voice had carried into the hall. Then she turned back to Henry, somehow expecting to see rage on his face, but the lights were still out. There was not even the courtesy of anger.

"Oh, Henry, I'm so sorry." A small sob choked her. "This isn't what I meant to do at all." She stood up, nearly knocking over her chair. "I don't know what got into me." But Hannah did know. She was going to do it. She didn't know how, but she was. "I think I have to go. Or want to go. I'm not sure which. On the trip, I mean. Please forgive me. I'll be back in three days. Just three. I promise." She bent down and hugged him. "I love you, Henry," she said. "Please don't be sad. I'll be back before you can even miss me." She knew if she lingered a moment longer, she'd change her mind. With one last look she rushed out and down the hall.

Mrs. Miller was sitting in her usual spot in the doorway. "Leaving so soon?" she called as Hannah neared.

"I'm… Yes," Hannah stammered, pausing as she reached her, not wanting to be rude. "I'll be going away for a little while. Just the long weekend." She stared at her shoes. "I'm…" She took a deep breath, willing herself to say it, to try it on. "Uh…my friends and I are going on a trip. To the beach." She glanced up, daring to meet Mrs. Miller's eyes, fearing judgment. Instead, the corners of Mrs. Miller's mouth curved into a smile.

"Oh, how wonderful!" she said. "I always loved a good adventure! Bring me something back, would you? A lifeguard perhaps. Preferably a young one. They'll need to keep up."

Hannah smiled with relief, with permission, and Mrs. Miller put up her delicate arthritic hand. "High five."

MAYA

Three states away in northern New Jersey, Maya stood in the middle of the ER and asked, "Where is everybody? It's too freaking quiet in here." The last two hours of her shift were always the deadest, the ones Maya liked the least. Being busy was one of the things about the job that worked for her, the constant running around. She liked to say it kept her thin, though of course it didn't, because she wasn't. Not that she cared. She was a firm believer in conscious self-deception as a life philosophy.

She'd gotten her job as a patient transporter through Blue and her endless connections right after she was fired from her last job. Which Blue had also gotten her. At the time, it had seemed like the worst idea in the world.

"I don't do hospitals," she'd said.

"You don't have a choice," Blue said. "Just be happy you have a job."

"I *am* happy to have a job. I'm just not happy that I actually have to do it."

Blue had sighed in acceptance of the fact that Maya was hopelessly irresponsible and that deep down this was one of the things she loved most about her. Or at least that's what Maya decided the sigh meant.

Now Maya slipped into the locker room for her purse, hoping to scrounge up enough change for a snack. She pulled out her wallet, which was empty, of course. It was always slightly surprising to find no money in it, such was the extent of her optimism. The foreclosure letter she'd received was jammed in the bottom of her purse, unopened. She'd known it was coming. But the sight of it still made her stomach sink anew. She stuffed her bag back into her locker, paused at the single, fraying picture she'd taped to the inside door—the girls in the photo booth at the Bridgehampton fair that last summer, their smiles so big, so easy. She glanced at the small mirror she'd hung above it, fluffed her hair, noticed the first signs of wrinkles under her eyes. She smiled to brighten her face. *Still the prettiest*, she said to the picture. She laughed to herself, imagining her friends giving her the finger as they always had when she said that.

The month of July always snuck up on her, skipped her thoughts and went straight into her body, like a quiet ache in an old broken bone before rain. She refused to give energy to memory, sure that this was why her friends were all screwed up now. They couldn't climb out of its dark well. But sometimes she could still feel it slipping under her closed door, not in words or images, but as a sense of dislocation, as if that night had done more than traumatize them all; it had ejected her from the only sense of home she'd ever known. Considering the letter in her purse, she felt that dislodgment now more than ever. Carefully she untaped the picture, tucked it in her bag, closed the locker door and returned to the insult of harsh lighting in the ER.

Two nurses were sitting at the station, chatting in low voices. Steve, a first-year medical student and world-class pain in her ass, was flipping through a chart, ever eager to find an exciting diagnosis, a patient with something other than the flu or chest pain, an opportunity to be a hero.

"Another day without a rare deadly virus to cure. How will you go on?" she said.

He stared unamused from beneath a mop of hair overdue for a cut. In return, she flashed him her most winning smile. Just to annoy. He gave her the finger. Victory!

"Seriously, though, where is everybody?" She glanced at her watch. She was antsy for work to be over so she could run home to pack. She'd planned on doing it last night, but then she'd bumped into the twenty-one-year-old who'd come in for a follow-up on his broken wrist. She wondered now if he was still in her bed and, if so, if she could borrow a twenty from him when she got home. In a matter of hours, she would be hopping the bus to Blue's and she needed some snacks for the road.

"I'm hungry," she announced to the room.

One of the nurses picked up the telephone; the other got suddenly busy with paperwork. Steve flipped a page in the chart as if he hadn't heard.

"Oh, come on, just a dollar for some chips," she said. "I promise I'll pay you back."

"If that was true, I'd be a rich man," Steve said.

"You'll be a rich man soon enough," Maya said. "Then we'll marry, and every night you'll come home to a freshly ordered-in meal."

"Quick reminder that I'm gay. Also, I'm not supporting your junkie habit."

She pouted in an obvious way, but he was immune.

He put the chart down, walked over, leaned against the wall, scrunching his shoulders to minimize the height gap. A patient was being rolled by. He waited until they passed, pushed his bangs back. "How'd it go at the bank?"

"Oh, fantastic." She pulled a lip balm out of her back pocket and applied it. "An absolute party."

In truth, her meeting with the loan officer had been more uncomfortable than she'd expected. Despite having an appointment, she'd had to wait in the lobby for half an hour watching a nature show play silently on the flat-screen, a hermit crab vulnerable without its shell scuttling across the exposure of beach toward some elusive shelter. She'd wrapped her arms around her stomach, smiled at the woman next to her. "They should serve cocktails and play a movie. If this was a flight, we'd be halfway to Los Angeles by now."

The woman didn't respond, and suddenly Maya wished she'd brought someone with her, someone more competent who could speak on her behalf, or at the very least make her laugh while she waited. She remembered that time Hannah had accompanied her on her first trip to the gynecologist when they were both sixteen. That was right around the age Maya started having sex, and Hannah suggested the appointment, then invited herself along. It was what her friends did. They occupied the space where a parent would be. It was never talked about, it just was—ever since the day Maya's mother had called her a good-for-nothing piece of garbage in front of her friends because she'd accidentally tracked mud onto the kitchen floor. Maya hadn't even flinched at the words, inadvertently telegraphing how often she heard them. That was when her friends knew how alone Maya really was.

There was so much a girl didn't know about the world when she didn't have a mother to teach her. How had her friends, so young themselves then, intuited this? Perhaps because they, too, were motherless in their own ways. All of them helping one another to fill the gaps. She wondered if that had been the original draw between them. Had they subconsciously sussed out one another's orphan needs? You find what you know—isn't that the theory? Either way, Hannah had taken Maya to Dr. Sheridan, the two of them giggling so hard at the absurdity of the stirrups and the cold cruelty of the clamp that she forgot to feel the pain.

How much she'd taken those friendships for granted. No one told her how much harder it was in adulthood to build a family out of nothing. How unmoored a person could be without those connections. But then, who would have?

It wasn't that Maya didn't have friends—she had plenty of them. But not like those ones. Not people who'd been the building blocks of her entire personality, who shaped her heart, made themselves her home. Not friends who would drop everything if she needed them, would accompany her to an icky appointment, be the grown-up when she didn't know how to be. They used to be her net. Now, in adulthood, with both Hannah and Blue in different cities and Renee who knows where, she was being asked to be her own net. It sucked.

Maya had considered mentioning this to the random lady sitting next to her at the bank when a man in a suit introduced himself as Donald and summoned her into an office.

"So," he said, taking a seat behind his large desk. "How can I help you?"

Maya stammered, tried to be charming, to find warmth

in the person sitting across from her. If she couldn't get this loan, she would lose her house. And though she never liked it much—a dinky one-bedroom shack in a less-than-safe New Jersey neighborhood—it was also the only security she'd ever been given by her mother. Her mother had left her with no life lessons, no wisdom, no basic tools of living, but she'd left her enough money to buy that place, and she needed to keep it. It was the only stability she had.

The problem was she couldn't keep up with the property taxes. She hadn't even bothered to open the bills after the first one. Somehow she'd convinced herself no one would notice. What else could she do? She didn't have the money. That was another thing that screwed you when your parents sucked—no one taught you things like money management. And when you don't get taught money management *or* self-soothing, well…it could be a bad combination for your bank account. She knew it was a problem, but once in a financial hole, fixing it was a whole other level of difficulty.

The loan manager had nodded patiently, then smiled that well-practiced, placating smile. "Let me pull up your account," he said.

He tapped at his keyboard, peered at his screen, leaving her to stare at the bone-colored walls, a set of framed awards, a series of pamphlets about credit cards and business accounts and money markets. The minutes swelled into tiny lifetimes. The room felt refrigerated and she, pink and raw inside it, a chilled shrimp.

"So, I'm looking at your credit score, and it's just… It's going to be hard to get you approved. Is there someone who can cosign? A parent? Or relative?"

Maya shook her head, swallowed on something hard.

"Okay. See, normally I would suggest a home equity loan, but I have to be honest... With your FICO score that's going to be tough. My advice really would be to try to clean up your credit. You have a lot of credit cards, a lot of credit card debt... If you bring that down, pay some of that off, you can—"

"Wait, how can I pay off debts if I... I mean, that's the whole reason for the loan. If I could pay off the old debts, I wouldn't need to—"

"Or you can develop a history of on-time payments. We just have to get your score up, because—"

Maya pushed against the threat of tears. "But I don't... I need this money now! Like right now. I don't have time to... to...to develop a history. I'll lose my house! Do you understand?" Her voice was rising, her grip on calm slipping.

"I do. I do understand. I'm sorry, but I can't just... See, we have rules for..."

A wide abyss blossomed inside her, a dark internal bleed.

"I have a job now," she heard herself say. "I'll probably be getting a raise very soon." A lie, but whatever. "All of the bad credit was from before. Look, I just need a few months. I need to keep this house. I... I don't have anywhere to go."

He smiled at her with compassion. Maybe even attraction. She relaxed a little bit.

"Let me mess around with these numbers," he said, "and talk to my supervisor. I'll call you this week."

She leaned forward. "I don't have a week." A sudden dazzle of panic.

"I'll do my best," he said.

"Thank you," Maya said standing, moving toward the door. "I would appreciate that."

"Miss Marino?"

She turned.

"I'm going to do everything I can. But don't get your hopes up."

"Hope is the only thing I have," she said. And it was. It would work out. They would give her the loan. She was sure of it. Then she'd just have to figure out how the hell to pay it back. But that was for another day.

That night she'd gone home and called Blue. It wasn't pride that stopped her from asking Blue for the money. It was that she'd asked so many times before that she wasn't sure Blue would say yes. And the thought of her saying no—she couldn't even think about what that would do to her, how deep that rejection would cut.

"Everything all right?" Blue had asked.

"Why wouldn't it be?" she'd said.

They'd chatted for a few minutes, and then Blue had mentioned that her mother put Nana's house in Montauk on the market. Maya was surprised to find her eyes well with tears. But she'd loved that place and their vacations together there. Nana's beach house was the last place they were innocent, the last place they'd been a family together. Just thinking about it summoned a sense of ease, the way being with your friends could feel like swimming a lazy backstroke beneath a warm embracing sun. How soft life had felt then, surrounded by her best people and a summer sea. No responsibilities. No burdens. No one trying to take the roof over her head. If only they could just go back to that...just for a little while. But then, they could, couldn't they? Before the house sold. That's what she'd realized. They should all go back. No, they *needed* to go back. One last hurrah! A chance to be wild and carefree like they used to be. To be a "framily" again. Man, she could really use that right now—to have her friends in her life. Really in it. Not just texts and calls, but together as one again. It could be like a do-over, a restart for all of them.

"So, listen, I have an idea…" She knew this would be a tough sell. She reminded Blue of the vow they'd made, of how long it had been since they were all together. She said that she'd been given a few days off—which wasn't true, but she could just call in sick. The hospital would understand. Technically it really was in the best interest of her health.

"Yes, let's do it," Blue interrupted. "When do we leave?"

Maya had stared at the phone in perfect shock. "Does Thursday work for you?"

Right after that they'd called Hannah. Got the "no" they were expecting but hoping against. Maya still wasn't sure what made her change her mind, but when she got a text from Hannah saying "What day are we leaving and what time are you guys picking me up?" she wasn't about to question it.

Now Maya stood in the ER twenty minutes before her shift was over and said to Steve, "About that dollar."

"Not happening."

"Have you no pity? My blood sugar is plummeting."

"I can probably score you a glucose tablet."

"There's no time," she said, putting a dramatic hand to her forehead, letting her knees start to buckle.

He laughed and then sighed and pulled the bill from his wallet. There was a clear understanding as the money swapped hands that Steve would never see this dollar again, but Maya liked to think she paid it back with her sparkling personality.

"Hey, by the way," she said, "remember that smokin' twenty-one-year-old who came in last week with a scaphoid fracture? We recently bumped into each other. In my bedroom. Who knew what one could do with a cast?" She waggled her eyebrows and then, knowing the power of leaving an audience hanging, skipped off to the vending machine.

"When are you going to have a real relationship?" he called after her.

She turned, smiled. "What the hell is that?"

She returned with a bag of Fritos to find him sitting at the nurses' station, doing a search on the computer. She stood next to him, peering over his shoulder, crunching loudly into his right ear to get his attention. "Do you think anyone will notice if I slip out early?"

"Yes," he said.

She sighed, glanced at her watch. Sixteen minutes left in her shift. Sixteen minutes and eight hours until she was off to Montauk. She'd tried to convince Blue to take today off so they could get an earlier start, but her great powers of persuasion could only go so far.

Steve stood, stole a chip from her bag and went to check on a patient. She glanced at her watch again, its unmoving hands like prison bars.

Screw it.

She slipped past the nurses' station, grabbed her purse from her locker and bolted for the door. She pulled out her phone, texted Blue with her designated arrival time. Together they would go get Hannah.

She stepped out into the dewy morning, shedding work and adulthood like a bad mood, eager to watch them shrink into the distance until finally she was at the beach, where the whole world would drop away the minute her feet hit sand. The beach would fix everything.

BLUE

Blue double-checked Maya's designated arrival time and grabbed her duffel bag by the door. She paused, glanced back at her apartment, at the sleek contours of her furniture, the spare open space, the walls hung with paintings her interior designer had purchased at auction from Sotheby's. The New York City skyline gathered around her windows, buildings of every height stacked deep, like a photo of a large family reunion.

The cleaning lady had come again that morning. Blue always had her come on the day she left for a trip. Part of it was so she'd have an immaculate place to return to, but ever since her father died and Nana moved into the home, there was also that creepy thought that if something happened to her, some unfortunate person would have to come and get her things in order. Who would it be? Surely not her mother.

No chance she and her new husband would fly in from Paris. She'd probably just send flowers to the funeral home with an impersonal note. No, Blue was being unfair. Of course her mother would come! It would look terrible to her friends at the country club if she didn't. Blue laughed darkly but then thought, *Seriously, who would it be?*

Maya and Hannah were the obvious. She hated the thought of them having to enter her place, how quiet and strange it would be without her in it. Maybe someone from work instead—ugh—one of the Wall Street bros on his lunch break, sorting through her personals while making deals on his cell. Or maybe her building manager.

What would a person think of her when they walked in here? What would her apartment tell of her life? *It looks like a showroom*, she thought. She caught her own image in the mirror, alone at the door, then locked up behind her as she left.

It was early evening and the city was gritty and seething in the airless heat. Cars and taxis nudged one another like a crowd charging for the exits, while swarms of people darted across streets and down sidewalks, cyclists zigzagging wildly in and out of traffic, everything jarring and intense and in motion beneath a vein of blue sky. The air smelled like pretzels and exhaust and urine. It always did.

Blue's doorman jabbed his arm into the air, and a yellow taxi swerved across two lanes amid an orchestra of angry, dissonant horns and pulled up beside her. She threw her bag into the back seat and climbed in beside it.

"Port Authority, please," she said while simultaneously composing a work email on her phone. She brought only a small leather duffel bag for the long weekend, packed "like a man," Maya always said. One pair of linen pants, a classic button-down, a couple of khaki Bermuda shorts and white T-shirts, a ten-year-old bathing suit she had no business wearing, toothbrush, underwear and a pair of flat comfortable sandals. She usually felt no need for makeup or hair products, if only because she'd decided years ago that they wouldn't help. But this time, because there was the possibility of seeing Jack again, she brought a few additional things: a necklace, a new leave-in conditioner her stylist had been trying to push on her forever, some fancy lingerie. When she thought of these hopeful little items in her suitcase, she cringed with embarrassment.

Her phone rang. She sighed, picked up. "I'm on vacation," she said. "Fine, okay, go. Mmm-hmm. Yes, I heard. Did you look at the reports? Well, look at the reports." She ended the call.

The phone rang again. "I'm on…okay. Yes, I heard. I told him to look at the reports." She sighed. Pulled out a cigarette. She wasn't a smoker. She just kept them around in case of emergencies.

"Do you mind?" she said to the driver, though she knew they never did. They could smell the wealth on her, the big tip.

She lit up, took a deep drag, creating a calm dampening cloud over her brain. Her email buzzed. Work again. She read it, responded, experienced a flash of dread at her overflowing inbox.

While she was there, she opened up social media, reread the message in her inbox for approximately the fiftieth time. It had come in at the end of a long day, in a long week when even a few hits of weed off her vaporizer couldn't quell a loneliness that made her skin hurt.

Blue, I don't know if you remember me. We knew each other many summers ago. I saw your profile in the Times and just wanted to congratulate you on your success! If you're ever back in Montauk, hit me up! Love, Jack Giles.

The first time she'd seen the message, she'd stared in a kind of blinking shock, the words *Oh my God* looping in her head. She'd stood, bewildered and giddy, wringing the nerves out of her hands as she paced, repeatedly returning to the computer to see if the message was still real. *No way*, she'd said to herself. *No way, no way*. He remembered her. All these years later. Thought of her enough to friend her, send a message. It had to mean something, didn't it? It had to mean a lot. She felt like a carnival ride had taken up residence inside her body, making her all lit up and twirly and nauseated. She wanted to call Maya or Hannah, ask their opinion, disperse the giant unfamiliar feelings she was having, hand them off. But it had been two in the morning. And besides, she was convinced that everyone she knew pitied her when it came to such things, thought she was a loser at love—which was absolutely true, she was—but it was one thing to know it and another to have other people believe it. If she told them, they would just make a huge mortifying deal about it. Instead she'd poured herself another scotch and then danced around her living room like the fool she swore she'd never be.

She'd stayed up half that night stalking him on the internet. There were no pictures, and she'd resented him for it. How did one make it to thirty without a single photo on Google Images unless they were in prison or the witness protection program? By the time she went to bed, she was already dreaming of their future courtship, the shared confessions of years they'd spent thinking about each other, how they'd never loved anyone else. Of course, she'd actually have to write

him back first, but she needed to come up with a perfect response. Something funny and just a little flirty. If only she
knew how to flirt.

The following morning, sleep deprived and wired, she'd
nearly put an extra zero in a million-dollar stock trade. Her
mind had been usurped. All she could think about was him—
this boy she'd met on a blue-bright summer day back when the
world was sharp and immediate. This boy who had kissed the
promise of love into her heart, unlocked a feeling of beauty
within her she didn't know she had. She could hardly bear
to remember how long she'd gone since then without being
kissed. Just the thought opened a cellar door inside her, dark
bottomless grief and shame underneath. Twelve years. Jack
had been the first and last boy to do it, the first to ever like
her, the last to know her before that terrible night had turned
her hard and sleepless and low lit as the moon.

The taxi pulled up to Port Authority, and Blue handed the
driver a hundred-dollar bill and waved off the change. The
surprise and delight on his face made it worth it. Her favorite
thing about money was the joy of giving it away. She often
fantasized about giving it all away, but then inevitably she
thought, *Without money what would I have?* No real friends in
her own city, no love, not even a decent hobby, unless smoking weed in her bathrobe at midnight could be counted as one.

She climbed out of the taxi and watched as an endless stream
of people who were not Maya emptied out of the building
into the steamy heat. She'd rushed to get here, assuming that
there would be some sort of unexpected traffic jam or holdup.
But of course, the holdup was Maya, who could cause more
chaos than an overturned truck on the highway just by being
herself. Blue was about to call her when a text popped up.

I'll be on the next one I swear!! ☺

She had to laugh. It was so utterly annoying but also so predictably Maya. There was an odd comfort in knowing and loving a friend so much that you not only accepted their flaws but found amusement in the familiarity of them. In that most basic way, Blue thought, all friendships were rooted in forgiveness.

This made her think of Renee. She abruptly discarded the thought.

Another email came in. *Jesus, I picked the wrong time to take a vacation.* Though on reconsideration she couldn't think of a more perfect time. In truth, it had seemed like fate—the most romantic, perfect fate—that just a few days after she received that message from Jack, while she was still trying to come up with a response, Maya had called with the suggestion about going back to Montauk. She would write to Jack as soon as they got there. Make it look spontaneous. Say something like, "Coincidentally happen to be in town for the weekend, you free?"

Now she walked alone down Forty-Second Street to the car rental place, something she and Maya had planned to do together. How unsurprising, she laughed to herself, that Maya was always miraculously absent whenever a credit card or cash was needed. But then, she thought, not *always*.

There was that one time in junior high school when Blue got roped into doing a bake sale auction. It was a charity event to raise money for soccer equipment for her team. Blue had played goalie. She decided she would bake Nana's famous cream pie, which happened to be her mother's favorite. Truth was she wasn't much of a baker. She was more of a wood shop kind of girl, but that was part of the problem. Blue suspected that her beautiful, feminine mother might actually love her if Blue was a different kind of girl—pretty and dainty with a knack for cooking and shopping and ballet. These were the kinds of girls her mother would dote on and adore, the ones with bows in their hair and frilly dresses, delicate boned and shy. But Blue was built like her father, athletic and husky. It was a quality she'd felt proud of until around fourth grade, when society's poisonous messages about femininity wormed their way in. That's when Blue had the epiphany that her mother felt about her the way society did—that she was the wrong kind of girl.

Somehow her thirteen-year-old mind thought that if she could just make a perfect pie, she could earn her mother's approval. She was always looking for the angle, the mathematical solution—as if she could rearrange herself in the exact dimensions that could squeeze into her mother's heart.

The night before the auction she invited Renee over to help her bake, and the two of them made sure to copy Nana's recipe to the letter. They made two pies to sell plus one to sample to "make sure it was right." As it turned out, she had a lot of fun doing it, especially the sampling part. It was delicious, just the perfect amount of sweet, and by the time she went to bed that night, Blue was imagining a big stage and an enormous crowd, everyone fighting to get ahold of her pies.

In reality the auction was held in a small hot tent behind the gym, the unimpressive crowd comprising the parents and siblings of the soccer team members. The girls got up one by one and described into the microphone what they'd baked, using the most mouthwatering descriptions they could come up with, and then the auctioneer (their soccer coach—this was a low-rent affair) would open up for bidding. As the auction began, Blue noticed that pretty much the only people bidding were the parents of whoever was onstage at the moment. Blue sat to the left with the rest of her team and scanned the crowd for her mother. She'd told her about it several times, and each time her mother promised to come. Just in case, she'd left the flyer on the counter that morning with the time and location circled in red to remind her. Her mother would be there, she would. Blue looked at the clock. Her shirt was beaded with sweat and her heart was starting to pound hard against its dampness. Her mother was probably just late. She was always late.

The line of girls ahead of her was quickly dwindling. Blue watched with panic as the girl two ahead of her finished her presentation, sold her pie to her own grandfather for a cool hundred. Still no sign of her mother. The next girl was called. Blue wanted to dissolve into the grass beneath her chair. What if she got up there and no one bid? What if she had to stand there, exposed and humiliated, with her stupid, unlovable pies?

The room went suddenly fuzzy, the coach's voice muffled in her ears. Her own name was called twice before it registered. She stood, her legs shaking so hard that one of her knee socks dropped to her ankle. Once at the mic she stammered into it, her wavering voice sounding so much louder than the girls' before her. She kept repeating herself as she tried to describe what she'd so proudly baked. She could see the audience quickly drifting, losing interest. Who would want a pie made by a sweaty, brutish girl whose own mother didn't like her enough to come?

Her coach opened the room up to bidding. There was silence from the crowd. *Please*, she thought desperately. *Someone.*

Anyone. A woman coughed. People looked around, shifted, waited. Sweat was pouring off her forehead into her eyes. *Oh God.* Then at last a hand was raised. Someone's mom she didn't know, some kind, beautiful person who took pity on her and bid ten dollars. Blue was so grateful. She wanted to run out and hug her. She wanted to be adopted by her. She started to walk off the stage when her coach said, "We've got ten dollars! Can we get fifteen?" Blue turned to him, pleading with her eyes, *Please don't do this to me. Take the ten and let me go.* She was so afraid she was going to start crying and make the humiliation worse.

Then suddenly a commotion from the back of the tent. A loud shout from just beyond it. "Fifteen dollars!"

Blue turned and peered out and there was Renee running in, waving her hand high, Hannah and Maya trailing behind her.

"We have fifteen!" the coach said excitedly. "Can we get twenty?"

There was a pause.

"Twenty!" Hannah called.

"We've got twenty, can we get—"

Maya's hand shot up. "Twenty-five!"

Hannah whacked her. "Do we even have twenty-five?"

"Oh, shit, good question," Maya said, completely oblivious to the judgmental looks from some of the parents. "Hold on a sec!"

Renee and Hannah pulled out crumpled dollars from their pockets, Maya retrieved hers from her shoe and they piled them together, holding up the auction as they counted. "Uh, never mind," Renee said finally. "Our bid is twenty-three dollars!"

"And ten cents!" Maya added.

God, they were just so unbelievably embarrassing. Just look at them, all grubby and weird and oblivious. But Blue didn't care! Because they were *there*, they showed up and now everyone could see that she had people. Ridiculous people but people!

"Sold for twenty-three dollars and, uh, ten cents to the young ladies at the back!"

"Suckas!" Maya said to the crowd. "You don't know what you're missing."

Blue covered her face with her hands. Maya always took it too far.

Afterward they sat on the bleachers and ate the pies with their fingers and fed some to the birds and it was just normal, that they did this for her; she could take it for granted just like people with loving families did. In retrospect that was the best part.

For a moment the memory made Blue soft—to think of how friends are life's greatest first responders, rescuing one another time and again from life's little atrocities. It was the big atrocities that no one could help with. Which was why Hannah was nuts now and Maya was reckless and imprudent and none of them had spoken to Renee in twelve years, Blue's anger toward her so solid and unmovable that even that moment of fond memory couldn't make a dent. Pie auction rescue or not, Renee didn't deserve her forgiveness, not after what she'd done.

She put away the memory and pulled out into the blare of car horns and the smoky breath of buses and an early evening sky as luminous and blue as the Hudson beneath the glow of bridge lights. The city had a particular lively beauty she could recognize but not connect with. She'd only moved here to be with Nana in her failing age, but she always felt like an outsider—a tourist who forgot to leave.

As she pulled back up to Port Authority, she spotted Maya on the corner, standing out among the throngs—the only person in New York without her guard up, the only person smiling. It was in part this careless beauty that drew people to Maya. There was something so compelling about an adult who was as trusting as a puppy on its back. Blue rolled down the window and shouted Maya's name twice before she noticed.

Maya took one look at the frumpy green sedan Blue had rented and then bent down to look at her with disgust. "You're kidding me," she said, climbing in. "You rented a Jolly Rancher."

"Sorry you're late," Blue replied.

Maya laughed and her eyes flashed with love. "Let's try this again." She leaned across the front seat and held her arms out wide and warm and welcoming as a beach. "Hi! You look amazing!"

"Hi!" Blue said back, and the feeling of having someone be so truly, openly happy to see her was like the sun shining right into her chest, brightening the place up a bit. In all her busyness it had been over a year since they'd last seen each other in person, and she'd forgotten what it felt like to see in someone's face that she mattered. She couldn't imagine why anyone would like her enough to give her such a reception. But that was the thing about old friends. The love was built-in to the innocent bones of youth, long before a proper assessment of each other's qualities could be made.

Now Blue accepted Maya's hug, then surrendered it just as quickly, aware of her own awkwardness, how she'd forgotten how to be close.

"It's been way too long," Maya said. "But really, you're joking with this car, right?" She eyed the roof like it had insulted her. "How are we supposed to re-create our fun trip without a convertible?"

"I think we'll be okay," Blue said.

"We'll just have to improvise. I assume you've got a chainsaw at the house?"

Blue rolled her eyes. "Buckle up. Poor Hannah is probably freaking out that we're not there yet."

"Wait, you didn't tell her we were going to be late?"

HANNAH

Hannah sat beside her suitcase with her phone in hand. On the other line, Vivian's voice buzzed with excitement.

"It happened again! I was wheeling Henry outside for some air and he looked up at me, his eyes so clear and present—you know how they can be sometimes—and he said, 'Hi, Mom'! Just like that! 'Hi, Mom.'"

The smile on Hannah's face was so big she could feel the stretch of it. "Ooh," she said, "that's amazing!" And there it was, just like every other occasion when Henry had spoken or squeezed a hand or flashed a smile—sudden irrepressible, delicious hope. On those days everything was okay again, everything was worth it, all the waiting and worrying and caretaking and loneliness and sleepless nights and gray despair, all of it worth it because he was still there, he was still *in* there, her Henry, her love, her one. He was still capable of coming back. Oh, how she wished she'd been there to see it!

She glanced at the clock, sorry to have to rush Vivian off the phone, but the girls would be here any minute. As soon as she hung up, she thought of Henry in the care facility, imagined him wide awake and conscious, back for good. There was still some brain activity. And advancing medicine. Miracles did happen. Even the doctors said that. There was that kid who woke up after eighteen years—turned out he'd heard everything around him. There was just so much they didn't know.

But then, another thought: What if he woke up again, even briefly, while she was away? She imagined him confused, disoriented, swallowed inside a lights-out loneliness in that sterile, loveless room. Imagined him saying "Hannah?" and getting no reply. It was the wrong time to be leaving for a trip. She couldn't even bring herself to mention to Vivian that she was going. She should back out of it right now. But her friends were already en route, driving a considerable distance in the wrong direction just to get her, knowing she'd never come if they didn't show up at her doorstep and drag her along. Knowing she wouldn't, couldn't, get behind the wheel of a car ever since that night she'd inadvertently driven them into a hell they couldn't have imagined.

She unzipped her suitcase, double-checked that everything she needed was in there. There were so many self-created systems that had to be followed for her to feel like she could go. She had to pack everything in plastic vacuum bags, sealed tight against germs and bugs. Any item of clothing taken out would need to be hot washed and dried in the dryer for at least an hour before it could be returned to the bag. The suitcase itself could not touch the ground or else that would have to be discarded. And of course, she needed her bleach packs, her Purell. And then all her medications—she couldn't go five feet without those. There was half a drugstore in her purse. Vicodin in case she got hurt, antibiotics in case she got an infection, muscle relaxers in case she got stiff, et cetera. And then there were the rules: no large crowds (terrorism), no driving through tunnels (claustrophobia), no swimming in the ocean (sharks, drowning), no shellfish (she could be allergic—who knew for sure?), no sharing utensils or towels or sheets or anything, really—oh, she had to be so careful not to slip, to stay ever vigilant. It was exhausting to live in a state of "just in case" and "better safe than sorry." To try to avoid more disaster and regret.

She checked her watch. Maya and Blue were almost an hour late. Darkness pressed against her windows, pushed into her thoughts. She considered calling to find out where they were, but to do so would telegraph her irrational fear/hope that they'd forgotten her entirely.

She glanced out the window overlooking the street, up at the stars glowing politely in the sky. Waiting was such an intolerable state for her, being in limbo, unable to relax and settle into any one place yet. Hell, sometimes just the mere transition of crossing from one side of the room to the other gave her a dim existential anxiety, like she could disappear inside the cavity of neither here nor there.

Years ago, in the early days of Henry's coma, she'd talked to her psychiatrist, Dr. Maloney, about this. She'd been failing to cope with the unendurable in-between place where hope was on one side, despair on the other, and she was never sure upon which side to wait. It wasn't even just the uncertainty of Henry's condition, she explained, but the uncertainty of everything, the way her whole life, every decision she made, forced an internal battle between possibility and dread, until the only choice seemed not to make a choice at all.

"You were alone that night," Dr. Maloney told her. "Just like in your childhood. You had no idea if anyone was coming. And yet you knew if no one came, you'd die. That gets wired into the brain. So now every time you're confronted with a stress situation, like a void of information or an undetermined outcome, your brain reacts as if it's life or death. You are launched back into that unbearable state, caught between the possibility of rescue and the threat of annihilation."

As he spoke, Hannah imagined herself as an abandoned baby bird, small and featherless, mouth open in a hungry wail. Waiting for rescue, waiting to be fed. She had actually thrown her head back and let out a little bird chirp right there in his office, trying to be funny, but he'd only stared at her gravely, then jotted a note in his notepad.

"But how do I fix that?" she'd asked.

She tried to remember what his answer had been. Something about rewiring. So much rewiring. Endless rewiring. At the end of the session, he'd written her a prescription for the Xanax that she now carried everywhere, and in high-stress situations—like, for instance, living—she put the small peach pill under her tongue and waited for that heavy calm to cover her like a weighted blanket.

The phone rang, jolting her out of her thoughts.

"Is this Hannah Barnett?" a nasal voice said.

Hannah hesitated. "Yes."

"I'm happy to inform you, Miss Barnett, that you have just won a grand-prize trip to—"

"Hi, Maya," Hannah said dryly.

"—Montauk, New York! Please come downstairs to collect your prize. Bring a chainsaw. Ask no questions."

Hannah was struck with a sense of relief, then dread.

It's only three days, she reminded herself. *I can do three days.*

She grabbed the handle of her suitcase, paused by her favorite photograph, one she'd taken on the beach in Montauk after they'd watched the sun's slow-motion dive into the ocean. It was a picture of Blue, Renee and Maya leaping off the lifeguard stand, their bodies in silhouette against the blue night, captured in tucked flight like some sort of ecstatic birth from the sky. For a moment she could almost grab that pure, perfect bliss she felt at that time in her life. She reached out and touched Renee's face, wondered where she was, hoped she was doing okay.

At the door now, she forced a smile. *This is going to be so fun!* she told herself. This was what Maya would do. This was what Maya would feel.

The girls were waiting on the sidewalk. She paused, startled by how different they looked, how much the same. Blue in her tailored clothes, her hair cut just below her chin, suddenly morphed in Hannah's mind into the eighteen-year-old she'd once been, oversize tie-dyed T-shirt (her Deadhead phase—short-lived, thank God), bangs always in her eyes, that twinkle in her eye and machine-gun laugh whenever she leaned in and whispered some dry, hilarious observation in Hannah's ear. It still surprised her to see how successful Blue had become, especially considering how unambitious she'd once been about anything but partying. She turned to Maya, instantly pictured her in her high ponytail and jangly bracelets, that unaffected sway when she walked, like she was slowing down time with her hips.

An entire childhood rushed to the forefront of Hannah's memory: sleepovers and late-night phone calls, a single shared school locker that spilled books and paper whenever it was opened, ski trips and summer nights and *he's the one who's missing out* pep talks and so much time, my God, so much free time just to be together.

Now Maya and Blue rushed her, arms open wide. *Don't mention that they're late,* she told herself.

Don't mention it don't mention it don't mention it.

"Hi!" they both said at once, pulling her into a hug. Their bodies, older now and almost a year unseen, were still such a comfort.

"You guys were supposed to be here an hour ago," Hannah blurted. She could feel them both stiffen, or maybe it was she who stiffened, bracing for them to be annoyed. Immediately she was angry at herself, fearing the withdrawal of the hugs, realizing she hadn't taken them in long enough and what a loss that was, to be separated from the heartbeat of them.

"It's Maya's fault," Blue said.

Maya shot Blue a look. "That wasn't what we agreed to say."

"I didn't agree to say anything. That happened in your head." Blue turned to Hannah. "You didn't think we'd just left without you, did you?"

"What? No! Are you kidding?" Hannah said a little too enthusiastically.

Blue and Maya exchanged a look.

"We should have called. We meant to call and got distracted," Blue said. "We suck."

"Well…Blue sucks," Maya said. "I was just late."

Hannah laughed, and Maya hugged her once again.

They climbed into the car, exchanging excited smiles. A

calm came over Hannah, a settling weight in her lap like a warm kitten. How had she gone so many years without being near the very people who mattered most? A flaw in human adaptation, we get accustomed to things too easily.

Around her the world was in motion, a parade of headlights and people strolling by, the waft of perfume and emissions on the breeze, all that life she usually watched from the safe distance of her window. She was in it now, in it again, and she imagined someone watching *her* from above, filled with that same wistful longing to be one of the moving pieces. In that moment all the dread and worry receded, and she thought that maybe this trip would be exactly what she needed: a yellow brick road where she would find her courage again.

"Beach house, here we come!" Maya said.

MAYA

"Isn't this fantastic?" Maya said. "God, we should have done this years ago!"

Her heart was so warm being back with her people. They were about to have a fabulous time, sunbathing at Ditch Plains Beach, drinking margaritas at sunset, playing beer pong on the back patio. They would do one another's hair and it would all go to waste in an hour anyway because of the humidity, and they'd hit the bars and meet hot surfers and, who knows, maybe she'd even bring one home. A rich one! It could happen. Throw a rock out there and you'll hit a millionaire… Wouldn't that be something if she brought back a millionaire like most people brought back T-shirts. All her problems solved. Of course, she'd have to actually like him. And she always went for the broke guys. But who knows? Who knows?

Man, she really needed this. What a brilliant idea she'd had.

She glanced in the rearview, caught Hannah looking back, stricken. "What?"

"Your driving," Hannah said, clutching the shoulders of the two front seats in a death grip.

"I assume you brought your Xanax?"

Hannah nodded.

"Might as well pop a few. We have a lot of time to make up."

Blue laughed, turned to Hannah. "Why are we friends with her again?"

"I ask myself that often," Hannah said.

"Let's face it," Maya said, "it's not like you guys had a lot of people clamoring for the job."

"Fair point," Blue said.

Maya made a sharp turn, a little too sharp, and watched Hannah shrink back into her seat, her shoulders pressed in as if she were being squeezed by an invisible crowd. A memory came to her of all of them at eighteen, driving home after their high school graduation ceremony, Hannah unbuckling her seat belt and standing up in the back of Maya's open Jeep, her white dress billowing, her red curls flying as she turned to watch the high school, their childhood, ebb into the distance. It was just before sunset and the clouds had flared ballerina pink, and Hannah threw her arms wide as if trying to catch that beauty and hold it, shouting "We're free!" into the wind, as if their innocence was a chain rather than a safety harness. Maya hit the gas and Blue and Renee cheered and Hannah yelled for her to go even faster until Henry yanked her down into his lap, wrapped her in his arms and kissed her.

Lovely youth. She could almost reach back and grab that feeling—the way they were trying to touch something then, not sky, exactly, but vastness. Like if they just went fast enough, they could grab it and hold on to it, be as big as it, and oh, even then she knew they were being reckless, driving too fast, but how could anyone fear death when they felt this alive?

"So," Blue said, turning around in her seat to face Hannah. "You excited?"

"I think so," Hannah said, smiling meekly.

"She is very excited," Maya said. "She just doesn't know it."

"I haven't been to the house in so long," Blue said. "First Nana got too old for the drive...and then work has been insane...but man, I miss it. My mouth's already watering for the lobster roll at Lunch. This really may be Maya's first good idea yet."

"Hey! I've had others."

"Name *one*."

Maya thought about it, came up blank. "You know I'm not good at pop quizzes."

Hannah leaned forward. "Hey, Maya, how's the new job?"

"Awesome," Maya said. She noticed Blue eyeing her skeptically, realized she might have oversold it.

"Please don't tell me you got fired already," Blue said. "It's been three months."

"I did not get fired already and I resent the implication."

"Good," Blue said. "Because I'm out of job contacts in Jersey."

"That's fine," Maya said. "I don't need your help again, thank you very much."

"And the house?" Hannah said. "Did you keep the purple front door?"

"House is great and the door is still purple!" Maya said with cheer. Granted, it probably had a foreclosure notice taped to it, but they didn't need to know that. It would all be fixed soon enough.

"So anyway…" she said, tapping her hands on the wheel. She wanted to change the subject, and besides, she had something important to tell them. All the way to Hannah's she'd tried to determine the best way to approach it. Perhaps if she made it seem like nothing, she could slip it by Blue without much fanfare. She certainly seemed to be in a good mood at the moment, so now might be the time. "Guess who I talked to?"

Blue's phone buzzed, cutting Maya off just as she'd carefully set the bait.

"I'm going to throw that damn thing out the window," Maya said.

"Sorry," Blue said. "Work stuff."

"It's nine o'clock."

Blue tapped at her phone and the message whooshed into the ether. "Okay, who did you talk to?"

Maya glanced at her. A mistake! She had telegraphed nervousness. "Renee!" she said brightly, as if there were glitter on the word.

A crash of silence inside the car. Tires humming beneath them. Maya bit her lip, considered her next move. She needed to sell this. Her toughest challenge yet. She looked back at Hannah for support.

"Wow," Hannah said finally, softly. It was quiet again before she dared to ask, "How is she?"

"It was a quick call," Maya said. "It's not a big deal. She's fine."

"Who called who?" Blue asked.

"I called her."

"Why?" Blue fired back.

"Because she's my friend? And I miss her?"

Blue stared at her. Maya returned her gaze, defiant.

"Watch the road!" Hannah pleaded.

"Anyway," Maya said cheerfully. "She says she's doing great. Engaged to some amazing guy. Living in Connecticut." She paused, looked at Blue's face. Made a judgment call. "Well, that's it. Just wanted to tell you! Moving on…"

"Good plan," Blue said and looked out the window.

Maya caught Hannah's eyes in the mirror. They looked the way her own must—sad.

BLUE

Blue couldn't believe Maya had called Renee. She lit an emergency cigarette, took a hard inhale as if applying pressure on a wound. She opened the window, turned to make sure Hannah wasn't getting blasted with fumes.

"You shouldn't smoke," Hannah said.

"I don't," Blue said, exhaling into the rolling night. Her hand shook as she took another drag. Her Rolex—a tacky gift from her company, but whatever, it told the time—glinted in the shine of passing headlights. She watched the smoke run out the window, wanted to follow it.

It wasn't even just the casual delivery. It was the utter disloyalty of the call in the first place. Yes, they were all adults and could do what they wanted, but *still*, the fact that Maya had talked to Renee felt a betrayal of some unspoken rule. The rule that Maya and Hannah had no right to a relationship with Renee if Blue didn't have one.

After all, it had been Blue and Renee who'd been best friends first. They were the two who'd known each other since practically the day they were born, had been referred to as "the twins," though they looked nothing alike. Renee was sleek haired and thin as an hour with a perpetual sense of hurry in her eyes, while Blue was broad-faced and sturdy, moved through the world with lazy muscle, like a piece of construction equipment. But she'd always felt that being with Renee was like being with herself, as if underneath they had the same sized hearts, beating at the same speed, creating a synchronicity of spirit, the way she imagined twins must feel, soothed by each other's rhythms in the womb.

Their parents had been best friends, too, at least until Renee's dad packed up his bags and walked out, fell in love with the secretary just like the cliché. Blue had actually been at Renee's house the night he left. Her mother was with Renee's mom, Sue, in the kitchen, the sounds of tinkling wineglasses and murmuring voices leaching through the screen door. Blue and Renee sat on the front steps, both ten at the time, preparing to toss Mentos into a bottle of Pepsi as precocious Renee explained the science behind the anticipated explosion. Even then Blue recognized the importance of friendship, of having a passenger along on your life, the way just sitting shoulder to shoulder felt like a buffering against things she could not name. She wanted to say something to Renee about it, but the night lowered in a hush, and Sue's voice from the kitchen turned into a loud, boozy smear. "I never should've had a kid," Sue said. "We were fine before that."

An awful silence followed, a period at the end of the cruelest sentence.

Renee chucked a Mentos candy into the soda bottle, and they watched silently and joylessly as it foamed and sprayed.

Blue couldn't look at her, couldn't bear to see the hurt in her eyes.

"They're so loud in there," Blue said finally.

Renee was staring off toward the street. "Did you know that when hippos are upset, their sweat turns red?" She usually took great joy in reciting strange facts, but now there was a remoteness in her eyes, as if she'd traveled somewhere Blue couldn't reach.

"Cool," Blue said, though there were so many things she wanted to say instead—she just didn't know how.

Renee jumped up suddenly, all long legs and long hair and eyes on the distance. "I'll race you to the end of the block!"

And Blue, who'd had no interest in moving, who was about as fast as a garden snail, had agreed. Somehow, she understood the request as an act of trust. That wherever Renee had to flee to in her mind to cope, she was inviting Blue to go with her. Of course, Renee had beaten her easily and then wanted to do it again.

She'd been a runner even then. She always wanted to run.

Now Maya said, "It's just... I miss her."

"I thought we were dropping the subject," Blue said.

"She was your best friend."

Blue let the sentence hang there, unanswered.

They moved out of the lighted city and onto the highway. The moon was high and indifferent. How strange, Blue thought, to be gazed upon nightly by a thing that does not know you, that stands over you as you sleep and dream, seeming benevolent but in truth neglectful, uncaring. It was like... well, it was like her mother, actually. Both her parents, really, but especially her mother. Like all of their mothers. Though truthfully Blue had no right to complain. At least her mother had been *around*. She wasn't abusive like Maya's mother, or casually cruel like Renee's or a depressive locked away in her room like Hannah's. She was just *uninterested*. And besides, Blue had Nana. Not all the time, but every summer at least.

Regardless, their commonality was the engine of her fierce loyalty, that deep gratitude for being allowed into the pack, four feral teenagers rearing one another like abandoned pups. Maya used to call their respective families "the Unchosen Ones." And it was true. People just got born into a house with a bunch of randoms and then were expected to love them regardless of personality or commonality or even, you know, decency. It didn't make sense. Sure, some people got lucky. But a lot of people didn't. The four of them had been the true family. They had chosen one another. It was why it mattered so much to Blue when one of them betrayed the contract. She didn't understand how Hannah and Maya could forgive Renee, how Maya's offhanded mention of her felt like asking Blue to do the same. In the back of her mind, a flash of dark night, that quickened heartbeat of terror. She blinked it away, climbed into the sky, letting the perspective shrink her into something tiny and irrelevant. It was a comfort—to be one step from disappearing.

Maya and Hannah were watching her. She knew they thought she was cold.

"It's no fun with you two fighting," Maya said. "We're supposed to be a foursome."

"We're not fighting. We don't speak."

"You know what I mean."

"I do, and no offense, I don't care."

It seemed to Blue that Maya was often sympathetic to the unsympathetic character, that friend who always, without fail, took the wrong person's side because she felt sorry for their weaknesses, regardless of how destructive they were to the people around them. On the one hand, Blue admired Maya's forgiving nature, but on the other she just wanted to be mad at Renee. Why was it so hard, Blue wondered, to allow other people their anger? Especially women. Women were always denied it. Told to be nice. To forgive. Screw that.

"Whatever she did to you, it was over a decade ago," Maya said. "How long do you plan on dwelling on this?"

Blue's jaw clenched. She took another deep drag on her cigarette. She wanted to strangle Maya for getting everything so backward. Part of her wished she could come out and say exactly what Renee had done, make Maya feel guilty for her casualness. But even if she wanted to, she couldn't. She had to sit on it like a suitcase that wouldn't quite zip, suffocate the air out of it. To speak of it would be to release its combustible content into the world, make what happened too real, too true. And once out, she could never put it back. To even think about Renee right now was stirring things she didn't want stirred.

For years she'd pushed Renee out of her head. The last time she'd even seen her was in the hospital—those weeks of keeping vigil over Henry. By then they'd already stopped talking. The last time they were actually friends was the night everything went so terribly, irrevocably wrong for all of them. The night after they'd returned from their last annual trip to Montauk, so blinded by their own happiness they didn't anticipate life's ability to take it all away.

It made everything worse—how happy they'd been then, how naive. It always made Blue hate herself to think of that. Like she'd let herself be duped somehow.

They'd gone to a party. A house they'd never been to before. Some guy Maya had picked up at the mall along with a new tank top and lip gloss. Chuck? Chet? Maya hadn't been sure—they'd called him Check.

Loud music from the backyard lured them toward it, heads turning as they entered through the back gate, her friends so tan and beautiful. She could see them as they were being seen—like sunbeams, like photons, so radiant and alluring, emanating some intangible spark. Another night she might have been jealous—she'd always been the approachable one, the buddy guys came to for advice about her friends. But that was before she met Jack in Montauk. With Jack, some part of life that had previously been closed to her was unlocked, allowed her to consider that she was desirable too. She even wore his sweatshirt that night, wrapped around her waist like a hug, like proof.

The party was wild and boozy with a kind of darkness at its edges—small groups slipping off into bathrooms or shadows, sniffing their noses as they rejoined the crowd. Maya ran off to find Check, leaving Blue, Renee and Hannah on their own among strangers. They were hesitant at first, shy and awkward. But then Henry arrived—and, oh, there he was, so crystal clear in her memory. That slight hunch in his shoulders as if stooping to listen, compassionate brown eyes, such genuine sweetness in his smile. His hair was cut short for summer and he was wearing a soft weathered T-shirt and khaki shorts, just filling into himself, becoming a man. She could almost reach out to touch the image of him as he kissed Hannah's head, then turned and greeted her with a brotherly squeeze. Henry. Henry. Two months from a tennis scholarship at UCLA he would never get to claim.

Renee dragged Blue off to get beers from the keg, then they wandered toward the pool. In the deep end, partygoers jumped in fully clothed, clutching their beers and pulling unsuspecting people in with them, everyone shrieking and laughing. Blue and Renee plopped down on the scratchy concrete edge of the shallow end, took off their flip-flops. Their bare legs dangled in the fire-blue water, swaying in unintentional sync. Renee's calves were long and lithe, her toes pointed gracefully like a gymnast's in midflip. Beside them Blue's legs looked scabby and thick. Somewhere along the way Renee had transformed from a tomboy like her into a coy, contained beauty and carried a new self-consciousness in how she presented herself, as if she was always aware of her angles. She'd become the exact opposite of her mother, who drank too much and always had stains on her shirts and lipstick on her teeth. Blue suspected that was the point. If Renee was perfect, if she was like a girl in a magazine, no one would leave her, no one would regret that she had been born.

Renee pulled her long, sleek hair into an effortless knot, and Blue wondered if femininity was an inborn trait she'd failed to inherit or something she'd just never been taught or bothered to learn. Just the fact of Renee's perfectly pedicured toes wiggling in the water seemed so mysterious—it would never occur to Blue to paint her toes! Or her fingernails for that matter. It seemed exhausting, and yet she often envied Renee for being the kind of girl her own mother had wanted, for looking the way the world insisted a girl should look. Life was hard on girls who existed outside that expectation. For years Blue had never faced any kind of reflection—mirror, window, photograph— beside Renee without feeling some dim, peripheral inadequacy. But that night it hadn't mattered. That night she had Jack in her memory and her best friend beside her, their legs kicking side by side in the water.

"I'm going to miss this," Blue said, staring ahead.

"Not me," Renee said. "I'm so ready to skip this town."

The words stung. Blue understood it wasn't about her, that Renee was running from her awful home life and toward a new version of herself, but still she wanted to say, "What about me?" She didn't understand wanting to leave. Here was where they had each other. There was where they would not. She felt ill equipped to be without her friends. How could Renee feel so differently? Beneath the din of the crowd, she could hear the quiet knock of water against the pool drains. A hollow, lonely sound.

"I'll miss *you*, obviously," Renee said. "But we'll visit each other all the time."

A sudden pierce of regret. If only Blue had studied harder, she could be joining Renee at Duke, the two of them in matching sweatshirts casting long fall shadows as they walked across a golden-lit quad. Instead she'd spent her high school years rebelling against her parents by screwing around in school. And while everyone else was charting their futures, she had no idea what she wanted to be when she grew up, only what she didn't want to be—a robot like her mom and dad, going to jobs they hated day after day just so they could take fancy vacations and drive a BMW and belong to a country club they never had time to visit. Blue wanted more than that—she just didn't know what.

"It's just not going to be the same," Blue said, staring into the pool. Emotions were hard for her to talk about and also to have, and she was suddenly congested with them. She took a huge sip of beer.

"You'll only be twelve hours away by car, twenty-three by train, three and a half by plane. Which means that if you ever...you know...want to be a pain in my ass, or miss my random trivia or whatever, the shortest distance is only two hundred and ten minutes."

Blue shook her head. "You mapped it out?" That made her feel a little better.

"And priced it."

"Dork," Blue said, laughing.

They bumped shoulders and watched the party grow and left the conversation at that. Soon the crowd turned friendlier with drink, and they found themselves pulled into a game of beer pong. Maya reappeared nearby, sitting on Check's lap and telling a story with her big hand gestures to a small crowd gathered around them. Blue spotted Hannah leaning against Henry's chest, his arms wrapped around her, her face relaxed and content. Blue waved, they waved back and then she saw Hannah tilt her head to Henry for a kiss, and Blue's heart torqued with feelings both painful and lovely, remembering Jack, missing Jack, the feelings so big she didn't know what to do with them. A Ping-Pong ball landed in her beer and she guzzled it down.

The night moved, blurred and swayed. Color and spin and murmuring voices, one occasionally rising over others. The air was charged, dense with humidity, lusty as an oyster. Blue went to the bathroom, lost her friends for a bit, wandered off to smoke pot behind the garage with a few guys she didn't know. She remembered looking back at the party, at her friends in their respective pockets of fun as she turned the corner and disappeared into the shadows. She remembered the electricity of youth humming inside her, that sense of ripeness, life plucking her from childhood into its mouth, all of them being pulled toward bright futures, tugged back by their love for one another, none of them knowing what horror was waiting for them on the other side of that night.

As she looked back on it now, she was struck by how detached she was from the memory, as if she was recalling someone else's life. She had walked into that night one person and came out another. Reincarnated into a colder world, a distrusting soul, an exhausted heart. And with a new enemy—Renee.

HANNAH

"I wish you'd just tell us what she did…" Hannah said.

Both she and Maya had always suspected they were missing a piece of the story, that what happened between Blue and Renee that awful life-changing night went deeper, darker than they knew. But Blue would never say, and now Hannah could tell she'd walked too closely to the edge. She could sense the barbed wire around Blue, feel its sharp prick. Blue could be remote, sometimes even harsh, when she was hurt, but Hannah understood that was how she protected herself. She suspected that was the case for most harsh people. Still it was the kind of thing that made her want to return to her apartment, close the door like a coffin, escape from people and their power to take themselves away. Too dangerous, the world.

And yet she missed Renee. She hated to think of her without them, of how lonely she must be. It wasn't hard to imagine. It was how Hannah had felt her whole life before she met Maya back in elementary school. Hannah had been on the swings by herself after classes had let out. She did this often, lingered behind until it got dark. It was easier to stay than to go home where no one even noticed she was gone. She liked to be outside where her aloneness was both visible and concrete. Sometimes if she swung high enough, the wind would seem to blow right through her chest and dissipate some of the heaviness there. At home, the feeling was concentrated, the air dense with it, the closed door behind which her mother stayed an ongoing rejection: Keep Out. How quiet she had to be as she passed that room where her mother slept and slept, how light and undemanding each footstep, each heartbeat—a soft little shadow without needs.

When Maya wandered along and sat beside her and started talking, Hannah was genuinely confused. Maya was so popular and Hannah was so...not. And yet Maya spoke to her as if they were already friends, which itself was a wonder—the simple way Maya assumed her presence was welcomed.

Hannah couldn't remember what they talked about, only that Maya kept daring her to swing higher and higher until soon they were racing each other into the sky, legs pumping, feet pointing into blue, and Maya beside her was just like the wind, dissipating her aloneness.

Then Maya leaped off the swing at its highest point and said, "Let's go to your house!" like this was something they usually did, like Hannah's apartment was a desirable place to go. How different the place had seemed once Maya was in it! Suddenly there was life standing in her kitchen. There was Maya with her long, sleek hair as black and shiny as a night ocean, her tea-tan skin and raspy voice—this fierce, wild girl with galloping bright energy, unleashed into her home like a horse through a graveyard. Maya wasn't worried about tiptoeing past Hannah's mother's door. Instead she walked in, announced, "What do you have for snacks?" and then flung open the fridge and the cabinets, pulling things out like she hadn't eaten in days. They'd decided on bagels—Hannah's favorite even then—and Hannah remembered being so surprised by the fact that Maya didn't know how to use the toaster and then again by how little butter she used for someone who seemed so comfortable helping herself to anything she wanted. "That's not how you do it," Hannah had said, almost affronted by Maya's under-buttered bagel. "Give me that." She slathered on a thick glaze. "Now make little slits like this." Hannah showed her with the knife. "So the butter melts all the way through."

Maya did as she was told, and when she took her first bite, Hannah watched her. "Good, right?"

"Oh my God," Maya had said, and her huge smile entered Hannah, lit her own.

After Maya left that day, Hannah worried what Maya would do when she found out how unpopular Hannah was at school—how leprous she seemed to be with her red clown hair. But it turned out Maya didn't care what other people thought. In fact, all the better if other people were against it. Maya threw other people's opinions out the window, not with a summoning of courage, but with a rush of glee. And anyway, Maya taught her how to tame her ridiculous hair, how to move through the world with her back a little straighter, how to ride a swing into the sky and then leap.

Hannah couldn't imagine not having Maya the way Renee no longer had Blue. The way Renee no longer had any of them. There had been a moment right after Maya mentioned

Renee was living in Connecticut that Hannah had wanted to say, "Let's go get her!" That's the kind of thing they would've done when they were younger—show up on Renee's doorstep with "Surprise!" and drag her off with them on an adventure. That instinct still lived in her somewhere. A small, mostly buried seed of spontaneity. But even if Blue would've gone along (never!), Hannah wouldn't have suggested it. She was too aware of how easily things could go wrong, how an unplanned detour could result in catastrophe. She'd already learned that lesson once. They all had. Her mind darted back to that night, the fork in the road. *"Which way? Which way?"*

The black highway unrolled. A fleet of headlights whizzed past at unsettling speeds. An unpleasant flurry in her chest, that small bird beating its wings against her rib cage. She should've known the peace she'd experienced when she first got into the car would be short-lived. Wasn't peace always?

She opened her bag, pulled out the Xanax. She would just take a half.

Blue turned. "Hey, can I get one of those?"

"Are you anxious?" Hannah asked as she tapped out a second pill into Blue's outstretched palm.

"Nope," Blue said, popping it into her mouth. "I just want to knock myself out so I don't have to deal with Maya the traitor."

"Good plan!" Maya said, unfazed. She switched the radio station to something light and easy, as if coaxing Blue into sedation.

Hannah suspected Blue really *was* anxious—that her impertinence with Maya was a cover for genuine distress over the mention of Renee. But she knew Blue would never admit that.

Hannah sighed and closed her eyes, tried to let the music soothe her. Everything would be great once they got to Nana's house. It always was. They'd gone every summer of middle school and high school, and each time they'd made the drive, that thrilling wind rushing through the open windows, Hannah would feel as if a big bright balloon were suspended in her chest, weightless and airy and flying about. When they hit the Sunrise Highway, she knew they were close, and this glow would fill her as if they were driving straight into light. And then to be at the house! Hannah loved all the noise and the laughter! There was always someone around to chat with or to go on a snack run with or simply to climb into bed with and lean her head against. She'd imagined this was what it must be like to have a real, loving family. And then she'd realized that she did have one, that nothing could stop her from claiming a family that wasn't blood born.

She tried to summon that feeling of safety now. To remember what it was to feel at home somewhere. She felt her body relax.

She must have dozed off for a bit, because the next time she looked at the clock, almost an hour and a half had passed.

"Why does that sign say we're headed toward Pittsburg?" she asked.

"What sign?"

Hannah leaned forward, pointed up.

"Uh-oh," Maya said.

Blue snorted awake in the passenger seat. "What's going on?"

The half Xanax was no match for Hannah's nerves, which were suddenly vibrating like the inside of a rung bell. She sat back and wrapped her arms around herself. It was too familiar, a reminder of another night. *You guys, I think we're lost...*

"Think I maybe took a wrong turn somewhere?" Maya said. "But not to worry! We'll just turn around at the next exit!" She pulled up the navigation system on her phone. Glanced at it. "In about fifteen miles..."

"Oh, Jesus," Blue said.

"Sorry," Maya said. "I'm freaking exhausted. I worked the night shift yesterday. You wanna take over?"

"Sure," Blue said.

"You can't drive," Hannah said. "You took a Xanax!"

"I'm fine," Blue said.

"No way," Hannah said.

"All right. Crap," Maya said. "Is there a place we can stop for the night?"

Blue sighed, pulled out her phone and asked Siri to locate the nearest motel.

"Wait, what?" Hannah said. "You're serious?" The thought of staying in a roadside motel, in a bed that other people had slept in, was just... Well, she couldn't. "Can't we just get coffee and keep going?" She could hear the rise of panic in her voice.

"I mean, we can," Maya said. "I'm just afraid I'll drive us into a ditch. Or to Alaska. You do realize we drove four hours already just to get to *you*."

"It looks like there's a motel a few minutes up the road," Blue said. "Another about twenty miles farther."

"Which place seems nicer?" Maya asked.

"Why?" Blue said. "You paying?"

"I don't mind paying," Maya said, which everyone in the car knew was technically true but also irrelevant since Maya never had any money.

They reached the first motel. A neon sign blinked Vacancy, luring travelers with a lobster buffet at the attached gas station–restaurant for $9.99. Hannah was pretty sure she recognized the place from an episode of *Cops*. "No," she said. "Keep driving."

"This is fine," Maya said. "It's just a place to crash for five or six hours. The other could be worse." She pulled in to the dimly lit semicircle parking lot, where the only two cars looked like incisors on an otherwise toothless and demented grin.

Bile rose in Hannah's throat. She hated being this way, hated it so much. She used to love motels when she was a kid, the cheap little soaps and upside-down plastic-wrapped cups in the bathrooms, the vending machines with candy bars and sodas, the dinky swimming pools with bottoms stained with mold—every motel so comfortingly the same. Now all she could see were the germs and filth. She remembered asking Dr. Maloney if the contamination fears had started because of all the blood. It had been all over her, on her hands and in her hair, Henry's blood. But he'd said that interpretation was too literal, that it was something far more poisonous that had gotten in. He'd sat back then, folded his hands across his lap and gazed at her in that penetrating way, waiting for her to figure it out. She'd stared back blankly until he announced her time was up. Whatever it was, she was certain she could not survive it. Whatever it was, her whole life was designed to avoid it. She thought again of the Xanax in her bag.

"I'll check in," Maya said.

"Wait!" Hannah said. "Can't we talk about this?"

Blue flipped Maya her credit card, got out of the car and

wandered off for another smoke. Hannah saw the small red glow of a cigarette in the distance.

She tucked her knees to her chest and attempted some deep breathing exercises. Already she wanted a scalding hot shower, maybe a precautionary antibiotic. And they hadn't even gone in yet. Which reminded her—who would be checking to make sure Henry's room was sterile without her to supervise the nurses when Vivian wasn't there?

She checked her phone, her mind lurching toward disaster. But there was nothing from Vivian. Nothing from the care facility. Just a bunch of Dear Miss Know-It-All emails, which made her feel heavy with answers she didn't have about questions she hadn't even read. Maybe by the time she got back—if she actually survived this trip—she'd feel less like a fraud offering other people wisdom.

A large truck rumbled up behind her, its square face glaring down with blinding yellow eyes. Hannah looked for Blue but could no longer find her. She inched lower in the seat, heard the sound of her own whimper. *Breathe, breathe, breathe.* She did this for as long as she could. When she finally opened her eyes, the truck was gone.

There was a sudden knock on the window. Hannah jumped, screamed.

Maya laughed as she held a key card up to the glass. "The key to paradise, baby," she said, spreading her arms wide across the parking lot, nearly knocking Blue, who had come up behind her, in the face. "I requested a room without a meth lab. But those were all booked up. I'm kidding."

"This place is seriously not safe!" Hannah said. "This creepy trucker pulled in right after you left. Scared the hell out of me."

"Your whole life scares the hell out of you," Maya said.

"If you saw the *Dateline* segment on roadside motels, you'd get it. They don't even clean the rooms!"

"Well, I haven't showered, so…it's a match," Maya said.

"And sometimes they don't even change the key codes, so anyone can get in."

"So it's a good thing you're staying with me," Maya said. "If anyone gets kidnapped, it'll be Blue. She's the low-hanging fruit."

"It's true," Blue said.

"I'm sleeping in the car," Hannah said.

"Please stop being ridiculous," Maya said.

Blue opened the car door, peered in. "You're definitely not safer alone in a car in the parking lot," Blue said gently. "Maybe the rooms are nicer than you think."

Hannah grabbed at Blue's compassion as if it were a parachute rip cord. She took another deep breath, clinging to the last-standing soldier of reason in her brain trying to fight back the stampede of irrational terror. One quick look at the room. If it wasn't okay, she would insist that they leave.

They wheeled their luggage toward the rusty metal staircase, past a vending machine with a ripped sign taped to it— "Out of Ordor"—the words *Eat me* scrawled below it. Even Blue looked a little uneasy.

"Here we are," Maya said, sticking the key into the slot.

Hannah peered over Blue's shoulder as Maya opened the door, causing an exhale of mildew and uncirculated air. Maya flipped the light switch to reveal two twin beds with bedspreads the color of vomit, a neat fold of white top sheet disguising all the human ick that had slept within.

Hannah froze at the door. "I can't," she said. "There has to be something else."

Maya dumped her luggage onto the floor. "There isn't." She kicked off her flip-flops, marched across the stained carpet and launched herself onto the bed.

"Oh my God," Hannah said. Her heart was hurtling. Her insides fizzing like a shaken can. Brain jumping from one terror to another. "Those comforters probably haven't been washed since the sixties." She could hear the hysteria in her voice, an onslaught of adrenaline and flight signals trampling over her capacity for reason. "Now you know why I always say no to everything. This is what yes looks like."

"This," Maya said, gesturing around her, "is what life looks like! Embrace it! Roll around in the shit of it!" She turned over and buried her face in the bedspread. "I love germs!"

Hannah screamed.

"You're an ass," Blue said to Maya. "She's right. They don't wash those things." Then to Hannah she added, "It's only one night. You can stay with me if you want. I'm more fun anyway."

"Ha! In your dreams!" Maya said, rolling over onto her back. "She's staying with me in the nondelusional room."

Blue laughed seemingly despite herself. "Well, I'm going to bed. I'll see you clowns in the morning." She turned to Hannah. "Remember, I'm right next door if it's too crowded in there with Maya's ego."

Maya threw a pillow at Blue.

Blue ducked, shouting "Nice try, loser!" as she slipped off to her room.

The second she was gone, Hannah realized there was no chance of them changing their minds about staying here. She looked at the bed next to Maya's but couldn't bring herself to move toward it. "I don't think I can do this," she said. Just standing there was making her itch.

Maya sat up. "What on earth do you think is going to happen?"

"I don't know… I just…" But there was no way to explain a phobia to anyone who didn't have one. It didn't matter that it wasn't rational, that the danger was imagined or overblown. What mattered was that it felt real and that the fear was a torture far worse than whatever had triggered it. She closed her eyes, picturing her bed at home, everything so clean and neat and safe. All she wanted was to be normal again. To not be so exhausted and exhausting. She started to cry.

"Stop!" Maya said, jumping up from the bed. The energy of her annoyance crowded the room, clashing with Hannah's distress, further abandoning her to it. "You are not going to do this. You are not allowed to break down on me. We're on vacation!"

"I'm trying!" Hannah said. She wept harder. "Do you think I *want* to be like this? Do you think this is a *choice*?"

Maya held up her hands in surrender. "Okay, okay," she said. "Hey, I'm sorry. Seriously, please don't cry. We'll figure something out. I'm going to help you." She scanned the room, frowning. Then her face lit up. "I know!"

"What?" Hannah said.

"Close your eyes."

"Why? Are you going to do something gross?"

"No. Just do it."

Hannah sighed.

"*Both* eyes, please. Thank you. Okay, take a few deep breaths."

Hannah tried, but her body resisted, didn't want to take

in the musty, moldy air, didn't want to take in any life at all. The sound of her own pathetic efforts made her only want to cry more.

"Now I want you to imagine you're walking into a… Where do you wish you could be?"

Hannah thought. *What is the opposite of this motel room?*

"Somewhere clean," she said over the mass in her throat. "Sterile." She heard the swish of the thick curtains being closed, could see the light behind her lids go black.

"Okay, great! So we're walking into a hospital."

Hannah thought of all those months with Henry in the ICU and squeezed her eyes against the image. She must have shaken her head because Maya quickly added, "It's not that kind of hospital though." And then, "I'm thinking it's more like an asylum."

Hannah opened one eye.

"Okay, sorry, kidding. Bad joke. It's more like a med spa. Not one patient there yet. You're the first person to ever enter it. Okay?"

Hannah nodded.

"Good. Now take a step onto the clean, bleached floor. You can do this."

Hannah kept her eyes squeezed shut. "Oh God, oh God." She tried to envision pristine flooring, but in her mind the carpet came alive, all those germs from all those people just waiting for their moment to get inside and pollute her. "This isn't going to work."

"It won't if you believe that." She grabbed Hannah's hand. "Now take a step forward. Ooh, watch out for all the cleaning supplies. Don't want to trip on that disinfectant. Do you smell all that bleach?"

Hannah giggled in spite of herself. She focused her attention on Maya's voice and the feeling of Maya's hot, dry hand in hers, allowing her to skid around the edges of the panic just a bit, just enough to take a small step, like dipping toes into a pool.

"Awesome. Now I'm going to lead you over to your bed."

Hannah stopped. "Can you check it first?"

"Check it for what?"

"Everything."

Maya sighed. "Stay there. Keep your eyes closed."

Hannah saw pink light behind her lids as Maya flicked on the bedside lamp. "Be thorough!" she called. She could practically feel Maya's eyes roll, and yet it was a comfort—her predictability.

After a minute Maya announced, "Perfectly clean," and switched off the light again. "Not a speck or a stain."

Hannah felt Maya's hand grab her fingers, drag her over to the bed.

"Now, I'm going to pull down the sterilized blanket and you're going to get under the nice, brand-new, hot-washed sheets."

Hannah sat on the bed and Maya took off her shoes as if she were a small child. Maya stroked her arm a few times.

"Now lie back."

Hannah slowly lowered her back down onto the bed.

"Spin a little."

Hannah turned and Maya took her legs and slid them under the covers. She realized she was trembling as Maya pulled the sheets up to her chin, tucked in the edges around her like a parent would do, left the dirty duvet at her feet.

Hannah opened her eyes. "You'd make a good mom," she said.

Maya smiled. "Thanks."

"We're all seeing in real time why *I* wouldn't."

They both laughed, and new tears pushed at the back of Hannah's eyes, born of gratitude.

"Xanax, please?" she whispered. "It's in the side pocket of my bag."

Hannah heard Maya's feet padding away, heard her curse as she stubbed her toe, heard the bathroom light snap on, Maya fumbling with the bag, the rattle of the bottle…padding back.

"Open," Maya said.

Hannah opened her mouth and the tiny, weightless tablet dropped onto her tongue. She swallowed it dry, anticipating the gentle warmth that would soon spread across her brain, making her limbs heavy, as if she could feel gravity pressing down on her, holding her in place. All she needed to do was survive the night. Six hours. She could do it.

She opened her eyes to see the outline of Maya's features, her familiar eyes compassionate and love-lit in the dark. "Thanks," she said. She let her lids go heavy. "Can you turn the bathroom light back off?"

"Your eyes are closed. You can't see it."

"No, I'll be able to tell."

"Not if you're asleep."

"But I won't be able to fall asleep with the light on."

"Yes, you will. Just let the kind pharmaceutical fairies take you away."

"But," Hannah said, "why does the light need to be on?"

"Gently taking you away off to dreamland…"

"Wait a minute." Hannah sat up. "Are you afraid of the dark?"

"What? No!"

"You are!" she shrieked. "I can't believe it. Is it the boogey-man you're worried about?"

"I'm not afraid of the dark."

"Boogey, boogey, boogey, boogey!"

They were both laughing now.

"I can't wait to tell Blue!"

"When did this become about me?"

"Oh my God, you're scared of the dark—and you know what's the best part? That's, like, the one thing I'm not afraid of."

"Oh, piss off."

"Speaking of being pissed," Hannah said, turning serious. "I feel really bad about Blue. I think she was genuinely upset about the whole Renee thing."

"Oh, whatever! She's being ridiculous."

Hannah sighed. "We don't know that. Maybe Renee did something really bad."

"What could possibly be that bad? Blue's just queen of the grudge. Remember that time she didn't speak to Renee for like two months because Renee ran over her pet lizard?"

"Well, yeah, but... Blue loved Edward."

"It wasn't intentional! As far as I know... Look, don't worry about it. I have a feeling they'll be friends again soon enough."

"Really?" Hannah said doubtfully. "I don't see how, but... good night, then." She watched Maya's shadow move to the bathroom. "Maya?" she said. She knew she shouldn't but couldn't stop herself. "Henry's okay, right? Do you think he's wondering where I am?"

She heard the bathroom door close.

MAYA

Maya stood on the other side of the door, leaned against it, breathed. She didn't understand the point of asking a question when you didn't want the answer. Sometimes Hannah's issues felt like a personal attack on her, forcing Maya to remember over and over again why they were there. She knew this was unfair.

She looked at Hannah's Xanax bottle. About ten pills left out of sixty and it was filled less than three weeks before. Maya envisioned shaking them out into the chipped white toilet, flushing them down like she used to do with her mother's pills no matter how many times it got her in trouble. She would do anything to exorcise the terrified animal who had taken over her friend's body, made her need drugs and plastic bags and antibacterial soaps. Anything to return the Hannah who existed before Henry had been stuffed into an ambulance

like a couch into a moving van, rushed to the ER in a dizzying blur of blue light and howling, the smooth black summer
night shattered with emergency.

Maya had been so sure in those first days when Henry was
in the ICU that everything would be fine, that Henry was
young and strong and that life would not allow such an injus-
tice. She visited, she talked to him, she brought him presents
for when he woke up. But once he was moved into a home—
his condition accepted as it was—she found excuses not to go.
There was always something she had to do, a reason she had
to put it off one more day and then another. Just like she'd
done with those bills that kept piling up on her kitchen table.
Better to stuff them into a drawer, pretend it wasn't happening. What else was she supposed to do? She couldn't fix it.
And she knew she had to keep moving or she'd end up like
Hannah, stuck inside that night, roaming the halls and rat-
tling the chains of fear like a ghost.

She sighed, looked around at the bathroom, the tiles skin
pink, the natty white towels neatly folded over the bar, the
white bath mat draped upon the tub. All the people who had
paused here on their way to somewhere else, on their way
home. She thought about her house, the only thing that had
ever belonged to her. *Why couldn't she hold on to anything?*

Don't pick at it, she told herself. This was what she thought
when something was wrong in her life. When she was a kid,
her father always reprimanded her when she scratched at the
scabs on her knees. It turned out to be the only useful thing
he'd ever taught her. Don't pick at a wound. It just makes it
worse.

A sudden familiar restlessness kicked up in her, an itch.
She'd always enjoyed attention, but in moments like this,

something happened in her, a craving so strong and wiggly that she had to sate it just to sit still again. She pulled out her phone, scrolled her contacts, called the twenty-one-year-old with the scaphoid fracture. *What was his name? Justin, Dustin? Jeff? Whatever. Irrelevant.*

"Yo." He picked up. His voice was thick with sleep.

Yo? She removed the phone briefly from her ear and stared at it, annoyed. "Hey, it's Maya!"

There was a silence, one second, two, eternity, and then, "Oh yeah, the nurse with the big boobs."

"Medical transporter with the big boobs."

"Right. Come over. I miss you."

Maya rolled her eyes and gave her phone the middle finger. Usually it was enough—the cheap thrill of men's desire—so easy to provoke—a momentary distraction. But tonight, a tiny sadness, the size of a single tear, welled inside. She didn't understand why. What was she expecting? She flashed back to Steve at work asking, "When are you going to have a real relationship?"

Was that what she wanted? A real relationship? She peeked her head out of the bathroom, saw Hannah's shadow in the dark, clutching her blanket to her chin.

No.

She wanted a good time. He just wasn't it.

"I think you have the wrong number!" she said into the phone.

"But you called—"

She hung up, smiled into the mirror to cheer herself. Behind her, the leaky bathtub faucet dripped—tock, tock, tock—the sound of insanity. She got undressed for bed, caught sight of the small constellation of scars on her back from the time when she was seven and her mother had thrown plates at her in a fit of rage. The lines were faded now, a mark of time.

Back in high school, after she and Hannah and Henry had gotten ripely stoned on the roof of Henry's house one night, the moon so low it was a fourth companion, she'd showed them the marks on her back. She'd never let anyone see them before. She feared pity, thought it contagious.

Now she closed her eyes, brought the memory into focus. She could see Hannah vividly, her cheeks so round back then, that peachy blush she used to wear, too orange against her pale skin. She could see herself, too, her T-shirt collar cut off at the neck, her arms wrapped around her knees, her long hair grazing them. Her mind flickered to Henry, the image of him smudgy. It was strange the way she could remember each of his features but not quite add them together to make a face. No matter how hard she tried, her mind would not let her see him.

Maya was laughing when she showed Hannah and Henry the scars, shrugging them off as nothing. What else could she do but make it not matter?

But then Hannah had put her hand on Maya's back, traced her soft fingers over the white raised slashes, and maybe it was the pot, maybe it was just that Maya was so fucking high, but something shifted inside her. She could feel Hannah's fingers penetrate her skin, her bones, probing until they found how deep the cuts actually went, pressing lightly on the wounds to staunch a bleed that had never actually stopped.

"You're like a whale," Hannah said, voice hoarse with the weed and with a kind of soft wonder.

Why did Maya feel like she wanted to cry?

"Henry, tell her she's a whale," Hannah said.

"You're a whale, dude," Henry said. He was lying back on the slant of the roof, looking at the sky.

"What the fuck does that even mean?" Maya said, taking another drag on the joint. It helped to say *fuck*, to carve her mouth around the hardness of the word. It was instinctual to reject softness. Isn't that what all the motherless did? Made themselves not need it, disdain it even. But it got in anyway, slipped in some side door of her. Thankfully, no matter how much Maya resisted it, Hannah and her softness always got in.

"Henry, tell her what it all means," Hannah said.

Henry shook his head in wonder, an unfathomably deep question to ponder.

Hannah sighed, exasperated that her profound pot-induced insights couldn't be followed. "Because whales are all scratched up from shark bites and orcas and whatnot," she said. She nudged Henry. "Remember that documentary we watched?"

"You watched," Henry said, gazing up at her. "I was watching you."

Hannah bent over and kissed him, then sat back down, reclined against him. "Whales are awesome, man. They're all like, 'Whatever. Go ahead and try me. I don't care.' They just keep cruising on, getting bigger and bigger until they're bigger than everyone, the biggest on earth."

"Whales are outrageous," Henry said.

Hannah sat back up then. "That's you, Maya. Inside I mean. You're the biggest person I know. No one can break you." She'd spread her arms as wide as the future.

Maya laughed it off, but then Hannah said, "Don't you get it? She threw plates at you and the plates are what broke. Not you. She was aiming for you but only destroyed her china."

And *fuck*, Maya really was going to cry then. She closed

her eyes, and the scars on her back, those marks of hatred and violence, of being unloved, they were reordering in her mind—*shit, was this pot laced?*—transforming into the shape of a whale. And where once there was her mother's fury, now there was a benign, resilient mammal tattooed on her skin, in her heart. Where once there was her mother's fury, now there was Hannah and her love, not replacing it—*if only!*—but covering it like a soldier lying over the wounded.

She wanted to say this but it was at once too corny and too meaningful. Instead she said, "You're stoned, Hannah."

"She is," Henry said.

"I am," Hannah replied, and then she threw her head back with that great laugh she had, so genuine and rewarding.

She thought of present-day Hannah, too frightened to even walk into a motel room. Was it possible to miss a laugh so much you sprained your heart? She could hardly fathom Hannah smoking pot, much less sitting on a rooftop or throwing her head back with such pure perfect joy.

She caught her reflection in the mirror. A whale. She rolled the word around in her mind like a pool ball, smooth and calming, knocking out worries of what she would do if the bank loan didn't come through. It would, of course—but just in case, it helped to be reminded that she was a survivor. She looked again at Hannah's Xanax, picked it up and tucked it in her own bag. She would prove to Hannah that she didn't need it. That Hannah was a whale too. She walked out, leaving the bathroom door open enough to create a strip of light across her bed.

"You still awake?" she said.

"Unfortunately," Hannah said. "Why?"

She had the impulse to tell Hannah about the situation

with her house, to say, "Look! Another shark attack." She didn't know why, who she was trying to convince that she'd survive it.

But then Hannah said in a small, tired voice, "You're not really afraid of the dark, are you?"

"Of course not," Maya said. She walked back to the bathroom, turned off the light. "Go to sleep."

She got into bed and pulled out her phone, checked her social media feeds, refreshing them several times in case something interesting should come in. It didn't. She cheered herself with the reminder of her secret plan. Fired off a quick text. She couldn't wait.

She listened for the sound of Hannah's breathing, noticed it had slowed. Then she got up and turned the bathroom light back on.

BLUE

Blue woke with no idea where she was. She blinked into the disorienting tilt of an unrecognizable room—stained walls, an orange paisley bedspread, a television set circa 1971. She was supposed to be in beautiful Montauk, waking to salt air and the rustle of the ocean, birdsong at her window. Instead she was in a cheap motel off some random highway. She had to laugh. She let herself be convinced by Maya of all people—the used car salesman of friends—of the perfect dream vacation and this is where they'd ended up. It was so typical. It almost wouldn't have been a real trip together if it had gone down as promised.

And then, less amusing, she remembered Maya's phone call to Renee. Also typical Maya. She rolled away from the spill of early sun through the blinds, yanked the sheet over her head. She knew it was childish to be upset about it, but the residue of betrayal lingered. Well, she wouldn't let it ruin her trip. It was a quick call, nothing more. If Maya had any clue what Renee had done, it never would have been made.

The sounds of low talking wafted through the thin walls, and Blue tried to listen in case Hannah and Maya were talking about her. But their voices were too muffled to make out. She'd forgotten how the invisible divide between her and them had always been there. Not that it was intentional. But sometimes, when they were all together, a vague loneliness slipped in like a fog, reminded her that Maya and Hannah were always each other's number one. She had lost the one person—Renee—who loved her best.

Well, it was no loss, really. The loss was in believing Renee had actually cared.

Her phone pinged with a text.

We need to get out of here before Hannah goes into cardiac arrest!!!

Always with the excessive punctuation. Maya herself was like a walking exclamation point. Blue got out of bed, washed up, grabbed her duffel bag and went next door.

Maya, wet haired and smelling like cheap shampoo, let her in. "Good morning, sunshine!"

Blue raised an eyebrow. "Is it though?"

Maya laughed. "It will be soon enough!"

In the background, Hannah was throwing her clothes into the trash bin.

"Don't ask," Maya said.

"Because it's what I slept in," Hannah explained, stricken. "Please, let's get out of here!"

Blue's heart tugged with pity. She couldn't imagine what

it would be like to live inside Hannah's terrified brain, to see the dark underbelly of life ever present, illuminated as if with a black light. She didn't know how to help, so she grabbed Hannah's bag and carried it out.

The day was gluey and overcast, the sun fuzzy and out of focus behind the clouds. In the parking lot, Blue stuffed their bags in the trunk and they all climbed into the car.

"This place looks even worse in the light of day!" Hannah said, staring back at the motel like it might give chase.

"Indeed, it does," Maya said cheerfully. "But we survived it! Now if we could all just lighten up a tad—" she glanced at Hannah in the back seat dousing herself in Purell, at Blue probably looking world-weary beside her "—on our *vacation*… because hello, we're on vacation…we might just have some fun." She started the car, flipped on the radio, cranked the volume up. "Road trip dance party!" She swayed toward Blue, snapping her fingers to the music, flashing a big, cheesy grin.

Blue stared back, unamused.

Maya sighed, turned down the radio. "Probably for the best. No one needs to be traumatized by your dance moves this early in the morning." She lowered the window, stuck her head out and yelled "Beach, here we come! Woo-hoo!" into the summer air. They peeled out of the lot.

In truth, Blue was pretty excited. She simply wasn't as emotive as her friends. But when she thought of the house, everything good she knew of life felt stored there. Funny to think that the first time her parents sent her there it had seemed like a punishment. She was being shipped off for the summer to another state and to a grandmother she'd never met. But something had shifted when she saw the house. It was rustic and square and as welcoming as an invitation, made of rich brown wood with a white second-floor porch that seemed to practically float over the water. And those steep steps leading to the dock—she could walk straight out of the house and down into the sea.

Nana had run out to greet her in one of her bright-colored muumuus, her arms outstretched, her smile warm and genuine. "Little one!" she said, and just that, to be called an endearment for the first time in her life, dismantled Blue's sullen defenses. In the kitchen there was iced tea and cookies set out for her and in her room a new boogie board still wrapped in its plastic, a teddy bear Blue was too old for waiting cheerfully for her on her bed. Blue was wanted here. She barely noticed when her parents left.

That first summer, Nana had made a great companion. She loved the beach and sometimes even joined Blue in the waves, wearing the most ridiculous bathing cap with flowers on it and a suit so bright it could be seen from space, whooping gleefully at the cold water as the gentle waves struck her. But even Nana could tell that the days were too long for Blue without friends her own age. The following year she told Blue to bring anyone she wanted. Blue had brought Renee and Maya and Hannah.

Had Blue understood back then what she was sharing? Probably not consciously. But in retrospect she could see how much lighter they all seemed in that house—where Hannah didn't have to tiptoe and Maya didn't have to duck a blow and Renee didn't have to exist where people wished she didn't.

Those first few years, Blue's father drove them out in his big black Lincoln Town Car, listening to news radio and smoking his cigars like the girls weren't even there, the four of them squeezed together in the back trying not to breathe too deep or die from boredom over the five-and-a-half-hour trip. But the minute they saw the sign for the Sunrise Highway, something about that magical name ignited their excitement. Even the road promised hope.

Once Maya turned sixteen, they drove out in her old ratty Jeep—the "heap Jeep," they called it—hair whipping, music loud, a whooping cheer every time they saw that favorite sign.

Each summer Nana had given them a little more space, allowed them to develop their independence in a way that felt both safe and giddy. Once she even let Henry come and stay the night. He'd been a counselor at a tennis camp in New York that summer and took the Jitney out. They'd all gone to the beach, dutiful Henry loaded down with all their towels and chairs like their own personal Sherpa. He was always such a good sport about things like that. It had been a hot day and the ocean was refreshingly cold and sparkly and they'd body surfed the waves like a pod of dolphins for hours. Henry and Hannah kept pausing to kiss between the sets while Maya and Blue made gagging noises at them. When the sun mellowed and lowered, Henry and Hannah had gone for a walk, holding hands as they disappeared into the distance, Hannah laughing into his shoulder. As Blue watched them, she'd pictured them strolling the same beach in middle age—a couple of kids and maybe a golden retriever trailing behind, then old age, Hannah gray and Henry balding, still holding hands, still making each other laugh. Back then it seemed like the only certainty she could count on.

"Hey, Blue," Maya said, interrupting her thoughts. "Remember that time you got stuck in a riptide and it pulled you into the middle of a surfing competition?" She was already laughing, had clearly envisioned it in her head before she spoke.

"Oh yeah. Some surf bro called me a speed bump and almost ran me over while I was drowning."

"They thought you were out there on purpose!" Hannah said.

"I know! I was waving for help and everyone on shore was waving back!"

They were all laughing now.

"We called you 'speed bump' for the rest of the summer," Hannah said.

"I remember," Blue groaned.

"Was it Renee who grabbed some random dude's board and paddled out to you?" Maya asked.

Blue knew the question was disingenuous. Maya was well aware of the answer. She could feel her blood pressure rise but refused to engage or be baited.

"That was some quick thinking," Maya added. "Probably saved your life."

Blue stared at her for an extra beat. Then looked away. "I would've been fine."

"Remember how you went and yelled at the lifeguard?" Hannah said to Maya. "Who you then proceeded to make out with like five hours later."

"Oh yeah, at the bonfire. He was cute."

"He was very bad at his job," Blue said.

"We had a lot in common."

An old Van Morrison song came on the radio and Maya said "Ooh!" and cranked it up and soon they were all swept up in it, singing along just like they used to. The wind was in Blue's hair and the day was in full bloom as the miles moved them closer to the girls they once knew, the house they once loved. When they hit the Sunrise Highway, they cheered.

Blue could've predicted with her eyes closed the minute

they reached the Hamptons. The air changed, turned sweet and clean like it was filtered through sunshine and honey. She inhaled deeply, the golden wash of afternoon sun glinting off windshields and dappling through the trees on the side of the road. They drove past vineyards and little farm stands with weathered wooden signs for corn and jam and fruit. Past the square, white shops of Bridgehampton, Water Mill, East Hampton, Amagansett. Then, unleashed from the traffic, they whipped across the natty Napeague stretch until at last they were up and over the hill and looking down into Montauk, the Atlantic a sparkly blue bowl below them, rippling sideways like a flag in wind, a perfect circle of sun standing above it.

They stopped quickly in the old fishing village for snacks and the town paper and soft ice cream cones with sprinkles at John's Drive-In. Then they drove out past the Montauk library and onto a sand-dusted road toward the beach. Finally they turned onto the pebble driveway of Nana's house.

"Bring on the beach, bitches!" Maya screamed, leaping out of the car.

On the porch next door an elderly couple glanced over, alarmed. Blue gave a small, embarrassed wave.

The wooden two-story looked almost exactly as it did in Blue's memory—smaller, perhaps, and more worn—the fence around it knocked down, probably by a tropical storm. The hammock still swung between the trees, but the netting looked ratty and precarious. Blue could see them again as they once were—bright and bursting out of the car in their short shorts and halter tops, their flesh so ripe and new, their laughter raucous and without edges, piercing the quiet. She remembered the last time they were there, how Hannah had run and jumped up on the front porch railing, walked it like a balance beam, did a little shuffle-hop-step, a cartwheel dismount. So fully present to the sunshine, to the smell of the ocean, to her friends beside her. She remembered Maya dashing out to the hammock, diving gleefully onto it, only to be flipped out, dangling by one leg as the others laughed. *A little help, assholes!* Her and Renee darting past Hannah up to the second floor to claim the best bedroom, doing their secret victory handshake when they got to it before Hannah and Maya did.

Now she extracted the spare key from the seashell key hider, left there for the property management and housekeeping services that came a few times a year to check the pipes, clean the house, mow the lawn and clear the gutters. The moment she unlocked the front door, Maya rushed past her into the foyer with its high ceiling and hardwood floor, its hollow echo. "I can't believe we're here!" Maya said as she threw her arms out and did a twirl. She took a big dramatic inhale. "Smell that—exactly the same." She waved the air under her nose like she was a sommelier. "A wonderful bouquet…soap…sunshine… and a touch of…mold…or is it mildew? What's the difference anyway?"

"Actually, they're two different kinds of fungi," Hannah said, "which grow on—"

"Oh, sorry, that wasn't a serious question," Maya said.

Blue took a deep breath filled with memory.

"I am literally eighteen again!" Maya said. "If we just cover all the mirrors, boom, we're all eighteen. Well, Blue's actually a grouchy old lady but, whatever…"

Blue tried to formulate a comeback, but Maya was already gone, running between the rooms on the first floor like a dog coming home. She returned breathless. "Everything looks the same. It's like being in a time warp. Come look!"

They moved into the kitchen, the cabinets now dated, the linoleum floor peeling at the edges. In the center, the round dinner table where they'd once played drinking games while classic rock played beneath their laughter—Skynyrd and Zeppelin and Floyd—music that felt like a secret passed down from one generation of rebellious teenagers to the next, songs that carried the tang of nostalgia for their youth even as they were experiencing it.

"Whatever shall we do first?" Blue said. Maya's gleefulness was catching.

"I need the bathroom and a shower," Hannah said.

"I was thinking we might—"

The sound of pebbles kicking in the driveway made them all turn.

"Who's that?" Blue said. "I'm not expecting anyone." She went to the front door where a shiny red-and-black Mini Cooper was now parked behind their rental.

Maya followed, Hannah behind them.

"That is…" Maya said. The car door opened and a slim woman emerged, slightly teetering on sandals with a heel an inch too high, a bottle of wine in one hand, flowers in the other. "Uh…surprise! Please don't kill me."

Blue was pinned where she stood.

"Renee!" Maya called, waving.

"Hello!" Renee waved back with the airy cheer of someone departing on a cruise ship. She made a few careful steps across the pebbles and then her eyes found Blue. Her smile wobbled and her wave turned tentative.

Blue's mouth hung open. A violent knock in her chest. Shock first. Then rage so hot and quick inside her, it could launch her head like a rocket. She looked at Maya, let her eyes speak for her: *Are. You. Fucking. Kidding. Me. Right. Now?*

Maya stared back, defiant.

Blue spun around, marched back into the kitchen. She didn't know what to do with herself. Where to go. How to manage this.

She heard Maya call, "Stay right there, Renee! I'll be right back. Hannah, talk to Renee."

Blue dashed out the side door. Folded over. She was short of breath as if she'd been running. A sharp cramp across her chest.

"Listen." It was Maya coming toward her. "I know you're pissed."

She was too angry to speak. Her fists were clenched so tightly she imprinted little crescents on her palms with her fingernails.

"Okay, you're *really* pissed. But come on… Twelve years ago we made a vow that we'd *all* come back. All *four* of us. A sacred vow."

Blue breathed through her nose. An image came to her—a game the four of them used to play over long, boring summers, tying rubber bands around a watermelon until it burst from the pressure. She could still recall that visceral squeeze, the anticipation of the explosion, not knowing when it would come, how destructive it would be. Now she imagined her own brain being wrapped in rubber bands, tighter and tighter.

"I cannot even believe…" She was still thin on air. "This is the worst stunt you've ever pulled. And that's saying a lot."

"That is actually saying a lot," Maya admitted.

Blue glared at her.

"I'm sorry."

"You're not."

"I honestly didn't know you'd react this way."

"Oh really? You didn't know I'd react this way? Right.

Then why didn't you tell me up front? You knew. And you did it anyway."

"Look. I knew you wouldn't be thrilled but I didn't realize... I invited her before we left—just for the day! But then when I told you about the call and you got so mad about it...well... I should've uninvited her then but I just...didn't know how."

"You say, 'Hey, sorry, I screwed up. You're not invited.' It's not hard. And why on earth would she think she *would* be invited here? It's *my* nana's house!"

Maya grimaced. "I may have possibly mentioned you were okay with it."

Blue gaped at her. She rubbed her hands over her face.

"Please just come say hi. I know you hate me right now but please."

"No."

"She's already seen you. Don't make it weird."

"Tell her it was a hologram. That I'm really back in New York."

Maya looked at her helplessly.

"I cannot believe you did this to me."

"I didn't do it to you—I did it *for* you. I love and adore you and I would never want to hurt you. I wanted to make things better."

"For you."

"For all of us."

"You can't. And it isn't your place to try."

"Okay. I get that now. It was ill conceived. I may have a habit of things like that."

"May?"

"But still, I would consider it a huge, humongous, gigantic, undeserved favor if you would just come say hi..."

"The favor was me agreeing to come on your spontaneous trip, paying for the rental car, supplying the house," Blue said. "The other favor is me not kicking your ass."

"I've seen you throw a punch. I'm not scared."

"No, you haven't. When?"

"Mark Tarrington. Eighth grade. He snapped your bra. You tried to punch him. He ducked. You lost your balance and fell into a pond."

"Oh, right. He was an asshole," Blue said. And then returning to the present moment, "And so are you."

"It's true. I am. Now come on. Ten minutes. Then I'll ask her—gently—to leave."

"No."

Renee was calling from the driveway. "Maya?"

Maya turned back to Blue, whispered, "Please."

Blue whispered back, "No."

"I'll give you twenty bucks."

"You don't have twenty bucks."

"But if I did, I would give it to you." Maya made a pleading puppy-dog face.

Blue sighed. It was so hard to stay mad at Maya—a fact that itself made her mad. And she knew it would make her look pathetic and petty *not* to go back out there. It would give Renee the impression that Blue actually cared. Which she absolutely did not. Not at all. "Go away. I need a cigarette."

"Okay," Maya said. "That's not a no, so I'll take it."

Blue watched Maya walk back to the front. She could see Renee through the bushes that separated the yard from the driveway. That profile so familiar, so deeply imprinted on her. She took in the changes in her face, her hair, her clothes— a glaring display of all the lost years. Time, usually so insidious and creeping, announced itself loudly. How inexplicably grown-up they were, how they had done this growing apart. There was a sudden ache in her throat made of history. The recognition of a different version of this story where that night hadn't happened. Where she would run out and tackle-hug Renee, both of them talking over each other in their excitement.

She looked at her cigarette pack, decided it wouldn't do enough, pulled out her vape pen, pressed the button and inhaled. It was all she could do, all she knew how to do, to let the pot fuzz the edges of her brain, settle like soft foam over her nervous system.

She should just leave. Go back to Manhattan. Return the rental car. Spend the weekend catching up with work. Let them figure out their own transportation! In fact, to hell with it, why not? She had better things to do than screw around at the beach.

But then—Jack. And besides, Hannah was innocent. It wouldn't be fair to her.

She leaned back against the house, followed the pot with an emergency cigarette. She was smoking too much but *whatever, screw it.* Everything was an emergency right now. Her life. This trip. She breathed deep, as if she could smother the slow rise of old things, that terrible susurrus of darkness rearing up. Wordless, imageless memory in her body, in her cells. The bottomless unanswered call of her eighteen-year-old self: *Help me, someone help me!*

She bit down on the memory, looked out at the blotchy sunlight through the canopy of trees, a kid on a bike in his driveway riding up and down, up and down, lonely as the moon's rise and set.

HANNAH

Hannah wanted to run after Blue. But there was Renee, who she hadn't seen in twelve years, standing alone in the driveway looking wide-eyed and uncertain, her arms drooping with the weight of the spurned wine and flowers.

She didn't know what to do. Just when she was settling into the trip, Maya had to throw in a plot twist. She was already stressed after the night at the motel, turbulent weather brewing at the edges of her. She could sense it like the first ripples of chop on a pre-storm sea.

Hannah made a decision. Hoped Blue would forgive her.

"Renee!" she said, stepping onto the porch.

Renee's face smoothed slightly. Hannah took in her stylish haircut, her effortful clothes in the latest fashion, her flawless makeup. There was something slightly different about her face. Older, of course, but something else that unsettled Hannah

because she couldn't put her finger on it. Botox? Plastic sur-
gery? Still it was Renee. Renee! And though her eyes needed
to catch up to this new version, her heart did not. Years could
pass, the mind could forget, but the heart always remembered.

They hugged and Hannah said, "Hi, hi, hi!" trying to talk
over the growing, obvious absence of Maya and Blue.

Renee kept smiling but her eyes betrayed her, had that look
she always got when any sort of conflict was present, flitting
around for somewhere to flee. She stepped back. Held Hannah's
hands in hers. "You look wonderful," she said. "I should go."

Hannah opened her mouth to say no. She didn't want
Renee to go. But then—Blue would be so hurt. She couldn't
betray her like that. Instead she tilted her head, met Renee's
eyes to convey her wish that it could be otherwise.

"It's fine," Renee said. "I actually have a million other
things I should be doing anyway. A wedding to plan, if Maya
didn't tell you." She lit up suddenly as if talking herself back
into joy. "I'm marrying the most amazing guy."

"Yes! I'd heard. That's so great—I'm really happy for you."
She smiled as warmly as she could, trying to mirror Renee's
sudden mood shift, sustain connection with her darting eyes.
Even when they were kids, it could feel like trying to lasso a
spooked horse once Renee's fear kicked in. She was the friend
they had to navigate a little more carefully. No direct confrontation. Constructive criticisms carefully Bubble Wrapped
inside layers of compliments. It was never discussed. They all
intuitively understood that Renee had a certain fragility that
couldn't bear the frankness they used with one another.

Hannah had never minded the extra work. When they
were thirteen, she'd slept over at Renee's house a few times.
After Renee's dad had left, her mother had taken a night job

at a restaurant and often stayed after her shift to drink with her coworkers. Sometimes she brought a strange man home who made Hannah uneasy when she passed him in the hallway. Eventually Renee's mom married the creep. Renee said that none of it bothered her, and yet every night she carefully lined up her stuffed animals like guards around her bed, a teddy bear fortress. "I can't sleep otherwise," she'd explained, embarrassed. Even at thirteen, Hannah recognized the need for a sense of safety, no matter how false. She couldn't have articulated it, but she felt it.

As Renee got older, the bears were retired and instead her fortress became that plastered smile, those fleeing eyes, her well-cultivated beauty. Very few people were ever allowed to penetrate the facade, and, even then, admittance seemed precarious, easily retracted. Only Blue had been trusted enough to be allowed complete access to Renee's heart.

Now Renee handed Hannah the wine and flowers. "Tell Maya—"

"Tell Maya what?" Maya said, reappearing in the driveway.

"That I'm leaving." Renee said.

"What? No, you can't!"

Renee shook her head. "You told me Blue was okay with this."

"She is!" Maya said. "She's completely fine with it."

Hannah shot her an incredulous look. Maya discreetly nudged her.

Renee glanced toward the side porch where Blue had disappeared, crossed her arms and gave Maya a pointed stare.

"Or she will be. Look, I'm not saying she's doing cartwheels about it—"

"Right," Renee said. "So I gotta go. It was great seeing you guys, but…" She held out her arms for a goodbye hug.

Maya grabbed Renee's wrists, lowered them. "Just give her a minute, would you? I sort of sprung this on her."

"And on me," Renee said, a momentary flash of emotion leaking out from behind her composure. She shook her hands free. "You lied to me. I never would have come."

"I did. But only because—well, because you wouldn't have come."

"For good reason."

"No, it isn't! Come on, Renee. You drove all this way. And you know you guys need to fix this shit."

"What do you expect me to do?" Renee eyed her car. "You saw her." She looked at Hannah for backup.

Hannah nodded vigorously. Blue definitely did not look thrilled.

"Look," Renee said, "maybe we can hang out some other time. Just the three of us." Her eyes perked at the thought. "We could do lunch in SoHo. That'd be fun."

"We're not doing lunch in SoHo," Maya said, and Renee's face fell. "I don't think you quite understand how hard it is to get this one—" she nodded toward Hannah "—to go anywhere."

Hannah was momentarily offended and then conceded this was true with a little side shrug.

"Listen," Maya continued. "Don't leave. It's too important."

"Not to Blue," Renee said.

"You don't know that. And if you go now, you never will."

Renee sighed, looked longingly toward the road.

The air was suddenly thin and difficult, gassed with sadness.

"This might be your last chance, ya know," Maya said. "The house is for sale. All three of us are almost never in the same

place. Right now you have me and Hannah as a buffer—and
I seriously doubt you and Blue will ever work it out on your
own. So it's kind of now or never. And if you decide you can't
come inside for ten minutes, then fine. That's your decision.
But just be perfectly clear with yourself that you're giving up
without even trying. On you. And on us. And on Blue. But
whatever. I'm not going to pressure you."

"Ha!" Hannah said.

She and Renee locked eyes.

"Just ten minutes," Maya said.

"But no pressure," Hannah said, getting a half smile out
of Renee.

"An hour, tops. What's the worst that could happen?"

Renee bit her cuticle, looked to Hannah for feedback.

Hannah felt Maya's elbow in her ribs. She elbowed her back
harder. Smiled at Renee. "I want you to stay too," she said
carefully. "It'd be really nice to catch up. I haven't seen you in
forever. *But* I also don't want you to be uncomfortable. And
I don't want Blue to be uncomfortable either."

Maya groaned. "What's so wrong with being uncomfortable? Sometimes it's necessary. You think pouring alcohol on
a cut isn't uncomfortable? But that's how you kill the infection. That's what starts the healing."

"Actually," Hannah said, "doctors advise that plain soap
and water is best."

Maya gave her a hard stare.

"Just saying," Hannah said. She turned to Renee. "Maybe
she has a point. It could be a good thing." Based on Blue's behavior, she wasn't sure that was true, but technically it couldn't
be ruled out. "I mean, if I were you, I think I'd do it. And
I'm afraid of everything."

Renee chewed her lip. She looked at the house, at her car, back to the house. There was something else, something new moving into her eyes. "Okay. Ten minutes. Literally ten. And then I'm out."

"Hooray!" Maya said.

"Hooray," Hannah said. She thought of what Blue's reaction would be. Wondered if it was too early for Xanax.

They headed inside in single file as if traversing a simple suspension bridge, everything tense and wobbly as they crossed the strange terrain of such a loaded reunion. Across Nana's driftwood floors scuffed by years of sandy feet, past the minimalist furniture in the living room, the mindless summer reads lined up on the shelf, and back into the kitchen. Hannah remembered the first time she'd walked into this house, standing in that beautiful foyer, the light so soft and pretty it felt staged for a photo. Her whole body had breathed, deep and free.

Now everything was stressful. The silence strained against her desire to break it. She couldn't think of what to say. She didn't know how to be around Renee anymore. It was so strange the way they were struggling with the most basic interaction when once they'd been like particles in a quantum entanglement. She tried to remember how it all went down, how they'd gotten so separated from Renee to begin with. In the aftermath of that night, they'd spent so many hours together, in and out of the police station giving witness statements, long nights in the hospital waiting to find out if Henry's condition would improve. Everyone operating in a zombielike daze. The anxiety was relentless, and whatever life there was beyond Henry was happening on the periphery of her consciousness. Dimly she recalled Blue actively avoiding Renee, the two of them sitting on opposite sides of the waiting room. But at the time Hannah had no energy for anyone else's dramas. All she cared about was Henry waking up. Then somehow amid all of that, September appeared, its sharp blue skies startling her with the reality that life kept moving, had not stopped for him. Her friends were, unfathomably, off to college. She remembered Renee stopping at her house to say goodbye, her car piled to the roof with luggage. They'd hugged each other tightly, made all the right promises, though Hannah had seen in Renee's eyes that she was already gone.

For a few years after she would occasionally get a handwritten card from Renee or a voice mail, always thoughtful, always concerned. But Hannah could feel a distance that lived beneath the words, and she understood that which went unsaid, that Renee was doing what Renee was best at—she was running. From that night. From the blood. From the taint of memory. From all of them. And both Hannah and Maya had let her run because what else could they do? And besides, Hannah understood it. Sometimes she wished she could do the same.

Now she looked around for Blue while Maya dug into the grocery bag of snacks she'd brought and ordered Renee to sit. Hannah grabbed a plate to put cookies on and whispered to Maya as she passed, "Blue's going to kill you."

"Blue's going to kill *us*," Maya whispered back. "You're abetting."

As if on cue, she heard the side door close and then Blue appeared stone-faced in the kitchen.

"There you are!" Maya said with a big ingratiating grin. "You done hiding the body?"

Blue ignored her, went over to the counter and leaned against it. She glanced quickly at Renee.

"Hi, Blue," Renee said, softly.

Blue nodded, quick and gruff. "Hey."

Twin souls, best friends, all those years of love and rescue before everything went wrong. Hannah held her breath, willing repair between them. If it was going to happen, this would be the place, in this house where they once bantered and gossiped as Nana quietly chuckled in a nearby room, enjoying their presence. Hannah had loved that—being quietly enjoyed. It made her feel so safe.

"So," Maya said. She smiled expectantly at Blue and Renee. "Here we all are."

"Cheers," Hannah said. She held up her Oreo, the only available object, and then quickly put it down when no one else did.

"Let's crack open that delicious wine Renee brought, shall we?" Maya said. "Blue, point me to a corkscrew."

Blue nodded toward a drawer and Maya went and retrieved it. She handed it to Blue along with the wine. "If you would be so kind as to do the honors, madame…"

Blue rolled her eyes, took the bottle, expertly uncorked it, handed it back.

"Effortless." Maya beamed. "You should've been a waitress." She pulled out four glasses and began to pour.

"I'm good, thanks," Renee said.

"Nonsense," Maya said, filling up her glass.

Hannah grabbed hers, took a big gulp, held it back out for a topping off.

"So Renee, did I tell you that our brilliant friend here—" Maya pointed to Blue "—was recently profiled in the *New York Times*? The paper of record. Our little Blue! Isn't that amazing?"

"That *is* amazing," Renee said, smiling tentatively at Blue. "Such an accomplishment."

Blue responded with a tight, close-lipped smile.

"She's going to be the next George Soros! Tell Renee how they named you number one in Wall Street's 'Top Thirty under Thirty.'"

Blue looked at her steadily. "You just did."

"Well, yes, but I thought you might want to elaborate."

"No thanks," Blue said.

"Okay, to be revisited," Maya said cheerfully.

Hannah and Blue exchanged looks, shook heads. Maya was undeterrable.

"Renee has great news, too, don't you, Renee?" Maya said, plopping down in front of Renee.

"Well, no one's calling me George Soros," Renee said.

"Nor me," Maya said. "Of that I can assure you."

"Who's George Soros?" Hannah said.

"Like I said, Hannah doesn't get out much," Maya said. "So Renee…spill the news." Before Renee could answer, Maya said, "Renee's getting married! Our very first wedding of the group! Isn't that great?"

Hannah smiled politely. Her face was beginning to hurt from all the polite smiling.

Blue looked out the window.

"Second, actually," Renee said.

Every head jerked in her direction. Even Blue's.

"I beg your pardon?" Maya said.

Renee gave a nervous little laugh. "Yeah. Technically I'm a divorcée." She paused, blushed. "It was… We were very young obviously. Just graduated—I had no clue what to do with my life. He was Italian and I was there studying art. We got married like a week after we met. Broke up in front of the Trevi Fountain, of all places."

"Wow," Hannah said. She and Blue exchanged a stunned look. She didn't want to criticize anyone's life choices, but getting married within a week seemed like questionable judgment. She'd never known Renee to be so reckless.

Renee must have sensed her concern because she squirmed in her chair and her cheeks turned red. She took a quick self-conscious glance around the room, those eyes reading everyone. Then she sat up straighter, smoothed her hair and smiled. "It was dumb, I know. But fortunately it all worked out in the end. And now I'm with my dream guy. Darrin is... I'm very lucky. You guys would love him."

Hannah's mind was filling with questions. Would they be invited to the wedding? If they were, would they go? She knew Blue wouldn't. And then she and Maya couldn't, could they? It seemed like another no-win situation, and her stress levels rose just thinking about it. The others must've been having similar thoughts, because the sudden return to quiet felt loaded.

"We actually met at a wedding," Renee said, as if rushing to fill the void. "I was the wedding photographer. We joke that now having a wedding is like coming full circle. Unfortunately the couple whose wedding it was are now divorced."

Hannah was reminded of how uncomfortable Renee used to be with silences, how she would scramble to fill them, how much it seemed like another form of running.

"Anyway," Renee said, seeming to run out of steam. She peeked at Blue and sighed. "George Soros, huh? That's amazing. Really, so cool."

Blue nodded, but her face was hard and inscrutable.

The refrigerator hummed. Renee drummed her long, perfectly manicured nails on the table.

"Oh, here, let me show you a picture of Darrin!" Renee

said. She took out her phone, pulled up a photo, passed it to Hannah. "That's us on my birthday. The night he proposed."

"Oh, wow," Hannah said. She didn't want to sound too enthusiastic for fear it might piss off Blue. "He looks nice." He had thick black hair and shiny eyes and the kind of seductive smile that she distrusted but knew lots of other women liked. She held the phone up to Blue behind her. She noticed Renee watching for Blue's reaction, seeming eager for her approval. Blue nodded at the photo and looked away.

Maya leaned over to have a look, as well. "Well, hello there, handsome!"

Renee laughed, more nervous than mirthful, and held out her hand to show them her ring. Something about the way she displayed it reminded Hannah of that stuffed animal fortress. "We live in this cute little cul-de-sac in Connecticut. Lots of trees and kids running around. I just love it. Maybe you guys can visit." Her eyes darted again to Blue.

"I like cul-de-sacs and trees," Maya said. "Just lock up the kids and that sounds great. Doesn't it, guys?"

Blue pulled out her phone, began scrolling the news.

Renee's face fell.

Maya frowned. "Something interesting happening in the world, Blue?"

"Just people being awful as usual," Blue said, without looking up.

Hannah slunk lower in her seat.

"People suck," Maya agreed. She turned back to Renee. "I gotta tell you…every Darrin I've ever slept with was a total maniac in bed. I mean that in a good way. And there've been like four of them."

"Ew," Hannah said.

"Seconded," Blue muttered.

Renee smiled and shook her head. "Oh my God, Maya," she said, "I've missed you." Then after a pause, quietly, sadly, almost inaudibly into her lap, she added, "I've missed all of you."

Hannah made a sort of cooing noise. She wanted to tell Renee how much she missed her, too, but then she caught the hardened look in Blue's eyes, her lips pressed thin with anger. Whatever went on between the two of them must have been worse than Hannah could imagine. Blue had always been as loyal as a rescue dog, only bit when provoked. *But what could possibly be that bad? To give up a sisterhood? To still be this furious after so many years?*

As Hannah wondered this, the room went suddenly blurry. It was as if she were floating away from it, above it, seeing it at a distance from her body. There was a bright flash of light behind her eyes. Then a clicking noise in her brain like a camera going off. She knew that light and clicking sound well. The warning signs. She squeezed her fists, trying to stay present, but the images came anyway.

The girls at the party. Blue and Renee playing beer pong while Maya danced. Henry's arms wrapped tightly around her, his lips grazing her ear as he sang to her the words of the love song playing on the stereo. Someone shouting over the music. Then Blue in a torn sweatshirt, bloody at the neck. A piercing scream—her own. Fear so loud in her ears it sounded like a waterfall. *Henry! Henry!*

She blinked, resurfaced with a silent gasp. A shiver of adrenaline went through her. Then the nausea hit. *Keep blinking,* she thought, *fast as you can.* It was what Dr. Maloney had taught her to do whenever she had flashbacks, because the mind can't see images in the midst of a blink. Her stomach listed. She stood and went to the window, opened it wide.

"You all right over there?" Maya said.

"What?" Hannah said, stalling. The last thing she wanted to do amid all the tension was mention anything about that night. "Oh yeah... I just... I think I might be getting sick."

Maya laughed. "You always think that."

"Right," Hannah said. She tried to smile but couldn't quite get there. Sometimes it was funny that she was the designated neurotic but other times it bothered her. There were *reasons* she was the way she was. It wasn't because she was weaker or less than or ridiculous—which is how they made her feel sometimes. Unintentionally, of course, but still. And yet they'd all seemed to survive so much better than she—Renee so in love, Blue and her success, Maya breezing through life like she was given the answers to the test while Hannah had studied and studied and still failed. Maybe this was why she didn't like being in the world. It forced her to realize just how messed up she was.

Breathe. Blink. Stay present.

She drank some water. Waited for the shakes to stop. Her body felt weak and drained. Her mind activated. A lingering sense of disorientation, like she was a time traveler stuck between worlds. Couldn't get her bearings in either.

She was used to the flashbacks by now. Not that they weren't always upsetting. *Trauma brain, it will pass*, she told herself. *Whatever happened has already happened.*

But this time something new had unsettled her—the image of Blue in the ripped and bloody sweatshirt. Usually the flashbacks were the same. But this was a piece she hadn't remembered before, couldn't place in her recall of that night. Why was Blue bloody? Why was her sweatshirt ripped?

MAYA

"Well," Renee said, standing. "I should hit the road."

"No, wait!" Maya said, jumping up. "We have to take a picture first."

She made them gather for a tense selfie and pretended not to notice Blue deliberately stepping on her foot. "Man, you guys need a tan," she said, shaking her head as she looked at the results.

"And you need an off switch," Blue said.

"I have one! It's right—" Maya dug into her pocket, pulled out her middle finger "—here!" She laughed at her own joke. Blue did not join her. Fleetingly Maya considered that she really might have been wrong to have invited Renee. Up until that point she'd figured the ends justified the means, but now she was starting to think she wasn't going to get the end she hoped for. It gave her an uncomfortable constriction in her belly, like her pants were too tight, so she discarded it quickly. Any minute now Blue would get over it. It was easy to maintain disconnection when you didn't have to look someone in the eye. That's why the internet was such a hellhole. But once Blue and Renee had some real face-to-face time together, Blue would be forced to see Renee's humanity, to remember the whole of her, their friendship. And that's what Blue needed—to remember Renee. In the end Blue would thank Maya. They all would. Maya just had to stall Renee.

"Okay, well—" Renee said.

"Oh! Speaking of photos," Maya said quickly, "look what I have." She ran to her bag, dug into it. Brought out the picture she kept taped to her locker at work, the one of the four of them at the fair the last time they were here twelve years ago. "Look how cute we were."

The other three moved in closer to get a look. The air changed, charged with wonder and wistfulness that they could ever have been that young, that carefree.

"Ah, the pre-cellulite days," Renee said.

"I miss my high alcohol tolerance," Blue said.

Hannah said nothing. They all knew what, or who, she missed.

"That reminds me!" Maya said, pulling out the list she'd made of all the fun things they'd ever done at the house so they could do them again. "Is there anything you can remember that I need to add to this list? I know we need to get wine coolers and cheap beer."

"We're thirty. How about vodka?" Blue said. "I'm sure there's plenty in the house."

"Nope. We're doing it old-school. Exactly like before. Also, we need stuff for a bonfire on the beach. Hey, Renee, remember that summer you accidentally set the beach grass on fire and almost lit up a multimillion-dollar mansion? Good times. I guess we can skip that part. And we need to go whale watching for sure, since we missed the boat last time…"

"Wasn't that because you got pulled over?" Renee said.

"She mooned a cop," Blue said, looking at Maya.

"You dared me!"

"To moon *someone*. Not a *cop*."

"You should've been more specific."

"Hey," Renee interrupted, "does your list include those cute boys we met?"

"Ooh, almost forgot about them," Maya said. "Remember that dark-haired guy who loved Blue?" She wiggled her eyebrows and Blue turned a stunning lobster red. "You introduced them, right, Renee? He was hot. What was his name again?"

"Jack," Renee said. She glanced at Blue as if hoping to see she'd scored a point. "Jack was his name. He was adorable."

"A local, right?" Maya said. "They were all townies."

Maya remembered how hard they'd been rooting for Blue the night she'd met him, eighteen, and never kissed. They knew it bothered her—not that she'd ever admit it. Even back then Blue never showed vulnerability. Which was part of the problem. You had to let yourself be vulnerable in order to be kissed.

And then to see her face after her night with him. The change in her. For days after she glowed like she'd swallowed the sun.

"I wonder where he is now," Renee said.

Blue shrugged, but Maya caught a glint in her eyes and, she thought, the hint of a smile.

"Anyway," Renee said. She made a move toward the door.

Maya stepped in front of her. "So—check this out—you guys are gonna laugh." She went back to her suitcase, pulled out a bright pink bikini and held it up. It was about four sizes too small. "Remember this? My thirty-year-old ass is going to be hanging like Christmas stockings, but see if I care!"

"Yeah, I don't think that's structurally sound," Hannah said.

Renee giggled. "That thing definitely won't meet code."

"Hmm, what's the inspector look like?" Maya said. "Might be worth having him check it out."

"I brought mine too," Hannah said. She dug into her bag and pulled out a pair of bikini boy shorts and a bandeau top. It looked two sizes too big. She'd lost so much weight in the months that Henry was first in the hospital and she'd never gained them back.

Maya watched Hannah hold the top up to herself and observe her reflection in the glass door. She was certain she saw a glimpse of the old Hannah in her eyes—that wide-eyed girl with the quick laugh, so easy to amuse and delight. She was sure Hannah had seen it too.

"What about you, Blue?" Maya said.

"I did not bring the same bathing suit," Blue said, "considering how much you guys mocked it last time."

"I didn't," Renee said softly. "I thought it was cute."

"That's true," Maya said. "See how nice Renee is! She would never make fun of your banana-colored old-timey swim dress, no matter how justifiable."

"I wasn't just being nice," Renee said.

For a moment Maya thought she saw Blue's face soften. It seemed like Renee saw it, too, because something like hope seemed to flare in her eyes.

Maya's "Uptown Funk" ringtone cut off the moment. She

looked down, didn't recognize the number. "Dammit! Hold that thought!" She brought the phone to her ear. "Hello?"

"Hi, I'm calling for Maya Marino."

"This is she."

"This is Donald Mason. From Mid-Atlantic Bank and Trust. We spoke on Tuesday."

"Hi!" A bolt of anxiety slashed through her, sharp and quick like the bright startle of a razor. "Hold on a sec." She stepped out onto the porch, let the screen door shut behind her.

The world was the color of memory, faded blue sky, fragile, liquid light, branches moving in a gentle breeze as if to some twinkling melody. From somewhere on the street, an eruption of laughter.

Maya started walking. Soft, harmless summer, open and forgiving. "Okay, I'm here," she said. "Please tell me I got the loan."

There was a pause on the other end of the line.

Time stalled, held its breath.

"I'm afraid that after a full review of your credit history and even taking into account your current employment…"

Oh no.

"Okay," Maya said. He continued talking but her heart was pounding over the sound of his voice. She didn't need to hear the rest anyway. "Not a problem. Thanks for calling."

"Miss Mar—"

She hung up.

The weight of it was so crushing. She wanted to put it somewhere—heave it off herself. She wanted to sit down. Give up. Cry.

There was nothing she could do. That was the worst part. She'd screwed up. Just like she'd screwed up a million other things. And now it was too late to fix it. One more loss in what had felt like an endless sea of them over the last twelve years.

She turned, stared up at the house, at the dark aging wood and cracking white paint on the shutters, the murmur of voices drifting out the kitchen window.

She felt so alone.

But no. She wasn't alone. And she refused to accept that there was nothing she could fix.

She put on her brightest smile and went back inside. "Okay, new plan!" she said to them. "Renee, you're staying for dinner."

BLUE

Blue realized she was mildly stoned the moment she did not murder Maya. Instead the suggestion of Renee staying for dinner seemed to move over her like a ducked punch. What were a few more hours of torture? She couldn't be bothered to care. Renee looked at her, her eyes asking permission. It was difficult, even when you hated someone, to outright deny them. What was she going to say, *no*?

"I'm going to my room," she said instead. Renee could take the obvious hint.

She marched up the creaky stairs, where thirty years of sand had settled in the cracks of the floorboards, to the second-floor rooms with their summery, mismatched furniture. The air was musty with uncirculated air, but throw open the windows, add a little polish and everything really was the same. If only people could be that easily returned to themselves.

As she entered the bedroom she'd slept in as a child—yellow curtains the color of morning sun, white chest of drawers with a handle missing, two twin beds quilted in a soft checkered gray—Blue knew Maya was right. She'd arrived at the last place she was truly happy. She could feel the lingering, pale wisps of daylight through the windows enter her, lighting up old spaces in her brain, time morphing between then and now so that she was looking out with the eyes of all the Blues she'd been—child, teenager, adult.

She threw her duffel on the bed by the window, sat down for a minute to decompress. She glanced at the empty one next to hers. Had a flash of Renee sitting on it in a camisole top and pajama shorts, her hair pinned up, a moisturizing mask on her face that made her look at once ghoulish and girly. Blue across from her in an oversize T-shirt and boxers, spots of acne cream on her chin. The two of them whispering late into the night as the ocean stomped outside the window. They were supposed to age side by side, grow into old ladies swinging on a porch, cursing the neighborhood kids and drinking spiked lemonade. That had always been the plan. Instead Renee had ended up with a shiny, perfect life while Blue carried all the damage, vandalized like a late-night subway car.

She shook off the thoughts. Felt something lumpy just underneath the anger. A swallow of sorrow.

It never got easier, mourning someone who was still alive.

From downstairs, laughter in a chorus of three. Apparently Renee hadn't taken the hint yet. Blue closed the door against the sound but still it lingered, a hollow echo in her chest. How did she end up being the one pushed to the outside? It was so unfair that her anger—her *righteous* anger—labeled her with a bitterness that was undeserved, that the script had been flipped so that she was the perpetrator for feeling wronged.

But then, self-doubt—was she right to still be mad? When was it time to forgive? Was it just a guess, a stab at a particular passage of time—a month, a year, a decade—or was forgiveness a feeling you could deliberately walk into like a room?

She pulled out her laptop, checked her brokerage account. There was always relief in seeing that large number staring back at her. The comfort of knowing she could be an island, utterly self-sufficient. No attachments, no need.

Of course the price of such self-sufficiency was a job she despised. She'd never meant to have this kind of career. It had started as a summer internship at her father's brokerage. She'd taken it only because it required less effort than finding something she actually wanted to do. Back then most of her energy was devoted to simply surviving the hours between sleep. Maybe it still was. But the talent for the job must have been in her blood, because she picked it up quickly and her instincts were good. She'd been hired on, moved up the ranks and eventually was poached by a rival company—a job she took, in part, to spite her father. At times she actually did enjoy the work itself, getting lost in the numbers, feeling she was good at something, having somewhere to go. It was the greed and corruption that bothered her most. She didn't want to be part of a system that seemed to glorify psychopathy. Some days she walked into the office and imagined jumping on a desk, delivering a grand speech about what dead-eyed, money-hungry, bottom-feeding, little-guy-screwing, status-seeking, sociopathic menaces to society some of her coworkers were, and the fantasy was so pure and gratifying she worried she might actually play it out at some point.

As if on cue, her email pinged—a message about an IPO her brokerage wanted her to push, one she suspected would not be in her clients' best interest. She chucked her phone on the bed and carefully, heavily, stood and began to unpack.

When she opened the top drawer of her dresser, she gasped. There, worn thin from age and still stained with chocolate, was the ice cream wrapper she'd saved all those years ago, a memento from the best night of her life. She couldn't believe it hadn't been thrown away.

She took it out. Sniffed it, though of course it smelled nothing but old. It all came back to her. The slow fade to memory, the beach re-creating itself around her. She was eighteen again, walking along the ocean's jagged seam, the sun riding her shoulders until they tingled. She'd left the girls back on their towels, their quest for beauty in a tan a ritual she'd felt left out of even then. Around the cliffs and over jagged rock she climbed to reach a spot that was empty, littered only with the carcasses of crabs and the cling of seaweed. A place that understood her.

On the other side of it, more people. A Frisbee landed at her feet. He came running up, shouting, "Sorry!" He had the bronzed skin of a lifeguard or a surfer, with brown hair tipped gold by the sun. She was immediately self-conscious of her pale body in her one-piece bathing suit with the flouncy skirt, the one the girls had been making fun of all morning, insisting she looked like an octogenarian cheerleader. Well, not all the girls. Renee at least had understood that Blue would rather die than expose too much, that Blue experienced her body as a place she didn't like to travel in, her own version of a dirty motel.

He stopped in front of her. "That didn't hit you, did it?" He pointed to his friend. "It's his fault. He does that deliberately to get the attention of pretty girls."

She opened her mouth to speak, but the shock of his sentence knocked the capacity for language right out of her head. He smiled at her, it felt like their eyes ignited in each other's gaze, and then she blurted, "Okay, bye" and took off. She wasn't sure if he'd called "Wait!" or if she'd only been thinking it, but by the time she found the courage to turn around, he was back to playing Frisbee. She walked back to the girls slowly so she could process their interaction, savor it.

No one had ever called her pretty before. She'd never dreamed that anyone ever would. It was impossible to think of yourself that way when your own mother thought otherwise.

And then that night she'd spotted him with his friends inside John's Drive-In. She was sure it was fate, and she stood at the counter with cheeks burning as she placed her order in the spotlight of his gaze.

"I think that guy likes you," Renee said, nudging her. "He keeps looking over." She grabbed Blue's arm and dragged her over to him. "I'm Renee," she said. "And this is my awesome best friend, Blue."

He smiled and his cheeks turned a bright, endearing red. "We've met," he said, looking only at Blue. "I'm Jack."

Jack.

She smiled at him. "Blue."

"So I've been told."

She laughed, embarrassed. "Oh, right."

They couldn't take their eyes off each other.

The ice cream cone was starting to melt down her hand.

He jumped up and grabbed her a napkin. "Let me know if you need help eating that," he said, grinning.

"Have some," she said, holding it out. She couldn't believe how bold she was being.

He took a lick. "Chocolate Brownie. My favorite." His eyes on her made her flustered and hot. "Next time I'll buy you one with sprinkles. It's even better that way."

Blue's head swam. *Next time? Buy you one?* "I don't like sprinkles," she blurted because she was an idiot and she didn't know how to flirt and now she was screwing it up.

Jack balked. Then his face turned serious. "Well, neither do I, then," he said. "Hate them, in fact. What kind of maniac likes sprinkles?"

Blue giggled so he kept going.

"Down with sprinkles. We don't need your waxy goodness. Hit the road, Jimmy."

He was making a list of all the awful people in the world who probably liked sprinkles ("Charles Manson—definitely a sprinkle lover...") when Maya and Hannah came over to join them. Eventually his friends and hers ended up cruising around town as a group, too young to go to the bars, too old to go home early. In Jack's truck they drove at a reckless, exhilarating speed around the small swooping hills of Old Montauk Highway. Eventually they found their way to Ditch Plains Beach, where the others ran toward the soft-breaking surf while she and Jack sat on a wooden bench overlooking their splashing friends, shouting "Shark! Shark!" to spook them. Once the humor of the joke wore off, they were left with only each other, their delicate, clumsy aloneness. The wind had been salty and sweeping, the night clear and deep with stars. A white lane of moonlight shimmered on black water. She shivered. He gave her his sweatshirt and put his arm around her, thinking she was shaking because she was cold. The act made them both suddenly shy. When she finally turned to speak again, he took her face in his hands and kissed her and she was stunned first and then struck with wonder, the ice cream wrapper still sticky in her fist and later tucked in the back pocket of her jean shorts so she could save it, so she would never forget that night and the delicious tremor of first, astonishing love.

Now she looked out the window, almost expecting to find Jack there, waving up at her. But there was only the dimming sky, a triangle of seagulls riding the breeze, winged shadows against the setting sun. She folded the wrapper, smoothing out the crease, returned to her laptop. She pulled up his profile to send a message and saw he'd uploaded a photo of himself.

A sudden commotion in her chest. To unexpectedly see that face, which had once looked at her so tenderly that her whole body yielded to it. Twelve years older and still so familiar.

Finally something good. She had the urge to drive immediately to his house—never mind that she had no idea where it was—and kiss him as soon as he opened the door.

But then the arrival of another feeling. It wasn't excitement, though it shared its features. It was excitement's sadistic cousin. She wanted to shed it like an itchy sweater.

She went to the mirror. Braced. Against the darkening room the half glow of early evening light through the windows illuminated the first sign of wrinkles under her eyes, the happy hours and business dinners around her belly. She touched her throat, a gesture she'd seen other women do, but found no fragility or beauty in her hands, in her collarbone.

What if he didn't think she was pretty anymore?

How had she failed to consider that before now?

A slump, something falling inside her. There was no way she could do this, risk rejection. All this time he'd been her island, the refuge she retreated to in her mind, a promise of hope—as long as she didn't try to cash in on it.

She pushed open the sliding glass door to the balcony, stepped out and lit an emergency cigarette. At the wooden railing she stood overlooking an ocean turned sideways with the threat of a storm. Loneliness flapping on the wind. The sun dropping into the water like a bright woman drowning in a slow surrender to the sea.

Now in more darkness herself, Blue was struck with a sense of doom, of doors closing all around her. She'd made a mistake, she realized, in allowing Jack to open this particular part of her life again. She'd learned to live without love. To make her need small, store it like a child's paper valentine in the attic of her mind. Now that she had opened the door, it occurred to her that perhaps the worst thing wouldn't be to go through life unloved. Perhaps the worst thing would be to have the opportunity for love only to discover you're too wounded, too self-protective to seize it.

HANNAH

Hannah sat with Maya and Renee at the table where they'd once all chugged cheap beer and played Truth or Dare until they'd gotten so drunk they ran down to the beach in the middle of the night—four girl-shadows dashing, so alive with the universe, claiming the breeze and every star and the shiny black Atlantic as they splashed into it. Whoop! Whoop! They thought they knew what their lives would be.

Now Blue was upstairs probably hating them all and Hannah was googling symptoms of Lemierre's syndrome on her phone.

Sore throat: check
Headache: check
Fever: ?

She turned to Maya. "Feel my forehead. Does it feel hot?"

"It's summer. So yes," Maya said without checking. "Now tell Renee she's staying for dinner."

"Renee, you're staying for dinner," Hannah said. Maybe it wasn't Lemierre's. Maybe it was the measles. Vaccinations could lose their potency after time, couldn't they? But that was stupid. She was fine. She'd been in therapy long enough to recognize that she probably wasn't dying, that her fear was simply triggered by the stress of being away from Henry and the current tensions between her friends. Too bad that being aware of anxiety's source never helped to quell it. Logic was happening in one part of the brain and fear in another and the two sections seemed to have no system in which to communicate with each other. It made her feel like she couldn't trust herself.

"I'll stay until Blue comes back down," Renee said. "Because it's nice to talk with you guys. But then I'm out. You wouldn't eat dinner with someone who hated your guts either."

"I would literally light myself on fire and toast a marshmallow off my own burning ass if it meant having lobster by the ocean with my lifelong best friends," Maya countered.

"Wow, that's specific," Hannah said.

Maya passed them each an Oreo. "And anyway, Renee, Blue doesn't hate you. Note that she didn't even try to kill me when I suggested it."

Renee fingered a small silver cross around her neck. Hannah didn't recall Renee being religious when they were younger, though admittedly she changed interests and beliefs just about every week, so it was hard to keep track. It used to drive Blue and Maya crazy. They hated how Renee adopted the tastes and hobbies of whomever she was dating—their favorite music or style of clothes or sports teams. They thought Renee was subjugating herself, letting boys dictate who she was. Hannah always suspected Renee distrusted that who she was would be enough. Or maybe she was trying to build a self from the outside in. It was hard to be sure because Renee had always been a bit of a cipher.

"That's a pretty necklace," she said, reaching out to touch it. She often wished she could believe in God. It seemed easier. "I didn't know you were religious."

Renee shrugged. "I didn't used to be." She paused, searched Hannah's face like she was peering around a shower curtain, making sure no one scary was lurking behind it.

Hannah smiled encouragingly and Renee continued.

"After my first marriage ended, I was walking down the street one night, crying, just lost. I didn't know what to do or where to go or who to call. It was pouring rain and there was this church on the corner with this warm glow of light coming from the open door. I ducked inside to get out of the rain and there was this organ playing and people were singing, and you know that feeling you get when a group of people sing together—that sort of rush of love for humanity? Anyway, I took a seat at the back and everyone near me turned and smiled at me, and it was like… I don't know… I felt this unconditional love there…like regardless of who I was or what I had done or how I had screwed up my life, all that mattered to them was that I was there. That was enough. And I just felt this sense of peace that I hadn't had in so long." She paused as if she'd revealed something she hadn't meant to. Hannah caught her eyes and they exchanged a knowing look. "Anyway, it was incredible. I felt so…relieved. I don't even know why. I guess because there was finally an answer. Someone had an answer to what I was supposed to do. I was baptized like six weeks later."

"That's lovely," Hannah said. "I'm so glad you found it." And she *was* glad the church had been there for Renee, that it had helped her. But also, she wanted to say, *Why didn't you call us? When you were lost and scared and didn't know what to do? Why didn't you call your best friends?*

"Last time I walked into a place of worship, I was sure I'd burst into flames," Maya said.

Renee laughed.

"But Blue goes to church… I think. You should talk to her about it. At dinner."

"You're relentless," Renee said.

"You miss me though," Maya said.

"I do. I miss all of you." She turned to Hannah. "Tell me about you. What have you been up to?"

Hannah tried to think of what she'd been up to. Worry. Phobias. Isolation. Loneliness. "Not much," she said cheerfully.

"Still working on the Great American Novel? You know, Darrin has a friend in publishing. I'm sure he could get him to take a look at your work."

"Oh…ah…nothing that's finished yet…" Heat rushed to Hannah's cheeks, her shoulders hunched over her shame. She knew she should be writing. Everyone was always asking about it like they were taking her emotional temperature. But ever since that night, her mind had turned on her, created dark terrifying pieces that always ended in disaster, until finally she realized it was making things worse—the stories she was telling herself. At Dr. Maloney's recommendation she'd tried journaling instead. But every time she stared at the empty page, she thought, *There it is. My autobiography.*

"I get it," Renee said. "There aren't enough hours in the day, as Darrin likes to say."

Hannah could practically hear what Blue's thought bubble would be if she were here: *Darrin, Darrin, Darrin—puke.* But everyone was like that when they were in love.

"You'll write it eventually," Renee said. "Hey, how's Henry?"

Hannah brightened. No one ever asked about Henry. She understood it was too hard for her friends—that like all difficult things in life, it was easier to avoid the subject. But understanding why didn't leave her any less alone with it. And now here was Renee with her warm receptive eyes, asking after him, treating him like he was still a person to be asked after. "Oh, he's…" She caught Maya eyeing them. Hannah often got the feeling Maya had *opinions* about Henry's condition that she was politely holding back. She had a good idea what those opinions were, which was why she let the subject be avoided. "He's good. Fine. Thanks for asking." She smiled painfully as her moment plunked and sank.

Blue reappeared in the kitchen. Her eyes were small and red. Hannah didn't know if she'd been crying or was stoned. She made a beeline for the snacks.

Mystery solved.

"I'm gonna call Darrin. Excuse me," Renee said, ducking outside.

"Tell him you're staying for dinner!" Maya called after her.

Hannah had a feeling dinner was going to be deeply uncomfortable. She swallowed. *Sore? Not sore?* Already she knew her obsessive, malfunctioning brain would chew on this question relentlessly. Forever on high alert because of that one time when she wasn't. She tried to forgive it, be grateful for its hypervigilant, if misguided, efforts to protect her. But the truth was she wanted a new one.

"So glad you could finally join us!" Maya said to Blue. "Care for a Funyun?"

Blue grabbed the whole bag, sat down and shoved a fistful into her mouth. "Why is she still here?" she said, eyeing the patio where Renee stood with the phone to her ear.

"You'll be happy to know she's leaving right after dinner," Maya said casually without looking up from the real estate section of the *East Hampton Star*.

Hannah marveled at Maya's ability to spin things. It was truly a gift.

"Look at these insane houses," Maya said, expertly changing the subject. "Ten bedrooms! Who even knows ten people they like? Hey, Blue, you ever think of getting into real estate?"

"Nope," Blue said.

"I hear it's a great investment. You could get a few houses. You know, smaller ones. Not necessarily *here*. I'm thinking like...Jersey. Get some renters in them..."

"I already have one job I hate, but thanks," Blue said.

"Well, just think about it," Maya said. "I may know of a place."

Renee returned and the air was instantly tense and charged again. It was like a storm front moving in and out. No wonder Hannah had a headache. She dug into her purse for both an aspirin and a Xanax.

"Jesus, you got a whole pharmacy in there?" Maya said, peering into her bag. "Is there a little man in a white coat in your wallet taking prescriptions? Can I order some opioids?"

"No, you're too happy," Blue said. "It's intolerable as it is."

Renee laughed and Blue looked up in surprise. Their eyes met. Renee had always been Blue's best laugh track. Both Han-

nah and Maya watched with held breath. Then Blue pushed
out her chair with a scrape and went to the window, turning
her back to them. Renee cleared her throat. Hannah sighed,
resumed her search for pills. She checked the pockets once,
twice. All the bottles were there except the Xanax. She felt another twinge of anxiety, a discordant pluck of her nerve strings.

"Maya, do you remember where you put my Xanax?"

"What?" Maya said.

"Please tell me you didn't leave it at the motel..."

Maya swallowed.

Hannah's panic spiked.

"Nope," Maya said. "I for sure did not."

Hannah breathed. It was somewhere around here.

Renee stared down at her phone. "Darrin's not answering
calls or texts."

"He's probably not answering because you've already called
and texted and you just left him like four hours ago," Maya
said.

"I just want to make sure he's not worried about me,"
Renee said.

"It doesn't seem like he is," Maya said.

"No, of course. Right. Why would he be?" Renee said,
with a quick smile. "Anyway, he's probably just at a movie or
something."

Hannah noticed Renee's brow still held the crease.

"I should reserve tickets for Sunday's whale-watching adventure on the high seas," Maya said. She pulled out her phone,
tapped at it, scanned the website. "Jeez. This shit is expensive!
Well, it *is* the Hamptons. The life preservers probably have
Hermès belts."

"I'm not going," Hannah said. "I can shop while you guys hunt Moby Dick."

"I will refrain from a hunting dick joke since there's some truth in it," Maya said, scrolling. "Anyway, of course you're coming."

"No way. You ever read the story of that guy who got stranded at sea and ended up eating half the crew?"

Maya didn't even look up. "He survived, didn't he?"

"And half the crew did too," Renee pointed out.

"All set," Maya said, putting her phone down. "Four tickets reserved."

"*Four?*" both Renee and Blue said at once.

"Three!" Maya said. "I meant three. Didn't I say three?"

Hannah suspected Maya in fact meant four and bought four, but she wisely kept her mouth shut.

"Now let's eat," Maya said. "I say we hit that overpriced tourist trap on the docks. My treat."

Hannah's jaw dropped.

Blue feigned a heart-clutching stumble backward in surprise. "You lift someone's credit card?" She checked her pockets for her wallet.

"I've got a job, remember? I'm very responsible now. One hundred percent trustworthy with money."

Hannah and Blue eyed her skeptically.

Maya grabbed Renee by the shoulders and led her out to the car like she was her prisoner—which she kind of was. The others followed, and soon they were all buckled in and oddly silent, and everything was super awkward again. They took Star Island Road to the docks where a small village of shops and restaurants huddled in a corner by the bay. The dark water panted, casting a slight fishy tang into the air. To the east, the sun's purple finale slashed the sky where it fell, black night dropping around it. A breeze swept up, warm and salty as a kiss.

Maya parked the car and the others climbed out. "Hold on," Hannah said. "I'm still looking for my Xanax." Maybe it had rolled into the front. Or fell out of her bag in the trunk.

"It'd be easier to look in the light of day," Renee said.

"I need it now."

"Well, I'm going to eat the maître d' if we don't sit down soon," Blue said.

"Go in," Hannah said. "I'll be right behind you."

She watched them leave and then pressed her hands under the seats. Nothing but the paperback she'd brought and Maya's empty candy bag. She searched the trunk.

Please be here, she thought. *Please.* Her body revved. The night turned ominous, seemed to breathe down her neck.

"Come on!" Blue called from the door. "They won't seat us without you."

A sudden flash of light. That clicking sound.

Henry at the party. *Come on! We gotta go!*

She blinked hard against it.

"In a sec!" she shouted back to Blue.

She gripped the back of the car, trying to ground herself here. Solid road under her feet. Dense, sultry air and swishing bay and friends nearby.

But it was too late.

Some part of her was back there.

The cops breaking up the party.

Henry desperate to leave. "I could lose my scholarship!"

The two of them running through the crowd to get the others.

They'd found Blue and Renee lying on lounge chairs by Check's pool, staring up at the stars.

"We gotta go!" Hannah cried.

"Shh," Blue said. "We're getting a tan."

Renee laughed. "She's stoned. She just told me she thinks she was a carrot in a past life."

"She's gonna be in jail in this life if we don't get out of here!" Henry said, gesturing toward the police officers silhouetted in the living room window.

They helped Blue to her feet, the four of them dashing and stumbling across the night, Renee out in front as always; she could've run laps around them, she was that fast, even drunk.

The beam of a flashlight swept over them. The cops had breached the backyard. Blue turned, pointed. "The po-po." She threw her hands up. "I didn't do it! I'm innocent!"

"Oh my God," Hannah said.

"Please shut up, Blue," Henry said, but he was laughing as he said it; he could not stop laughing as he ran.

Hannah was laughing, too, and trying not to, because it was taking the air she needed to flee, but she wasn't really scared, or rather only scared enough for it to be fun. The sense of pursuit reminded her of childhood—of playing games like Manhunt and Kick the Can on hot, summer nights, life in her lungs, every game an excuse to be chased.

Down the too-dark road they flew to where Hannah had parked her car and Henry his.

"Wait! Where's Maya?" Hannah said, and then they heard a voice shout "Here!" and there was Maya running up behind them, waving her bra in her hand, her shirt on inside out, breathless with the uncharacteristic exertion. Henry looked to Hannah and burst out laughing all over again. He loved her ridiculous friends so much.

Hannah glanced back at the house. The cops were preoccupied with other partygoers. They were in the clear.

Henry kissed her. "You all right to drive?"

"Totally sober," she said.

"You can come back to my house if you want. My parents won't be home until late." He wiggled his eyebrows and she laughed.

She looked back at the girls. She'd hardly seen them all night. "I'll see you tomorrow," she said.

"Be safe," he said.

"Always," she said.

She hadn't known it was a lie.

Now standing in the parking lot as Blue walked impatiently toward her, Hannah wanted to scream back to the teenagers they once were, *Stay at the party! Don't leave! Turn yourselves in to the police!*

If only.

If only.

If only.

Hannah blinked and blinked.

"I have weed back at the house, if that helps," Blue said as she neared.

"I really need my Xanax." Just having the bottle in her hand could sometimes soothe her nervous system.

"Where was the last place you saw it?"

"Maya had it."

They exchanged a knowing glance.

"I'll help you find it when we get back, okay?" Blue said.

Hannah nodded. Blue's uncharacteristic gentleness made her throat swell with that particular kindness-induced grief. She wished she could tell her about the memories, seek comfort in the shared experience. Instead she pushed her thoughts into the present. The glow of restaurant lights and the long, rocky arm of the jetty stretching into the bay, the happy vacationers that would be dining inside, her friends nearby. *It'll be fine*, she told herself. *I can do this.*

"Sorry you had to come and get me."

Blue shrugged. "Spared me five minutes with Renee."

"Sorry about that whole thing too."

"Yeah. Not the trip I was hoping for," Blue said.

"Story of my life," Hannah said, and their eyes met and they both laughed and for a moment Hannah really did feel better, she felt recognized. She could tell Blue did too.

They went inside, the restaurant all shiny beer-colored wood and thick white tablecloths, windows on all sides overlooking the shimmying water. Families everywhere wearing lobster bibs and sunburns and smiles. Instinctively Hannah went to sit next to Maya—a mistake; Blue would be stuck beside Renee. Blue lurched in front of her as if the seat next to Maya's was the last in a game of musical chairs.

Renee folded her napkin into her lap, stared out at the bay.

Hannah slid in beside her, looked at Maya. "The Xanax wasn't in the car." Her palms started to sweat just saying that out loud. "I'm really starting to freak out. Are you sure you didn't—"

The waiter materialized, red faced, with a bread basket. "Can I start you ladies off with drinks?" he asked with an Irish accent.

"Four vodka tonics, please," Maya said.

"Oh no, I just want water," Renee said.

Maya frowned at her, turned back to the waiter. "Three vodka tonics—" she pointed to Hannah "—and make hers a double. She lost her drugs."

"Sorry to hear that," he said, flipping his order pad closed. "Coming right up. And, uh… I may know a guy…"

"Thanks, I'm good." Hannah smiled politely.

"I might hit you up later," Blue said to him.

Hannah turned back to Maya. She didn't know how to impress upon her how necessary her Xanax was.

"Wait!" Maya called to the waiter, dodging Hannah's gaze. She surveyed the table. "Do we want to order appetizers now? Let me answer that—yes. Last time we had that amazing calamari, right?"

"Actually, I don't eat squid anymore," Renee said. "Darrin read that they're really good at problem solving, so…"

"Is that right?" Maya said. "Well, until they figure out how to stay off my plate, I'm eating them. An order of calamari and some crab cakes, too, please."

"I just want a salad," Renee said, placing her napkin in her lap. "No tomatoes. Or actually if I could trade tomatoes for grapes, that would be wonderful. Dressing on the side, please."

Blue lifted her gaze to the ceiling. Hannah sensed that her high might be wearing off.

The waiter nodded and retreated again.

"Please focus, Maya," Hannah said. "You gave me a pill in the motel room and then…what? Where did you put the bottle? Did you throw it away? Did you put it in your bag? Think!" She could hear her voice rising against her efforts to maintain self-control. The flashbacks threatening to seize her again without warning. "It's really important."

Maya opened her mouth to answer just as Hannah's phone rang.

Hannah looked down at it. Then up at the girls. "Oh no."

MAYA

Maya watched as Hannah barreled out of her chair with wide, worried eyes and disappeared onto the patio. *Christ, was it too much to ask to have one thing go right on this trip?*

"Probably Vivian," Blue said.

The table was quiet for a moment.

"Henry's mom?" Renee asked. "I hope he's okay."

"He is," Maya said. She wasn't concerned. She was frustrated. The last thing Hannah needed right now was a call from Henry's mother.

"By the way," Blue said, "did you take Hannah's Xanax?"

Maya was indignant. "What? No. Why on earth would I do that?"

Blue shrugged. "Seems like something you would do."

Maya was about to protest but of course it was something she would do, because she *did* do it. And she should've just admitted it. She was very bad about fessing up. Always had been. She blamed her crap childhood for that. It was pure survival mechanism—hiding mistakes that could be used against her. But she was thirty now and should probably get around to fixing that little character flaw.

Still. All she wanted was to help Hannah and, okay, now she could see it was wrong to take her Xanax, just like maybe it had been wrong to invite Renee, but her intentions had been good! That had to count for something, right? She planned to sneak it back into Hannah's purse as soon as they got back from dinner. Even though she didn't want to believe it was a mistake. What she wanted was for Hannah to see that she didn't need it, that the world wasn't as frightening as she believed. And she wanted Blue and Renee to be friends again. She wanted everything to go back to the way it was. This was her family. Didn't they get it? She needed them. She also wanted a loan from Blue so she could save her house but that was a whole other self-inflicted headache. The sudden thought of it, of being homeless—not out on the street—but without a home, was a peek into some interior darkness, a kind of bottomless falling.

In the past she'd always just borrowed from Blue, no problem. Each time she genuinely believed she would eventually pay it back. But this was different. This was a catastrophic screwup. She didn't even want to say the number out loud because then she'd have to sit in it, and frankly, she didn't like sitting in bad feelings, especially about herself. But perhaps she could mention it and hope that maybe Blue would *offer* to lend her the money. She knew Blue would be pissed, but then again, it could be argued she was giving Blue an opportunity to look like a big shot in front of Renee. To swoop in as the hero. Show off how successful she was. Technically, Maya decided, she was doing Blue a favor.

"Is it terrible that sometimes I think it would be better if something *did* happen to Henry?" Blue said.

"I think that often," Maya said. "If it was me, I'd want you guys to yank the hell out of that plug. It's not a life."

"For either of them," Blue said.

"That's a terrible thing to say," Renee said. "They could find a cure tomorrow. He's still young. And technology is advancing."

Maya saw Blue's jaw set. She locked eyes with her, tried to discourage what she sensed was coming.

"Just out of curiosity, Renee," Blue said, as Maya slunk lower in her seat, "when was the last time you saw Hannah? Or Henry, for that matter?"

Renee opened her mouth, said nothing.

Blue folded her arms, pinned her with a steely look. "Right," she said.

A seagull swooped down just outside the window, snagged a bread crumb someone left on the railing, flew off.

Renee watched it go, shook her head. Finally she turned to Maya. "I told you this was a mistake."

Maya sighed.

In the distance a night fishing boat glided by, its white lights shining like little moons on the black bay. Maya imagined jumping fully clothed into the water, swimming out to it, drifting away like a lazy afternoon. Perhaps a cute captain on board. Destination unknown and irrelevant. She loved this thought—that an entirely different life was one crazy leap away.

"Hey, remember when we went fishing at the lighthouse?"

she said, scrambling for a way to keep the peace. She hadn't thought about that in so long.

That was their first summer out here together, before boys mattered too much and alcohol was a few years away and they were all still trying to discover what they loved to do.

"None of us wanted to go," she said to Blue, "except you." The rest of them thought it would be gross and dull and way too early to wake up. "But then Renee saw how important it was to you, so she made us." They'd laughed at Renee when she came downstairs that morning all ready to fish in platform sandals and a white summer dress like she was headed to the Bridgehampton polo classic.

They'd tiptoed out of the house and down to the beach. The predawn sky was an electric violet—the color lightning makes in a nighttime storm. The sand was soft and cool. They'd been out there only a few moments when the sun began crowning out of the sea, igniting a fiery road of light across the water. It seemed as if they could walk right out and touch its glowing head.

"Look," Hannah had said. "It's the sunrise highway!"

"I love it," Blue had replied. "It totally is."

They cast their lines and watched the swimming sun and stood shoulder to shoulder inside the stillness of that ocean light. After about ten minutes Maya decided she was bored and soon after Hannah, too, was complaining. Renee was clearly suffering in silence. Blue tried to teach them that this is what fishing was, patience and quiet and reflection.

"It's dumb is what it is," Maya had said. "I'm over it."

"Wait!" Renee yelped. "I think I have a nibble!" The line pulled again. "Oh my God, what do I do?"

The fish was tugging hard. Blue rushed to help, shouting

orders about when to reel and when to let, adding her own hands to the pole when the fish gave a vigorous yank. Suddenly they were all excited.

"It's probably a tuna," Blue said. "And a big one, the way it's pulling. In fact, I'm certain of it, a bluefin, I bet—over fifty pounds for sure!"

Maya was impressed with Blue's depth of knowledge.

"I think it's a shark!" Renee kept saying. "It's going to pull me in with it!"

"You're going to need a bigger boat," Maya quipped.

There was a great deal of carrying on. Hannah had her camera at the ready while Blue and Renee engaged in the tiresome struggle. Maya left after twenty minutes and returned with doughnuts just as Renee managed to reel it the last few feet to shore. They whooped and cheered as Renee gave one last tug of her pole. Then suddenly they all went quiet.

"Wait." Maya said. "What *is* that?"

It took a split second for it to register and then she laughed so hard she choked on her doughnut as Renee pulled from the sea a man's rubber fishing boot. She ran out to it, held it up. "It's kind of cute and maybe my size. Do you think you can catch the other one?"

They'd all dissolved in giggles then, calling Renee Captain Ahab and suggesting they phone the local papers to report the impressive catch. They even brought it to the pier and weighed it on the fish-weighing scale. Somewhere there was still a picture Blue had taken of Renee proudly holding up that rubber boot and grinning ear to ear. When they returned to school in the fall, the story of that "fish" grew and grew. By the time they graduated, it was a five-foot mako.

That was the same year Blue had made a sign in her shop

class and then nailed it above the door of Nana's house the following summer. It was a big wooden arrow pointing toward the ocean, and in hand-painted letters it said "To the Sunrise Highway."

Maya smiled now, remembering. "That was so great, right?"

Renee sighed.

Blue flagged down the waiter. "Can I get a shot of tequila, please?"

"Me too!" Maya said. "And those problem-solving calamari as soon as possible." She looked between her feuding friends. Wished they would just get over this stupidity, remember all the good. Reminding them didn't seem to be working, so for now it was probably best to try a new tactic, direct the heat onto herself. "So…a funny thing happened on the way to paying my property taxes."

Neither of them looked at her or acknowledged that she'd spoken. Both had disengaged entirely, were staring off in opposite directions, stewing in their own silences.

"Hello!" Maya said. "Anybody home?" She threw up her hands. "Oh, for God's sake. I'm going to the bathroom." She grabbed her purse, marched off. Nothing was going as planned, and she felt suddenly light-headed and floaty, precarious as a balloon in a child's hand.

Just outside she could see Hannah on the patio, clutching the phone to her ear as she paced between the white plastic tables. Maya skipped the bathroom and made a beeline for the bar. Several men turned as she entered. She zeroed in on a young guy in the corner. He looked about her age, maybe a little older, a lonely, soulful fisherman she decided, judging by the weathered lines around his eyes. She smiled at him and his whole face lit up with happy surprise. He raised his glass.

"Oh, hello there," she said under her breath, enjoying the way his smile grounded her back into her body. She sat down next to him, and the lightness in her head became substance and clarity again. He was exactly who and what she was looking for, a cute boy to have a flirtatious spin with, maybe even make out a little, clear her head of all the drama.

He watched her settle in, his face full of unguarded hopefulness, and as they grinned at each other once more, she had the urge to lean over and kiss him, to disappear into that black, thought-free universe where kissing took her. She glanced back at Renee and Blue slumped at the table, telegraphing misery like actors playing to the balcony, over to Hannah pacing outside. She thought of her house in foreclosure, her dead-end job, her fractured friend-family, everything real and closing in on her. "Save me," she said.

"Happy to," he said. He scanned the crowd to locate the threat, then turned back to her. "From what exactly?"

"Where to begin? Let's start with sobriety." To the bartender she said, "Light beer on tap. He's buying." She turned back to the guy. "Please tell me you're having a good night."

"I am. Sort of. Well, actually...my dog died. I came here to raise a glass..."

"To your dead dog."

"Indy. Yeah. He liked Bud." He gave a little chuckle as if remembering.

"Interesting," she said. "It wasn't a drunk driving accident, was it?"

"Nope, he had his own chauffeur. Paws couldn't reach the pedals. Oh, and it gets worse." He pulled out a small metal container with a paw print on it.

"That's not..." She poked it with her finger, leaned in toward it, whispered, "Indy, is that you?"

"He doesn't talk so much anymore. Used to be quite the conversationalist."

"Well, I should probably leave you to your mourning."

"He had a good life. Let's call it celebrating." He grinned at her.

"You don't carry that everywhere, do you?"

"Nope. Not yet anyway. Just picked it up on my way home from work. I'm planning to...spread them somewhere. But don't know where yet. It'll come to me."

"This is by far the strangest bar encounter I've ever had. And believe me, that's saying a lot."

Her beer appeared on the bar top. She took a sip and raised her glass. "To Indy," she said.

He smiled and his gaze fell from her eyes to her lips and there was a lift in her stomach, like she was taking hills at speed. "To Indy," he said, raising his glass. "And to the sudden appearance of beauty in unexpected places."

Cheers erupted from a scatter of patrons watching a ball game on the TV above the bar.

"I think you just scored," she said, smiling as she clinked his glass.

She was not usually such a drinker, but tonight the alcohol was a wonder, tasted like summer parties and old boyfriends, tasted like a past worth remembering and a future worth looking forward to. "I'm Maya by the way."

"Andy."

"Let me ask you something, Andy. How do you feel about whales?"

"Whales? I like them."

"Excellent. You'll do, then."

She noticed the helmet beside him.

"Yours?" she said.

She had never ridden a motorcycle, had never even known anyone who owned one. Once when she was driving Blue back to college after a holiday, a guy had pulled up beside them on a bike and performed tricks for them. Blue had laughed at him, called him a tool, but Maya loved the various ways men tried to impress her, the humor, the peacocking. Now she looked at the helmet and imagined the night blowing through her, the muscle and roar of the engine beneath her, her worries shrinking to the size of the rearview mirror, disappearing behind her like tailpipe smoke.

"Take me for a ride," she said suddenly.

"Yeah?"

She glanced over at the girls, her lifelong best friends, her most important people. None of them looked back.

"Yeah," she said. "Let's go."

He laughed and motioned to the bartender to pay the tab.

BLUE

Blue was wondering how the hell she wound up alone at a table with Renee. She'd been so preoccupied with her anger she barely even noticed Maya leave. Now she and Renee were stuck inside this stroppy silence that Blue had neither the desire to sit in nor put an end to by way of conversation. The waiter was taking too long with her drink. And she was starving—a gnawing emptiness where her hope of Jack had lived. She eyed the bread basket. She could eat it all, including the wicker. In fact, she would've gone right ahead and done just that if Renee hadn't ordered a salad. She didn't need the judgment. Besides, now that her high was wearing off, she was pulled back to how she'd felt earlier when she looked in the mirror…saw the bumps and swells of her body in all the places society insisted only smooth lines should be. She'd always vowed never to be one of those women who worried about her weight and yet here she was, because for one fleeting instant the hope of love had beckoned, and like all women, she'd been taught that only the beautiful and skinny could receive the call. And Blue was not either of those things. Oh, she'd learned that lesson in the hardest way possible.

She often thought of the cruel trick society played on women, inundating them with messages that they weren't enough and then telling them they could fix it by starving themselves, knowing that, like Harlow's monkeys, people needed love and comfort even more than food. And all along what women carried, what they perceived as excess weight, was merely the shame they'd been force-fed before they could identify its taste.

It made her angry. It made her hate.

And still some part of her bought into it.

Across from her Renee reapplied her lipstick and then glanced around at the other diners with that tranquil half smile that had been her camouflage since they were teenagers.

Blue imagined the curse of beauty was the constant maintenance. It was like driving a Mercedes. No point in having it if you didn't keep it clean and polished, if you weren't *advertising* it. But who had the time or energy? It could flatten a person. She'd already seen it happening to Renee at the end of high school—how she'd started disappearing into her prettiness, making it the centerpiece of who she was, the thing society told her she should be and nothing more. It had become at once her defense and her deepest vulnerability.

Renee shifted uncomfortably, the silence clearly getting to her. Blue knew it was only a matter of seconds before Renee broke it. She did a countdown in her head from three.

"It's so pretty here," Renee said the instant Blue hit one. "I'd forgotten."

"Mmm-hmm," Blue said. She picked up the list of specials, pretended to study it.

"I always loved the nights. They feel so…promising or something. I don't know."

"Mmm-hmm."

"So…can I ask how you are?"

"Great," Blue said flatly from behind the menu. "Never better."

"Good," Renee said. "That's good. You look good."

"Thanks."

The silence stretched. She made no effort to fill it. Renee sighed, began drumming her fingernails on the table. Anything to fill the void. Over the top of the menu, Blue could see her desperately scanning the restaurant for rescue.

"So, um…how're your parents?" Renee said finally. "They good too?"

"My mother's in Paris. I assume she's fine." Now Blue put the menu down, looked directly at her. "My father's been dead for three years, so I wouldn't know how he is. Hot, probably."

"Oh." Renee's eyes had that wet shock to them, like an open cut just before it bleeds. "I didn't know."

"How would you?" Blue said.

For years after their falling out, Blue had waited for Renee to reach out to her. All she'd wanted was an apology, acknowledgment of what had happened, a sign that Blue was a loss that Renee was not willing to incur. She kept hoping. And was angry at herself for hoping. And still hoped, because so often the only person who could heal a wound was the one who caused it. Eventually she burned out her emotions on the cycle and stopped thinking about it entirely, which in some ways felt worse—the emptiness where feeling should be. Then when her father died a few years ago, all that hurt resurfaced.

Who else but the friends you'd grown up with would understand the complicated feelings around losing a father who was, at once, not a good father and also the only one you had? Renee should have been there. She should have at least *known* about it. Called. Or sent flowers. Even just a card. Something.

Blue stood abruptly. She couldn't sit in this anymore. Some vaporous feeling was swelling, threatening to saturate her like a cloud turning to rain. "I'm getting a drink. The waiter is taking too long."

As she headed to the bar, she saw Hannah still outside with her phone to her ear, her red hair wild as ocean spray, her white summer dress trembling in the breeze. She made such a sad portrait. Blue considered going out to her. But then Hannah looked up, lifted her free hand to wave and returned her attention to her call. Blue glanced back at the table, at Renee looking stranded as a shipwreck.

Whatever. Good.

The bar was loud and crowded. She carved a path to the bartender and raised her hand to alert him. He was handsome and surfer-tousled, looked like a wealthy college kid on summer break.

"Scotch and soda and a shot of tequila, please."

He rested his forearms on the countertop. "Can I see your ID, young lady?"

"What? Oh…" She went for her wallet, a pleasant blush heating her face.

"I'm just joshing ya," he said, laughing, as he went to pour her drinks.

The blush turned to a sting. *Right. Of course.*

He put the drinks on the bar and she slammed down the shot. Handed him cash with a big tip he didn't deserve. As soon as the money left her hand, she realized she'd done it to make herself look important and instantly she was sick with herself.

Around her the restaurant was emptying of families with children. Now it was mostly couples dining together, first dates and long-term marriages, everyone paired. Blue tried to remember the last time she'd even had a crush on anyone. There was that one guy at the bar on Fifty-Second who she thought might like her—he'd chatted her up all night and she was sure he was going to ask for her number. But then he'd followed her into the bathroom and asked her to go down on him. Called her a fat bitch when she refused. She tried to let herself cry in the taxi home but she couldn't. By that time all of her tears had solidified into some dense, immovable block in her chest.

Oh, and there had been Patrick at work. He had a sweetness to him, a bit of low self-esteem, but he wasn't bad looking and sometimes he made her laugh. A coworker had mentioned that he liked her—though Blue found that hard to believe— but no door had ever opened to cross over into a relationship. She didn't know how to act like anything except a buddy. In fact, the more she liked a guy, the more inclined she was to chum it up. She had no clue how to flirt or seduce or even show mild interest. That was the part that was too hard. To dare to let herself be seen as a woman, a potential lover, to risk revealing her own want to be seen as that. She always imagined it being met with revulsion. Anyway, the new secretary had made her move on Patrick. Candy was her name. Jesus, it was like a bad porno. And maybe that's what he wanted, because Blue had attended their wedding last year.

On some level Blue knew she was complicit in her singleness, recognized the hardness in herself, knew that it was people's softness, their tender spots that made other people love them, and she had those—it wasn't that she didn't have soft spots, too—only she didn't know how to show them. If one slipped out for even a moment, she'd rush to cover it with a joke or a curse word. She didn't know how to stop doing that. It felt like survival.

Instead she'd trained herself to make love not matter. And while sometimes when she was alone in her apartment she would lie on her couch in a ball, her arms tucked inside her knees so the squeezing weight would feel like a hug, for the most part she'd accepted that there were some things in life she wouldn't get to have. But now because of Jack...because his reappearance online made her remember, made her miss...

I'm such an idiot, she thought, *to have let myself dream.*

She sighed, headed back to the table hoping Maya and Hannah had returned.

She found Renee still alone, fiddling with her engagement ring. Twisting it to the left. Twisting it to the right. Twisting Blue's guts right along with it. Not that she wanted to be engaged. God, no. She had no interest in marriage. But she wanted love. To even know it for a moment, just once in her adulthood. It seemed so little to ask. But instead Renee had found exactly the love she always dreamed of while Blue had spent the last twelve years totally, profoundly deprived of it, her once bright hopes torn down like drapes. And Renee to blame for it all.

"Look," Renee said as Blue sat down without speaking, "can we just start over?"

It was so Renee to want to pretend nothing had happened. To clear it from the record like a questionable call in a Little League game.

"Hi, I'm Renee." She smiled, encouraged Blue to play along.

Blue just stared. Early on in her job she'd learned that silence was often the most powerful response. It shrunk other people. Made them squirm with discomfort. She could actually see the uneasy fidget in Renee's eyes. She tried to enjoy it, this momentary revenge. Instead, a guilty twinge. Why did acting in anger always make her feel like a bad person? Even when it was justified. Men probably didn't feel that way—they weren't conditioned to always "play nice" and "be soft." As if denying women their rage made them less likely to be prey. Just the opposite, in fact. She took another gulp of her scotch.

"Okay...that's a no then," Renee said, smile falling. "I just thought... I mean, we were best friends for like thirteen years..." Renee shook her head. Looked like she might cry. "Whatever. Never mind."

Blue made herself impenetrable. She could do that with her mind. Erect an invisible shield around herself that no words— not even *best friend*—could breach. It felt like a superpower. She wondered if everyone had it. "That was a long time ago," she said.

Renee winced. "Not *that* long ago. I still know the name of every crush you've ever had, every teacher you ever hated, every band you ever obsessed over. Yes, even O-Town."

She was clearly looking for a smile but Blue wouldn't give it. She wondered why Renee suddenly cared so much when she couldn't have been bothered for twelve years. She'd ask her but then it would look like the answer mattered.

"I also know you love peppermint ice cream and hate the word *chunk* and that there are exactly nine goldfish buried in your backyard, every one of them named Freddy. You were like a sister to me."

Blue scanned the restaurant. Still no sign of Maya. She was probably hiding out in the bathroom, texting some random dude, imagining a peace treaty might be drawn up in her absence. "I don't know what you want me to say."

The waiter appeared with their food and drinks. They re-treated into themselves like two boxers into their corners as he set everything on the table. "Let me know if you need anything," he said as he backed away slowly, sensing tension, and then turned and darted off.

"I don't know either," Renee said, defeated. "Forget it."

An unexpected and traitorous lump blossomed in Blue's throat. She swallowed it back. Hardened herself against it. "I will."

Renee was playing with her engagement ring again. She was like freaking Gollum the way she kept gazing at it. She caught Blue eyeing it.

"You know," she said, "I was always a little bit jealous of you."

Blue was too surprised and curious to resist. "Me? Why?"

"Oh, I dunno. You were just so much tougher than me. Still are, obviously."

"I hate that word," Blue said, surprised by her own dis-appointment. What had she wished Renee would be jealous about?

"It's supposed to be a compliment."

Blue eyed the bread basket with longing. All she wanted was to stuff her face with carbs. "In my experience, people who define women as tough don't let them be anything else."

Renee considered that. "I guess I'm just saying that I… admired how you were never desperate about boys the way I was. You never needed to be in a relationship. I don't even know who I *am* when I'm alone."

I don't know who you are either, Blue thought, anger return-ing. She reached past the calamari for the bread, slathered a roll with butter, shoved it into her mouth. *To hell with it.* "Anyway, who says I'm alone?"

Renee's face lit with surprise. "You have a boyfriend? I didn't know... I just assumed..."

Blue sat back, folded her arms. *Of course you did. Also screw you.*

"Sorry. I just...hadn't heard you mention anyone. So...so you're seeing someone?"

"Look, I really don't feel like talking, if you don't mind," Blue said.

"Okay, then, that sounds like no. It's fine. There's nothing wrong with being single." Renee grabbed some of the calamari she'd said she wouldn't eat and shoved it into her mouth. Shook her head. Looked out the window where the last glow of purple sky had been swallowed by darkness.

"Jack."

Renee turned. Squinted. "What?"

Blue's stomach buzzed, electrified. "I'm seeing Jack. You remember Jack. Superhot guy from the last time we were here. We have a date tomorrow night, actually."

Renee's mouth dropped, just as Blue hoped it would. Only Blue didn't feel the satisfaction she was looking for. She felt positively sick with the fact that she'd said that, that she'd lied, and worse, that she'd felt she *had* to lie to prove she wasn't unlovable. Only she hadn't proved anything except that she was subscribing to some stupid patriarchal idea that her worth was determined by having a man.

Thank God Renee was leaving after dinner. Otherwise she'd have completely screwed herself. Otherwise she'd be expected to produce Jack.

HANNAH

Hannah had ended the call with Vivian, then stood for a moment in a state of numb detachment listening to the knock and slosh of water against the docks, the bustle of people going in and out of the restaurant, the music floating out and drifting over the water. By the jetty a large tugboat glided solemnly past, like something from another era, old and mournful as the sea.

As she started back, she saw Renee and Blue framed within the restaurant window, and she was struck by how old they looked, older than their age, or at least older than how they lived in her—those young girls she once knew with all their effervescent hope.

Her own reflection floated in the glass. Ghostly, disembodied, true.

The phone call with Vivian had left her guilty, especially

the surprise in Vivian's voice when Hannah explained that
she wasn't in DC. She and Vivian had spent so much time together over the years as they teamed up to care for Henry. But
it was complicated for Hannah. When she and Henry had first
started dating, Vivian had taken her in almost like a surrogate
daughter. She went out of her way to include Hannah for dinners and holidays, even got her a birthday present each year.
Hannah loved being a part of Henry's family. At Christmas
they sang carols around the piano and on the Fourth of July
Vivian would make a picnic and they'd all go down to the
National Mall and watch the feathery plume of fireworks light
up the Washington Monument. Sometimes Hannah would
catch his parents nuzzling or laughing with Henry over an
inside family joke, and it was all so warm and also confusing.
In some way Hannah found it hard to trust, didn't quite understand it. Happy families seemed almost fake to her; there
was no part of her brain that had developed to understand
this strange phenomenon. It was so far from what she knew.

After what happened to Henry, Hannah had few people to
turn to. Her own mother was too fragile, too absent, had no
empathy reserves to offer. Their relationship persisted as one
of avoidance—a polite phone call once a week where nothing
was ever really said because nothing would be heard. Hannah
accepted that it would never be any other way. But Vivian
was available to her; she not only understood her sense of loss
but shared it. The two of them lived it together, day in and
day out, in that care facility. She knew Vivian blamed herself
for what happened to Henry, for being out late that night, for
leaving him home alone. And probably his dad had blamed
himself too. He'd suffered a fatal heart attack only a few years

after. Vivian said the grief was what killed him. There were just so many endless repercussions to that night.

But Hannah couldn't imagine that Vivian did not blame her as well, blame her the most. After all, it never would've happened if she and Henry hadn't been dating. She assumed Vivian was still nice to her simply because she needed an extra hand with Henry. If anything happened to him, she was certain Vivian would have no more use for her. Maybe that's why she hadn't told her she was going away for a few days. She was too afraid to remind her of the vast difference in their fates, that she'd be on vacation with her friends while Henry was stuck in a long-term care facility, his mind a turned-off TV. And all because of them.

A piece of memory broke free, floated up.

The four of them driving home from Check's party that night. Her hands on the wheel, Renee adjusting the radio beside her.

"Maybe we should cruise around a little so we can sober up," Renee had said. "And by 'we' I mean Blue. I think she's having a harder time with the separation than she's letting on."

"From Jack?" Hannah had asked. They all knew Blue was lovesick over him, had talked about little else ever since they'd returned from Montauk.

"No, from us. College. That we're all leaving each other."

Hannah glanced in the rearview mirror, saw Blue slumped like a rag doll in the back seat, eyes closed, lost inside a boozy, weedy spin. Hannah understood it. She was struggling with their impending separation too.

"It's still a month away!" Maya said, poking her head through the divider. "All the more reason to live it up while we're still together." She leaned forward and cranked up the radio, and soon they were singing along to it, loud as a crash, the black night rushing through the windows as they sailed across Rock Creek Parkway, an aisle of infinite sky above the tree line.

The music seemed so right, and that sultry summer air was pouring into the car through the open windows and so Hannah drove on aimlessly, no rush to get home anyway. She took a right turn and then another. How many times had they done that? Just taken right turns until they landed somewhere interesting. They knew DC by heart, or at least Hannah thought she did. But she was distracted by the music, the laughter, and somewhere she lost track of the turns, and then the neighborhoods started to look unfamiliar, seedy, the sky blacker, the streetlamps fewer—surrounding them in that darkness of neglect.

"You guys," Hannah said, "I think we're lost."

Now as she slammed through the noise and the restaurant crowd toward Blue, who sat with her arms folded across her chest, toward Renee looking longingly at the bay as if she wanted to throw herself into it, Hannah understood, really understood, that they'd been lost ever since.

Blue and Renee looked up as she snaked her way over to the table.

"Everything okay?" Blue asked.

Hannah took her seat. The room was heightened with laughter and high chatter, the lighting softer now, the black night hugging the windows.

"She said it was," Hannah said.

"Oh, good, I was worried," Renee said.

"No reason to be," Hannah said.

The tears came, immediate and unbidden, like breathing.

"Oh no," Blue said. She looked helplessly at Hannah and then at a waitress passing by as if somehow she might be able to help. Finally she grabbed the napkin in her lap, shoved it at Hannah. It was covered with crumbs and cocktail sauce.

Hannah wanted to laugh. Thirty years old and Blue still didn't know what to do with emotions. But instead her tears only came harder.

Renee offered her a clean napkin and then reached out and grabbed her hand.

"I don't know why I'm crying," Hannah said. "She said he was okay." But something was wrong. Some unidentifiable piece. *What was it?* "I just have a bad feeling."

When was the last time Vivian had called for no reason? She couldn't remember. And now her mind was replaying the phone call, the moment she'd asked if Henry was okay. *Had there been a pause before Vivian answered?*

Dread, heavy, the color of ash, settling inside her.

"She never said why she was calling," Hannah said. "When I told her I was here, she said she didn't want to bother me. Just to call as soon as I got back. But she didn't say *why.*"

"But she didn't mention a problem?" Renee said.

"Right." But there had been a pause. Hannah was sure of it now. "I shouldn't have come. That's the bottom line." She should've known there would be a price to pay for leaving him.

"I think you're worrying over nothing," Blue said.

Over nothing.

She knew Blue didn't mean it like that. At least not consciously. But how could she explain to them how essential Henry was to her, even in his condition? How could she make them see that he still gave her so much when the notion of love was consigned to what a person could do rather than just the fact of them being there and always there and never stopping. The times when she would climb into Henry's bed, feel his heart thump against her own, nestle her face into the comforting sleep-smell of his neck, were the only times she was ever truly at peace, the only times her breathing settled and the fears retreated and everything in her stilled.

He was still the love of her life, her whole world. If anything happened to Henry, she wouldn't survive it.

MAYA

In the restaurant parking lot, Maya strapped on Andy's helmet, the breeze off the water blowing warm and gentle as a whisper.

"Where to, ma'am?" he asked, wearing that same boyish grin he had when he first spotted her in the bar.

"Take me to the place your dog loved most in the world," she said.

"You really want to go to Tucson?"

She gave him a look.

"I'm serious, he loved it there. He was smitten with a labradoodle named Bernice. Wouldn't look at me for a week after we left."

"Maybe the place he loved second best..."

"That would probably be my neighbor's pool. Which is why they put a big lock on the gate." He climbed onto the bike.

Maya got on behind him and pressed herself into the strength of his back, feeling a sense of deep relief in the touch, like stepping into a hot shower after getting caught in bad weather. "Take me to the pool," she said. "I know how to break a lock."

He laughed and revved the motor and flipped up the kickstand with a practiced flick of his boot. Soon they were launching onto the unlit road toward town, roaring past the moonlit gleam of the bay, faster and faster, as if they were winged.

"Woo-hoo!" Maya yelled into the night. Glorious and wild and set free. This was what mattered. Not bills, not loans, but soaring, but life. The ephemeral lust to touch something bigger, to merge with it. The wind moved through her, ignited her. She was a sparkler. She was the Fourth of July. She was bursting out of herself in the same way she'd felt the first time she had sex, bungee jumped, stole her parents' car before she had her license, moments that felt lifted from life, in defiance of suffering. At sixty miles an hour in open wind, the boundary of her body disappeared. She was air and night and speed, vast as the universe, lit up as the stars.

"Do a wheelie!" she called over the roar, though she wasn't sure he had heard her. She laughed to herself imagining Hannah's horrified face if she could see her now.

Andy pulled onto a side street near town, the bike slowing to idle, the ride over and yet somehow still happening inside her. He parked in front of a modern A-frame house, the sudden quiet like a dive under a wave, and led her by the hand into the backyard. There a floodlit pool glowed in the dark as if a small corner of blue sky had been carved into the lawn.

"All right, Houdini, let's see your skills," he said as they reached the gate.

Maya tried the lock, considered her options and then simply scaled the fence like a criminal.

"Resourceful," Andy said, laughing, as he followed. "I like that." He walked up to her, stood so close she could feel the heat coming off his body, feel the charge between them in that one inch of space. He smiled down on her, adoringly, the way one might smile at a puppy, with gentleness and generosity and forgiveness for anything she might ever do, and something softened and yielded deep within her as if all she'd ever wanted was to be forgiven. For what, she didn't know. His hands found her hips, his fingers grazing them gently as he drank her in, and then he leaned down and kissed her. He smelled like mint gum and beer, his chest earth solid against hers, and she became all body, no thoughts, only bliss and wanting as he led her down onto a lounge chair.

She opened her eyes.

They gazed at each other.

"Hi," she said.

"Hi," he said, goofy and sweet. As tough as he looked, there was something deeply vulnerable and unguarded about him, like a little boy sleeping. Her heart tugged, a sudden rush of tenderness unlike anything she'd ever felt.

She pressed her hands against his shoulders, nudging him off. He was a quick summer hookup, nothing more. "What if your dog is watching?" She pointed to his jacket pocket where the small box of ashes was jutting out.

He rolled over with a sigh and lay on his back beside her. "That's okay. He's seen a lot more action than this." He flipped his jacket over, covered the container. "There. Privacy."

She laughed. "Much better." The dizziness she'd felt as he kissed her lingered.

They were quiet for a moment.

"Do you think he's, like, around you somewhere?"

"Indy? Well…he's not coming when I call his name, so…"

She smacked his arm. "You know what I mean. Do you think there's just nothing left of the barking and running around and happiness to see you?"

She searched his face. A strange sense of urgency was grinding inside her. Lately she was too aware of the tenuousness of everything. She couldn't stand the idea that nothing lasted.

She thought of her friends, of that night, lost in that dark neighborhood. The obliteration of light. She pushed it away.

"I don't know," Andy said. "I hope not. I hope I'll see him again someday. In heaven or wherever. He was a great brother."

She sighed. A stillness settled over them as they gazed into the black expanse above, the crowd of tiny stars, the mottled moon suspended in the sky as if someone had batted it there. A particular kind of ache settled in her chest, something about the beauty and sadness of existence being so inextricably bound. "I'm not a God person," she said. "I think we die and that's it. There's nothing."

"That's grim."

She turned to him. "Is it?" It was. But. "Maybe it just makes this life more important."

Their eyes caught. She felt something like love. Though she knew it couldn't be. She turned back to the sky.

"I have this theory," she said, "that your degree of faith is based on your prebirth relationship with your mother."

"Okay, I'm listening."

"That's our first experience of another being, right? In the womb. A presence that can be felt but not seen—one that is hopefully, but not necessarily, protective and benevolent. And that's when our brain starts developing, so…"

"Right…"

"Anyway, that's about all I've got."

"Wait. That's your whole theory?" He laughed.

She laughed too. "Just that maybe you either learn to trust in something bigger than you early on…or you don't."

He frowned, considering.

"Look, I'm not saying it holds up, but it certainly would explain *my* lack of faith."

"I mean, but even by your example, doesn't the womb just prove the limits of our perspective? I'm sure when we were in it—which is really weird by the way—I'm sure we thought that *that* was all there was. We had no idea there was this whole universe out here." He gestured toward the pool, the house behind them, the trees shivering lightly in the breeze.

"My friend Hannah thinks that when you die, your soul merges with those of everyone you've ever loved. Like you know how sometimes when you hug someone you're in love with you feel like you can't get close enough, you want to crawl up inside them? She thinks death is like one giant soul hug. Like our bodies are the prison and death is the freedom." She paused, thinking about Henry. "Anyway… I'm not actually sure she still believes that." She needed to stop thinking about sad things.

"I hope it's something good," he said. "I'm sort of afraid of death. Or at least of dying in a gruesome way. You?"

"Not at all. Don't intend to ever do it."

"Good plan," he said. He leaned over and kissed her, and then his weight was on top of her and his weight was the certainty, the salve against all the instability in her life and the strange feeling she'd been having of being too light and loosely tied, made of dandelion feathers. He squeezed her and she wanted to say "Don't let go," wanted to glue herself to him so she wouldn't float away on a breeze. She suddenly understood what Hannah meant about souls hugging.

"I could lie out here forever," he said.

"Wait, how long have we been here?" She thought of her friends back at the restaurant, imagined them as she hoped they'd be, halfway through dinner in their lobster bibs, laughing and talking as they cracked claws, dipping their mini forks in butter, all of their differences set aside.

He looked at his watch. "About forty-five minutes."

"We should probably get back."

"Yeah, for sure."

Neither of them moved.

"Okay. Off we go."

"Back on the road."

"It was fun while it lasted."

"Yep, we should do this again sometime."

Finally, Maya sat up, looked around at the manicured lawn, the white lights strung like musical notes across the patio, the glowing ripples of the pool reflected on the house. "It's pretty here. I can see why Indy liked it."

"Mmm-hmm," he said, though he was looking at her and not the surroundings.

"We should get married here."

"Indy would've loved that. He was a romantic at heart."

"You think the homeowners would mind?"

"Yes."

"Then we won't invite them," she said.

He smiled, and she was surprised to find that she could

picture it all. She had never actually thought about marriage. She'd only been teasing. And yet. When she'd said it out loud it made sense. There was just something about him… she didn't know what.

She'd had too much to drink, that's what, she decided.

Still, it was sort of fun to think about.

"A fall wedding, I think. Small. Twenty people or so. I don't want anything fancy. But I want a pretty dress. I want to be the prettiest girl you ever saw."

"You already are."

"So you'll marry me, then?"

"Of course," he said, and he said it just like she had, like they were merely playing a game—but there was an earnestness beneath the conversation, as if they realized that rescue had come for them both. Blue would hate her for a thought like that, think it was weak and dependent, but Maya was starting to think that all people were in need of love's rescue and women were sometimes just more honest about it.

Not that this guy meant anything though. She understood how chemicals worked in the body.

She jumped up, went to the pool, bent down and ran her fingers through the still water. He followed her.

"I guess you can't exactly spread the ashes here. That would be kinda gross for the owners. But any last words for your pooch?"

He smiled, considered. Their eyes locked for a moment before they both looked away. "Nah," he said. "He already knows."

"Okay, then, I'll say something." She stood, raised an imaginary wineglass. "To Indy," she said, "who always liked to make a splash."

She turned and pushed Andy into the water. He pulled her in behind him, the two of them crashing into blue, coming up laughing. The water was warm and rousing. He grabbed her, kissed her, her stomach whooshing, her heart floating in her chest like a beach ball. Making her forget everything but the moment.

Suddenly the night flared white, spotlights glaring at them from every direction. They heard a window open in the house.

Their eyes widened as they looked at each other. Then, giggling quietly, they scrambled to the pool ladder.

The back door flew open. A man was yelling, charging toward them.

"You goddamn kids!" he shouted, which, at the moment, they felt like they were, and then they were running across the patio and scaling the gate, leaving a guilty trail of dripping water behind them.

They reached Andy's bike and he handed her his jacket before they both hopped on.

"Go!" Maya yelled happily as she tucked her wet arms into the sleeves. She clutched his damp back, shivering with cold and adrenaline, life swelling like a laugh in her throat, everything pure, simple, fun. Perfectly what she needed. And two more days lined up like this, a boy and her best friends and summer on the wind. It was going to happen. Then Blue would lend her money for the house and everything would work out okay just like it always did.

"You all right?" Andy shouted over the roar of the motor as they pulled back onto Montauk Highway.

She was.

BLUE

Blue paid the check as Renee fired off texts to Maya that went unanswered. "So much for Maya buying dinner," she said to Hannah. "Mystery of her disappearance solved."

She told herself Maya was fine. Hannah had seen her talking to some guy earlier, and now, knowing Maya, she was probably off in a secluded area making out with him. Which was all the more annoying considering she'd been cornered into lying to Renee about Jack because Maya had left them alone together. Oh, it didn't matter that it had been her choice to lie. She was fully aware that it wasn't fair to be mad at Maya about that. But she had enough legitimate reasons that she didn't mind adding some illegitimate ones to the list. She should've never let Maya drag her on this stupid vacation. And okay, fine, she hadn't technically been "dragged." It was another spurious claim, but still, *still*. Maya left her with Renee!

Who she didn't want to share a country with, much less an evening. And now Blue was stuck dealing with the fallout.

"I'll check the parking lot," she said, throwing a cash tip on the table.

A sudden sick feeling turned her stomach.

A glimpse of memory, darting like a shadow across her periphery.

The recall of danger.

"I'll see if she's on the dock," Renee said, nervously fingering the cross around her neck. "Maybe she went into one of those little stores."

"I'll double-check in here," Hannah said.

A look of dread passed between them.

"She always does crap like this," Blue said. "I refuse to worry."

But she couldn't help it. That night lived in her. Rose up like a rogue wave and crashed down in irrational, all-consuming terror. She could see it in Renee's and Hannah's eyes, too, that quick leap to panic. One night, a few minutes, was all it took to rewire a brain.

And even back then Maya had been too loose with the world, too obtuse to its realities.

Even back then.

She didn't want to think about it. About that creep in her spine when eighteen-year-old Hannah had said, "I think we're lost." About the way her body had seemed to sense what was coming.

But no, this was not the same as that. Maya was fine. Everything was fine.

And yet hadn't she thought the same thing back then, when they pulled in to the convenience store that night to get directions? She thought they would be rerouted back to safety. And instead. Instead.

God, why didn't Maya ever learn?

Drunk and high as Blue had been after Check's party, she knew enough to force herself sober the minute they'd gotten lost. And when they'd spotted that convenience store and got out to ask for directions? Blue had been acutely aware that the neighborhood was unsafe, that they should not draw attention to themselves. But not Maya. Oh no! She'd been as loud as a jet engine as she clambered out.

"Who's buying me a Slurpee?" she'd shouted.

"Shh," Blue said as they stepped around a homeless man on their way into the store. She still remembered the way he swatted at imaginary flies, his wide, electrocuted eyes looking out upon some unknowable horror.

"Who's buying me a Slurpee?" Maya repeated in a whisper and then burst out laughing.

Maya got her Slurpee and directions from the cashier and the girls pushed back out into the night. Blue paused to give the homeless man her change, and that's when she noticed that another car had joined theirs in the parking lot, a scratchy-looking guy leaning against it, sucking on a cigarette. His two friends sauntered past them into the store. Even before the man spoke, Blue felt something, an antenna standing at attention inside her, tuning in to some unnamable danger.

"Hey, baby," he rasped at Maya, his voice perverse, violating, as if he was rubbing up on her with it.

Blue shot him a look of disgust and he laughed. His smile was a jack-o'-lantern's, his rotted, broken teeth suggesting the meth pipe. He stuck out his arm and grabbed Maya's ass as she went by.

Blue wanted to say something, punch his ugly face, but alarm bells sounded in her head. She was too aware of where they were—lost. How dark the night was—crow black and underlit. How vulnerable four girls alone would be inside it. "Ignore it," she said, pushing Maya toward the car.

"Fuck that," Maya said. "He doesn't get to put his nasty hands on me." She shook free of Blue, turned to the guy. "Listen, needle dick—"

"Ooh yeah!" the man said, cackling. "I like 'em with a little fight." He grabbed his crotch. "Whatchyou got for me, little girl?"

"Maya!" Blue said. "Come on."

Maya squared up on him. "Keep talking and I'll knock out your last tooth."

The man licked his lips. And again that laugh—it sent a shiver up Blue's spine, the way it had a slime to it, slick with hate. She turned and moved faster toward the car, pushing Maya in front of her. She shoved her into the back seat and scrambled into the front. Turned to Hannah. "Let's get the hell out of he—"

"Blue! Watch out!"

Blue turned as a blur of greasy hair and rotten teeth lurched toward her. She yanked the door closed just as his grimy hands slammed down on the glass in front of her face.

He went for the door handle.

Hannah dove for the locks.

"Go!" Blue cried.

Hannah fumbled to get the key in the ignition. "I'm trying!"

"Fuck, Hannah, go!" Maya said.

He pounded on the window so hard the car shook.

Renee leaped forward, blasting the horn to alert the store clerk. Blue saw it draw the attention of the man's friends in-

stead. They turned and pointed, abandoning their stuff as they
ran for the door.

"Oh my god," she said.

Hannah was fishing around on the floor.

"What are you doing?" Blue said.

"I dropped the keys!"

The man made a lewd gesture with his tongue, rattled the
door handle as Hannah scrambled for them in the darkness.
"Shit."

He pressed his face against the window, baring that nasty
shattered-glass smile.

"Hurry!" Blue shouted.

"Shut up!" Hannah cried.

His friends reached the car just as Hannah found the keys,
got them in the ignition. One creep pounded the hood. She
slammed the car in reverse. Screeched out of the parking lot.

"Jesus," Hannah said. "Is everyone okay?"

"We're fine," Maya said. "Everyone's fine. Those slimeballs
don't get to ruin our good time."

But Blue wasn't fine, couldn't shake the look in the man's
eyes. She'd never been that close to pure hatred before, the way
it bored into her, black and parasitic, hunting for a new host.

They'd been on the road only a minute when Blue noticed
Hannah glancing in the rearview mirror.

"What?" she said.

"Nothing."

Blue turned. Saw two pinpoints of light stabbing the darkness, growing bigger, coming faster. She knew it was them
even before the beat-up car came into view. She could feel
the darkness, darker than the night around them, spilling toward them. "Oh my God."

Hannah sped up. Much too fast for the road. Almost missing curves in the darkness.

Soon the men were beside them. Swerving threateningly into their lane. Nearly pushing them off the parkway.

The light ahead turned red.

"Run it!" Blue shouted.

"I am!" Hannah yelled as the car shook with too much speed. "Which way?!"

"Make the next left!" Maya said. "I think."

"You think?!" Blue said. "What street?"

"Whipple or...I don't know...Whitehall? Begins with a *W*...maybe... I don't... She was talking so fast!"

"You didn't write it down?" Renee said.

"You've got to be kidding me!" Blue said.

"Everybody, shut up!" Hannah said.

Blue frantically checked her phone for cell service.

Renee screamed as the car pushed back up behind them, riding their bumper.

"You guys..." Hannah said.

Before she'd even gotten the words out, Blue understood by the tremor in her voice that they would be bad.

"We're running out of gas."

Now as Blue scanned the parking lot, she felt the way she always did when she remembered that night—that dark, disorienting descent, a scuba diver in murky waters, losing her sense of which way was up. How quickly that blackness could engulf her, steal even the direction of light. She thought of her unfinished second drink inside the restaurant, missed it like a limb.

Hannah and Renee approached, grim faced.

"We looked everywhere," Hannah said.

Blue pulled out her emergency cigarettes, shook one out of the pack and lit it. That night was so close to her now, the thin veil between past and present dissolving. *Bright, useless moon, the guttural bark of a dog, Renee, help!* She needed something… she needed… She inhaled slow and deep, studied the ribbon of her exhale as it curled and drifted and finally disappeared. Smoking was meditation and forgetting. A few drags were all that was necessary to suffocate the feelings.

Hannah was hugging herself, rubbing her arms like a child self-soothing. Renee looked pale, her hairline damp and curling with sweat.

"Should we call the police?" Renee said.

No one moved. Their eyes met, wide and spooked. The awful unspoken thought pulsing between them once more: *Jesus, not again.*

The roar of a bike broke the pall of dread, a single headlight zooming toward them.

"Please tell me that's not her," Blue said.

"I hope it is," Hannah said. "It'll mean she's still alive."

"Right," Blue said steadily, "but then I'll have to kill her." It was all stirred up in her—everything, all of it. That night, this night, the burden of loving people.

The bike skidded to a stop in front of them with a little fishtail flourish. Maya, on the back, wearing a man's jacket, took off her helmet and flashed a big smile. Beside her some random dude with slicked-back hair, a wet T-shirt clinging to his chest.

"Did she pick up a stripper?" Renee whispered under her breath.

"Hi!" Maya said, scrunching her own wet hair. "What are you guys doing in the parking lot?"

Blue wanted to punch her. Her fists were balling as if she might. She was relieved too. Of course she was relieved! But her whole back was soaked with fear sweat and her heart wouldn't calm and all she had wanted, all she'd freaking wanted, was a quick getaway with her friends, with Maya and Hannah only. And just maybe to have a little tiny romance, just for a few days, to be kissed for freaking once, just one more time in her stupid life. And instead here she was, the walking credit card, dealing with other people's BS as usual, terrified that Maya had been murdered. She might as well be back at work fixing the mistakes of all the Wall Street bros who outearned her while underperforming her.

"Andy," Maya said. "This is my fr—"

"You're dead to me right now," Blue said with the controlled menace of a cocked gun.

Maya flinched with surprise, recovered. "Oh! I am? Okay, well, can I not be dead until Monday? Because I haven't even had a day at the beach yet. Or a last meal, for that matter. Plus, we've already had one loss." She pulled out the box of ashes from Andy's jacket pocket. "This is…well, was…Indy."

Blue scowled. No one spoke.

"All righty, then. Guess you're not dog people," Maya said.

"You're such an asshole," Blue said.

"Should I…ah…" Andy thumbed toward his bike.

"No," Maya said. "Just wait over there a sec." She motioned to the edge of the parking lot, and he dutifully headed that way.

"What were you doing?" Hannah said as soon as he was out of earshot. "We were seriously worried."

"We thought you'd been kidnapped or something," Renee said. "Think of where our minds went."

"I went swimming! I wasn't gone that long." She paused, glanced at Andy and back to them. "I mean, come on, did you *see* him? What choice did I have?"

Blue was so mad she thought she might stroke out. "What choice? Oh gosh, I don't know. You could've chosen not to scare the crap out of your friends, I suppose. You could've chosen to be considerate. You could've... I'm just spitballing here...*not gone.*"

"Could you possibly overreact more? Excuse me if I didn't want to share in the misery party you guys were having. Maybe if you weren't fighting—"

"Oh, right!" Blue threw her hands up. "It's *our* fault. You had no choice but to run off with some random drifter you met in a bar."

"You could've at least told us you were leaving," Renee said.

"You guys would've stopped me!" Maya said. "Whatever. I'm not going to apologize for trying to enjoy my vacation."

"*Your* vacation?!" Blue said. "Okay, hold on, everybody, let's all take a minute to remind ourselves that we are on *Maya's* vacation and *we should not interfere with her fun if she wants to take off and abandon us to bang some loser on a bike!*"

She saw Andy turn, look dumbfounded. It gave her a sick pleasure to know he had heard.

"Real mature, Blue," Maya said.

Blue gave her the finger.

Maya gave her the finger back.

A young couple hurried their children past.

"Okay, you guys..." Hannah shook her head.

"Blue's right, Maya," Renee said.

"Thank you," Blue said.

Blue and Renee exchanged a look, realized they were on

the same side. *Oh, whatever.* Blue didn't have the energy to be mad at two people at once and right now her fury at Maya trumped everything. "You know what? To hell with this. I'm out of here." She started toward the car.

"Excellent plan," Maya said. "This is stupid. Let's go fight it out with a dance-off at the Talkhouse."

"I mean back to the city," Blue said over her shoulder. "You're absolutely right. This trip *is* miserable." She stopped, turned. "And by the way, how about giving Hannah back the Xanax you stole from her?"

"What are you talking about?" Maya said.

Blue just stared.

"I didn't take it!"

"Oh, really? It's just a coincidence that for years you've been going on about how she needs to stop, and it's a crutch, and now—poof—it's gone, when you were the last person to have it?"

"Wait, what?" Hannah said, wounded. "That's really what you think of me, Maya?"

"No!" Maya said. "Okay, yes. No. It's complicated. I'm sorry. And I did take it. I'll give it to you as soon as we get back to the house."

"You stole her medication? Seriously?" Renee said incredulously. "Jeez."

"I was only trying to help."

Hannah and Renee looked at each other, started toward the car.

"It was a mistake, okay?" Maya said.

Blue walked back to her. "Give me the keys."

"All of this because I met a guy? It was nothing! Just a laugh."

Blue extended her hand.

"But—"

"*Keys.*"

"Whatever," Maya said, lobbing them at Blue. "Leave, then! What do I care?"

"We *are*," Blue said.

She hit the remote key with flare, unlocking the car doors. Hannah and Renee exchanged glances before climbing in.

"No, wait!" Maya cried.

They all turned.

"What about the beach? The sunsets? The happy hours? Just screw it all? Forget the friendship? See you later? The whole point of this stupid trip was to fix us! To go back to the way things were before everything got all messed up. And we were happy. And normal. And best freaking friends! Remember?"

Blue opened the driver's door. "Sorry," she said, "but your plan didn't work."

"You didn't give it a chance."

"It never had one."

"Look, I apologize, okay? I shouldn't have left without telling you! I admit it!"

It wasn't enough. Even if Blue wanted it to be, it just wasn't.

"Tell me what you want me to do to make you stay," Maya pleaded.

I want you to have kept your mouth shut that night, Blue thought. But that wasn't fair. She knew it wasn't fair to blame Maya. "You know what I want?" she said instead. "I want you to grow up. I want you to consider people. I want you to keep a job for more than three months. I want you to pay me back the four thousand six hundred dollars and twenty-five cents you've borrowed from me over the last ten years."

"You kept a tab?"

"I did. But no more. The days of me bailing you out are over. You need to act like a responsible adult for once in your life."

"Fine," Maya said. "Consider it done. All grown up. I'll be so mature I won't even laugh. I won't even *smile*. Okay? If I agree to that, can we just try—"

Blue got in the car, slammed the door shut. Renee and Hannah joined her.

"You guys," Maya called.

Blue gripped the steering wheel, stared straight ahead. The anger was out of her. Now all she wanted was to drive away. From everything. From all of it. Just go and go and go until nothing felt hard anymore. It seemed like she'd been wanting to do that for so long now. Even before that terrible night. But who was it she wanted to leave? Her parents, yes. Herself, probably even more so. But not her friends. They were what had kept her sane, possibly even kept her alive. But that was before. When they weren't so damaged and life so complicated. When they didn't hurt her. Not in a real way.

And yet it tugged at her. Those things she tried so hard to deny—her love, her dependency. That endless devotion to her old friends that she sometimes wished she could cut out of her heart and toss away. It hurt to stay. It hurt to go. In equal measure.

She sighed, rolled down the window, motioned toward Andy. "Him or us," she said.

Maya looked sadly at Andy, back at Blue. "But—"

"Five seconds to decide," Blue said.

Maya didn't move.

Blue started the engine.

HANNAH

Hannah sat in the back seat, momentarily away from the noise and the tension and the cavity of night sky. She was exposed wire, a downed telephone line, spewing high-voltage electricity. She couldn't believe Maya took her Xanax! Not that it mattered now. Between this and the call from Vivian, she was so out of there. Henry needed her. Or she needed him—she wasn't sure.

"I seem to remember much less fighting last time we were here," Renee said dryly.

"Yeah," Hannah said. "And more fun." They both stared wistfully ahead.

Outside the car Maya stood stubborn and conflicted.

Blue honked and she jumped a little, glared into the headlights. "Do you think she practices being a pain in the ass?" Blue asked.

"Yes," Hannah said.

"I think it comes naturally," Renee said.

Hannah pulled out her phone, pulled up Google to search for train and bus schedules. She wondered which would be more likely to be the target of a terror attack. A bus, she bet. She decided to go with the train.

Blue lit a cigarette.

Renee discreetly rolled her window down.

Hannah pulled up the train schedule. Checked the times. It was too late to go tonight. But she could take the first one out in the morning to Penn Station, a second to DC. She swallowed. Weirdly her throat no longer hurt. Just in time, now that she was leaving.

Blue shined her high beams on Maya. "Should we just leave without her?"

Before Hannah or Renee could answer, Blue backed up, steered left, let the car roll forward without Maya in it.

"Wait! Don't," Hannah said. "Even though she probably deserves it."

Blue sighed, stopped the car.

Maya marched up to the window. "Let me just say goodbye," she said, and stomped off to the edge of the parking lot where Andy stood.

"I almost feel bad," Renee said. "He *was* pretty hot."

"She'll find another one in ten minutes," Blue said with a shrug.

They watched as Maya and Andy embraced.

Blue honked the horn again, and Maya's middle finger shot up behind Andy's back. Finally Maya returned to the car, climbed in beside Hannah, slammed the door shut.

They pulled out of the lot, and Maya turned to wave goodbye with an expression that Hannah had never seen on her. It almost looked like longing. Hannah hated longing. It hurt in such a physical way, like your heart was reaching outside your chest, came just short of its desired target. But no, she was probably projecting. Maya never got attached to men.

They drove in silence, not even the radio to camouflage the strife, and everything had a lonely quality to it like the howl of a wind. Hannah scanned the side of the road for deer that might bolt out in front of them. It was so dark out here, the night.

"So that's it?" Maya said. "We're all just going to hate each other and be miserable for the rest of the weekend?"

"No one hates anyone," Hannah said.

Blue cleared her throat.

"Am I seriously the only one who cares about fixing this?" Maya said.

"Some things are past fixing," Blue said as she pulled up to a stop sign.

Hannah felt this in her chest. She felt this in her life.

"Do you believe that too?" Maya said to Renee.

"I don't know what I believe," Renee said.

They turned onto Montauk Highway. The air near the beach was salty with sea and the stir of memory. It was as if summers lay dormant in the body, awoken again by that smell. Hannah wondered what the memory of vacation smelled like to people who lived here full-time.

They turned onto the street where Maya had once ridden Blue's skateboard straight into a sewer. They passed the beach where Hannah, wading in the night ocean, had turned to see Blue getting her first kiss. They reached Nana's street and Hannah saw them as they were at eighteen, coming home after a bonfire at Ditch Plains, singing at the top of their lungs and stumbling drunkenly into one another, Renee trying her first cigarette and gagging and coughing so violently that she fell down a small ravine.

Now Blue spun into the driveway. The house was a dark, unwelcoming silhouette. They'd forgotten to leave the lights on. The engine ticked and settled, made the quiet louder as if they'd parked underwater. As they got out, Hannah could hear the waves booming like the thundering footsteps of giants. Storm surf. Angry ocean.

Renee looked at her watch. "Oh, shoot. I missed the last ferry from Orient Point."

"Oh no," Hannah said.

"It's fine," she said wearily. "Just adds another hour to the drive."

"It's already late though," Hannah said. She looked pleadingly at Blue.

"All I know is I'm going to bed," Blue said. "You guys can do whatever."

Maya grinned at Renee. "I've got a big T-shirt you can sleep in!"

Renee paused, finally conceded. "Okay. I'll leave first thing in the morning." She looked at Blue. "Thank you."

"Actually," Maya said, "I was thinking that tomorrow we can—"

Hannah tuned out, thinking about how she would break the news that she, too, would be leaving in the morning. This trip meant so much to Maya. And even though she was pissed about the Xanax, Maya was still her best friend, still the one who'd tucked her into bed at the motel when she was scared, who never stopped inviting her into the world no matter how many times she refused it, who loved her when she couldn't find much to love about herself. But Henry...

"I won't be here tomorrow," Hannah blurted.

"Beg your pardon?" Maya said.

"I know you're going to think I'm ridiculous—"

"Too late," Maya said. "I've thought that for years."

Blue unlocked the front door.

Hannah braced. "I'm going back to DC."

"Oh, come on!" Maya said. "Because I took your Xanax? I'll give it back right now." She headed toward the stairs. "It's in my top drawer."

Hannah looked to Blue.

"She has a bad feeling about Henry," Blue said for her.

Maya turned. "What do you mean, a bad feeling?"

Hannah gave a little shrug, stared at the floor.

"Feelings are not facts. It's in your head. The last thing you should do is listen to yourself."

Hannah closed her eyes. "I know you don't understand."

"You're right," Maya said steadily. "I don't."

"He needs me."

"Oh, bullshit, Hannah," Maya said. "*I* need you. *He* doesn't even know you're there!"

"Maya!" Blue said.

The room went still. Or Hannah did. She didn't actually know which. It just seemed like there was a moment where Maya's words hung, suspended in the air before they landed. She had a weird instinct to laugh, but darkly and with horror. That Maya could say that to her. That her best friend could say that. Try to take away her hope when the only thing more painful than hope was to be without it.

She pulled herself taller, looked Maya right in the eye. "You have no idea what you're talking about." She turned to Renee and Blue, who both bowed their heads. "None of you do." She ran past them up the stairs.

Behind her she heard Maya say, "Shit."

Then Blue said, "You're on a real winning streak, Maya."

Hannah slammed the bedroom door shut, grabbed her Xanax from Maya's top drawer. She opened the bottle, but it wasn't anxiety she felt, so she closed it again. She sat down on her bed, got up. The room was dark and grainy but for the moon through the window and the light from the hall. She could've flipped a switch but she didn't want to. She had the strange sense that she'd been punched out of her own body, the pain so big and detonating she'd gone numb.

He does know I'm there. He does.

She let the evidence play out in her mind. Every moment when she felt him with her, a sudden smile, a single word, a brief light behind his eyes before flickering out again—all these little signs—they were like proof of God or proof of fate or proof of anything that required faith; little clues and then gone, so much space in between those moments to fill with doubt. But they happened—they did. What the hell did Maya know?

She heard footsteps on the stairs. The door flew open. All three of her friends stood in the entrance.

"Hannah," Blue said.

She went to the closet, pulled out her suitcase, threw it onto the bed. "Whatever," she said. "I know you probably all think that about him."

No one said anything, which only confirmed it.

"Must be nice. To believe that." She moved to her night-stand. Dumped her medications into a plastic bag. "Because,

like, if he's just gone, if he's just…'brain dead'—" her hands
shook as she sealed the bag, threw it into her suitcase "—then
you don't have to think about him. Or worry about him. Or
visit him. Or have any responsibility for him at all. Everything's settled and you get to go on with your lives."

"No." Renee reached toward her.

"Don't," Hannah said. She marched past them and into the
bathroom. She gathered her toiletries and makeup except for
her toothbrush, which she'd need in the morning. She was
a robot, utterly detached from emotion, and she marveled at
herself, at the way her brain had snipped off all of her feelings
at the root because they were too big to bear. She suddenly remembered a time when Henry had gotten so upset during an
argument with his dad about school that he ran out the door
and dry heaved on the lawn. It had startled Hannah and hum-
bled her and filled her with such tenderness for him. When
life felt hard, he tried to expel himself. She shut herself down.

The feelings were there though. She was simply in the eye
of it. An almost eerie calm within her. If only she could stay
there. Just this once. And also forever. She returned to the
bedroom, focused only on her mission to pack.

"You can think whatever the hell you want," she said, yanking her stuff from the dresser. "But you're not the ones who
sit with him every day." She tossed her first aid kit into her
suitcase. "You're not the ones who see him smile. Or feel his
eyes follow you around the room sometimes." She chucked in
her vitamins, her antibacterial wipes, her extra charger. "You
don't have to see a tear roll down his cheek when you wheel
him outside to see a sunset, or hear him suddenly say 'Mom'
or 'Yes' or 'Hi' and then be told by your friends—by people
who are *supposed* to be your friends—" she fought the sudden

choke in her voice, the calm crumbling "—that there's no hope. That you're an idiot for holding on."

Maya sat down on the bed in front of Hannah's suitcase. "You're right."

"I know," Hannah said. She returned to the drawers. The one convenience of her neurosis was that all of her clothes were already neatly packed in her large plastic freezer bags.

"I didn't know he did some of those things," Maya said quietly.

Hannah slammed the top drawer shut. "Because you never want to talk about him."

"Yes, well, I need to grow up," Maya said. "We've already established that."

Hannah checked under the bed for anything that might have fallen under it. "Look," she said. "I came. I stayed in a disgusting motel for you. We had fun."

"No fun has been had yet," Maya said.

"Well, whatever, I did it. I tried."

"Oh, please," Maya said.

"What?" Hannah shot back up.

"You didn't try."

"Maya," Blue warned.

"Sorry, but she didn't. No part of trying involves packing up your plastic bags and going home."

"Why are you on my bed?" Hannah said, suddenly registering that fact. "Please get off my bed." It was all she could do not to physically remove her, displace the contamination. Maya probably hadn't even washed her hands.

Maya didn't move. "Look, I get that there's a chance for Henry someday. I get that there are medical advances and all that...but until then...when do you get to live your life?"

"I am living," Hannah said. "So maybe mind your business, okay?"

Maya didn't even flinch. "I don't even think you believe that."

Hannah stared at her.

"She has a point," Blue said quietly.

Renee bowed her head.

"I just think—" Maya started.

"Get the fuck off my bed right now!"

The room hushed, the air retreating to the corners like frightened children.

They stared at her in shock.

Hannah didn't care. She was a fucking grenade.

"Fine," Maya said, standing. "Jesus." She put her hands up in mock surrender.

They glowered at each other.

Hannah went to speak but the spell of rage broke and she was small again, smaller than before, and there was nothing left in her to fight the truth. She slumped down next to her suitcase. Stared at the contents of her life. All that plastic. All those medicine bottles. What she had become.

She felt something tear, a tiny, terrible rip on the seams she held so tightly together.

Because it was there. The want. Too painful to own. And yet. Now named out loud? To live. Not just function. To have experiences. To feel things, big things. To have life happen to her. It was there—a hidden yearning and regret for all she'd already given up. So many years. So much of her youth. And she couldn't be sure Henry even knew she was there. Not when his eyes were blank and distant. Which was most of the time. And, oh God. To live! She'd felt it when they left DC, and again when they pulled up to the house and she remembered what it was like to be excited, to be fearless, to feel her future as wide-open as a prairie. But to move toward life—she understood this—would be a move away from Henry, every step in its direction a step away from him. And that seemed impossible. Unbearable. To detach herself even a little from the one certainty in her life. The only safe thing in a world of dangers. Wasn't that why people stayed in bad marriages? Because to untangle from a person was to let go of the tether, and without it, however one-sided, however painful her relationship with Henry was, there was nothing, there was falling. If she opened the door, even an inch, she would never be able to return. Not in the same way. And then where would she be? It was the only life she knew. When she tried to imagine any other, she saw herself in the car on that night turning to her friends. *I think we're lost.*

"But what if I stay and something goes wrong?" she said.

"No," Maya said. "See, you just did it again."

"Did what?"

"Stopped yourself from living."

"No, I'm just saying—"

"Nope." Maya stuck her fingers in her ear. "Lalalala."

"But!"

"Lalalala!"

"So much for growing up," Hannah sputtered.

"Stay. You can do this." Maya grabbed her arm. "You can."

Hannah considered. Could she? Which regret would be worse?

MAYA

It was still dark when Maya woke, her eyes heavy and dry with a fatigue that had depth to it. Renee had crashed out beside her, Hannah next to her in the other bed, Blue, who was more than happy to have her own room for the night, just across the hall. All of them together. It should have felt right.

It felt like loss.

It was loss.

It could not be loss; she refused it.

She had to fix it. What could she do?

Well, she could grow up, for starters. But that wasn't exactly a small order. And besides, she didn't want to. And besides, she didn't know how. They should teach that in high school, she thought, a class for orphans and the unloved and the unparented about the basic fundamentals of being a grown-up. Then again, she would have cut that class anyway.

She had to try something.

She climbed lightly out of bed, slipped downstairs into the kitchen. Stared into the darkness there until she could find the shape of action. What moved Hannah? Cleanliness, she realized, a sense of home. She flipped on the light, pulled out the bleach spray from below the sink and began to scrub. Countertops, fridge, table, windows, floor. Wash, polish, shine until the light broke through, until the sleepy sun tiptoed in through the leaves in the trees. Would it help? She didn't know. But she had hope. She always had hope. The girls would be up soon. She headed out, bought bagels and butter, still Hannah's favorite.

She found herself looking for Andy's bike as she drove down Montauk Highway and passed through town. Already the streets were crowded. A jaywalker darted out in front of her, shot her the middle finger when she honked. *The only thing more aggressive than a honey badger is a New Yorker on vacation*, she thought. She looked again for Andy inside the bagel shop, somewhat surprised he wasn't there. It felt like fate had betrayed her. She should've given him her number. He'd asked for it as they stood at the edge of the parking lot saying goodbye, his large hands thumbing her hipbones. "It might be hard to get married if I don't know where to find you," he'd said with a grin.

But the girls had been waiting in the car, watching her. She'd taken this trip to be with them. They were what mattered. And besides, it just seemed easier—to keep their night together untouched by love's erosion—a mint coin of memory she could take out and look back on whenever she needed a smile. But man, she hadn't expected to miss him so much. She didn't even understand it. They'd spent only a few hours together. She ordered the bagels, headed back to the house. She was just finished setting out the spread when Hannah appeared in the kitchen.

"Look," Maya said. "I cleaned! And I'm making coffee." She held up a tray of carefully arranged sliced bagels. "And I went out and bought your fave." Their eyes met. A flash of surprise across Hannah's face. A spark of hope in Maya's chest. Then she noticed the suitcase.

"The train leaves in twenty minutes," Hannah said. "I just called a cab."

"Oh." Maya lowered the tray. It would be stupid to cry, so she didn't. Instead she took two bagel halves, stuffed them into the toaster, wiped her hands against her thighs. "Call them back. I'll drive you."

"Maya," Hannah said.

Maya moved to the fridge, pulled out the butter.

"Okay, well. I guess I'll put my stuff in the car," Hannah said.

Maya nodded without turning. A moment later, she heard footsteps on the stairs and then low talking in the foyer. Blue and Renee were awake. Maybe they could convince Hannah to stay.

Maya tried to listen but the bagel popped up, startling her. She cut little slits in the tops, slathered it in butter, wrapped it, stuck it in a brown paper bag. She smiled brightly to herself for practice and then walked out into the foyer and repeated the gesture.

"Ready?" Hannah said.

"Yep," she said, smiling. Sometimes you could make a thing less bad by pretending that it wasn't bad at all.

"Do you want us to come?" Blue said.

"No need," Hannah said. "We can say goodbye here."

"I got this," Maya mouthed, winking at Blue. She had to believe she could still convince Hannah to stay. Aloud she said, "I'll be in the car."

She grabbed the keys and walked out.

It was going to be a hot day. The air already smelled like a furnace. She slipped into the driver's seat, looked away as Hannah hugged Blue and Renee. The passenger door opened and Maya handed Hannah the bagel and coffee.

"Thanks," Hannah said, peeking into the bag and setting it on her lap. "Smells good."

Maya backed out onto the street. Too fast. Hannah braced. The car filled with the weight of impending separation. They passed the beach, the ocean, the promise of vacation. They passed two young girls on bicycles. They passed the girls they'd been.

"There's gotta be something I can say that'll change your mind," Maya said.

Hannah was watching the girls recede into the distance. "I wish."

"You do?"

"I know he's probably fine. If it was something really bad, Vivian would tell me to come home."

"Right. Okay. I don't get it. Why leave, then?"

"Deer!" Hannah said.

"What? Oh, crap!"

Maya slammed the brakes. The deer, stopped in the middle of the road, stared at her with blank, unblinking eyes.

"Jesus Christ on a cracker," she yelled. "Why do they just freeze like that? Dumb animals."

"She can't help it," Hannah said. "It's how she's wired."

"Seems counterproductive," Maya said. The whole point of

life was to keep going. Any living creature was bound to get run over if they didn't know that. "So, if you know Henry is fine, are you leaving because of me?"

"No," Hannah said. "That's not it at all. I don't know how to explain. It doesn't even feel like a choice, honestly. Everything just gets too…much. Like the world gets in too far. I can't keep it out. There's no boundary. And then it's too painful to stay. To stay anywhere, really."

Maya pressed lightly on her horn. The deer ran off into the shrubbery. She pulled out onto the tree-lined highway, the low early sun throwing light in her eyes. She tried to imagine what Hannah was describing but she couldn't. Not at first. But then she remembered herself in the bank, trying to get the loan. The sense of something intolerable building inside her. What was it? The possibility that she wouldn't be okay. That some pressurizing force would shatter her to bits. She considered mentioning this to Hannah but she couldn't bring herself to. She didn't want to give darkness a voice. She wanted to forget it. "That sounds awful," she said.

Hannah held her gaze. "It is." And then she added, "There are worse things."

Maya thought of Henry. Maybe they both did.

She didn't want their last moments of the trip to be sad.

She turned and cracked a mischievous smile. "Do you realize we just left Renee and Blue alone together?"

"With access to kitchen knives," Hannah said. She made a stabbing motion and they burst out laughing.

The air lightened. Hannah took the bagel out of the bag, unwrapped it. "Just what I needed, thank you." She gave half to Maya and then took a bite of the other half. Briefly closed her eyes to savor it. "Mmm, perfectly buttered."

"I used your trick," Maya said. "Remember when you taught me that?"

"Aww," Hannah said. "I totally do. We were so little."

"It's stupid, but it's the only food trick I know. It's like being passed down a special recipe. And it really does make a bagel taste better." Maya cleared her throat. She wasn't saying what she meant. What she meant was that it had felt like mothering when Hannah taught her how to butter a bagel. What she meant was that Hannah was important to her in a way that other people could not be, in the way that only the people who raised you could be. And sometimes friends raised each other. Sometimes they were the only ones who did. But unlike family, there was no shared home to return to for vacations and holidays. As soon as they graduated, they were off on their own, no longer a unit but four divided parts. And this was what she hated most about being a grown-up—not having a gang to experience the world with. Her friends used to be her net. Without them there was nothing, there was falling.

Don't go, she thought. But she couldn't make herself say it. She'd always been good at asking for things—for a couch to crash on or a ride or a job lead. But it was asking for heart things that she had trouble with. It would reveal too much, hurt too much if anyone said no.

They reached the station. Happy people with weekend bags were stepping out of train cars, reuniting with their already tan family and friends who'd come to retrieve them. Summer joy in their faces.

Hannah put her hand on the door, turned to her. "I love you," she said.

"I love you too," Maya said over the words stuck in her throat.

She hugged Hannah hard. "Give Henry a kiss for me."

Hannah nodded and climbed out, her slender figure moving toward the ticket booth. She turned and waved and Maya waved back.

Maya waited until Hannah paid her ticket and disappeared inside the train. She kept waiting as the train pulled away with its loud goodbye, just in case, just in case.

But Hannah was gone.

BLUE

Blue stood on the front porch, leaning against a pillar, smoking a cigarette. She peered out at the grassy yard, the cars passing beyond the fence like a slow-moving train. A large cloud ambled above, washing the color out of the day as if with a sponge. It was way too early for smoking. It was all she could think to do.

Back in high school if any of her friends were struggling, Blue knew exactly how to fix it. A quick dose of fun with a pinch of recklessness was always the cure. Cut school together or drive just fast enough to cause a little scare or do something a tiny bit illegal—shoplift a candy bar or jump a Metro stall or sneak into a movie theater. Things that said *we are young, we are alive, nothing can stop us, none of this matters!* It was so easy, then, to move through things, to exist only in the present. Before too many losses had accumulated. Before the world got in.

But no more. Hannah had taken something with her when she left—not just a piece of the whole of them but some secreted hope that, with time, the damage of that night would lessen rather than root and grow tentacles. Blue felt hollowed out by it and surprised by how heavy a feeling emptiness could be. This was the problem with people leaving. They didn't just go away—their absence created a phantom presence, a haunt of sorrow in their place.

She sighed—the body's effort to expel the ghost.

Renee was upstairs somewhere, behind a closed door. Which was good. A good thing. They were two soldiers sticking to their respective sides of the border. But why was Renee still here at all? She should just march up there and tell her to leave. Why didn't she? The thought occurred to her that maybe she didn't totally want Renee to leave, but that was ridiculous. Of course she did.

Christ, this trip was a disaster.

At least before she came, she still had the fantasy of Jack, ridiculous and self-deceptive as it was. Now that, too, was a hollow.

One last long inhale, letting the smoke linger and burn in her lungs. Then she stubbed out her cigarette, reentered the numb silence of the house. It reminded her of her apartment in NYC, of the too-quietness there as well—like she was walking around in a world on pause. What a desolate thing it was to be the only sound in a room. She couldn't wait to pull the covers up to her neck, close her eyes. Maybe later would be better. She and Maya could have one drama-free day at the beach, a bit of sun, nothing happening but the fold of waves on sand.

She trudged up the stairs—radar tuning into Renee's location. The strange tension of sharing a house with an enemy.

Halfway up she stopped, listened. Was that retching? Had Renee been drunk last night? Blue hadn't noticed her boozing, but then again she hadn't been paying much attention. She was almost at her bedroom door when she heard it again. Yep, retching. At least it was best that Hannah wasn't here to hear it. There wasn't enough Purell in the world to get her through that situation.

The bathroom door flew open. Renee appeared, looking uncharacteristically disheveled.

"Help! I think the toilet's about to—oh, you're right there." Renee pointed shamefully in the direction of the impending disaster. "Um...yeah."

Blue pushed past her. "What did you do?" The room smelled like vomit.

"Nothing," Renee said. "I don't know... I just flushed it and it started..."

Blue averted her eyes from the toilet, removed the tank's lid.

"It must have been something I ate," Renee said.

"We all ate the same thing, and I feel fine." It wasn't fair to be mad at Renee for getting sick, but then life wasn't fair. She tugged on the flush lever in the toilet tank and the water stopped running. She started toward the door.

"Wait. What did you do?" Renee said.

Blue paused, suppressed an exasperated sigh. "I jiggled this thing."

"Oh, right," Renee said. "I think I remember this happening last time."

It had. Only the last time, Maya had been the one to use it and failed to notice the water rising until they all went to the beach and came back to a flood.

"If I recall correctly, Maya hit on the plumber," Renee said.

"Yeah. Who was like fifty," Blue said. She couldn't resist.

"Right. Because she was hoping for a discount."

Blue tried not to laugh because laughter seemed like weakness, like opening a door, but she couldn't help it, it was still funny. It was so hilariously Maya.

She saw a glimmer of hope in Renee's eyes. Abruptly she turned, put the lid back on, snapped back into business mode. It was easier when her anger was the barrier between them. But take it away, even for a second, and the underbelly of love and hurt could be exposed. Anger was the Band-Aid, loss the wound.

"Guess he wasn't much of a plumber," Renee said. "If it's still broken twelve years later."

"I'm sure he was fine," Blue said dismissively. This wasn't a bonding session—she wanted to make that clear. Though it was admittedly odd that Nana hadn't bothered, in all the years since, to get it properly repaired. Maybe at a certain point everyone just sort of accepted broken things. Jiggling a lever became a reflex, so integrated into daily routine that it became unconscious. It was actually kind of scary, she thought, how long a person could go without noticing everything falling apart around them.

She started toward the hall.

"Do you think Hannah will be okay?" Renee said to her back.

Blue paused. Like all the other broken things, she'd simply stopped noticing how much Hannah had been damaged, accepted it as if it had always been that way. At least until today. She didn't have an answer, so she didn't give one.

They both turned at the sound of the front door creaking

open downstairs. Soft footsteps approached, and then Maya appeared looking grim. "She's gone."

Blue sighed. "So much for your powers of persuasion."

"Every superhero has their kryptonite," Maya cracked, but Blue could tell her heart wasn't in the joke and her smile looked jerry-rigged to her face.

Renee leaned against the open bathroom door. "That sucks."

Maya nodded outwardly, Blue inwardly.

"And I just barfed," Renee added.

"Oh no," Maya said.

"I'm fine. Probably just a little food poisoning."

"Weird," Maya said. "I wonder why no one else is sick. I guess those clever calamari found a way to escape after all."

Blue groaned.

"What? That was funny."

"I hope Hannah isn't yakking on the train," Blue said.

They all looked at one another, and the pall of Hannah being gone fell over them again.

"Well, I should probably hit the road," Renee said.

"You're going to get on a ferry right after you just puked?" Maya asked. "Why don't you give it a few hours?"

Renee looked at Blue.

What was Blue going to say, *No, go puke on the ferry*? She shrugged. "So…now what?" she asked.

"I guess we could mope around the house," Maya said. "Or we could mope at the beach."

"Mope and tan?" Renee said.

"Yeah, like multitask," Maya said.

"I could do that," Blue said.

"I have an extra bikini," Maya told Renee. "It'll be three sizes too big, but—"

"Actually," Renee said, "I have one in the car. I didn't know what the plan was for yesterday so I brought one in case."

"Perfect!" Maya said.

They went to their rooms to change, and Blue considered a quick hit off her vape pen. But first, her bathing suit. Which...ugh. She loved the sun, she loved the beach, she hated its clothing requirements. And the fact that other people had to be there. That she had to be exposed in front of strangers. And she hated that she hated it. It was not an inborn trait to be ashamed of your own body. It was taught. It was learned. That old rage rushed up again. She lit her vape pen, took a hit to squelch it, threw on her suit away from the mirror. She was going to make it a nice day if it killed her.

It was still a bit cloudy by the time they reconvened on the front porch, but the sun was trying hard and the air was sweet with honeysuckle and fresh-cut grass and the suggestion of the sea. Blue chucked Maya the car keys, climbed into the passenger seat, spotted a book on the floor. She picked it up.

"Hannah's," Maya said. "She forgot it."

"I'll mail it to her," Blue said. She opened the book— self-help, of course—to a random page and scanned it. Hannah had underlined a quote: "Our consciousness would be broken up into as many fragments as we had lived seconds but for the binding and unifying force of memory."

She snapped the book shut. She didn't want to be made of memory. Didn't want Hannah or any of them to be made of it either. If only a person could cherry-pick—turn their mind into an Instagram page made up of only the highlights. She wondered if that's what Maya's inner life looked like.

It was a short drive to their preferred beach, and they reached Ditch Plains just as the clouds disappeared. The swarm of cars in the parking lot meant there was a decent swell. Every half-assed surfer came out for a wave over two feet, turned a paddle-out into a contact sport. Blue couldn't help but think of Jack, of the morning after their first kiss when she'd watched him etch graceful zigzags in the surf with his board.

Now Maya slipped into a questionable parking spot that may or may not get their tires stuck in the sand and they piled out.

It had been a long time since Blue had been to the beach. The sun was sharp and white above the cliffs, the ocean tipping and shuffling to the shore, and people were scattered on towels beneath lollipop-colored umbrellas, surfboards lined up like fence posts against the dunes, the smells of coconut oil and salt water and sunshine baked into the air.

"It looks exactly the same!" Maya said as they stopped at the threshold of sand, taking it in.

To Blue, Ditch Plains seemed more crowded, a little hipper, no longer a place for old-school surf bums but for wealthy city moms with sand strollers, expensive SUVs in the parking lot, models preening in tiny bikinis. Wealth had taken over, had chipped away a little bit of its soul. Or maybe it was just time that did that, altered the chemistry of things, took away pieces and added others. Still she understood what Maya meant. The bones of the place were the same. It still felt lazy, a beach that had no interest in competing with the more elegant beaches of the Hamptons—a B-personality beach. And maybe there was comfort in that, in the way that some changes rarely went all the way to the bones.

"Let's sit by the lifeguards," Maya said.

Blue shot her a look.

"What? For safety reasons, I mean."

Blue plopped down where they stood and Maya sighed and joined her.

A toddler ran past, kicking sand as he waved his small green shovel back and forth.

"Why do people have children?" Maya asked. "So much work. So much drool."

Blue didn't know either. Sometimes she wondered if wanting to be a mother required actually having had a mother.

Renee sat down next to them, wrapped her arms around her knees. "I bet you guys'll want them eventually."

It was always so annoying when people said that. Like somehow they knew you better than you knew yourself. Blue never wanted kids. She'd screw them up rightly.

"Who was it that used to say they wanted to adopt high schoolers?" Renee asked. "Hannah?"

"Blue," Maya said. "But only so she'd have someone to pick up her dry cleaning."

"Ha!" Renee said. She turned to Blue. "Does Jack want kids?"

Blue tensed. With all the drama that went down last night, she had completely forgotten about her lie.

"Jack?" Maya said. "How would Blue know something like that?"

Shit.

Blue jumped to her feet. "Not everyone wants kids, you know. And it's kind of sexist to assume Maya and I don't know how we feel about it." To Maya she said, "I'm going down to the water." She marched down to the shore, making a show of it, hoping her feminist outburst would distract Maya from pursuing her question. *Stupid Renee. Why did she always have to remember everything?* If Renee mentioned it to Maya, she'd need an out. She couldn't very well fake going on a date, could she?

If it came to that, she could say she was sick. That it was just so disappointing, but she couldn't possibly go out on a date with a stomach flu. She'd have to fake vomiting, but whatever, she was an old pro at that from all the times she tried to get out of going to school. Renee had inadvertently set the whole story up. She was good for something after all.

How sad though. That she had to cover one lie with another. How pathetic.

She stepped into the water, let the shock of it jolt her out of her self-pity. It had been a while since the Atlantic had rolled cold and welcoming over her feet. The tide was rising, gathering higher and higher around her ankles. The fortepiano of waves crashing and retreating sounded like cars swishing through rain. This was where she'd first met Jack.

She closed her eyes, breathed in the salt air. For a moment she imagined him coming up behind her, turning to see in his face that same expression—the look of a man who found her attractive. And oh, that look. It could hold you like a parent, make you feel as wanted as a newborn. She'd never known it before she met him, how aligned those pathways were in the brain. She knew only that whatever she'd experienced was a thing she'd been missing her whole life without knowing it. For years after, she'd forgotten what it felt like, her heart in hibernation until she'd nearly convinced herself that love didn't matter, not really. But she could see now that it did. That it always had.

If only she knew how to get it. If only she were capable.

She pushed away the thought, went back to the towels. Maya lowered her sunglasses, eyed her warily, then returned to her gossip magazine. Blue relaxed. Clearly Renee hadn't mentioned anything about her having a date. Otherwise Maya would be harassing her for details. She went to grab a water from the cooler and, finding none, glanced up at Maya. "Wine coolers and beer? Really?"

"I picked them up on the way back from the train station. You're welcome."

"It's barely eleven."

"And…?"

Blue sighed. "I'm gonna get some water at the Ditch Witch."

"Ooh, I want a treat," Maya said, jumping up.

"I'll come too," Renee said.

Oh yay, Blue thought with an inward eye roll.

The food truck was a staple of Ditch Plains Beach. When Blue was younger, she believed that running the Ditch Witch would be the ideal job. Days spent overlooking the bucking sea, the air sweet with suntan lotion and hot dogs, happy wet-haired kids shoving their parents' crumpled dollars over the counter, hungry surfers stopping to chat her up about some tropical storm that would bring waves their way.

It made her wistful to think about how logical such work had once seemed, when money meant little and she dreamed only of being happy, of extending the easy pace of childhood indefinitely.

They waited at the end of a long line of sun-mellowed surfers and packs of kids and overburdened mothers. Maybe her dream hadn't been so impractical after all—this place must really make a killing. Maya moved closer to read the menu scrawled on an old surfboard.

"You're paying, since you skipped out on dinner last night," she called to Maya.

"You should've told me before we left!" Maya said. "Who brings their wallet to the beach?"

"Clearly you assumed someone did," Blue said dryly.

"Hey," Renee said, "isn't that…"

Blue followed Renee's gaze to a guy tying an old-school wooden long board to the rack of a classic VW van. He was shaggy haired from the sea, a little round about the middle but nicely built…

For a moment Blue could only stare, her heart racing. "No," she said, turning away. "It's not." And it probably wasn't. Likely it was just someone who resembled him. Although it *was* a small town. And Ditch Plains his favorite beach. And the waves *were* up. So. It wouldn't be totally improbable…

Blue didn't want to peek again to find out.

She did and she didn't.

"I think it *is* him." Renee cupped her hands. "Jack! Jaaack!"

"Oh my God, shut up!" Blue hissed.

As if in slow motion, he turned.

Oh God.

"I knew it!" Renee said, waving him over. "I never forget a face."

Blue grabbed her arm. "Stop!"

"What? Why?"

"Because I…I don't want him to see me like this."

Too late. Jack stepped down from his truck and headed toward them.

Renee grimaced. "Sorry." She wiped a spot of sunscreen from Blue's cheek. "You look great. Don't worry."

Blue was detaching from her body. The noise around her fading into the background, the sun a cruel spotlight. Forget how she looked. Which was hideous, but still. What if Renee mentioned the date? If only a sinkhole would open up beneath her. Or a tsunami would strike. Either one.

She considered her options. Or tried to. But her mind sputtered and stalled.

Jack squinted as he neared. A small thrill briefly disrupted her horror. Jack, her Jack! Right here, in front of her! And from what she could tell, the years had been kind to him.

But no, this was not good. Very, very bad. She pulled her hat lower.

"Blue?" he said. "No way!"

"Hey there," she managed. Her voice sounded dumb and weirdly pitched. Her brain kept looping it, beating her with it.

"Wow." He shook his head. "I almost didn't recognize you in the…" He gestured at her hat and sunglasses, and she was so acutely, unbearably self-conscious, shriveling under his gaze.

They exchanged a clumsy hug, followed by an awkward pause. She could feel Renee looking at her strangely. Surely she was catching on that something was amiss. Blue's tongue seemed to be swelling, blocking words from exiting her mouth.

Renee stepped forward. "Good to see you, Jack. It's Renee, in case you forgot."

"Right, Renee!" Jack said. "I remember. Great to see you too."

He wore faded board shorts and scruff on his chin—a good sign, Blue noted peripherally; she hated vanity in men. And maybe it meant there was no girl in the picture.

"Blue," Maya called obliviously from the front of the line. "I need your credit card."

Blue chucked her wallet without looking, heard a kid go "ouch."

"We were literally just talking about you," Renee was saying.

Oh no.

"You were?" He looked at Blue.

"Uh…yep," Blue scrambled. "We were reminiscing about… um, summers. All the summers. Good times and whatnot."

Renee frowned. "No, we—" She stopped herself when she saw the look on Blue's face.

Jack blinked.

Blue was dissolving into the pavement. "I can't believe the Ditch Witch is still here!" she said quickly. "Who knew food trucks would become all the rage?"

A kid with a boogie board ran between them. Blue and Jack smiled shyly at each other as they dodged him. Renee kept looking between them with a puzzled expression.

Maya returned with three ice cream bars and a tray of sodas. "Oh, hello there, handsome."

Jack laughed.

Renee nudged her.

Maya did a double take. "Wait. Is that…Jack?"

"Hey there," he said.

Maya glanced gleefully back and forth between Jack and Blue.

Blue shot her a murderous look.

Maya handed her an ice cream, cheerfully bit into her own. "This is so great! The two of you after all these years."

"We really should get back to our towels," Blue said.

"What? Why?" Maya said. "Unless you want to come sit with us, Jack? I have booze in the cooler."

"I'd love to," he said, running a hand through his drying hair, "but I actually gotta head to work."

"Oh, totally," Blue said, trying not to sound relieved. "Of course. Well, have fun."

"Work, shmirk," Maya said. "Maybe we'll see you later?"

"*We* won't," Renee said. "But Blue will, right?"

Blue froze. Horror zoomed in, circled her in a panoramic close-up. A buzzing sound in her head, like she'd poked a nest of bees.

Jack raised his eyebrows, glanced between them.

"I'm confused," Maya said.

Renee looked at Blue, who was going to die on the spot. She was sure of it. She *hoped* for it. The sun beat down relentlessly, melting her ice cream bar in her hand. *Say something,* she thought. But what could she say?

"Oh, wait! You mean at Surf Lodge?" Jack said finally. "You're going?"

"No," Blue said, then looked at Renee. "I mean, uh—"

Everything happened in that quick glance, the wordless language of lifelong friends resurrected. Blue confessed she'd lied, conveyed her humiliation. Renee absorbed the information, made a quick decision.

"Yes," Renee jumped in, coming to her rescue. Just like she would have when they were younger. "She is going. You'll be there, right, Jack?"

"Wait, why is only Blue going? I want to go to Surf Lodge," Maya said, still oblivious to all of it.

Renee elbowed her.

"Ow!" Maya said. "Why do you keep hitting me?"

"Definitely," Jack said. "You guys should all come. It's reggae night. Super fun. Everyone goes." He stole a look at Blue.

She could tell he was trying to see past her hat and sunglasses, and she was grateful for how much they hid.

"Well, I'm heading back to Connecticut and Maya has... uh...a thing to do," Renee said. "But you'll look out for Blue for us, right?"

"Of course," he said. He glanced at his watch. "I gotta run. But, hey, great to see you guys, and I'll see you later, Blue."

"Not if I see you first," Blue said, then wanted to throw herself over a cliff.

He started back toward his car and Blue turned back to the beach. She was having so many feelings at once, her thoughts speeding and colliding, becoming a high white noise. She was at once humiliated about the lie she'd told Renee and relieved that Renee hadn't exposed her. She had to reluctantly admit that was really nice of her. And somehow Renee had even managed to get her, if not a date, then at least a chance. And Blue wanted this. To see him tonight. It was more than she could've hoped. And she did not want this at all. For him to see her.

"I still don't understand what 'thing' I have to do or why Blue gets to go and we don't," Maya complained.

"You're not joining them on their date, silly," Renee said. "I'm going home and you're staying at the house."

"Whose date?" Maya said. "Blue and Jack have a date?"

Renee shot Blue a knowing look. "They do now."

"It's not really," Blue said. "You can totally come, Maya."

Renee frowned. "But don't you want to be alone with him?"

"Oh, right," Maya said. "Wacka wacka."

Blue rolled her eyes but inwardly felt an awful slither. She was already exposed and full of shame and now Maya had to throw sex into the equation. Just the thought of it made her mind unhook from her body, hover above it. Her friends didn't know she'd never done it. They just assumed she had. Because everybody had sex—it was, at some level, the main function of existence. Only a freak wouldn't want it or be able to get it. Society let her know that every single day. So what if women had been conditioned their whole lives to equate sex with violence—from bra snaps in middle school, to keys turned into weapons against rape, to an endless stream of TV shows and movies about women being victimized, tortured, murdered by men. You were still supposed to want sex and do it and not be afraid. And if you didn't, you were a sad, desperate old maid and you should hate yourself. It was so messed up, and still Blue felt the shame of it, the stigma. And also the longing. To want to want it. And now it was too late. She didn't know how to do it. And how would she ever be able to explain *that* to a man? Thirty years old and she couldn't even remember how to kiss, much less how to move her hips.

One wrong turn, so many years ago. That's what it all came down to. Was it possible to alter the course now? Sometimes she thought yes. Other times it just seemed hopeless.

She reached into the ice chest, grabbed a wine cooler, took a swig.

"You guys," Renee said. Her eyes were wide, her mouth agape. "Am I seeing what I think I'm seeing?"

They all turned to follow Renee's gaze.

HANNAH

Hannah hadn't been on a long-distance train since she was a little kid. There was something bleak about it. Her childhood memories of them were romantic and exciting but now she saw they were dirty and hard-seated like a subway. At least it had been easy to navigate her travel. She was always expecting everything to be difficult—though maybe it was just the drag of fear that made life seem tedious and exhausting. Or maybe the anticipation of problems was merely an instrument to avoid doing anything at all. Probably both. But as it turned out, there'd been a quaint and obvious ticketing station and a map of all the stops and a conductor whom she could pepper with questions. And since they were at the end of an island, there was no chance of going in the wrong direction. Or if they did, getting lost was the least of her problems. If only everything could be like that—so clear-cut and defined.

The doors closed, the next stop was announced and the train started up with a low moan and a whistle. Hannah watched the scenery chug by, her face staring back at her in the dirty, water-spotted window glass. A slant of sun knifed across her lap, turned her pale legs ghostly. Suddenly she was trapped and unsure. And alone—this most of all. Her friends were probably heading to the beach right now, decked out in sunglasses and hats with their big beach bags, their big laughter. They'd spend all day there under a broad blue sky, trading gossip magazines and memories, taking a midday stroll along the ocean as the white water sprayed upward like a young girl's hair in wind. Simple togetherness, simple joys.

The train pulled forward, then picked up speed, greenery and desertlike shrubs rushing past as she was bumped and rattled along toward the city. She shouldn't be on it. In retrospect it had been nice to be with her friends. Even though all they'd done was fight and aggravate and worry her, she had been in the presence of people who really knew and loved her and there was such comfort in that. It was only now, returning to her aloneness, that she'd noticed the difference. Worse, she'd left just as it seemed the trip might finally get fun. In fact they'd probably have *more* fun now that she was gone. Realize she was just a drag on their good times. Stop even bothering to invite her anywhere.

The long trek home loomed. She would have to take a second train to DC and then hail a cab to her apartment and then hot wash all her clothes, scrub her body. Then back to Henry at the long-term care facility where there was nothing left to fear, but nothing left to be excited about either. Just days that blended into each other and passed and made her older and only that. It was safe. It was comfortable. It was known. And—

it was not enough. Oh, if only being aware of a problem actually fixed it. She was making the wrong decision. She was sure of that now. And equally powerless to stop it. Once the momentum got too far in the direction of fear, she couldn't rein it in; she had to oblige it like a menacing boss.

She adjusted in her seat, pulled her bag closer, reminded herself that she would have equally regretted staying. How were you supposed to know which way was right?

Well, that fortune-teller at the Bridgehampton fair had told her once, and she had failed to listen.

To think of how much she and her friends had laughed at the oracle's eerie prophecy!

Never for a moment had she taken it seriously when the woman had said, "You will come to a fork in the road and darkness beyond it..."

And yet there had been exactly that.

So much the psychic had been right about...

"On the one side of the fork, a boy who makes you feel safe. On the other..."

Hannah shivered at the memory.

And a few days after, after their return from Montauk, there she was at a fork in the road, just as the woman had warned her.

There she was shouting to her friends, "Which way? Which way!"

There she was saying, "We're running out of gas..."

And the men were closing in.

And a decision had to be made.

Right or left?

Right or left?

She had gone right.

Some instinct drove her, a faint recollection that she'd come upon this road before with Henry. That they'd gone right at the fork.

Almost instantly she'd recognized familiar landmarks. They were nearer to home than she thought. They probably even had enough gas to make it. Her cell service came into range. She called Henry. Told him about the men. He knew exactly where they were. Guided them to his house.

"Stay on the line with me," he'd said, and so she had, glancing nervously in the rearview mirror until the sleazebags disappeared from view. What relief when they finally turned onto Henry's well-lit street, pulled in to the driveway, no one behind them!

He was waiting at the door for them, her handsome Henry looking so huggable in his sweatshirt and boxers, his brown hair lopsided from sleep, matted on one side, sticking up on the other. The others leaped out and raced toward him, clamoring about the scary chase, giddy with release. She watched him tilt his head and furrow his brow as he listened in that charmingly befuddled way he always seemed to have around her loud, squealing friends, looking, to her mind, like a new dad, adoring and sleepy and confused. She remembered thinking as she observed him that Henry was her home, the truest home she'd ever known, and how lucky she was to have found him so young, when their whole lives were only beginning, when their love was a springboard launching them both into a shared and promising future.

She stepped out of the car feeling like a surprise gift the way he smiled when he took her in. She smiled back, wanting nothing more than to press herself to him, to feel his heart beat steady and strong and soothing against hers. To walk toward the shelter of a hug.

But then he turned his head, just slightly, his gaze sweeping past her to something beyond. She turned too. Saw the blinding headlights careening up the driveway. For a split second she thought it was Henry's parents back early, a trick of the brain.

Then Blue and Renee were screaming at her from the doorway.

"Run, Hannah!"

"Hurry!"

The piercing yip in their voices went through her like a shiver, stopped her heart in that animal way, trilling the biological alarm of nearby danger. She looked back at the car. It felt like slow motion, that head turn. The men were climbing out, rising like shadows in a child's darkened room, and all at once her mind exploded, her thoughts disorganized, scrambling to catch up to what was happening. She needed to run. But her legs refused to work. They came toward her, slow moving and dangerous, a dark current of menace approaching from three sides. She turned back to her friends. To Henry. Their mouths were open but their words traveled over her as if she were underwater.

"Run, Hannah!" Henry shouted then, his voice so loud it splintered her shock. It was as if a switch went off. Her legs came to life and she ran for him, ran toward love, toward the safety of Henry. He reached her, grabbed her hand, pulled her to the house, shouting to the others to get his father's gun from the closet. She tripped on the front steps, fell to her knees and the men were just behind them, so close she braced for them to grab her. Henry pulled her to her feet and they plowed through the door, and she couldn't make out the words of her friends over the sound of her own terror, could only join the screams, the chaotic squawk of birds and beating wings in the presence of a hunter.

They slammed the door shut just in time, but as soon as it was closed, it crashed open again, evil men spilling through, smashing into Hannah's safe world with their demented smiles, their greasy, sweaty faces and unwashed clothes. Their smell of booze and rot. There was so much movement then. Everything happening too quickly and too slowly all at once. Time warped and the volume was turned up on faces, bodies, sound, everything so immediate, hyperreal. She remembered Blue and Renee splitting away, running toward the kitchen, chased by one of the men. And then a crack and a stunned stillness as her head hit the wall, a sudden eerie quiet, one quick pause and then everything was in motion again. A large man with dull eyes stood over her where she'd fallen or been knocked down, and another one—the scratchy-looking one who had started it all back at the convenience store—laughed at her, his spit flying from his mouth, landing sour on her face. The large man pulled her to her feet and she had this strange moment of hope when she thought that maybe they wouldn't hurt them, that they were just trying to scare them. It was a hope she would never allow herself again. About anyone. About anything.

"Leave her alone!" Henry shouted.

"Leave her alone," the scratchy one mocked in a high, squeaky voice.

She could see him only in profile, light hair slick with grease, face meth pocked, body skinny and slithering. He laughed again and then his voice turned low as a prowl.

"Or what, tough guy?" he said. He shoved Henry so violently that his feet left the ground and he fell into the couch, and then Large Man who still had Hannah by one arm grabbed her other one and held them behind her back.

Their eyes met, hers and Henry's.

"Let go of her!" Henry screamed again.

"Or what? Or what, bitch?" the scratchy one said, turning to laugh with his friend at their fear. His eyes were unsteady, dangerous. He was the one to worry about.

"The police are on their way," Hannah lied, trying to steady the tremor in her voice. "We already called them."

"Oh yeah?" the scratchy one said without concern. "We better hurry up, then."

In a flash, he had a gun to Henry's forehead.

The scream that came out of Hannah was disembodied, unearthly. It haunted her, that scream, the piercing shriek of her own helplessness. She could still feel it in her sleep, the way it tore through her body and smashed against the air, trying desperately to shatter the moment, stop it from happening.

"No!"

It was all she had. That scream. She tried to wrestle her hands free, but Large Man's grip only tightened.

Henry pressed himself into the back of the couch as if he could disappear into its cushions. His eyes were haunted as he stared, quivering, into the barrel of the revolver. He had never looked so young, so unbearably, frailly human.

"I'll give you whatever you want!" Hannah cried. "I know where all the good stuff is." It wasn't true, she didn't know what Henry's parents had or where it was or if it would even make a difference, sate evil. But she had to say something, stand in the way of the nightmare, change the direction of its inevitable unimaginable end. And maybe, she thought, maybe that was all they wanted, just to rob them. And then they would leave. They would leave. Please, God, they would leave.

"Talk." The man turned to her, his gun still pointed in Henry's face.

She made quick calculations. *Could Henry grab the gun? Where were the others? Could she make a run for it and distract them?* But she saw that there was no other move to make. She was trapped. "I'll show you. Please."

He moved toward her, away from Henry, sidling up to her like a hiss. She refused to look at Henry, only at the man, willing him to put the gun away. *He's going to rape me*, she thought. Something in his face made her think that. His eyes hate-black and dead. She started to whimper, but still she was grateful he was moving away from Henry, glad for that gun to be out of his face. "I'll show you," she heard herself say, so much braver than she felt. "Anything you want."

"Hannah," Henry said, and she knew by the desperate clutch of her name in his voice that he understood the sacrifice she was making, that he wanted to save her as much as she wanted to save him. There was so much in that one word, all their love, all their despair locked together in this unbearable moment. She wouldn't look at him. To look at love in a room so suffocated with evil would break her. And then the man turned, she didn't know why, and the shot was so loud, mixed with a scream that was at once coming from her and outside her, the sound of her scream and the shot mixed as one, slashing open the night, her whole world, and then Henry slumped on the couch and they pushed her up the staircase as if there was still life left in her, as if the bullet hadn't ripped straight through everything that mattered.

"Henry!" she screamed, her voice annihilating all but its

own sound, clawing at the air to make the nightmare stop. She saw the red stain spreading across the tan couch like an ink spill, and everything was warped, happening in some alternate universe, unreal because it had to be unreal, because she had just been at a party and now love was gone and she had failed to stop it.

The train shrieked to a stop in Amagansett. Jerked her back into the moment. She found her breath. Deep, deep. It never worked. She didn't even mind, in a weird way, the piercing pain, the way her heart pounded. Sometimes it was purging to relive the horror, like she was sick with memory and had momentarily expelled it. Well, she was, really. Sick with it. And to look at it head-on reminded her—*this is why I am the way I am.* She could be gentler with herself, forgive herself her neurosis, her inability to live. *Of course, of course, how could it be otherwise?* Unless she had listened to the psychic. Gone the other way at the fork. It would have been otherwise then. They wouldn't have even *been* at Henry's that night if only she'd done that. Or was that magical thinking? She didn't know, she didn't know.

She thought of that flashback—Blue in a ripped and bloody sweatshirt…where did that fit in? Blue wasn't in the room when Henry was shot. Unless she was remembering it wrong…

She leaned her head back. A man in tennis clothes climbed on, took the seat across from her. Why did people do this when there were other open seats on the train? He pulled out a copy of *Dan's Papers*, flipped it open, made her invisible. Good. Just the way she liked it.

She wished she had something to read—remembered she left her paperback in the rental car.

She shouldn't even be on this train. It was rash and stupid.

She was missing everything. But the constant haunt of *what if* had forced her hand. If something happened to Henry, she would be responsible. She already was. *On one side of the fork will be a boy who makes you feel safe. The other side is uncertain and unknown. Take the harder road or you'll regret it for the rest of your life.* Hannah had taken the safe road. And the psychic was right: she'd regretted it ever since. Oh God, so much regret.

The train restarted its loud, lulling chug.

The man across from her wetted his index finger and thumb and flipped the page. She shuddered. She braced for him to do it again, put his fingers to his mouth after touching the dirty newspaper. But something caught her eye. A jolt in her chest like her heart had been hooked and yanked upward. She leaned forward. The man lowered the page and eyed her with irritation.

"Oh, sorry," she said, sitting back. She was surprised by how steady her voice sounded. "Would you mind if... Can I see that for one quick sec?"

He raised an eyebrow, reluctantly handed her the paper. She looked closer at the picture in the ad, checked the date. She felt her face animate with shock. It couldn't be her. Could it? But it was. She was almost certain. She was definitely certain. It had to be a sign. Right? That she should see this now, when she was once again at a fork, uncertain if she was going in the right direction. It was the most perfectly obvious sign imaginable, really. No room for doubt. She sat with this, her body vibrating. It was energy coursing through her, unfamiliar, long lost. She recognized it now—hope. The train pulled in to East Hampton. She got up, paper clutched in one hand, bag in the other, and ran for the door.

"Hey, you can't just take that," the man shouted after her.

She stepped out into sunlight, warm and welcoming. Instantly she felt relief. For once she was not exhausted. She was exhilarated. She was free from worry. Because finally, finally a certainty. A sign. A direction.

She called the girls but no one was picking up—they were probably at the beach, their phones in their bags. She couldn't bear to wait for a train. She flagged a waiting cab, threw her bag in the back seat, gave the driver the address. It was so strange to be going back the way she'd just come, like the world was a movie on rewind, only more vivid, everything sharp and immediate. What if she was being foolish? Well, of course she was! And yet. Despite the irrationality of it all— a psychic, my God—she had that rare, too-rare feeling, that gut instinct of rightness. And wasn't it true that life sometimes did that? Just put something in front of you that was too uncanny, too coincidental, too perfect to deny. The whole way back she kept looking at the newspaper page in her hand, energy thrumming inside her as she played back the random circumstances that led her to see it just when she needed it most. These were the kinds of moments that could almost make her believe in God. Or in something anyway.

The cab pulled up to the house and she handed cash to the driver and climbed out. The girls weren't there, just as she expected. She changed into her suit, slathered on a thick application of sunscreen, a cover-up over that, then ran to the beach, clutching her giant hat, her flip-flops nipping at her heels. She couldn't wait to surprise her friends.

She dodged cars going in and out of the parking lot, then reached the edge of the sand. She scanned the beach, body after body; so many bodies that they became indistinguishable from one another, just masses of pink and bronze skin and bright-colored bathing suits merging into a mosaic. She turned and turned, shielded her eyes against the glare. A clench in her gut. It was hot in a violent way, like being stalked by the sun, no refuge anywhere. She wobbled toward the water, checking every face. Two teenage girls eyed her hat as they passed.

"I wonder if she gets Netflix with that thing," she heard one of them say before they both burst out laughing.

Oh whatever! she thought. *Enjoy your premature aging!*

She tried Maya's cell phone. Listened for her ringtone among the chattering throngs. Nothing. She'd been so stupid to think she'd be able to find them on such a crowded beach. Now what was she going to do? This was a mistake. Maybe that ad for the psychic hadn't been a sign after all. The clench in her gut deepened.

She was about to give up when she heard "Hannah?!"

She turned and there was Renee holding a half-eaten ice cream bar. Her whole body loosened. "Renee? What are you doing here? I thought you were going home."

"I thought the same of you."

Blue and Maya came up behind Renee, looking slightly shocked.

"There you are," Hannah said. "I thought I'd never find you guys!"

"You're kind of hard to miss," Maya said. "Only person on the beach in a lamp shade."

"Is everything okay?" Blue said. "Did you come back for your book?"

"She didn't come back for her stupid book," Maya said. "She couldn't stand being away from me!"

"Exactly," Hannah said cheerfully.

"But seriously…" Renee said. "What happened? Didn't you get on the train?"

"Yes," Hannah said, "I got all the way to East Hampton, but, well, this guy who got on in Amagansett…"

"Ooh, a guy?" Maya said.

The girls were rapt with attention.

As Hannah looked into their faces, she was suddenly unsure that her explanation would be received in the way she hoped. Her friends were not exactly open-minded about such things. They'd think she was unhinged. Well, they already did. But they would laugh at her, make a joke of it, unwittingly rob her of that feeling of rightness. They didn't know how the oracle's words had haunted her all these years, wouldn't understand how much she needed to see her again, assess whether she was real or a fraud who had made a lucky guess. She couldn't do it, couldn't risk her hope being punctured. "I just changed my mind, that's all. I was on the train and I realized this is what I want…to be with you guys." As soon as she said it, she had a sickening thought. "It's okay, right?"

"No, we already rented out your bed," Maya said. "Of course it's okay, dork! I mean, it would've saved us a morning of moping around if you hadn't left in the first place, but it hasn't seemed right since."

Hannah grinned and they led her back to their umbrella. "Oh, and guess what?" She tried to sound super casual. "That fair is in town again. That one we went to last time, remember? I saw an ad in the paper. We should totally go…"

"That dinky little kids' fair in Bridgehampton?" Maya said.

"Remember how fun it was? We can get another photo booth pic. Pet the llama?"

"That freaking llama spit on me, thanks for reminding me," Maya said.

"I'd go back just on the off chance that happens again," Blue said.

Hannah bit her lip. Worry seeped in. What if they refused to go? She couldn't go alone! "We're supposed to be re-creating the trip, right?" she tried. "That's the whole idea. Unless you're too old."

"I am not old," Maya said.

"Okay, good, because the thing is...tonight's the last night."

Her friends looked at one another dubiously. Clearly none of them wanted to go.

Hannah's spirits crashed. She had not anticipated this. Her eyes welled behind her sunglasses. She caught Maya looking at her.

"You know what?" Maya said. "You're right. Of course we should go! I literally can't imagine anything more fun."

"Really?" Blue said. "Not one thing?"

"It'll be great," Maya said. She widened her eyes and nodded slightly in Hannah's direction as if to suggest they were dealing with an unstable person and should play along.

For once Hannah didn't mind the characterization.

"Blue can't go," Renee said. "She has her date."

"Date?" Hannah said. "What date?"

"See what you miss when you leave," Maya said. "Okay, so Blue will tragically have to forego the face painting and the ring toss for a raging party and a hot man."

"I'll just come with you guys," Blue said.

"What?" Renee said. "Why?"

Blue shrugged and smiled but her eyes looked sad. Something unspoken passed between her and Renee.

Renee frowned, seemed to pause carefully before speaking. "If you want… I could stay. Go with you to the Surf Lodge. Just so you don't have to go alone, I mean. Maya and Hannah could meet us after. If it would make you more comfortable…"

Blue folded her arms, shrugged like an angsty teenager. "That would be fine, I guess."

Even Hannah could see that Blue was relieved. She glanced back and forth between them. "I have questions," she said.

MAYA

Back from the beach and freshly showered, Maya grabbed the car keys from the kitchen counter and stepped into her flip-flops. Blue was upstairs. Renee in the hammock. Hannah pacing the driveway.

Early evening had arrived in its slow summer way, the sun powering down to a small fading glow, the sky settling soft and gray and melancholy as old age. Maya pushed out the screen door, singing "Scarborough Fair" but cleverly, she thought, changing the lyrics to "Bridgehampton Fair." She sang with real zest and, as far as she was concerned, raw, undeniable talent, trying to work herself into excitement for their carnival adventure. It wasn't as promising as a night at Surf Lodge, but what did it matter? Hannah was back! Renee was staying and she and Blue were going out together, just the two of them! Her plan was finally working. She sang louder.

Hannah shot her a pained look, covered her ears.

"Jealous," Maya said.

They got in the car and Maya started the engine. "So… give me the real deal on why you came back. And why you want to go to the fair. This is about the cotton candy, isn't it?"

Hannah laughed.

Maya eyed her. "Spill," she said.

"Huh?"

"I don't buy that you just changed your mind on the train out of nowhere. I know you." She backed the car out of the driveway.

Hannah bit her lip, looked out the window. "You'll make fun of me."

"Probably. But tell me anyway."

Hannah shifted to face her. "Remember last time? That psychic we went to?"

Maya thought. "Vaguely. Called herself Oracle something?"

"Oracle Lauren. She's there. Tonight. I want to see her."

"You came back to see a carnival psychic? I don't get it."

"Because she predicted everything…that night. The fork in the road. The decision to go to Henry's. Everything." Hannah looked at her earnestly.

"Hmm," Maya said. She'd thought that Hannah's return was a positive sign, one of growth, but now she was a bit worried that psychics might be a new manifestation of Hannah's neurosis. She'd seen that kind of thing happen before. A perfectly normal girl she'd once worked with had moved to Los Angeles and returned with a suitcase full of crystals, a self-diagnosed gluten allergy and a boyfriend who channeled fairies. It had all started with a tarot card reading on the Venice Beach Boardwalk. "Okay. Well, can I ask you something?"

"That depends," Hannah said. "Is it a real question or just a setup for you to give me unsolicited advice?"

Maya considered this. "Maybe both?"

Hannah sighed. "Go."

"What are you hoping to get out of this? Would you rather find out what happened was inevitable? Or…"

"I'd rather it never happened."

"But she can't give you that."

"I know," Hannah snapped. She sat back and leaned her head against the side window. "I know that," she said again, quietly. "I just need to know if she's for real. And I know she probably isn't… I just need to know for sure because of the things she said…if it was just a lucky guess…or if there was something I could have done to change it. And if somehow she is real—"

"Then she can tell you if Henry will ever wake up."

Their eyes met.

"Yes," Hannah said.

Maya felt a small ache, almost like a bruise, in her solar plexus. She wanted to say "I can answer that." She wanted to say "No, he won't wake up," because she was certain that he wouldn't. But then, what made her so sure? Miracles happened. Medicine really was advancing every day—she'd seen that firsthand at work. It was just that to wait for either of those things meant sitting every day for twelve years in failed hope with no end in sight. Maya preferred to cut her losses. Snip, snip, just like her relationships. Get ahead of the letdowns and inevitable goodbyes. Now she considered that maybe false hope and no hope were two sides of the same coin—a way to avoid the uncomfortable ambiguity of uncertainty.

The traffic was crawling as they neared town. The shadow

of that night hitchhiking along, creating a dusky gloom inside her. "What if you knew there was something you could've done differently?" she said. "Something that would've stopped it from ever happening?"

Hannah looked stricken.

"Hypothetically. I'm not saying you did—you didn't. I'm just saying what if. Like, if you knew you messed up. If you were sure it was your fault. Could you ever forgive yourself?" There was something wrong with her voice. It sounded strange to her own ears.

"I don't understand why you're asking me this."

"Forget it," Maya said. "Dumb question. We should definitely talk about something else." This was why she never wanted to talk about Henry. It made her blood move too fast, like she was dangling over the edge of a steep precipice, a dark swallow below.

"Would you?" Hannah said after a long silence. "Forgive yourself?"

"I don't know," Maya said. "I don't know if you're supposed to."

They were both quiet for a moment.

"Anyway," Maya said. "It wasn't either of our faults, so no need to think about it. Those dirtbags are rotting away in prison—right where they belong."

"Yeah," Hannah said. "If only that made me feel better. I mean…obviously I'd feel worse if they weren't, but…"

"It doesn't change anything."

"Exactly. Yeah." She bit at a cuticle, stared off. "Do you ever think about the fact that they'll be eligible for parole in a few years?"

They shared a loaded look.

"No," Maya lied. Sometimes the thought ambushed her in the most random places—at work or the grocery store or standing in her kitchen. She'd feel a prickle in her spine and she'd turn suddenly, half expecting to find them standing there, a gun in her face. She knew it was irrational. Blue kept frequent tabs on their parole status and the lawyers had assured them they'd be unlikely recipients of early release based on their long rap sheets. But still, the possibility shadowed her. "It's not happening, trust me."

Hannah nodded, worried her lip.

"And even if it did, it's not like they'd come looking for us. It wasn't some personal vendetta. It was meth."

"True," Hannah said, though she hardly looked reassured. "Hey, I've been wondering about something. Do you know why Blue's shirt was bloody that night?"

"Huh?" Maya took a sip from her water bottle, trying to wash away the black feeling. She really, *really* wanted to change the subject. But how many times had she done that on Hannah? It wasn't fair.

"I had a memory of Blue from that night. Her sweatshirt was ripped and bloody," Hannah said.

Maya shook her head. Tried to recall—or rather found herself recalling before she could stop herself. She'd been in the bathroom when the men came in the house, had crouched by the door, fear-still, all the life in her turned off so they wouldn't hear it. Her purse was in the car, her phone. She was frantically calculating a way she might get to it. Or at least to the gun in Henry's closet.

She rolled down the window to let some air in. "Maybe it was Henry's blood?"

She didn't want to think about it.

But the memory came back again anyway.

The muffled sound of the men through the door, taunting her friends. Hannah's voice, terrified. Henry trying so hard to sound tough. Maya's own heart beating so loud in her chest. In a moment of quiet, she'd accidentally leaned against the tub, knocked over a shampoo bottle. She froze. Braced. Waiting. Nothing. And then a sudden gunshot. So loud it blew the thoughts right out of her head. She was only seizing heart and blaring adrenals and splintering mind. Then Hannah was screaming "No!" And, *oh God*, Maya had never heard such a sound. Everything in her tightened. She was caught inside a horror she could not yet grasp. All animal terror and human regret. And then an awful thought had come to her. *Thank God*, she'd thought, thank God it had been Henry and not Hannah.

She had been grateful. God help her, what a thought to have.

By the time she heard the men go upstairs and she'd dared to run to the closet for Henry's father's gun, the police had arrived. But it was too late, in some way, to save any of them.

"Blue wasn't in the house when he got shot," Hannah said, pulling Maya from her thoughts. "She ran, remember?"

"I don't know," Maya said. She was agitated and light-headed at once. "Maybe we should ask her." The grainy gray sky deepened around them. Already she missed the daylight. "Look." She pointed to a small Ferris wheel peeking above the car line on the side of Montauk Highway. As she pulled in to the parking lot, tents and rides suitable for small children came into view. She tried to summon that feeling that carnival lights usually gave her—the way it took her back to

that dizzying life-lust of her youth, but her mood had damp-
ened too much.

"I'm nervous all of a sudden," Hannah said.

"If by 'all of a sudden' you mean every day of your life,"
Maya said.

Hannah pressed her hand to the window like a child watching snow fall. "What if she tells me something I don't want
to hear? I hadn't really considered that."

"She won't," Maya said. "I won't let her." But now she was
worried too. Hannah was so susceptible.

"Maybe I should take a Xanax," Hannah said.

Maya said nothing, turned in to the lot.

"Why did you take it anyway?" Hannah said.

"Just don't think you need it," Maya said. And yet even as
she said it, she was aware of some internal alteration, her certainty fraying at the edges again. It wasn't a comfortable feeling, left her exposed to self-doubt. But it also allowed her to
see that her certainty, which she'd always thought a strength,
was sometimes actually a crutch. It separated her from other
people, put the world and everyone in it into boxes, created
judgment. Without it she was aware of feeling vulnerable, but
also spongier, more attuned to life's mysteries, where answers,
like humans, were not so cut-and-dried. "Scratch that. Maybe
I just didn't want to believe you needed it."

"Why?"

"I don't know." *Because it makes me feel guilty*, she thought
but could not say. *Because I don't want you to become my mother.*
"I just wanted you to live."

"I'm trying," Hannah said.

"I know you are."

"The meds help."

"Then I'm an asshole."

"You are," Hannah said, smiling. "That's accurate."

Maya laughed, but also she felt the truth of it. She had to stop trying to force people into living the story that she needed them to. It wasn't fair. She pulled in to what was hopefully a legal parking space—though she wasn't going to look too hard to be sure—and the two of them got out and joined the crowds.

Maya pointed to the left. "They still have a photo booth! We are definitely hitting that before we leave." She would put it in her locker at work with the original photo of the four teenage girls they'd been—giggling as they piled in and flashed their innocent, hopeful smiles into the future. She could almost summon what it had felt like to be that age— oblivious and unbound—life so impossibly shiny before it had been dulled by overuse. But as soon as she grasped the feeling, tried to keep it, it slipped away. Left her with more sadness.

The fair looked so rickety and more run-down than she remembered, like an aging man with bad knees. It suddenly seemed foolish that she'd thought they could re-create the trip they'd had, go back to seeing only the brilliant lights and forget the rats scurrying in the shadows, or the fact that the games were rigged, the prizes cheap. What were you supposed to do with the underbelly that adulthood revealed? If only she could unsee it.

Hannah scanned the vendors, and Maya felt both her worry and hope that the psychic might have answers for her. The dark feeling in her spread. "Maybe this isn't a good idea," she said, though her words got carried away in the crowd.

Hannah pointed to a sign over a booth:

ORACLE LAUREN: Tarot, Palm, Crystal Ball. We take credit cards!

There was a small line of people winding around the table, partially blocking their view. They craned their necks to see over the crowd.

"Is that her?" Maya asked.

Hannah nodded. "Yep."

"I actually predicted that it was," Maya said. "All right, well, let's see what she has to say for herself."

"Maybe we should walk around for a minute first," Hannah said.

Maya noticed Hannah's hands were shaky. "Okay. You can buy me an ice cream."

Hannah gave her a look.

"What? We have to re-create this *exactly*, and last time you bought me ice cream. I don't make the rules."

They wandered through the throng, the smell of popcorn and cotton candy and the briny Atlantic on the breeze. Above them, big mechanical arms spun kids up and down, backward and forward, throwing chips of colored light onto the pavement.

They each got soft serve cones as well as cotton candy to share. Maya ate quickly, burying her worries about Hannah under a thick layer of creamy sweetness and airy sugar. They sat down on a bench and soon the night came down solidly around them, the small, tragic carnival lit up and swirling, alive with the shrieks of happy children, the crank of machinery, the ring of prizes being won. Everything seemed heightened as if Maya herself were aloft on a ride and being whisked around like a glow whip, everything both bright and dark, thrilling and seedy, twirling toward an inevitable end when the rides would be over, the carnival packed up, everything gone except silence.

It was the silence part Maya couldn't stand. The dark breath that lived under everything, wordless and terrifying. That place inside herself she could not, would not enter. And yet it was too present tonight. Had been since they arrived. She looked over at Hannah now wiping her hands with a disinfectant towel she'd kept in her purse, her eyes fixed on the psychic's tent. Something in Hannah's face cleaved at Maya's heart.

"Let's go on the Ferris wheel first!" she said suddenly, dragging Hannah toward the ticket booth. She wanted to be dizzy and unthinking, wanted them both to be.

"Do we have time?" Hannah said.

"It's only eight thirty. It'll take five minutes."

Hannah hesitated.

"Please tell me you're not scared of a Ferris wheel. It's small." Which was true. But it had those spinning cages that made it more fun, and what it lacked in majestic heights and thrilling speed it more than made up for by questionable construction and code violations. This was the real thrill, Maya thought, that at any time a bolt could fail and they would plummet to their deaths in a sea of funnel cakes. Not that she would say that to Hannah.

They bought the tickets and within minutes they were at the front of the line handing them off to the teenage ride operator. He led them to a cage and then pulled the safety bar over their laps. Hannah made him check the lock twice before he sealed them in.

A sudden whir.

"Oh God," Hannah said.

And they were in motion.

Slowly they rose, spoke by neon spoke, Maya grinning with that particular bite of tension mixed with delight, until they were throned high above the crowds, the perspective strange and joyful. Soon the ride was moving faster, suddenly swinging them back and forth, then all the way around in their cage as the wheel made its arc. They squealed and gripped the bar and their screams joined those of the other riders, floating up like balloons into the summer night. Spinning, spinning, Maya looked over to see Hannah wild-eyed and emitting terrified, gleeful shrieks, the primal thrills and terror of the ride overpowering everything but the moment. Their eyes met and they both laughed. They were children, adults, best friends all at once, and Maya's heart was a swell and then a whoosh and a scream as the wheel spun around again and again until the world was nothing more than a blur of lights and sound, her mind free of everything but merriment. It was exactly what she needed.

Suddenly the ride ground to a jerking stop, the two of them perched precariously near the top. Their cage swayed and tilted downward. The ride shuddered forward for one moment, flipping them upside down.

Then it stopped again, leaving them dangling.

Maya looked over, saw Hannah blanch. "Don't worry," she said. "It'll start back up in a second." She didn't want to be stopped, she wanted to be moving again, wanted to be inside the spin and the noise. The blood was rushing to her head.

"Any second," she repeated. The Ferris wheel creaked. "See?"

But nothing happened.

The bar was too distant from her lap. She was hanging out of her seat against it. It seemed like she could slip out of its protective hold so easily. She wondered if the cage would break her fall or if she would crash right through it, the force of her body pushing it open, launching her like a missile into the pavement. Hannah's fears were rubbing off on her.

"This is how you get an aneurysm," Hannah said, clinging to the safety bar.

"No, it isn't," Maya said.

The Ferris wheel made a strange groaning sound, tipping them farther.

"Oh my God," Hannah said.

"It's fine," Maya said.

Someone in another car was screaming, the rest of the riders suspended in awful silence. A small crowd gathered below, looking up.

"I knew we shouldn't have done this."

"Any minute now."

"I seriously hate you for this," Hannah said.

Maya knew she didn't mean it, but still the black feeling she had earlier returned, sinking and formless.

Blood pooled in her head, a building pressure.

Hannah was breathing strangely, making whimpering sounds.

"You're fine. We're fine!" Maya said.

Dammit, why had she suggested they do this?

In the distance, sirens and flashing lights. July night and still that person screaming. Too familiar. She closed her eyes against it. Her fault. Hannah's words: *I hate you.* Hannah *should* hate her. Maybe it would even be easier if Hannah *did* hate her. How could she not? How could Hannah not hate her for what had happened. She wanted to say *I'm sorry*. She wanted to say *I know I should've just kept my mouth shut*. If only she hadn't said anything to that scumbag at the convenience store… It was always there, hanging a thumbnail below consciousness: *I'm sorry, I'm sorry*. And just above it: *It's not my fault! How could I have known what they would do? I had the right to defend myself when he grabbed my ass. I am not to blame for what those sick men did.*

The cage swayed.

"Stop," Maya yelled. Her mind was suddenly bright with screaming, a hard, blazing sunshine breaking inside her skull. "Let us down!"

"Please. Shh," Hannah said, clearly terrified.

Maya closed her eyes, breathed. "Okay. Sorry. Sorry. Okay."

Distraction was what they needed, Hannah especially. Something light and funny. This was a thing Maya could do. A way she could help. And she needed to help. To fix the mistake she'd made. "Hey," she said. "Remember that ski trip in eleventh grade? When we spent the whole weekend in our room high out of our minds?"

Hannah shook her head. A bead of sweat on her brow. "Not really…"

"Oh, come on, you must. Don't you remember how the last day we decided we should get a few runs in so your new skis would look slightly used and your mom wouldn't get mad?"

"Ha, no," Hannah said through fear-gritted teeth.

"We were so stoned we couldn't figure out how to get off the chairlift at the beginner hill. We just panicked." Maya was laughing now, which was sort of an uncomfortable thing to do while she was upside down. "We just kept going up and up. All the way to the top of the mountain. Double black diamond. Vertical incline. Super icy. We were all, 'We're gonna diiie.' I can't believe you don't remember." She looked over at Hannah. Maybe it was helping. It seemed like it was. "What could we do but ski down?"

"Oh no. It's sort of coming back to me now. Wasn't that the trip when Doug Penny got his head stuck between the toilet and the tub looking for his phone?"

"Yep. He's probably still there, actually. Anyway. We convinced ourselves we could do it. Of course, it took us all of two seconds to wipe out, and then we were both just sliding down the hill, bouncing off every mogul like pinballs. I think you lost a ski."

Hannah let out a little laugh and Maya was pleased. She looked down to see several men had joined the teenage ride attendant and were examining the controls. A fire truck pulled in to the parking lot. If she could just keep talking until they fixed the wheel.

"I remember trying to get up and then just straight tumbling down the mountain. It was so crowded. People were literally leaping out of my way to get to safety."

Hannah laughed again.

"I knew I should be scared because I was falling fast. Or at least it seemed like I was. But I was so stoned that I just thought it was hilarious."

"I definitely remember losing a ski."

"We ended up just sprawled on the hill, cracking up. Every time we tried to stand, we'd fall again."

"Weren't people yelling instructions at us from the chairlift?"

"Yep! And skiers kept stopping to offer a hand. Everyone was so worried, trying to help, but we couldn't stop laughing long enough to let them."

"Such idiots."

"So great," Maya said.

"If only I was high now maybe I'd think *this* was funny."

"I'm just going to pretend we are…whee, upside down, yay, so fun!"

"Does that really work?" Hannah said.

"It could," Maya said cheerfully.

The Ferris wheel lurched suddenly and the cage swung in the wind. A rider across from them screamed again.

"Hoo," Maya said. "Fun!" She tried to make them both believe it.

Hannah whimpered anew. "Keep talking. What happened? How did we get down the mountain?"

"Oh, we ended up just taking off our skis and sliding down on our asses. It took us like an hour. Literally the same skiers kept passing us on their second and third runs, waving as they flew by."

Hannah laughed. "Oh man, how did I forget that?"

Their eyes met briefly in sadness. So much lost to that one night.

They were quiet again, the air still. They could see all the way to the ocean. The reflected lights from surrounding houses floated like tea candles on the water.

"If we die on this dumb ride before I get to see Oracle Lauren…" Hannah said.

"We're not going to die."

The Ferris wheel turned suddenly and with it their cage righted.

"Hey, we're moving!"

"We are. See? Fun!" Maya said.

The rotation delivered them chair by chair to the bottom,

Hannah's fear seeming to dissipate quickly in the descent. The ride operator unleashed them from the cage. "Sorry about that, ladies."

"Ugh, we're 'ladies' now," Maya said as she climbed off with wobbly legs. "When did that happen?"

Hannah looked at her phone. "Come on, it's getting late." She started walking fast in the direction of the psychic's tent.

"Wait," Maya said, grabbing her arm. "I have a question."

"Talk while we're walking."

"How do you know you made a wrong turn?"

"Huh?"

"That night. At the fork in the road? How do you know it was the wrong choice?"

Hannah recoiled. "Seriously?"

"I'm not saying it was the right choice. What I mean is… how do you know it was even a choice at all? Like, if the psychic really could predict it, then it must have been fated, right? Otherwise, she couldn't know."

Hannah considered this a moment. "I guess," she said finally. "But maybe if I'd actually done what she'd said, things would've been different."

"Right. But see, that's what I'm saying…maybe you never would have." Maya was feeling around in her brain for her thoughts. "Maybe a hundred times out of a hundred you would have done the same thing because that was the script. If fate could be altered, it wouldn't be fate. I'm not saying I'm right, but…" Maya didn't know if she was saying this more for Hannah or for herself. But it seemed important, like the possibility of removing some quiet burden from them both. Just that. Not a certainty but a possibility that maybe neither of them were to blame.

Hannah nodded thoughtfully. "I still want to see her."

"I'm not trying to stop you. I'm just saying…if stuff's going to happen where there's literally nothing you can do to change it, what's the point of knowing ahead of time? If it was bad, you'd just have longer to dread it and be miserable. And if it was good, you would be less excited when it happened because you'd already know it was coming. Either way you still have to live your life in the meantime, right?"

"I guess," Hannah said.

They reached the tent. It was dark and shuttered.

Hannah looked around frantically. "Where is she?"

Maya glanced at the hours listed—3:00 p.m. to 9:00 p.m.— and then down at her phone. It was just after nine.

Hannah stared in disbelief. "Wait. No." She looked at Maya and back to the tent. "I don't understand." She seemed like she was going to cry. "This doesn't make sense. I was meant to see her…this was the sign."

"What sign?"

"Just… I dunno…a sign! A direction." She was pacing now, circling the tent as if Oracle Lauren might suddenly return. She was definitely going to cry.

"Hannah," Maya said.

"We have to find her."

"Okay," Maya said. "But I mean, I think she's gone. I guess we could google her. See where her next gig is…"

Hannah stopped, put her hands to her eyes, began to sob. "It was hard enough for me just to come here."

Maya moved to comfort her but Hannah shook her head.

"What am I supposed to do?" she said. "Why won't life help me? I'm trying so hard…"

"Hannah," Maya said. "She's just a dumb carnival shill…"

But Hannah was inconsolable. "Don't you get it? Now I have nothing. I'm just going to be stuck in the same place! In the same exact place of 'What if he doesn't wake up? But then what if he does?' Every day. Every single minute of every day. It's consuming me. It's swallowing my whole life. Will he be okay? Will *I* be okay? My head is a constant debate. Hope, fear, hope, fear. Back and forth, up and down. And there's no answer and there's no door. It's just a circular room made up of circular questions and I'm locked inside, I'm trapped! And I don't know how to get out." Her body sagged. "I thought maybe life was giving me an answer..."

Maya didn't know what to say. What could she say?

"I know she's not real. Probably."

"Very probably," Maya said.

"Possibly probably."

"Possibly probably she just made a lucky guess that one time."

Hannah sighed. "I know," she said. "I know that's probably true." She plopped down on the grass and wept anew. "I was just desperate. I *am* desperate."

Maya sat beside her, put an arm around her shoulder. The world spun and twinkled and bustled around them.

"I wanted so badly to believe," Hannah said.

"I know."

"And instead everything went wrong. Total disaster. Just like I always fear."

"I mean, I wouldn't say disaster, but..."

Hannah laughed through her tears. "I tried, right? I came all the way back." She looked pleadingly at Maya.

"You did."

"And I'm fine. It didn't kill me. I guess that's something."

"You are fine."

"It's just that for once I didn't worry if I was making the wrong decision or that something terrible would happen. I was so sure it was meant to be...that my brain stopped arguing itself. It was such a relief." She wiped her eyes, her body shuddering. "Sort of like how we weren't scared on the ski slope because we were stoned."

Maya nodded, trying to understand.

Hannah hugged her knees. "Ugh, life is so hard sometimes."

"Yep," Maya said. "Sometimes it is."

"I don't know...maybe...even though I didn't get an actual answer, I did lose the questions, and that's something. I was out of my head and in the world. For a little while anyway. It always seemed like I couldn't really move...like in my life...without the answer first. But I did a little. Which I guess means I can again."

"And you're here with me," Maya said.

"And I'm here with you."

Maya smiled.

"Thanks," Hannah said. "Good talk."

"Yeah?"

"I mean, not as good as a psychic, but whatever."

Maya laughed. Then she gave Hannah a mischievous look. "Come on, let's go crash Blue's date."

BLUE

Blue showered until the water ran cold, then got out and went to her bed, where she'd carefully laid out the outfit she would wear—the off-the-shoulder yellow blouse Maya had insisted she borrow, the necklace, the white capri pants, the fancy underwear. It looked so much like hope lying there that she threw it all on as quickly as she could to escape the embarrassment of seeing her wishes laid out so barely. She went to the mirror, turned one way and then the other, trying to be objective. She could stare and stare and stare and still not know what she looked like. Not really. The words that came to mind were not her own. She knew that. But when she looked in the mirror, that's what she saw. She saw the memory of hatred, swallowed and then regurgitated by the voice in her head. But knowing that didn't help.

She needed a countervoice.

She went downstairs. Renee was in the kitchen, her back turned. She had a different dress on, presumably borrowed from Maya based on the way it hung on her. Renee had belted it, wore it with a stylish slouch, managed to look perfect and enviable.

She turned. "Hey." She held up a framed photo she'd been looking at. "Look at this."

In it fourteen-year-old Blue and Renee were lying at opposite ends of the hammock, their sun-bronzed legs tangled in the middle, each of them engrossed in a book. Blue was smiling as if she sensed Nana was taking the picture, a strip of sunburn across her nose and cheeks. They both looked so happy.

"That's exactly how I remember you," Renee said, handing it to her.

Blue barely glanced at it. She didn't need to see the girl she'd been blinking up at her from the photo, surprised to see the kind of person she'd grown up to be. She put the picture on the table, held her arms out stiffly. "Do I look okay?"

It seemed demeaning and pathetic to need Renee in this moment. But not having input was worse. She couldn't trust herself to have objectivity or even know what would be appropriate to wear. She had to focus on the night at hand. It was bigger than her grudge. It was too big, in fact. Her one shot at love.

Renee looked her over.

"Never mind," Blue said, before Renee could answer. "I give up." She started back toward the stairs.

"What are you talking about? Blue, you look…amazing!"

Blue turned. "Oh, please," she said. It was exactly what she wanted to hear. And exactly what she couldn't believe. Besides, she still didn't want Renee to think her opinion mattered. Just because Renee was being nice didn't fix everything.

She marched over to the fridge. Fished a wine cooler out. Uncapped it and gulped some down. "Disgusting." She held one out to Renee.

"Sounds tempting, but I'll pass."

Blue shrugged. "More for me." She sat at the kitchen table. "Let me guess—Mr. Perfect doesn't drink."

She saw Renee tense.

"Actually, he does." Renee turned and began wiping down the already clean counter. "And so do I. I just...can't right now." She paused. "Because I think... I mean, I know... I'm pregnant."

Blue froze.

Renee turned, watched her face.

"Wow," Blue said, averting her eyes. She took another huge gulp, tipped the bottle in a half-hearted cheer. "Congrats."

Renee came and sat across from her. "I started getting morning sickness—as you saw—and I'd noticed my nipples were browning. So I took a test last week. And well..."

There was an eager searching in Renee's eyes. Something she wanted.

"It's actually why I came. Here, I mean. To see you guys. The minute I saw that test...I just...wanted to talk to someone. I called my mother. That's what you're supposed to do, right? It's like an instinct. So automatic I still forget how pointless it is. I mean, she was nice about it, I guess. In her own way. But you know. It's like her being nice to me now is sort of too late. It didn't *mean* anything to tell her. And then I knew who it would mean something to tell. And I wished I could call you. It made me realize how fast time is passing. Like we were *just* teenagers. And now I'm going to be a mom and—"

As soon as Blue met her gaze, Renee looked down as if she realized she'd exposed something.

Blue didn't know what to say, what she was supposed to do with this. Act happy? Pop some champagne? Or sparkling cider? It shouldn't have taken Renee twelve years and a pregnancy test to realize that she mattered. "Well…like I said, congrats. I'm happy for you."

Renee blinked. Then stood abruptly. The mask of perfection back on her face. "Yeah, thanks. I'd appreciate it if that stayed between us. At least for now. Anyway. It's almost nine. Should I call the cab?"

"I guess," Blue said. She opened the second wine cooler, then realized she needed something stronger. Why did Renee have to put this on her right now when she was already freaking out? It was too much to take in. She grabbed the bottle of vodka from the freezer and OJ from the fridge, made a screwdriver you could see through.

Renee recited their address into the phone. Blue downed half the glass, visited the hall mirror for one last hopeless fix of her hair, smiled a practice smile into it.

Jesus Christ.

Why am I doing this?

I can't do this.

By the time the cab announced itself with a kick of pebbles in the driveway, she was pregnant herself—only with dread—an inch shy of her own run to the toilet. They climbed in and Renee told the driver their destination.

"Maybe we should skip the bar and go to the fair," Blue said, as they turned onto Montauk Highway. The drinks hadn't helped. Her nervous system was like an anxious dog recognizing landmarks en route to the vet. She rolled down the window, let the black Montauk night fly in.

"Why do we do this to ourselves?" she said. "Why do we

bother with men?" She wasn't really talking to Renee so much as thinking out loud, expelling her anxiety into the air. So many women she knew were cheated on or abused or simply in the wrong relationship. When she was younger, she could never understand why women stayed with men like that. But now she could see how easy it would be to sink into an offering of love, no matter how inadequate. Just for the relief of not having to look for it anymore. Of not having to hope for love only to be disappointed over and over. But of course, Renee wouldn't understand. Renee had found one of the good ones right away. The only thing that had saved Blue from the heartache of men was that she'd learned early on how to withstand the wet weight of loneliness that sat on her chest until she almost stopped noticing it there. Only now she *was* noticing it. Now it was heavy, so heavy. Now she wanted. But it was terrifying—the possibility of wanting and not getting. Of opening your heart only to be knifed with rejection. Such sharp, precise pain. It took her breath away to even imagine it. "I'm sure Jack's a womanizer. Or a commit-phobe. Or can't love."

"Can't love?" Renee said. "Or can't love you? Because it sounds like you're preemptively rejecting him."

Blue shrugged. "Both. Probably. No one ever stays." The alcohol was making her too loose. And too loose to care that she was.

"That's not true."

"Seems like it."

"People stay," Renee said. "Some of them anyway. Some leave and come back."

How can you tell which from which though? How do you stop

from getting too broken before you find them? For a moment Blue wished they were still friends so she could ask that.

"I don't know," Renee said as if Blue *had* asked the question. She leaned her head against the window, staring impassively out at the passing world. "You just have to find a way to trust."

"Trust who?" Blue said.

Renee shrugged. It was like they were having two different but matching conversations. "Maybe just yourself. That you'll be okay no matter what other people do."

The thought was a comfort. Renee was a comfort. Like returning to an old beloved book, remembering its solace, its happy if complicated ending, the way it spoke to something true. She hated it. She should be strong enough to resist Renee's pull. But she didn't have the will right now. For a moment she even wanted to confess the whole truth, that she hadn't been on any other dates, never had sex, that Jack was the last boy she'd kissed. She longed for Renee's advice. Or at least for the safety net of love she'd once had with her.

But all that did was remind her—to be known and loved and then left as Renee had done to her. It was so gutting—speared a person in all their old wounds, unearthed that primal internal wail that sometimes lived in deep silences. *Why don't you love me? How could you do this?* You had to drown out the noise of it with so much stuff, cell phones and social media and TV and movies and music and work and still it came lurching up when you least expected, when you were just trying to have a relaxing weekend or a quiet moment on the subway.

How could she risk her heart again? With Jack? With anyone?

The cab pulled up in front of the restaurant.

The nervous pit in Blue's stomach grew.

"Ready?" Renee said.

"Yep," Blue said, but did not move.

They sat.

"This is where you wanted to go, right?" the cab driver asked.

"She's nervous. It's a date."

"I'm not nervous," Blue said.

The cab driver hooked his arm around the back of his seat, turned to her. "You want my advice?"

"No thanks."

"The thing I learned after four marriages," he said, "is it either works or it doesn't. There are people in life who get you and people who don't. You can't make someone be in your 'psychic clan'—I trademarked that, by the way—who's not in your psychic clan. So if he doesn't like you, not in your PC. On the flip side, if he *is* in your PC, there's not a whole lot you can do to screw it up."

"Good stuff," Blue said, though her dread was so loud in her head she could barely hear herself.

"Thanks," he said proudly. "I wrote a book on it. You can buy it off my website…hold on…let me give you my card. There's a discount code on the back."

Renee hustled her out of the cab. "Okay, let's do this."

Blue handed the driver a wad of cash through the front window, and she and Renee headed toward the Surf Lodge. Her heart was hammering, blood roaring in her ears. She was swept off in it, half-blinded by it, everything rushing at her in a loud blur. She'd imagined a night like this so many times. Long before she'd even heard from Jack again. For twelve years it had lived in her as a hope that someday they would find each other, that she would bump into him on a street corner in Manhattan, or at the wedding of one of her summer friends or somewhere truly unexpected, like an African safari. And now here she was. And here he would be.

She followed Renee inside, an embarrassing sweat breaking out on her forehead and the back of her legs. She thought of her apartment back in NYC. She thought of the size of her bank account. She tried to stand on these things like an island, but they were thin ice, unable to bear her weight. It was terrifying how easy it was to lose herself, to summon everything she knew when she was alone and find it too slippery to hold in the face of other people, becoming only the thing that they valued or didn't.

Renee led the way through the crowd. The light was soft, strung like a mimic of stars, the room crowded with the chatter of guests and the chime of silverware, the salty air off the bay reaching through the open doors. Everyone was in their Hamptons whites, girls with sweaters tied over their delicate shoulders, bleached teeth laughing against tan, taut faces.

Blue was being assaulted by her own inadequacy. She was lumbering and odd looking, a spectacle here. Each person she passed looked through her on their way to talk to someone who mattered. Renee, on the other hand, looked like she completely belonged.

Why was she doing this to herself? It wasn't worth it.

She gave a cursory glance around the room. "Doesn't look like he's here," she said. "Let's go."

Renee grabbed her arm. "He's right over there. Look."

Jack was waving at them from a table. Blue's heart backfired and her legs were suddenly loose and unreliable. She waved back and tried to smile but her mouth spasmed and she imagined she must look insane.

I can't do this. I don't know how to do this.

Her head seemed to be filling with water, distorting light and sound.

She started toward the patio for a cigarette. Reached into her purse for the pack. It was empty. *Of course.*

She rerouted to the bar.

"Where are you going?" Renee said, tripping after her.

"I need a drink." *And a minute to calm the hell down.*

Blue glanced back at Jack. He was talking to his friend, making him laugh, looking like every other person in the place, perfect and good-looking and at ease. She was so ridiculously in over her head. She could barely even manage small talk, no less be cool or coy or charming. What on earth would she have to offer someone like him? Nothing, that's what. It made her want to cry. Foolish, stupid girl. She waved a large bill at the bartender to get his attention. He ignored her and served two beautiful women at the other end of the bar.

"I don't think you should have another," Renee said. "You need to be lucid."

"I'm unbearably lucid," Blue said.

Finally the bartender came over.

"A shot of gin and tonic. And a tequila. Please."

"You mean a shot of tequila and a gin and tonic?" he said, taking the cash.

"Sure, whatever."

Renee hid her eyes.

Two glasses were set in front of Blue. She turned her back to Jack's table and gulped down the shot. She grabbed the gin and tonic, downed that too. The booze seemed to rocket into her brain almost instantly. "Better," she said.

They weaved their way through the crowd.

Jack saw them coming and stood. Up close, in the dim romantic lighting, he looked doubly handsome and intimidating, immediately robbing her of all her liquid courage. "You came!" he said.

"Heyyy," Blue said. She was trying to sound cool, but she was struggling to modulate her voice over the blood-rush of adrenaline in her ears. "What's happenin'?"

He put his hand up and Blue appallingly found herself throwing him a high five before she realized he was just waving to Renee behind her. He paused, puzzled, then met Blue's hand with his and held it rather than slapped it.

"You look different without the hat and the glasses and the…morning ice cream bar, ha ha," he said.

She was sure she saw a shadow cross his face as he observed the sad reality of her.

He thinks I'm ugly, she thought, and the awful notion drifted down into the depths of her and lodged itself there. *I should leave. Walk out with my dignity intact.* Already she hated him. Already she hated herself.

"Hey, again," Renee said, holding her arms out for a hug.

"Hey," Jack said, pulling her in. "You came after all."

Blue watched, burning. "She's engaged," she said. It just fell out. Because of course he would want Renee and not her. Wasn't that always how it went? Two beautiful people. They looked like they belonged together.

"No way! Tonight? Where's the lucky guy?"

"No, not tonight…ah…" Renee looked askance at Blue.

"Well, congratulations. This is my friend Peter." Jack gestured to the shy-looking guy beside him wearing a crisp white shirt and a clear desire to be elsewhere. "Peter, this is Renee and Blue."

"Howdy," Peter said, and Blue considered he was the male version of herself. In fact, Jack probably brought him to match them up. *Oh God, seriously though, he probably did.*

They sat. Blue was so nervous she misjudged the distance, landing heavily in her chair. She couldn't bear to look at Jack, to catch any hint of disappointment in his face. She decided she was still too sober, tried, to no avail, to get the attention of a passing waitress. When she turned back to the table, Jack had said something that made Renee laugh.

"So what do you do, Peter?" Blue said, angling away from Jack. If he was going to fall in love with Renee, then she was going to ignore him and flirt with his sour-looking friend and pretend she was having a blast.

"Real estate," Peter said, glancing around the room.

"Commercial or private?"

"Private."

"I would have guessed commercial."

He looked at her strangely. "No. Nope."

"Nice. Well. I love real estate. I have a great apartment, a large penthouse, actually. Across from Central Park." She heard herself talking loudly, trying to sound important, but she couldn't stop the train. She snuck a furtive look at Jack. He was showing Renee something on his phone. *Hello. Did he not see the massive ring?* She plowed on. "And I work in finance. Many real estate deals. Big money deals." *Jesus Christ.*

"Oh." He shifted uncomfortably. "So, uh, how do you and Jack know each other?"

Jack turned, tuned in. His eyes met and locked on Blue's.

"That's a good question, actually," Jack said. "Where did we meet? Ice cream shop, wasn't it?"

Blue stiffened. "Actually, the beach first."

"We did?" Jack said. "The beach. Really? Oh, wait, that's right! Didn't my buddy almost hit you with a Frisbee?" Jack threw his head back and laughed. "Wow, I totally forgot about that."

Blue looked away, the memory shifting inside her. It had been so important to her—that moment when the Frisbee almost hit her and Jack had rushed to the rescue, called her pretty. She'd put a frame around the memory, kept it near. All this time she'd believed he felt what she felt. That instant, blush-inducing connection. That pull in the chest. That *wonder*. But it was all in her head. It meant nothing to him— *she* meant nothing to him—he didn't even remember it. She probably hadn't even been a real person to him, just another conquest in a long summer of them, a way to pass the time.

"Fortunately for me, I was still able to win her over with my charm," Jack said. He leaned back and smiled at her.

She did not smile back. "Hardly."

"Oh, come on." He tilted his head, searched her face. Then he turned to Peter. "It was love at first sight."

Wait. Did he like her? Was she reading this all wrong?

No, he was just mocking her. She was sure of it.

"Please. It was a meaningless summer fling," she said. She wasn't going to let him get over on her again. She wasn't going to let him see all the stupid hope she had.

"Okay, if you say so." He was still smiling, though his pupils darted uncertainly as he watched her.

Blue felt a kick under the table.

"You wore his sweatshirt for weeks!" Renee said, staring hard at her.

"No, I didn't!" Blue snapped. She tried to kick her back and accidentally moved the table, knocking over Renee's water glass.

Everyone lurched back in their chairs.

"Sorry! Sorry," she said, hearing the slur move into her voice. "I'm not drunk, I swear." She grabbed a bunch of napkins and squashed them against the spill. "It's just water, people. Chill!"

Jack stood, grabbed some more napkins from a nearby table. Their hands touched, a flash of electricity as he helped her mop up. She pulled away as if stung. "I've got it," she said. She dabbed at the spill and then sat back down into an uncomfortable silence. They were all looking at her. A remaining trickle of water dripped into her lap.

"We should get you a real drink anyway," Jack said to Renee. He put his hand on her forearm and Blue felt the knife twist in her gut.

"Oh, no thanks," she said. "I'm okay."

"Why don't you tell them why, Renee," Blue said.

Renee shot her a wounded look, shook her head no.

"She's with child," Blue said, happy to deliver the killing blow to Jack and Renee's burgeoning romance. "Her nipples are brown. That's how you know apparently. Crazy, right? Have you ever thought about having kids, Peter?"

She saw all three of their mouths fly open in shock.

"Ah…excuse me. I'm going to…get a drink at the bar," Peter said before nearly hurdling over her to escape.

"Well, uh, congratulations," Jack said to Renee. He tapped his thumbs on the table, glanced nervously around the club.

Renee gave him a tight smile, stared into her lap.

The uncomfortable silence expanded.

"Blue!" someone shouted, and they all turned to see Maya and Hannah heading their way, big grins on their faces.

Blue was at once relieved for the interruption and horrified to have more witnesses to this disaster.

"We're crashing your date," Maya said.

"You mean Renee's date," Blue said.

"What?" Maya said. Their smiles fell as they reached the table and caught the vibe. They stopped, stood awkwardly, eyes darting in search of explanation.

"Sit," Blue said. "Have a drink. I've offended everyone else. Might as well join the fun."

Maya and Hannah exchanged looks, then pulled up two seats and sat down warily.

Jack glanced at his watch, took a sip of his beer, smiled grimly at no one in particular.

To Renee, Maya mouthed, "What is happening?"

Renee made a drinking gesture, tilted her head toward Blue.

"I caught that," Blue said.

Suddenly Renee's eyes bulged. "Excuse me." Her hand flew to her mouth as she got up and ran across the restaurant.

Maya watched her. "Is she drunk too?"

"Pregnant," Blue said. "Drunk is how you get that way."

"Pregnant?" Hannah said. She looked at Maya.

Maya looked at Blue. "For real?"

Blue shrugged. "Apparently."

"Oh, wow," Hannah said.

"Hell yes!" Maya said. "We're having a baby! This is such an excellent shit show of a vacation. I *love* it."

"Yep, so great," Blue said bitterly, throwing a half-hearted fist into the air. "So glad I came."

Maya shot her a questioning look, Hannah a worried one.

Jack shifted uncomfortably, kept taking nervous, furtive glances at Blue.

"So how's it going, Jack?" Maya said.

"Good," he said. "Yeah, really good."

"Cool."

They both nodded at each other for several beats too long.

He glanced at Blue again, as if trying to catch her eye. She ignored him.

He watched her for one more moment and then cleared his throat. "Well… I should be going," he said, inching out of his seat. "Pete and I have…ah…a thing we're supposed to…"

"A thing," Blue said.

"Yeah…uh…"

"You can't go," Maya said. "We just got here."

"No, Maya," Blue said. "They have a thing to get to."

"Blue," Jack said, "can I talk to you alone for a—"

"No, you don't want to be late for your thing," Blue said.

Jack sighed helplessly, shook his head.

"Blue…" Maya said sternly. "Jack, you should stay."

"No, he shouldn't," Blue said. "Besides, we have a thing to get to too."

"We do?" Hannah said.

Blue saw Jack signal to Peter at the bar.

"Well," he said to them. "It was great seeing you guys. Keep in touch or…whatever." He glanced one last time at Blue, seemed to sigh, then walked away.

Renee came out of the bathroom, saw what was happening, looked to Blue as if willing her to stop it.

But by then Jack was already at the door, exiting Blue's life as quickly as he'd reentered it.

For a moment no one spoke.

"Well then," Maya said.

A horrified quiet sat with them amid the detritus of empty glasses and sopping napkins.

"Good riddance," Blue said too loudly over a quiet, building grief. She picked up Jack's abandoned beer and took a sip. "Nostrovia, everyone! That's Russian for 'let's get drunk'!"

They stared at her. She chugged the rest of the beer.

"You're cut off," Maya said.

"Okay, but first a round of shots." She was desperate for more booze, desperate for oblivion. Jack was gone. The serrated edges of that reality sharpened inside her chest with every breath.

She saw Hannah reach for the half-full drink Peter had left and slide it out of her eyeline.

"Maybe we should go," Hannah said.

"Screw that! We just got here," Blue said.

A man at the next table leaned over. "Excuse me? We're trying to have a nice dinner here."

"I'm so sorry," Renee told him, looking mortified. "We were just leaving."

"No, we weren't," Blue said. Taste of vinegar in her mouth. Renee aligning with this stranger in shared horror at her behavior. *Apologizing* for her. Her focus narrowed. This was all Renee's fault. This whole disaster of a night, all of it.

Maya stood, grabbed Blue by the arm. "Come on, babe."

Blue tried to make herself deadweight but gave up almost instantly. Maya was strong, and also, she suddenly didn't care, wanted to go, to be gone from this place, to be not home but nowhere. Maya got her to her feet. Blue pitched slightly as if caught in a gale and then righted herself, marched out.

The others followed her.

"I'll bring the car around," Maya said. "I had to park down the street."

"I'm calling a cab," Blue said, fumbling for her phone.

"What? Why?"

"Don't wanna be near her." She pointed at Renee.

"Me? What the hell did I do?" Renee said.

Blue rolled her eyes so hard she almost lost her balance. "What the hell did I do?" she mocked. She rifled through her bag, hoping for a stray cigarette. "You'd think that someone with a fiancé might have the *decency* not to flirt with someone's date," she muttered. "But no. Not Renee. Renee has to take everything."

"Are you kidding me right now?" Renee said. "I wasn't flirting. I was being *polite*. Because *you* wouldn't talk to him."

"Whatever," Blue said, zipping her purse, glancing around for a stranger with a smoke. "Go away. You've ruined my life enough."

"I've ruined your life?" Renee said. She turned to Maya and Hannah. "I have single-handedly *ruined* her entire life, now?"

"Yep," Blue said. "Ya did."

"Oh, for God's sake," Maya said. "What is with you? Look, I don't know what happened between you two—"

"Right," Blue said. "You don't." Her mind felt clearer than it had in hours; the alcohol seemed burned off by the torch of her sudden fury. "So maybe stay the hell out of it."

"Okay," Maya said. "I can do that. Or…here's a crazy thought…you could just go ahead and tell us! Just put it all out there—"

"Oh yeah. That's…that's brilliant. Can't think of anything better than spilling my guts to you guys so you can tell me again to get over it. I'm gonna go ahead and take a pass on that."

"Fine. Don't tell us, then," Maya said. "But then you don't get to hold us hostage to a question you refuse to answer and then blame us for not understanding you."

"Right. Whatever," Blue said. She turned and stormed back

toward the restaurant. *Screw this.* She needed another drink now. But no. The engine of her anger was gunning, already set on its course. She doubled back. "Did it ever occur to you that it was too painful to tell you? Or, like, that I was worried you couldn't handle it? Did you ever think that maybe, just maybe, I wanted to know you even gave a shit? 'Cause you know what? As far as I could tell, you didn't want to know."

In the distance, the sound of amateur fireworks. They all instinctively flinched.

"Well, you're wrong," Maya said. "We do want to know. We're your best friends and you're important to us so just freaking tell us, for God's sake."

Blue tilted her head back, found the moon. Nope, that made her dizzy. Instead she sought its reflection on the water. So much noise. Everything so loud inside her.

"Blue," Hannah said, her voice soft. "There was blood on you that night. I remembered that on this trip. Is that true?"

"Yeah," Maya said. "Why was there blood on you?"

"What did he do to you?" Renee said.

Blue laughed bitterly. "Oh *now* you want to know? *Now* you're concerned about what he did? Go to hell, Renee."

"Blue, *I'm* concerned. What did he do?" Maya said.

"He didn't…?" Hannah said.

"Please no," Renee said.

Blue knew what they were asking, blinked against the words. Of course they thought it was rape. If she told them the truth, they would probably say she was lucky it wasn't. Renee might even offer up an infuriating "Thank God!" And it was true—she *was* lucky, if you could call it that. And that was the worst part in some way, because she sure as hell didn't *feel* lucky, and that made her feel guilty and ashamed of her own suffering.

"You really want to know?" Blue said. They were all watching her. Hannah, Renee, Maya—all of them so still and expectant. Her head felt clear and sober, though she knew she couldn't possibly be. "Will it make you feel better? Sate your... your...curiosity? Comfort you if I say no he didn't rape me?"

"We really want to know," Hannah said. "And not because we're curious. Because we care."

Blue looked away. Tried to imagine saying the words out loud. But there was so much resistance, like a weighted dumbbell sitting on her chest, asphyxiating the words before they could be spoken. She couldn't have pushed them out even if she wanted to. She thought back on that night, her mind stumbling into a darkness black as a grave, tripping over moments of that horror still so alive, so vivid.

"Blue," Maya said.

The men chasing Hannah up the walkway. Her friends screaming. Though in Blue's mind there's just silence, open mouths and fear-lit eyes, their hands and bodies lunging to grab Hannah, pull her in to safety. Henry shouting for someone to get his dad's rifle in the closet. And then they were falling backward, the door flying open, the men inside the house.

Oh God. She could still taste the hot panic. Sour and corrosive.

Now she forced herself to look at Maya. But instead of being comforted by the new softness she saw in Maya's eyes, Blue was enraged. Because it was too damn late. It had all come too late and all she wanted was to hurt someone, to stab with words, to discharge all the poison that had been put inside her. All these years she'd held on to the secret, and now what she wanted was to wield it as a weapon. A weapon against Maya for asking her to forgive. A weapon against Renee for deserving no forgiveness. Screw it. Screw them. They wanted her story. Well then, they should get it, they should have to live with it. Renee should have to live with it.

She looked at Renee, saw those darting eyes. Saw the way her arms were wrapped around herself, defended against what Blue might say. The anger Blue felt in that moment acted as a Heimlich maneuver, suddenly propelling the words out of her. She wasn't going to let her escape this again.

"We ran." She jammed her finger toward Renee. "She was in front of me." Through Henry's kitchen and out the back patio door. The night air like freedom. The sleeping neighborhood oblivious to their terror.

"They were chasing us. One of them at least. I could feel him behind me but I didn't want to turn. I just kept my eyes on Renee. She jumped the bushes into the neighbor's yard. I was right behind her. Running so fucking hard. Thinking if I could just get over those bushes. If I could just...like they were some kind of...magic divider he couldn't cross. I was right there. He grabbed my shirt. I tried to shake him off but I couldn't. I was screaming, 'Renee, Renee!' And she stopped and turned. I saw her stop and turn. He told her to come back. He told her he'd kill me if she didn't. Remember that, Renee? Remember him saying that?"

Blue looked away, tears so long unshed, now pooling.

"She looked right at me. I was so scared, so scared." Blue paused, the weight of the next memory almost too heavy to speak. "Then she turned around and ran."

The air was thick with their silence.

"Blue," Renee said, moving toward her now.

Blue backed away. "I watched you go. I watched you leave me there with that…you left me there to die! How could you…how could you just—" She shook her head against the slimy tentacles of memory. Nauseated with emotion but there was no turning back. "He told me he was going to have some fun with me first."

Hannah's eyes were wet, tears threatening to spill over.

"Next thing I knew, my face was in the dirt." Blue could still taste the damp grass when she hit the ground—that familiar smell of childhood play and softball games in center field—only turned dark and wormy as a burial pit. Even now it was the first thing that came to her, that damp green smell, his stale breath, her own rancid fear.

"He flipped me over, pushed my sweatshirt up to my neck, tore at my bra. I fought." He hadn't been terribly strong, only just stronger than her own adrenaline-fueled body. "I kept thinking Renee would come back. That help would be coming." *I just need to stall him.* "But then he pinned my arms above my head. I tried to kick him. I was thrashing and kicking, trying to get away. He put a knife to my throat." She hadn't remembered seeing him hold it, only felt the poke of the blade against her skin. "I begged him to stop. 'Please,' I said. 'You don't want to do this.'"

He'd pressed it into the thin skin of her clavicle, just enough that she could feel the sting, the tickle of blood tracing its way down her breast.

"Do you know what it felt like to have to say that? To have to beg?" Her voice caught, remembering how she'd loathed the sound of her own whimpering, so meek and cowed, in the face of such revolting evil. "But I had to do it… I had to stall. Because Renee was coming back, right? She wasn't going to just *leave* me there. I kept thinking, *What's taking so long?* I kept thinking, *Hurry! Hurry!*" The words looping over and over in her mind, a refrain against his body on top of her, against his sickening odor, his enraging weight. "He pushed up my skirt." She'd never worn skirts before. But she had that night because she'd dared to believe she could be a pretty girl, had dared to embrace her own femininity in the face of Jack's attention days before.

"And then…" He'd been removing his belt when he'd stopped suddenly, froze like a squirrel sensing danger. A million times she'd tried to remember what had made him pause, but her mind was a skipping stone, jumping from one disconnected moment to another. What she remembered next was him looking at her, staring deep into her eyes, into her vulnerability, as she lay utterly helpless and exposed beneath him. "He said…" She stopped. Shook her head. She couldn't say it. How could she say it?

"Blue," Maya said.

She swallowed. Her body shaking with the force of keeping the words in. "He said, 'You're too ugly to fuck anyway,' and he stood up and ran."

She looked at her friends.

They stared back, mouths hanging open. A hush over the group like a winter.

"Oh my God," Maya said.

Blue breathed. It seemed the first time she had done so since she'd started talking. But she didn't feel better. She didn't feel purged. She was still, in some way, trapped there, stuck in time, the old film playing to its inevitable end, only to start over again. She remembered the relief of weight being removed, not just of his body but of a nightmare ending. Or so she had thought. It was only later, after the adrenaline had worn off and the men were captured, after a plea bargain of second-degree attempted murder had been struck to spare the girls from testifying, after the attention around the case had faded and things had gone back to "normal," that she'd realized he was still on top of her, all that weight crushing her and the disgusting residue he left on her that made her feel as hideous as he said she was, hideous to the core. One of the worst parts was that it wasn't even new. He'd just reinforced the belief about herself she'd been raised with.

She turned to Renee. "I waited for you." She was trying so hard to fight off sobs, to climb over the lump in her throat, to stand solid and big in her anger, not liquefied and reduced by grief. "I waited for you to help me. I believed that you were coming back. That you were my friend. That you were the one person, the one person in my life…" Tears were bubbling over now, burning as they spilled out of her eyes. She wiped them furiously away. "Well, *friend*, congratulations! He didn't rape or kill me. Your conscience is clear."

As soon as the words were out, something broke in her, all her defenses crashing in one instant, leaving her with the devastation of having been abandoned by the one person she'd always believed loved her. Her body crumpled as if struck.

She pressed her palms to her eyes, waiting to hear dumb platitudes. But when she looked up, she saw that not only Hannah but Renee and Maya were crying.

"No!" Blue said, all of her anger returning in a rush. "You do *not* get to cry, Renee. Do you hear me? *You* got away. You went to the neighbors—*safe and sound!* And you never once apologized. You never once even bothered to ask what happened to me after you left me there!"

Renee sobbed harder. "I know!"

Blue scoffed. "You know."

"I was too scared to ask. I knew you must hate me. I swear I was just trying to get help. And I did. That should count for something, right? That I got to a phone? That the police came. That that sicko is in jail now? But I know I left you. I can only imagine how that felt. And I have to live with—"

Blue laughed short and hard like a scrape. "Oh, you've got to be kidding me. Poor Renee. What *you* have to live with. Tell us. Go ahead. What do you have to live with, Renee?"

"That I'm a coward! That I couldn't be there when you needed me. I know I should have said something. I know I pretended like it didn't happen. I just didn't know how else to live with the guilt."

"You left me."

"It was stupid and selfish and messed up. I get it. I let you down in a way I can never be forgiven for. I failed you. Totally and completely. And I hate myself for that. And I have to live with that."

"Good. I hope it keeps you up at night," Blue said. She felt hijacked by hate, everything ugly around her, in her. And yet she kept amplifying it, justifying her hatred in her mind in the hopes that it might finally find release. Because here she was, thirty years old and incapable of the kind of soft, vulnerable love that didn't nip in fear, incapable of being loved in her own soft places, of being in a relationship with a man, of loving herself. And as far as she was concerned, it was Renee's fault just as much as that scumbag's who ground her into the dirt. If Renee hadn't left her, Blue wouldn't be so broken. If she'd just said she was sorry afterward, allowed Blue to confide in her the horror, Blue wouldn't have felt so abandoned, her ugliness confirmed.

"It's always the same with you, Renee, even now as I confess something I've been holding inside for twelve years—you have to make this about you. Even now you're only thinking about yourself." Blue didn't even know if this was true but she didn't care, didn't give an ounce of concern about anything but unburdening herself.

Renee's tears stopped instantly as if she'd been slapped to her senses. Her voice took on a wobbly sort of anger, daring herself to allow it.

"Really? I only think of myself? Ever? What about everything I ever did for you before that moment? Why can't you remember anything but that?"

"*Because for me there is no other moment!*" Blue screamed. The air seemed to ripple with the force of it. They both stood there in the wake of it, in the shock of all that rage. Then Blue slumped with the exertion. She had hoped to feel better, finally free of it all. Instead she was just empty and dried out. Alone. Ashamed. She turned away from Renee's gaze.

Maya stepped between them. "Okay, listen, you two," she said. She addressed Renee first. "I get why you ran. It was an impossible predicament. But it was weak and uncool that you never talked to Blue about it."

"Thanks, I'm aware," Renee said.

Maya turned to Blue. "And it's weak that you have defined a person—your best friend—by one moment, because it's easier to hate than to accept someone's different ways of coping and to be powerless to change them. We all fail each other. We fail ourselves."

"Great, so you all agree that I'm weak," Renee said. "Good to know."

"At least you're just weak. I'm weak *and* ugly," Blue said.

"Oh, for God's sake," Maya said, throwing her hands up.

"Wait," Renee said to Blue. "You know it's not true—what he said. You know you're not ugly, right?"

Blue looked at her, then past her, past the streetlights, the restaurant lights, the summer moon. She hated that she believed it. She knew it meant that that scumbag had won. But no matter what she told herself, no matter how much she didn't care what some psychopathic dirtbag thought of her, she couldn't escape the greasy psychic film he'd left on her, the way it made her feel turned inside, like rotten fruit. The way it leaked out and drove people away. "Sometimes I wish he *had* killed me."

"Blue!"

"I don't even know why he didn't."

"Maybe he heard the sirens," Hannah said.

Blue looked up, surprised. She'd actually never considered that before. But that kind of made sense. The sirens are what stopped him from...well...everything. The sirens that were there because Renee had run to a neighbor's and they'd called 911. She felt something shift, a piece of missing information altering the narrative. It changed things. Not a lot. But a little. Still. "If it wasn't true, what he said, I wouldn't be alone."

She sat down on the curb, the weight of that thought too heavy to bear. "It isn't fair," she said to Renee. "You have it all and I'm still back there. Alone and scared. I lost my best friend. I lost everything. And now, on top of that, I ruined my one chance with Jack."

It was too much. Too much.

Renee sat down beside her. "Listen to me. Look at me. I need you to hear this. I'm so sorry. I'm so, so sorry I hurt you. It's the last thing I ever wanted to do. I have missed you every single day for the last twelve years. And hey, if it makes you feel any better, my life's actually not that great either. If you want to know the truth, I didn't get pregnant on purpose. And as for my 'perfect relationship,' I think Darrin is cheating on me." She swallowed. "I haven't been able to admit that out loud until now."

"Wait, what?" Maya said.

Renee laughed, an almost hysterical yelp. "Yep. With the neighbor! I found texts. And my first husband cheated on me too. Two days after our wedding. And I still stayed. He was the one who left me. And you know what? Deep down I think I deserve it. Or at the very least expect it. Because...who could love me? I mean, I don't even know who 'me' is. Like, what are they even loving in the first place? And whatever, so what. I'm not asking you to feel sorry for me. I'm just saying..."

Blue stared at her. They all did.

"I didn't know that," Blue said. "Obviously."

"That bastard," Maya added. She sat down beside them and sighed. "Since we're playing whose life is worse, I'm losing my house because I sort of forgot to pay the property taxes and I can't get a loan because I've blown my credit so bad, and on top of that, I don't feel like I have you guys either."

"Wait. What?" Blue said.

Maya squeezed her eyes shut against whatever Blue was going to say next.

"I'm going to kill you," Blue said.

"Please do," Maya said. "And just to be clear, I know you're not going to give me a loan, so don't worry, I'm not asking."

They all turned to Hannah.

"I feel pretty good," she said.

HANNAH

A damp mist was settling over the night, wisps of fog slipping off the bay like souls. Cars pulled in and out of the lot, passing treacherously close to them.

"Let's go home," Hannah said. "We can talk about it all tomorrow."

Blue flicked her lighter on and off. "I don't feel so hot," she said. "I might've had one too many."

"I know that feeling," Maya said. "Only with Cheetos."

Hannah watched Blue take a last hopeful glance at the restaurant as if Jack might return, saw a dark, sober anguish flash across her face. *Poor Blue*, she thought. *Regret is such a tireless wound.*

"You okay?" Hannah said. "Maybe tomorrow you could send him a text. I bet he'd understand if you apologized."

"Maybe," Blue said, though Hannah could tell she didn't mean it.

They climbed into the car and Maya pulled out of the lot.

The fog was so thick now, rising smoky from the street like the exhale of a winter breath. They pulled over twice to let Blue puke and eventually rolled up to the house and filed out. Blue went straight upstairs and was passed out within minutes. Hannah put an empty bucket on the floor beside Blue's bed, a glass of water on her nightstand. As the others got ready for sleep, she lingered in the darkness of Blue's room.

She wanted to say something about fear and regret. About forgiving yourself for making mistakes born of trauma. About how the more broken you'd been, the more things you were likely to break, like a computer rewired to self-destruction. She wanted to tell Blue it only made it worse to turn on yourself about it, to be without self-compassion. But what were words? She knew they would never reach the place where it mattered. She pulled the blanket over the now snoring Blue. "You went," she whispered. "Remember that. At least you went to see him. And that was very brave." She nodded to herself. Knew that even if Blue could hear her, it wouldn't comfort her, that she wouldn't be able to see this night as anything but a catastrophe. It was always easier to see small successes when they belonged to someone else.

Hannah moved back into the room she shared with Maya, climbed under the covers and stared into the swell of darkness. She wondered what it would be like to go on a date again, if it was as daunting as it seemed. Not that she'd ever go on one. She just wondered.

In the morning she heard Blue tiptoe in and then bang her knee on the edge of the bed. "Ow!" Blue hissed.

Hannah sat up.

"Sorry!" Blue said. "I was just seeing if you were awake." Her shoulders were drooped, her expression like a basset hound. "I'm so humiliated."

Maya stirred, sat up yawning. "What time is it?" She looked between Hannah and Blue.

"I'm having flashbacks of what an asshole I was to Jack," Blue groaned.

"Hey now," Maya said. "Some girls play hard to get. You were playing hard to like. It's just a twist."

Hannah and Blue stared at her.

"I'm just saying maybe he likes the challenge," Maya said. "Sheesh."

"I think I'm going to throw up again," Blue said suddenly, sprinting out of the room.

A moment later there was banging on the bathroom door. "Renee," Blue said. "Open up, I'm gonna hurl." A pause. "Are you puking in there?"

Hannah and Maya exchanged a look. They heard the thunder of feet down the stairs, the front door flinging open, Blue running out. The guttural bleat of retching coming from both inside the house and outside it.

"Is Blue...in the driveway?" Hannah asked.

"I don't know, maybe the front lawn?" Maya said.

They listened more closely.

"Driveway," Maya said. "You can hear it hitting the pebbles." Hannah gagged.

From the bathroom, a loud retch from Renee.

Maya turned to Hannah. "This reminds me of that time we ate that bad chicken and—"

"We don't need to talk about that."

Renee emerged from the bathroom and appeared in the

doorway looking pale. "Pregnancy," she said. "All of the hang-
over, none of the booze."

Hannah patted the bed and Renee sat.

"So…" Maya said.

"So…" Renee said.

"You really are pregnant," Hannah said.

"It would seem so," Renee said with a sigh. Her eyes were
glassy from vomiting or sadness or both.

"And that asshole is cheating on you," Maya said. "I could've
told you all Darrins are dirtbags."

"You said they're all good in bed," Hannah pointed out.

"From all the cheating," Maya said as if it was obvious.
"Why didn't you tell us?"

Renee shrugged. "Oh, I don't know. I guess I wanted you
guys to think I was…who I wished I was. Surprise! I'm a fail-
ure at everything."

"Him being a cheat has nothing to do with you," Hannah said.

"Part of me knows that," Renee said. "The other part of
me—the part of me that wants to fix it and stay with him, I
guess—is unconvinced. I know that should be a no-brainer
but…nothing ever feels that simple when you love someone.
Pathetic, huh?"

"Very," Maya said.

"Says the girl who's losing her house," Hannah pointed out.

"I like to think of it as giving the house to a bank in need,"
Maya said.

"Hey, what happened to Blue?" Hannah said.

They listened. Silence.

"Blue!" Maya called.

Still nothing.

They got up, went to her last known location in the drive-way. The elderly couple across the way saw them searching and pointed politely to a body in the grass.

The girls approached Blue, who was lying on her back, one arm strung over her eyes. "Who's up for breakfast?" she said, without moving.

"Not you," Hannah said.

"I'm fine."

"You're light green."

"But she was forest green a half hour ago," Maya pointed out. "Also, I have bad news."

Blue squinted up at her.

"We have tickets for the whale watch in an hour."

MAYA

Maya insisted they make a quick stop at the farmers market for breakfast just as they'd done twelve years before. There they browsed the kaleidoscope of shiny fruits picked from nearby fields, sampled the thick loaves of butter-brushed bread and gourmet jellies in homemade jars, ogled the chocolate scones and crumble-crust pies, everything fresh and sweet, the tastes of summer. They made their selections, and Maya coerced Blue into buying her an everything bagel with cream cheese. Then they all sat cross-legged on the grass, people watching amid the bustle of morning traffic in town.

Mostly they were quiet, letting the day wake them slowly, fixed on their coffee and food. Maya noticed Blue holding her fist to her mouth as if she might be sick again.

"Blue, eat something," Maya said.

She held out a piece of her bagel. Blue glanced down.

Suddenly her eyes bulged and her cheeks ballooned like a pufferfish.

"Oh no," Maya said, yanking the bagel away.

Blue's face settled back. "False alarm."

"You're in bad shape, my friend," Maya said, but Blue wasn't listening. She was staring off into the distance, her mind carried elsewhere.

Maya followed her gaze to a quaint old restaurant across the street with a for-sale sign on the front.

"I used to love that place," Blue said wistfully. "Best fried shrimp ever. And Nana always let me order two desserts. Can't believe they're selling it. The hipsters will probably turn it into a bowling alley."

"Or something French and overpriced," Hannah said as she peeled a banana and took a bite.

"Or a fedora shop," Renee said.

"The freaking fedoras," Maya said. "What is with that?"

"Literally no one looks good in a fedora," Renee said.

"I mean, I do," Maya said. "But I get your point."

"What they should really do is turn it into a bar," Blue said. "There're no good divey bars in town." As soon as she said it, she gagged again.

"Maybe not a good time to be thinking about alcohol," Maya said. "What time is it?" She grabbed Renee's wrist to check her watch. "Crap! We gotta go."

They gathered their trash, fled back to the car. Blue trailed them, one arm covering her eyes, the other outstretched to ward off the sun. "I'm going to die," she moaned repeatedly to no one in particular.

Maya took Old West Lake Drive to the docks, passing the

sleepy bay, the wind soft through the open windows, the morning light wan and tired as a mother before coffee.

"Look," she said as they passed Surf Lodge. "Scene of the crime."

"Ugh," Blue said, without looking. "Kill me."

Maya and Hannah exchanged pitying glances in the rear-view mirror.

"I have aspirin if you need it," Hannah said, rifling through her purse and showing Blue the bottle.

"Got anything for self-loathing?" Blue asked.

Hannah seemed to consider this, handed her a pastry.

The air changed as they neared the docks, salt thickened and fishy. They passed the bait and tackle shops, the dilapidated restaurant where old local fishermen hunched over the dark bar to day drink.

Maya parked in the lot and then they dashed toward the boats, their beach bags bouncing, their flip-flops nipping at their heels.

"Too much running!" Blue groaned as she pulled up the rear.

Soon the old wooden planks were underfoot, the bay sloshing and slurping beneath them, the squawk and glide of seagulls overhead.

Just ahead of Maya, Hannah stopped abruptly to gape at an enormous, lifelike great white shark hanging by the entrance, its jaws open, mouth painted blood red. "Uh…"

"Cool!" Maya said, dragging Hannah along before she could have second thoughts. "I hope we see a live one today. Look! There she is!" She pointed at an old white boat with aqua trim bobbing and creaking against the timbers, the words *Viking Star* painted across the cabin. It was already loaded with tourists in beach gear and binoculars, a scrawny teenage deckhand untying the line from the docks.

"Wait!" Maya called to him just as they reached the boat.

He paused, held out his palm, eyed them impatiently. "Tickets," he said.

Hannah bit her lip, looked nervously out at the water. "Is it safe?" she asked.

"Put it this way," he said. "If you were actively trying to die, whale watching probably wouldn't be an efficient way to do that."

Maya laughed. "I like you. Are you single?"

He raised an eyebrow.

"He's twelve, Maya," Renee said as she handed him her ticket.

"Seventeen," he corrected her indignantly.

"I can't personally think of a more efficient way to die today than whale watching," Blue said, shuffling up behind them, her face scrunched with misery. "Bury me at sea, please."

"It would be an act of compassion," Maya said to the deckhand. She turned to Blue. "I'm not convinced you're not already dead. I've seriously never seen anyone that color before. Your face is like a mood ring the way you go from green to gray."

"What mood is this?" Blue said, holding up her middle finger.

Renee laughed, looked sympathetically at Blue. "You sure you want to go? It's only a four-hour wait in the car."

Blue gave a thumbs-up. Continued her slow death march onto the boat.

Suddenly Maya felt a tap on her shoulder. She turned.

"Looking for me?" he said.

It took a second for her brain to catch up to the skip in her heart. "Holy shit. Andy!"

The night came back to her in a rush—her chest pressed

against his strong back as they rode on his motorcycle, the two of them lying side by side beneath a ceiling of stars, tumbling together into the swimming pool—that blissful, scary suspension of the fall. The way his kiss felt a little bit like love.

A small, feathery spin in her stomach. And with it, surprisingly, a swell of relief. Like a wrong had been righted, an unnatural separation fixed.

"What are you doing here?" She was nervous. Which she never was. She ran her hand self-consciously through her hair, remembered she hadn't combed it before she left.

"I work here," he said. He stepped up to her, just close enough into her space that she could feel the way he towered over her. She looked into his eyes, acutely aware of her body's desire to breach the inches between them. "I was hoping you knew that and came looking for me."

"We're looking for whales, actually," she said.

But he was staring at her and she was staring at him and it seemed like words were in the way and neither of them were really listening.

Crap, she really liked him.

He leaned in closer. "I thought I'd never see you again."

"You would have missed me," she said.

"I already did."

She smiled, looked away.

"Guess this means fate has decided," he said.

"Could be coincidence," she said with a shrug.

"Hey, lady," the deckhand called. "You in or out?"

Andy arched an eyebrow. "Good question," he said. "You in or you out?"

She smiled, called to the deckhand, her eyes still on Andy. "In," she said.

Andy grinned. Time stopped. Just for a minute.

"You should probably give me your number," he said.

"We're leaving in the morning."

"You'll be back."

She laughed at his confidence. "Give me your phone."

She put her number in.

"Okay, then," she said.

"Okay, then," he said.

They gazed at each other for one more lingering moment and then she hopped onto the *Viking Star* and blew him a kiss.

She joined her friends at the stern as Andy stood watching. The deckhand threw the coil of ropes onto the dock and the boat rocked and bounced off the old tires on the pilings. Hannah grabbed Maya's hand nervously and squeezed.

There was a sudden swirl of white water as the motor purred, growing into a frothing wake. The diesel engines hummed, low at first as the boat moved slowly from the dock and then changing pitch as the captain hit the throttle. The horn blew as they slid into open water, the white sun flashing on the ocean. The wind picked up as the shore receded, Andy on the docks growing smaller, waving one last time before walking away. Something in Maya's chest fizzed, reached back to him like the boat's wake.

They moved starboard, their faces pitched toward the sea. Hannah took a deep breath, let go of Maya's hand.

"You all right?" Maya said.

Hannah clutched the rails. "Trying to tell myself this is fun," she said. "Like falling down the ski hill stoned. What about you? You're looking a little flush." She laughed at her own teasing, her hair whipping across her face as the boat picked up more speed.

Maya scoffed, tried to make her smile smaller. It seemed so embarrassingly big.

"You always get the guy," Blue said, staring queasily into the water. "It would probably make me sick but—" she paused as the boat heaved over a small swell, looked like she might retch into the ocean "—I already am."

"Please," Maya said. "I never *want* the guy. I'm a free bird, baby." But she didn't feel free. She felt the tug of longing, of Andy back on the docks, pulling her into port. She was surprised by how nice it was. How much it caught her off guard, introduced her to a part of herself she didn't know was in there.

"I remember that feeling," Hannah said, reading her thoughts.

Their eyes met. Hannah smiled lovingly, but Maya could see the sadness.

She wanted to say something, to apologize, to take back everything that had just happened with Andy so Hannah wouldn't have to see it, be reminded of what she'd lost.

"I'm gonna hurl," Blue said suddenly. She ran off the deck, pushing sightseers out of the way with such force that Maya pictured them being thrust overboard in her wake.

The other three looked at one another.

"I'll go," Renee said.

"Guess we won't be seeing her again this trip," Maya said as she watched Blue disappear down the stairs, Renee at her heels.

She turned back to see Hannah headed toward the ship's bow in her big sun hat and glasses. She seemed determined, white-knuckling the rails as she went, passing a mother and her toddler feeding bread crumbs to the seagulls. The birds glided along at the boat's pace, dive-bombing to snatch the crust out of the kid's hand as he squealed in fearful delight.

Maya watched Hannah reach the front, square herself against the expanse of ocean as if issuing a challenge. She saw her lift her face to the sun as she held her hat. There was something so poignant and solitary and heroic about her in that moment. At this distance Maya could see the whole of her—how the bubbly feeling inside Maya once belonged to Hannah: romance, innocence, hope, all taken in an instant. Hannah turned as if she could sense Maya watching her. She smiled and waved. *Look at me!* she seemed to say. *I'm doing it!* Maya smiled back, felt a pang. She forced herself to forget about Andy, put him away. She had to.

She joined Hannah at the bow.

"It's so pretty out here," Hannah said.

The salty wind pattered their faces, the boat cutting across the sparkling water like scissors on a cloth.

"When I saw you before with Andy," Hannah said, "it reminded me of how good life can be. Like, not just pleasant or fun but that really euphoric good, you know? That juicy…" She reached out her hands as if trying to grab at something. "I don't know…center of it all." She laughed. "What am I trying to say? I'm babbling. Just maybe that I'd forgotten that."

Maya stared out over the ocean. She didn't know how to respond. It didn't feel right that she got to have the juicy part.

"I thought I was protecting myself. Being so conscious of all the bad things that could happen," Hannah said. "But I'm beginning to think that anxious voice in my head isn't even mine. It's those men. It's like they're everywhere, around every corner in my brain, dangling a new fear, saying, 'We're out there. We're going to get you again.'"

Maya turned. She could feel Hannah's eyes behind her sunglasses, searching her face.

Hannah gave her a small smile, looked out on the water, let go of the rails. "I know I shouldn't be talking about it. That we don't talk about it. It's just... I've been waiting for them to go away. I think I secretly hoped that if I just came here, if I...stepped out of my comfort zone, they would stop. But I get now that they're not going to. I just have to know what they are, live over them, in defiance of them. Be brave, I guess."

The boat lifted over a wave and Hannah squealed and reached out desperately to clutch the rails again, which made them both laugh.

Maya wondered if she herself had ever been brave. She always thought she was, but then, life never felt as hard for her. She glanced back at the dock but it had slipped out of sight, only open sea in every direction. She imagined Andy standing exactly where she'd left him, waiting for her return. *It wouldn't work anyway*, she thought. *Long distance relationships never do.*

Renee found them at the bow. "Blue's begging everyone who walks by to throw her overboard," she said.

"That'll teach her not to binge drink," Maya said.

"I think that's only half of what's making her sick," Renee said. They all got quiet.

"Well," Renee said. "See any whales?"

"Not yet," Maya said. "I want to see a blue whale. Those are the biggest, right?"

"Biggest animal to have ever lived on earth. Their tongues alone can weigh as much as an elephant."

"Ooh la la," Maya said.

"Ew," Hannah said.

"Seconded," Renee said.

Maya scanned the horizon.

Around them, tourists had their binoculars out as the captain came over the loudspeaker reciting all that they might see as if he'd given the same speech three times a day for thirty years and just wanted to move to Colorado and never see a whale again. The girls' excitement grew upon hearing the possibility of seeing dolphins leaping in the boat's wake, leatherback sea turtles dining on jellyfish, packs of seals with their doglike faces, poking their slick gray heads out of the water. And of course, the whales: minkes and humpbacks, pilots and sperm—the last making them laugh like prepubescent girls.

They stood watch, waiting, ready. The anticipation nurtured their excitement as they scanned the waterline. The boat chugged on. Hannah went below to check on Blue, returned twenty minutes later with drinks and a grim report. They ate fruit from the farmers market and drank their colas and Hannah read Dear Miss Know-It-All questions off her phone and recruited answers from Maya and Renee.

"Okay, here's a good one. Should Anonymous pursue her dream job in LA or stay with dream guy in Chicago?"

"Dream job," Renee said.

"Dream guy," Maya said.

Hannah and Renee looked at Maya in surprise.

"Who knew you were such a romantic?" Hannah said.

"I'm not," Maya said. "I just hate work. Next question."

"Dana from Oregon wants to know when it's the right time to have sex with a new guy."

"As if there's a wrong time," Maya said.

"Whenever you actually *want* to," Renee said.

"After he's been tested for STIs," Hannah said, making a note in her cell phone.

The sun rose higher. The salt started to sting against their

sunburns. Soon the beauty of the world they were gazing upon
became monotonous. Flat and blue.

"Dear Miss Know-It-All, where the hell are the whales?"
Maya said, getting restless.

People began looking at their phones, retreating to the bar
below. The kids on board were getting cranky, the energy
turning bleak.

"Come on, whale!" Maya whispered to the ocean. Just one.
Even a fin. She would be satisfied with a glimpse. She felt the
pain of wanting. The urge to shut it down and accept that she
would not get to have it.

Time stalled, the sun turning sharp and hard and relentless,
stealing color, casting a layer of white over everything. Another hour passed. They ate more food, wandered the deck,
blinked out at the unchanging landscape.

Hannah picked at the chipping paint on the rails with her
fingernail. "Don't think we're going to see any today," she said.

"Don't say that," Maya said.

Renee sighed.

Blue reappeared. "Any—" She retched. "Any whales?"

The three of them shook their heads.

"Of course not," Blue said. "Story of my life."

"Oh, stop," Maya said.

"Nothing to see for miles and miles in any direction," Blue
continued.

Maya shook her head, sighed. But as she looked at her
friends, thought of their lives over the last twelve years,
thought of her own meandering future, she understood what
Blue was saying—the way monotony could seep into adulthood. No one had ever warned her about that.

The captain came over the loudspeaker. "Well, folks," he

said, "I'm sorry to say the whales have eluded us today. We'll be heading back now."

"Shoot," Hannah said. "We didn't even get to see a freaking dolphin."

"Let's sit down," Maya said. Her face burned and her eyes felt gritty with salt. She headed toward the benches. Tedium and disappointment—she couldn't think of enemies greater than those. She thought of Andy. *If only he lived closer.* But even then, an internal resistance, something in the way. She closed her eyes.

Almost as soon as she shut them, a collective gasp from the boat.

"Maya, look," Hannah shouted.

Maya jumped to her feet, turned just in time.

Euphoric eruption! Life bursting from below into the air. Its fins outstretched like wings. Its grooved white belly arced toward the sun. *I live!* it seemed to shout at them with its enormity, its acrobatic grace. *We live!* It paused, midair, suspending time for a moment. Its skin oil-slick and gleaming. Water raining off its barnacle-covered flanks. Then with a thunderous splash, it landed back on the ocean's top, slapped the surface playful as a child, carbonating the white water. A show just for them, a circus act at sea. The passengers cheered, electric with awe, witness to some impossible majestic beauty, some seemingly fabled creature of an underwater universe. A magical communion between life forms. *Oh glorious, mysterious, nonsensical world.*

Maya's heart buoyed in her chest.

"Boom!" she said. "Just when you least expect it. When you think you know how it will all turn out." She turned to Blue. "Story of everyone's life."

BLUE

Blue watched as the water stilled, the whale slipping back into the deep like a dream quickly forgotten. Around her the mood on the boat had changed. Seagulls gathered and gossiped like old ladies, frantic with excitement over the humpback's visit. The passengers became at once celebratory and serene, as after a birth. The boat steered toward the docks, everyone chatting about what they'd seen. Some guests disappeared below, switching from colas to cocktails at the bar, before reappearing on the deck.

"I gotta admit," Blue said, "that was pretty spectacular. Almost worth all the puking."

"I knew we'd see one," Maya said. "I never lost faith."

"Did anyone get any pictures?" Renee asked.

Blue shook her head regretfully.

"I didn't even think to," Hannah said.

"That sucks," Maya said. "If only there was some genius who remembered to… Oh wait! There is." She held up her phone, grinning.

"Oh, yay!" Hannah said.

They all gathered around Maya's phone.

"Make sure you text me all the good ones," Blue said.

They looked on eagerly as Maya began to scroll and scroll, picture after picture.

Their smiles faltered.

"I don't understand," Renee said.

Maya reached the last photo, looked up. "They're all of Hannah's hat. That damn thing is bigger than the whale."

Blue looked closer and, sure enough, every picture was of Hannah's yellow brim plus a slice of blue ocean and a tiny splash of white water beyond it.

"Wait," Blue said. "Is that the tail?"

"Yes, I think…" Maya peered closer. "Nope, that's her ribbon."

Hannah made a hangdog face. "Sorry."

They all shook their heads, returned to the bench.

"We still love you," Maya said. "Just a tiny bit less."

Blue leaned back, stretched out her legs. Her nausea had subsided just enough that she had resumed replaying every dumb thing she'd done the night before. Each recollection was worse than the last—the drunken spill of water, the look in his eyes, all the stupid things she said. She wanted to find a small closet in herself, safe from memory and self-recrimination, step inside it, shut the door.

In front of her a sleepy toddler eyed her warily from over his mother's shoulder. *Who are you to judge me?* she thought, staring back. *Things are easy now, but just you wait, it's all downhill from here.* He shoved a biscuit into his mouth with his chocolate-stained fist and glared at her. *Yeah, that's right, teethe on that, little man.* She had reached a new low. She was having silent wars with two-year-olds now.

"I don't want to go back," Renee said. "Can we just stay on this boat forever?"

"Why not?" Maya said. "Can't get much more adrift than I already am."

"Try getting pregnant," Renee said. "With a cheating fiancé."

"You win," Maya said.

"On the plus side, I haven't thought of Darrin in like five hours."

"Who?" Maya said.

"Exactly," Renee said, and they laughed.

Blue closed her eyes for a moment, the night before looping in her brain. She thought of that moment of elation when she'd received the message from Jack last week, of the lacey underwear she'd packed so optimistically in her suitcase. Of how hope could turn so swiftly on her. A flash flood of despair. She blinked it away, thought she might be sick again. "You guys," she said. The ocean was wrinkled with wind now. In the glint of sunlight, it looked like crumpled tinfoil. Meringue-like peaks of white water formed and scattered. A light mist was dampening her outstretched legs. "What if Jack was like that whale?" She wasn't asking in the hopes of an answer. She didn't know what she was hoping for.

"What does that even mean?" Maya said.

Blue examined her feet in their flip-flops. If she looked at Maya directly, she might cry. Grief gnawed at her, carnivorous, insatiable. It seemed both about Jack and utterly separate, a false corollary.

"You wait and wait and wait for good things to come

along. The really big things—love, the perfect job, some great victory—but what if one of those things shows up and you just…blow it?"

"Oh, Blue," Hannah said.

"First person who says 'there's more fish in the sea' gets thrown overboard, by the way," Blue said to cut the seriousness.

Renee sighed, twisted her engagement ring nervously. "You should text him."

"No way," Blue said.

"He's not your one big thing," Maya said. "He's just a guy. Who you've attached too much meaning to."

"What's the saying?" Hannah said. "Don't confuse a lesson for a soul mate."

"So what's the lesson, then?" Blue said. "And how do you know the difference?" She looked into their blank faces. "And why the hell doesn't anyone ever have the answers to anything that matters?"

"Technically Hannah gets paid to have the answers," Maya said.

Blue arched an eyebrow at Hannah. "Do I need to send you an email or do you dispense advice on the fly?"

"Please," Hannah said. "You're looking at a girl who sought answers from a carnival psychic."

Blue sighed, regret weighing on every inhale. If only she could have a do-over.

"If it makes you feel better, I think every guy is my whale," Renee said. "It doesn't even occur to me to wonder if I actually like them. It's just, you know, here's *somebody*. I bet a lot of people miss out on the right person by thinking that way. Because, God, who has that much patience to wait? That much faith?"

"Maybe," Blue said. But it didn't make her feel any better.

They all got quiet.

In front of them, the woman with the toddler was now wiping his chocolate-covered hands with a napkin from her bag. Blue noticed Renee watching them.

"I'm going to raise this kid without a father," Renee said slowly, as if that reality was only now settling in. "Just like my mother. Literally a repeat. Why can't we ever get away from our past?"

"I don't know," Blue said, wondering the same.

"I'll end up screwing this kid up for life."

"No, you won't," Hannah said.

"Please," Renee said. "Look at me. I run from conflict. I panic in an emergency. I make dumb choices..."

"All true," Maya said calmly, then seemed to notice them gaping at her. "What? It is. Not the part about being like her mother, obviously, but I mean, of course she's going to screw the kid up." She uncapped her water bottle and took a long, slow sip, unfazed by the continuing looks they were all giving her. "Everyone screws their kid up. It's a fact of life. Fortunately there will be other screwed-up kids. Like we were. Who Renee's screwed-up kid can be screwed-up friends with. And they'll have good times and bad times. And the cycle continues."

"But I don't want to screw anyone up," Renee said.

"Then don't be a mother," Maya said.

"Anyway, I thought we were talking about me and *my* mistakes," Blue said.

"Actually, we were talking about me first and then you interrupted," Renee said.

"Enough about anyone's mistakes!" Maya said. She jumped to her feet, startling all three of them. "Seriously, look where we are." She thrust her arms wide.

Behind her the horizon was slowly resolving back into slender white beaches and bursts of plush, tree-lined coast, the sun on its slow dip to the west.

"I wonder if we can see Nana's house from here," Hannah said.

They all moved to the rails, squinted toward the shore.

"Is that...Blue's dignity floating over there?" Maya asked. "Oh, never mind, it's just a buoy."

Blue whacked her on the shoulder.

"Let's take a picture," Hannah said.

"Okay," Maya said, "everyone move closer. Hannah, take off the hat."

Blue and the others smooshed in beside Maya, and Maya flipped the phone camera so they could see themselves in it. Immediately Blue looked away, unable to bear her own image. It was impossible not to imagine how differently this day would have gone if she'd handled herself better the night before. Maybe Jack would even be with them on the boat. Or she'd be meeting him afterward for a walk on the beach, holding hands by the shoreline as the afternoon lowered behind the cliffs. If only she could have at least kissed him. Just once. Just to know again, just to remember that sweet, blissful aliveness. She would've been okay with that. One kiss.

"Okay everyone, smile," Maya said.

Blue forced a smile over the ache. After all, she was with her best friends, her first responders. And if life was going to hurt, then at least there was this, there was sunshine, there was love. She looked at Maya with her disarming smile and warm eyes, at Hannah with her big sunglasses and red curls, at Renee leaning tentatively in beside her. Couldn't it be enough that she had this? Why did the heart always want more?

HANNAH

It was half past five as they left the docks, the hour turned golden and baked to softness. Hannah was drowsy, her body relaxed in a way it usually was not, like she was stoned on so much sunlight.

"Anyone up for a late-day swim?" Maya asked.

"I might be up for that," Hannah said.

Their eyes caught in the rearview and she saw the surprise and delight in Maya's face, and it made her want to do that more often, say yes.

The parking lot was in transition, the all-day surfers strapping their boards to their cars, unhurried and happy, the postwork evening shift pulling up in their trucks and Jeeps, jumping out to check the waves.

Hannah approached the sand, the Ditch Witch closed for the day, the old wooden bench beside it empty, the seagrass waving in the onshore breeze. The lifeguards had retired. Only a scattering of families remained, a scrappy wet terrier chasing a stick, a girl packing up the tie-dyed shirts she'd been hawking out of her beach bag. Hannah watched two kids running toward the water with their bright boogie boards. It made her wistful to think of how their lives would be filled with many things, love and heartbreak, loss and joy, laughter and regret. This, she understood now, was all that could be predicted. It could be predicted of every life. Every one.

The sun was tiring now, creating a deeper blue to the ocean, a September-like chill blowing onshore. The air smelled slightly turned, a hint of rot in the sea. A reminder that everything ended. She saw a flash of herself returning to her apartment. Saw her life close and lock. She shivered. Remembered Maya talking about choices.

"Can't believe we have to leave tomorrow," Renee said.

"Let's just stay," Maya said as she and Blue joined them. "What's another day or ten? I hear the weather will be beautiful."

"Say the word and I'll cancel work," Blue said.

Hannah would love to stay on but of course she thought of Henry. Even a few more days would feel like an indulgence. Instinctively she glanced at her phone. Saw a missed call from Vivian. Her nervous heart flinched.

"Last one in buys dinner," Maya shouted, throwing off her cover-up. She turned and looked at Hannah and her face changed. "What?"

Hannah shook her head, hit Return Call and began pacing. Something was wrong. She could feel it. Dread rising, pouring in. She could sink to her knees, be swallowed by life like it was quicksand. She swore it could happen.

Vivian's phone went to voice mail. Hannah was panicking now, in need of her Xanax, in need of Vivian to answer the damn phone.

She called again as the girls stood silently watching.

"Hello?" Vivian finally answered.

Hannah headed toward the ocean. Her instincts drove her there, to its monotonous, heaving efforts, its break and rebuild. *It goes on*, she remembered someone once saying about life. *It goes on*. She took a breath in order to brace against a moment that might rob her will to do so.

"Hannah," Vivian said.

It was in the way Vivian said her name that Hannah knew for sure the news was bad, and there was a shock in this even as she'd anticipated it. She gripped a rock on the jetty, lowering herself onto it, her body heavy and arthritic with impending sorrow, with resistance to it. She squeezed her eyes shut, trying to block out what was coming.

"I'm so sorry to interrupt your vacation again," Vivian said.

Shrieking erupted out of two small children chasing each other in the sand, an absentminded mother beside them gazing past the sea to something beyond it.

"What is it?" she heard herself say. She was suddenly two Hannahs at once, the Hannah living this moment and the Hannah observing herself in it, aware that something enormous, dark, nuclear was about to crash into her life, drastically change it, change her, that nothing would be the same after. Oh, it was so awful—that awareness—watching your heart lunge for hope, that last desperate clutch on the life you knew.

She looked at the children, wanted them to have their innocence and joy for as long as possible.

"There was an accident."

It was as if all of her systems stopped at once. Heartbeat, lungs, thoughts. The terrible purgatorial pause.

"An aide was moving Henry into his chair and I guess he lost his grip on him and he fell. They took him to the ER. They ran tests. There was a minor brain bleed, which is why I called you the other night. I assumed it would resolve. But there continues to be some swelling on the brain. On his breathing center." Vivian paused. "He's on a ventilator now."

The world seemed to dilate around her. Too big, too loud, too much. And she too small to hold so much sorrow. But just as quickly, hope leaked in. "Okay...that's not good. Obviously. But he's still okay, right?"

He had been on a ventilator once before. He still had the trach scar.

Eventually they had gotten him off. He'd been okay.

Silence on the other end of the line.

Tears sprang. "They can treat it, right? I mean, even if he has to stay on the machine for a while?"

Hannah's throat constricted.

She heard a sigh. "I had a long talk with the doctors again today," Vivian said. "Hannah, I think we need to consider whether..."

Hannah braced. "Whether what?"

"We've held out hope for so long," Vivian said finally. "He wouldn't want this. For him or for us."

"What are you saying? No—you can't."

"Please consider—"

"There's nothing to consider! Vivian, please!" People on the beach were looking at her. She didn't care. "You're not thinking straight."

"I think it might be time to come home," Vivian said. "It

would be good for you to see him. And then we can talk about it in person. And you can talk to the doctors. I'm really sorry. I didn't want to disrupt your trip."

"I'll be there in..." She tried to remember how much time the drive to DC took, but her brain was shutting down. "Like five or six hours. Please, I beg you, don't make any decisions without me."

She hung up, returned to her friends, aware only of the dissonant joy all around her, of carrying her body in a new way, like an overfull glass. The sky brightened and sparked, jarring and surreal in its absolute separateness from her. Tears pushed. She shoved them back. No time. She would drive there; she would stop this.

Maya held her arms out when she saw her.

Hannah thought she might collapse, that her bones would not hold her anymore.

"We need to go. Right now."

They stopped at the house, packed quickly and silently, shoved their bags into the trunk. If they left anything behind, Blue could have it sent.

"I'm driving," Hannah said. She did not wait for their response, though she felt their surprise. She didn't bother to address it. She just knew she needed to be in control of something.

Maya handed her the keys.

Hannah got in, put her hands on the wheel, reoriented herself to the driver's seat. She heard the sound of three seat belts clicking as she backed out and onto the road. She felt no apprehension in driving—only necessity—as if her fear had always been one of speeding into the inevitability of this moment when tragedy would strike again. And now that it was here, her mind was so preoccupied with trying to survive it that her body became a separate automatic animal, quietly taking over all functioning without thought.

Almost immediately they hit traffic, vacationers leaving the beach, and all at once she was slamming her palms down on the wheel. "Come on, come *on*." Lying on the horn at cars that were just as helplessly stalled as she. Honking at the unfairness of everything, at the cruel randomness of the world.

"It's okay," Maya said. "We'll get there."

"I never should have left him," Hannah said.

"You didn't cause this," Maya said.

"They've never dropped him when I was there." She slammed the horn again. "Go, dammit!" To Maya she said, "Don't try to make this better for me."

She slipped into herself as if behind a door, trying to manage feelings too big to share. She couldn't bear to sit in the uncertainty again, this most violent of places.

At last the traffic eased slightly, just enough. Soon they'd be off Route 27, and she could press down on the pedal, make the minutes fly. There was no caution in this car today. No frightened Hannah. Only determined, only racing, only *please, please, please.*

MAYA

Maya watched as they sped through the streets that had carried them here, framed in the last tangy light of sunset. The fruit stands on Montauk Highway were already closed and boarded for the day. The sky ahead was turning dim and gray as the road, as if evening were a city they'd soon be passing through. In her mind she kept going over everything she'd packed, unable to shake the nagging feeling that she'd left behind something important. *What was it?*

She wanted to turn on the radio, the silence too loud, Hannah's desperation radiating off her like a nuclear spill and nothing Maya could do about it. Never before had she been so aware of love's limitations—how it could soothe but not save, help but not fix. How some sadnesses were so big they came with a moat around them, stranded a person in their grief. She was right beside her best friend and utterly helpless to stop her pain. How did anyone accept love's false promise—an end to aloneness? How to forgive people for that? And how to be forgiven in return?

They merged onto the Sunrise Highway, where the traffic was lighter. Maya watched the speedometer rise as Hannah pressed down on the gas. *Slow down a little,* she thought. *We're going too fast.* But it wasn't even Hannah she wanted to say it to.

She glanced at Blue and Renee, their faces tight and worried.

Would it be so bad? she wondered. *To let Henry go. Wasn't he just a body now?*

And yet the thought of just losing her house was so gutting, to say goodbye forever to a place that held her memories, provided security and comfort. And what was a body if not that? What was a body if not love made tangible by borders so that it could be recognized and touched, provide refuge, contain history inside it? Without Henry, Hannah would be homeless, totally and utterly. The thought made her swallow on something sharp.

Hannah's phone pinged. Maya reached for it, read the text from Vivian out loud so Hannah could keep her eyes on the road.

"Still stable," she said. She watched as Hannah breathed with relief. There was time.

The hours stretched long and tedious, the usual landmarks startling and strange somehow, at once familiar and foreign, the way a place sometimes looks when it is intensely the same but you are not. Hour after hour they drove and life passed and something inside Maya grew and grew.

Off the highway now and winding through the streets of DC until she saw the lights of the hospital, the white slab of it stretching for half a block. She remembered so vividly those long nights in the waiting room, her friends like corpses with coffee cups, haunting hallways and sleeping in chairs. The presence of death everywhere.

Hannah pulled in to the lot. "Okay," she said. She took a deep breath. "We're here."

Maya had a sudden vision of herself running. Away from the hospital. Fast as she could. The black shadow of her tearing across the nearly empty lot. Just like Renee had run from Henry's house, blind, unthinking, desperate. Just like Hannah fleeing into the cocoon of herself in that claustrophobic apartment, clutching her Xanax bottle like it was mace against all the terrors of the universe. Just like Blue working away the hours of her life, letting them pass by unlived, unfelt, without dreams attached. She was desperate to run. It felt like survival.

Instead she climbed out, followed the others inside. Through the glass doors, left at the end of the lobby.

"There's Vivian," Hannah said, and Maya looked down the hall where Vivian was standing by the elevators clutching a coffee cup.

Maya was saddened to see how time and grief had aged her. Vivian had always been a presence with her regal stature and winter-blond hair. Even after that night she'd remained sturdy and in charge as she dealt with doctors and bad news and hope and more doctors. But the ensuing years had left her frail and faded, her hair turned white, a shell-shocked look in her eyes like she couldn't quite grasp where her life had gone, why she couldn't find it.

"I think we should wait in the lobby," she said to Hannah. "So you two can talk."

Hannah nodded, took a deep breath. She seemed to be searching Maya's face for something she needed. Hope, maybe. "Wish me luck," she said.

"Good luck," Maya said softly. If only she knew what that might look like today.

BLUE

The lobby had long been updated since the last time they were here, but to Blue the air still carried the weight of that traumatic night, those weeks of visiting Henry in the ICU, his body barely visible beneath all those tubes and wires, the only sign of life the small tidal rise and fall of his chest. All of that terrible waiting.

"Sometimes I forget how much we went through," Renee said as if reading her thoughts. "I don't know if that's good or bad."

"Good," Maya said.

"Bad," Blue said at the same time.

"Who wants to dwell?" Maya said. "I never want to think about it again. I never want to be *here* again."

"There's a difference between dwelling and remembering why we are the way we are," Blue said.

"How are we?" Maya asked.

"Fucked up," Blue said.

"Speak for yourself," Maya said.

"You can speak for me too," Renee said. "I'm a total mess."

Blue glanced down the hallway. "What do you think they'll decide to do?"

Maya shrugged, shook her head. For all her bravado, Blue noticed a pallor beneath Maya's tan, an unusual tension around her mouth as if the strings had been pulled too tight.

They fell back into silence, the air too heavy for talking.

There was a dull buzz like the sound fluorescent lights make, only it was happening inside Blue, an underlying current of anxiety. The news played on a TV mounted high on the wall, something about a former child star turned drugged-up teenager being arrested for sending an unsolicited nude Snapchat to his Uber driver. In the corner a gray-haired couple held hands as they sat on an upholstered couch and frowned up at the TV.

The walls closed in, as claustrophobic as blindness.

"Be right back," she said. "I'm going to have a smoke."

"That shit will give you cancer," Maya called after her.

Blue hurried down the hall, stepped out into the summer air, into the surprise that the world was still there. Sometimes you could sit in a room that made you forget that it was.

She walked over to a low retaining wall, lit a cigarette, sat down and inhaled deeply.

The night was huge and she felt the black emptiness of the sky as if she had swallowed it.

"Hey."

She turned to see Renee. She looked tired and somehow younger, her makeup almost gone, her hair pulled into a messy ponytail.

"Thought you might want company," Renee said.

Blue remembered Renee's pregnancy, put out her cigarette.

"Oh, thanks," Renee said. "You didn't have to. I can just stand over there."

"No, it's fine. I should quit anyway. Not that I really smoke."

"Right," Renee said as she sat down beside her, the two of them so small inside the night.

In the near distance, a chorus of crickets. Blue pictured a male cricket running one of its wings across the teeth of the other, opening both to create acoustic sails, calling for a mate across the dark titanic night. It seemed at once lonely and beautiful—the need to connect reduced to the level of an insect, the way it never got too small to disappear entirely. Even though Blue sometimes wished that it would.

"So weird that we were on the boat just this morning," Renee said, leaning back. "Seems like forever ago."

Blue nodded. It was as if sorrow was its own country and they'd been rerouted to it, forced to make an emergency landing here. She stared up at the parenthesis of moon, how little light it gave. "When does it stop being so hard?"

Renee sighed. "I don't think it does. I don't know that it's supposed to." She kicked her heels lightly against the wall. "I wish there was, like, a weather report you could get for life. 'Dress warmly, there's going to be a monster storm for the next ten days, but then you'll have sunshine for three straight months.'"

"Seriously."

"But then if I tried to prepare for everything, I'd be Hannah. Never leave the apartment."

"Prepare to be unprepared," Blue said, using finger quotes.

"Or accept maybe."

"So easy to know that, so hard to do it." Blue flicked her lighter mindlessly with her thumb, the flame stoking and dying again and again. The sky seemed deeper and wider and darker than Blue had ever noticed. So infinite and impersonal. She was suddenly acutely aware of her own impermanence, of a world with none of them in it. "Sometimes I think about the fact that, like, right now, at this very second, there's a lion lying in the grass in Africa, or…a…a penguin waddling across the Antarctic ice, or a camel roaming in a desert. It's weirdly comforting that the world is so big. So many creatures, so many lives. Sometimes it's when it feels too small that it's… I don't know…harder, like magnifying or something. I don't know what I'm saying."

A car passed them in the parking lot, its headlights illuminating them for one quick moment and then gone.

"You have to call him, you know," Renee said.

"Jack? And say what? I completely humiliated myself."

"Oh, come on."

"I high-fived the man, Renee."

She tried to make light of it but underneath she was all ragged shame and loss.

"I think you have to at least try to make it right."

"I don't even want to think about that right now," Blue said. "Nothing matters but Hannah and Henry."

"I know," Renee said. "But it will."

They sat without speaking, the city air so still—it never moved in summer in DC.

"Why does any part of you want to stay if Darrin's cheating on you?" Blue asked.

Renee sighed. "Because I'm weak? No, that's not fair. I mean, I think I am, sort of. But also just human. You know, want to save him, want to save myself. All that stuff you can know you shouldn't do and still do. Or maybe you should. I don't know. I'm still trying to figure out where forgiveness fits in."

"It's a tough one," Blue said.

They looked at each other.

"There has to be room for mistakes, you know? The question is how much room, how many mistakes? When is a mistake too big to forgive? I don't know. Sometimes I think we're all too tough on each other. Being a person is *hard*. For everybody. Other times I think the opposite—that we accept behaviors we shouldn't because loneliness sucks."

And sometimes, Blue thought, *we accept loneliness when we shouldn't*. She sat with this for a moment. Then she reconsidered. Maybe that was too simple. Maybe most people just accepted what they could tolerate because it was familiar. She thought about Renee. How she found a guy just like her father. She thought about herself. How she couldn't have anyone, just as she'd never had anyone in her own family. Maybe it was just too frightening to be loved in an unfamiliar way. Maybe most people were stuck their whole lives on the same song, playing over and over, sung by different people. Or by no one at all.

Who the hell knew?

She stood. "We should go back."

Renee nodded and they headed back into the building, found Maya where they'd left her, staring up at the TV.

"What took you so long?" Maya said, though they'd been gone only a few minutes.

Blue was about to answer when she looked down the hall, saw Hannah turn away from Vivian and face them. Even from a distance she could see a deeper strain on her face.

HANNAH

Hannah moved down the white antiseptic corridor toward her friends feeling like a foreigner in her own life, a reluctant tourist to it. She was no longer in her body but somehow above it, watching herself traffic through her experience the way an author might observe a character, with interest and remove and best wishes.

Against the numbness, a sudden piercing longing for Henry. Not hospital Henry but the Henry in the before who would've held her in his arms until she felt contained, squeezed her whole again. The Henry who would have listened to her concerns, helped her know what to do.

What should she do?

Blue, Maya and Renee met her halfway.

"What did she say?" Maya asked.

"She wants me to think about it more," she said. "So I

said I would. Even though I still plan on saying no. Obviously."

"Okay," Maya said.

"They did an MRI and an EEG. There's almost no brain activity at all anymore." The words rubbed at her throat. She saw a jagged sadness in the eyes of her friends, reflecting her own. "I think I'm going to throw up," she said suddenly. "I need water."

She stumbled over to a water fountain in this strange body of hers. Cried as she drank. Tears mixed with the splash. She wiped her mouth, her eyes. Turned to her friends behind her, looking for hope, finding only more sorrow.

"I just need a minute," she said. She had to pull it together before she saw Henry. She was so afraid that he would sense her fear, that she would cause him distress. The doctors would say this was impossible. It worried her anyway.

"Do you want to maybe go to the chapel?" Renee said. "It's quiet. Might be a good place to think."

Hannah nodded, wiped new tears at the fleeting, absurd hope that she could pray this away with magic words. That if God existed, he might somehow...

They located the chapel behind a simple white door, a small wooden sign above it. Hannah hesitated. "I don't believe," she said. "In God. I used to..."

"You don't have to," Renee said. "It can be whatever you need." She opened the door and Hannah entered.

The room was small and dim, quiet as a cave. Rows of benches lined up in strict formation, electric candles cast their muted glow on the walls.

Hannah slid in beside Blue, Maya beside her, Renee on the end. A bubble of silence surrounded them, the room a held breath. The profound stillness evoked in Hannah a primal sense of being supported, if not by a deity, then by a human-kind that understood the need for places like this. Places to contain anguish. Built across thousands of years to carry people through.

Hannah closed her eyes, falling into the deep quiet, letting herself be held by it, tender and raw. She became aware of a dense grief in the room, the reverberation of all the desperate prayers that had been issued from these benches. She listened, tuned to the frequency of universal despair. To her surprise, it felt like love and her chest filled with it. She felt love for all the hurting strangers who had preceded her here, for the humanity that had brought them to their knees. And somehow their love echoed back.

She leaned into the love and the grief. Got down on her own knees, called to do so by her need to surrender to her helplessness—to send an SOS into the void and hope that it would land in the right hands. Her friends kneeled beside her. Their eyes met. They bowed their heads. Maya's shoulder brushed against hers and Hannah edged away to give her space; but a moment later she felt Maya lean into her again and she realized it wasn't a mistake. She leaned back.

Hannah paused, trying to find the words for her prayer. To find an answer to her question. How could she be asked to give up hope? How could anyone know when it was time to do that? To pull the plug on a person? On a life?

She took a breath and in her head she began. *I'm not perfect, but I'm trying. I know I don't deserve any better than anyone else. And I know you have other things, other people, to worry about. Bigger problems. But…* She paused, the thought unbearable.

*Please don't take anything more. Please don't ask me to do this.
I can't. I can't.*

Even as she prayed this, prayed as hard as she could, she
heard a voice in her head just beyond her own. It was Maya's
voice, small, offstage in her mind, telling her that she would
be giving up *a* hope, not *all* hope. Giving up the hope that
Henry would get better, that he would get to have a real life
and that she would get to share that future with him. And in
that moment Hannah understood how she, just like Henry,
had been stuck in a holding area between life and death. How
maybe she'd conflated her aliveness with his. Maybe keeping Henry here was selfish, her way of avoiding that awful
in-between place where one hope had died and another had
not yet been born. Perhaps all this time she'd been keeping
him stuck as well, preventing his passage to somewhere better. *Was there somewhere better? Somewhere they would meet again?*
She knew Renee believed it. And though she was inclined
to disagree, she also knew that her perspective was as limited
as any other creature's, as limited as that of the octopus who
knew nothing of the craggy fisherman above him, nothing of
planes swimming sharklike across the moon at night, of giant
trees whose branches bobbed in a breeze.

She thought now of the Henry she knew when they were
younger, his warm, safe hugs and the way he smelled like
laundry detergent and how he absently stroked her arm when
they were together. The boy who used to put an extra packet
of cream cheese in her bag at the bagel shop when they first
met, who moved her out of the rain to kiss her, who gazed
at her with such soft, loving eyes that she came to see herself
through them. She asked this Henry, the Henry in the before,
what he would have wanted if he knew what was coming.

Twelve years kept alive. How many more would be enough? How long would he ask them to hold on? And she knew the answer clearly. It had already been too long.

No! she thought, a howl in her chest. *Please no.*

She couldn't take it. It was too much. *God help me*, she thought. The primal wail. Her body racking. *I can't. Please God, I can't.* Her pain was a universe, her whole being made only of sorrow.

She felt a hand on each shoulder. Maya on one side, Blue on the other. And she wanted to say, *Please make it stop, please if you love me, please help me.* But she understood that this was what was happening, what had to happen, and no one could change it. She sat up, wiped her cheeks, forced her breath to slow and regulate. "I have to go," she whispered. "I need to see him."

She walked out, moving down the hall as fast as she could. Her grief was giant and unwieldy, like airplane wings careening and crashing into everything she passed. She could almost feel the strangers walking by sensing what it was, stepping out of the way of it.

They took the elevator up to the fourth floor. Buzzed into the ICU. Entered the awful theater of urgency, of patients tubed and wired like aliens in purgatorial rooms, the beeps and sighs of machines, the low murmur of doctors and nurses talking over the terrifying undercurrent of the lottery, of maybe life, maybe death.

Vivian was standing at the nurses' station. She turned and saw them, her shoulders sagging with exhaustion, an almost ancient sadness in her eyes.

Hannah ran to her and Vivian held out her arms, hugged her tight.

"I get it," Hannah said into the cloth of her shirt. "I understand now. We have to let him go."

"Yes," Vivian said, and Hannah could hear the choke in her voice. "Yes, sweet girl, we do."

She stepped back, took Hannah's face in her hands and gave a determined nod, as if summoning courage for them both. Then she held out her hand to the others. "My girls," she said, "I'm so glad you're here." She hugged them all. "I think I'm going to go to the chapel for a bit. Take as long as you need."

But I need forever, Hannah thought.

Together the girls walked to Henry's room.

She looked at Maya, saw the helplessness in her eyes.

"He's still here," Hannah said. "Right now. That's what I keep telling myself."

But she knew that soon there would be an empty bed, eventually taken by someone else's loved one, another set of family and friends gathered around. How could it be? Her brain wanted to shut it down and so she did.

She went to Henry, took his hand in both of hers. She watched as each of her friends bent down to him, put their lips tenderly on his forehead, told him goodbye. Maya put her hand on top of hers. On the other side of the bed, Blue and Renee added their hands, as well.

They sat like that for a few moments, quiet and sad and together.

"Did you know sea otters hold hands while they sleep?" Renee said. "It's so they don't float away from each other."

"I like that," Maya said, squeezing.

"Me too," Hannah said.

"We'll be right outside if you need us," Maya said.

Hannah nodded, watched them go with the awful understanding that it was time. She sat alone with Henry, the sky at the window dressed in mourning black, the room mostly dark but for a soft shell of light over Henry's head, the dull glow of machinery. A hollow, sterile quality to the air, as if life had already been suctioned out of it. She took in Henry's beautiful face, the way his hair, in need of a trim, curled near his ears. She traced his big hands, put her head on his chest— the safest place she had ever known.

He was her first love, her first experience of tenderness and also of ecstasy. He had taught her how to drive, fixed her computer when it broke, listened to all her sorrows and dreams. He was her person, her one. After that nightmare night he'd become even more her safest place, in some way her imaginary friend, the one who never got mad, who never hurt her, who would never leave, a benevolent and steady presence in her life like Renee's Jesus. Without him she would be untethered.

She climbed into his bed, lay on top of him. Sobbed quietly so that he wouldn't know. Just in case. Just in case he was still in there, she didn't want to frighten him. She wanted to scream, *Why? Why?* and *Fight! Fight!* And against those words another voice in her head said, *Maybe this happened because he knows you'll be okay now, maybe he was waiting for that, maybe he sensed that it was time for both of you to let go.* She didn't want that and yet she understood. Even as she grieved, she understood.

She stayed like that for a long time, touching and pressing her body against his, memorizing the feel of him, his strong and steady heart, still here, still beating. She was ripped. She was full of love. She held on and held on and held on. She kissed his cheeks, sniffed for the sleep smell at his neck, but it was already gone, replaced by something medicinal.

It was too much. Too much. He was all she knew.

Finally, reluctantly, she climbed off. She sat beside him again, watched him breathe, memorizing each rise and fall of his chest. Stroked his arms, his hair. *I love you, I love you, I love you.* She raised his hand to her forehead and pressed it against her, imprinting its warmth there.

From the doorway, Vivian's soft voice. "Hi," she said.

Hannah looked up to see her enter. "Hi," she whispered back.

"Are you okay?"

Hannah shook her head, *no*, new tears brimming. "Are you?"

Vivian shrugged, gave a sad smile as she moved into the chair across from Hannah. "We're setting him free," she said. Her eyes welled. "I don't want to. I don't want to." She looked so old in the fragile light, as if loss made gravity stronger, stretching faces, casting shadows. She caressed Henry's face and Hannah imagined how many times she must have done that when he was just a newborn in her arms.

"The doctor will be in soon," Vivian said.

"I can go," Hannah said, though it was the last thing she wanted. "If you want to be alone."

Vivian reached across Henry's chest. "Stay," she said, grabbing Hannah's hand and squeezing. "He would want you here. I want you here. It won't be much longer."

A nurse came in quietly, double-checked if they were ready. A morphine drip and sedative were added, explained. The nurse's kindness brought on fresh tears. They waited. Hannah clung to each moment. Even as she suffered in the terrible anticipation, it seemed better than the finality. She forced herself to watch when the nurse unplugged the respirator, to bear witness to the end of everything that mattered to her. It was suddenly strikingly quiet. Her hand left Vivian's, found Henry's again. She watched his peaceful, undisturbed face. *I love you, Henry*, she thought. *It's going to be okay now.* His body gave a small shudder beneath her hand.

"He's going," Vivian said.

They each kissed his face and Hannah clutched his hand tight so he would know she was there.

"Goodbye, Henry," she whispered.

Goodbye.

EPILOGUE

They buried Henry on a quiet blue day in July amid mourners whose grief had been suspended for so many years it became relief. The four of them seemed to inhabit their own atmosphere, private and removed. Maya did not recognize herself as she moved through the ceremony, how subdued she could be. Beside her, Hannah was stoic, her shoulders pushed back as though she were once again at the bow of that whale-watching boat, at war with a fear that extended in every direction and beyond the horizon. Blue and Renee were calm, quiet presences throughout and, like Maya, watchful as spotters should Hannah fall apart. She did not.

When it was Maya's turn to say goodbye, she approached the casket, put her hands on the wood and imagined it as a small ship taking Henry on an adventure into another world. An ache of grief, pure and uncomplicated, filled her, felt not entirely bad, somehow satisfying in its truthfulness. It was as if memory had finally attached to some free-floating torment she'd been wrestling with, made it into an enemy more knowable and defined. For twelve years Henry had become something bigger and more nebulous in her mind, lived inside her as a formless accusation, an abrasion of guilt on her conscience. Now that he was gone, she could remember him as more than the constant quiet reminder of that night; she could remember him as her friend.

There would be no return to innocence. If she'd hoped, which of course she had, that the damage those men had inflicted would die with him, she was quick to realize it would not. It would never be fully gone for her, for any of them. It would sometimes be bigger and sometimes be smaller, but it was impossible to remove the psychic shrapnel of that singular bullet. Their bodies absorbed it, functioned around it.

And maybe innocence was overrated and resilience the opposite. Maybe there was beauty, not in suffering itself, but in the depth of intimacy it fostered with other people. Maybe that was the trade. She could tell herself that anyway. She could make it be real.

That night after the funeral, they crashed at Hannah's apartment and stayed up late sharing warm, funny memories of Henry. Maya tried not to think about anything but the present—not the eviction notice awaiting her, not Andy back in Montauk, not the yawning future or how little she understood of what she would do about any of it. For the next few days at least, she'd be staying on with Hannah to make sure she was okay.

The following day the four of them woke up late to the sun banging at the windows. Blue and Renee brought their bags down to the rental car and hugged Maya and Hannah goodbye.

Blue was, more than anything, relieved to be going home. It had all been so much and she needed time alone to process. Still, she was happy to have the company of Renee for several hours as she drove her back to Connecticut. She'd send a service to pick up Renee's car at Nana's, have it delivered to Renee's house. They were both too drained to take on the extra drive time themselves.

They were not suddenly back to being best friends. The deep trust they once shared had been shattered, for Blue, on that night long ago. Even if she wanted it to, her heart would not open too wide for Renee. But she was beginning to understand that life had a lot of pain and loss in it, so when the potential for repair was there, she should try to take it. She would leave space for something new to grow, not expect too much, nor dismiss the possibility of what could be.

When they reached Renee's, Blue parked the car and they sat for a moment.

"I wish we could just keep driving," Renee said.

"I can take a few more spins around the block," Blue offered.

Renee smiled sadly. "Not far enough." She flipped the visor mirror down and began to fix her hair. Her dress, the one she'd worn the day she arrived in Montauk, was wrinkled, her face drawn from sleeplessness, her makeup faded, and yet somehow she looked younger, or at least less guarded. She pulled out her lipstick, then sighed. "Hopeless," she said as she shoved it back into her purse without bothering to reapply it.

She glanced up at the house she shared with Darrin and back to Blue as if reminding herself there was someone there, more in her life than just him. "You think I should leave him, don't you?"

"You're asking my opinion on a love relationship?" Blue replied with a laugh. "I don't know what you should do."

"Part of me thinks I should just run. The other part of me thinks that's what I always do. I don't know which instinct is right. Either could be."

"I guess you'll know what you're going to do when you do it," Blue said.

Renee nodded. "Yeah. We'll see what he says when I confront him." She puffed up her cheeks, blew her bangs up on a big exhale. "This should be fun. I haven't even told him I'm pregnant yet."

"Good luck," Blue said. "You've got this. Let me know how it goes."

Renee climbed out of the car, ducked her head back in, smiled. "Thanks."

As Blue drove back to Manhattan, she imagined what was happening inside that house, whether Renee had walked in and confronted Darrin or whether she had paused just outside the door, pulled out her compact, reapplied her lipstick, put on her Renee smile, and said nothing. Blue was sure she knew what she would do if it were her, but everyone was always sure what they would do in a hypothetical.

It was almost evening by the time she reached the city and dropped off the car. She walked into her apartment, set down her bag in the empty foyer, and realized, not for the first time, how much she hated living there. And, too, how easy it would be to forget that, to once again be habituated into the familiarities of her life, accustomed to her misery. She called in sick the next three days and wandered her hallways, staring at the walls and out the window and in the mirror. She drank too much and got high and checked Jack's social media channels a dozen times a day and felt shame about it and reprimanded herself for being a stalker and then kept doing it anyway. She didn't know what she was looking for there.

The following week an offer came in on Nana's house for higher than what she'd asked. Blue took it off the market instead and turned in her two weeks' notice.

In September she packed up her stuff and left the city behind.

Early fall settled over Montauk, blowing in waves the color of dolphins and winds like chilled glass. Blue turned the corner onto Nana's street, now her street, with the last of her belongings. Fear zapped her in intermittent surges. What was she going to do out here? She had no plan, no direction. She'd been rash making so many drastic changes at once. It was so unlike her. But death had been undraped from denial in the days after Henry's funeral. And death did that—it made you scramble for life. Grab without thinking.

She'd noticed, as she drove through town, that the restaurant she'd once loved so much was still up for sale.

She could afford it.

Of course, she didn't know how to run a restaurant.

And restaurants were a bad bet. Everyone knew that.

But the idea of a place where people would gather for joy, a place she could come and go and always belong—she liked the thought of it.

Probably she wouldn't do it.

But maybe she would.

And of course, in the back of her mind, Jack. She knew it was inevitable she would bump into him somewhere in town.

She'd finally found the courage to text him an apology. His reply had been muted. "Don't worry about it. It's all good." Blue knew it was a blow off. Whenever she thought about it, it was like a slow, sharp razor across her chest. Still, she fantasized about the day when she would maybe own that restaurant and he would happen to walk in, see the afternoon sunlight spilled like a drink across the polished bar, surfboards riding the beechwood walls, a large aquarium in the corner teeming with fanciful fish. And be impressed. This was as far as she could walk it. With him or any other man. Love was still too dangerous a hope to carry. For now she'd settle for making her life better and hoping someone would notice.

She pulled in to her driveway, got out and looked up at Nana's house, her house. She did love it so. Dust motes floated in the panels of light through the windows as she entered. A chaos of boxes and paint buckets and cleaning supplies was scattered everywhere. She put down the grocery bag of sandwiches and snacks and drinks she'd bought for the girls and put them away. The clock on the microwave said noon. They'd be here any minute. She went outside, lit up. She'd promised herself she'd quit after the move, but then life hadn't quit and there was too much stress and *tomorrow*, she told herself, *tomorrow I'll do it.*

The traffic out front had thinned to a dribble. It was so quiet here after Labor Day. Soon early darkness would take over, the air would smell of wood smoke and then of snow, and only the locals would remain.

It would be lonely. But then that wasn't new.

And, too, she needed it—the quiet and the clean air and the open space. It was so hard to know yourself or what you wanted when there was so much noise and too many people and every city breath engaged her lungs in extra labor.

She heard the familiar sound of pebbles hopping under tires followed by cheerful honking as Maya, Hannah and Renee pulled in. One last drag on her cigarette, then she stubbed it out and stepped forward to greet them.

"Hey!" Renee said, climbing out. She hadn't started to show yet but there was a flush in her cheeks that made her look more like the teenager Blue remembered. She moved as if to hug Blue, then paused, unsure. The bond was still so fragile.

"I'll grab your bag," Blue said instead.

"I could kiss the ground!" Maya said, stepping into the sunshine. "Grandma—" she pointed toward Hannah "—drove the last leg, clocking five miles under the speed limit and wouldn't let us turn on the radio because it was 'too distracting.'"

"I told you guys you could drive if you wanted," Hannah said.

"Technically Maya did," Renee said. "From the back seat."

Blue shook her head and laughed.

Hannah smiled through tired eyes. Blue noticed the subtle drag in her movement and took her bag, gave her shoulder a squeeze. "I'm just happy you're here," she said. "Seriously, thanks so much for coming out to help, guys. I should probably warn you…"

Blue let the mess in the foyer finish her sentence for her. Maya let out a low whistle as they waded through the minefield of supplies and unlabeled boxes. Blue shot her a warning look. She'd given Maya a loan for her house on the condition she get a second job to pay it back. And Maya had actually done it, gotten herself an additional job selling paint or something random. Still Blue knew that whenever Maya had money, she spent it. If Blue was lucky, she'd see half of that loan returned, so she planned to hold the debt over Maya's head as much as possible.

Now she sighed, overwhelmed. "I didn't even bother to sort it. Just moved all my junk here. I don't even know where to start."

Renee put her hands on her hips, surveyed the scene. "We should probably throw out everything you don't need first," she said. "Then we can work with whatever's left."

They all nodded.

A daunting task.

But a start.

Perhaps even a life philosophy.

They headed upstairs to drop off their bags.

Hannah was the last one up and with an effort that belied her years. Grief, she was learning, moved in slow, heavy turns, made a shipwreck of its inhabitants, pinned them in its murky aquatic hold. But today, or at least in this moment, the ache was accompanied by gladness. It was like a fluid leak into the wrong engine, the way hope could find its way into sorrow.

She entered their room and Maya turned and gave her an encouraging smile. She gave one back. "You look tired," she said, just noticing now. Maya never looked tired.

"I worked fourteen hours yesterday," Maya said.

"Ugh," Hannah said.

Maya shrugged. "It's temporary."

Hannah knew Maya's optimism was sincere, that Maya's greatest strength was her refusal to get pulled down by life's hardships. Their whole life Maya had always been one step ahead of suffering, in the place of possibility where things were better. Still, it seemed that Hannah could see the vulnerability in everyone's eyes lately, even Maya's, and this, too, was a product of loss—the deeper attunement to struggle. She felt the shared question inside them, in every person she passed—*will I be okay?*—the uncertainty more conscious in some than others but each tending to it in their own way, this baby in need of constant soothing. And this thought gave her a great empathy for humanity and for herself and for all the various ineffective tools that people use to beat back the terror of their own fragility, of life's unpredictability and potential for pain. For the first time in a long while she felt that she was not alone, not crazy, that she was just coping, getting by like everyone else.

They unpacked their stuff, ate lunch at the picnic table under birdsong and the gaze of a doe who had wandered into the yard and a September sky the saturated blue of oceans on a globe.

Then they began the work.

Hannah was put in charge of cleaning, Renee organizing and rearranging with her decorative eye, Blue tossing out all that was useless or old or didn't belong to her. Maya moved between them, lending a hand and pausing with unnecessary frequency for refreshments. The light shifted across their conversations, their silences. Hannah was grateful for the work, for the way it occupied her mind, pushed her back into her body and against grief's propensity toward inertia.

She saw Renee repeatedly check her phone, and something in the furtiveness of the act raised Hannah's suspicion that she was communicating with Darrin. Blue and Maya must have noticed, too, because each time it happened, they glanced at each other with a raised eyebrow.

"He wants to go to therapy," Renee blurted finally.

Maya sighed. "They all say that when they're caught. Men like him don't change."

"I think they can," Renee said. "If they want to enough." She looked to Blue.

"I'm inclined to agree with Maya," Blue said. "But I concede that anything's possible."

"I have to try at least," Renee said.

Hannah understood. It was so hard to know when to give up on a person. To know who could be fixed and who could not. Nothing was ever as simple as it seemed. And so often the only answer, the hard but only answer, was to wait and see.

Still, she hoped, they all hoped, Renee wasn't just settling because it was easier to deny a problem than to truly face one. The cost for that was always higher, both in pain and lost years. They'd seen that play out before with Renee, and Hannah worried this was merely a new version. But she couldn't be sure. Change was often incremental, almost imperceptible to the observer. Failing to see it didn't mean it wasn't happening.

The light shifted again. Shadows crossing the room and quiet descending like weather. Everyone preoccupied with their work and their thoughts. Hannah surveyed her friends. They were inhabiting such different lives from what she had once imagined. Not that she'd ever had a particular picture of what they'd all become. It was just that she never expected their adulthood to be so...ordinary. Somehow youth had made her friends seem larger than life, destined for greatness. But then, what was that?

Where would they all be ten years from now? she wondered. *Would the answer surprise her?*

Renee stood up, looked around at the few remaining boxes in the foyer. "I'm starving," she said. "Anyone up for dinner?"

"I hear there's a great place for lobster rolls on the docks," Maya said. "I'd be happy to pick some up...if Blue gives me cash."

"Can't possibly imagine why you'd want to go to the docks," Blue said.

Maya smiled, the grin of a girl falling in love. "I did mention we'd stop by. And hey, maybe Andy has cute friends."

"Not for me," Hannah said. "It's going to be a long time before I'm ready for that."

"As if you know what life will do," Maya said.

Hannah thought of Henry then, and her heart was pierced with such sharp longing that it took her breath away. The girls continued discussing dinner plans but the thought of going out left Hannah suddenly exhausted.

"If you guys don't mind, I think I'm going to stay here," she said. "Close my eyes for a little while. Bring me something back?"

"You got it," Maya said.

Hannah placed her order and headed upstairs. But instead of lying down, she pulled out her laptop and sat down at the desk by the window. Ever since Henry died, she and Vivian had been meeting once or twice a week for coffee and Vivian had been gently encouraging her—the way a mother might—to work on her novel. She'd even read some pages and given Hannah constructive feedback. Whatever fear she'd had that Vivian would have no use for her if anything happened to Henry had quickly been assuaged. She understood now that they would always be deeply important to each other, that, like the girls, Vivian was her chosen family.

It was so essential—she understood this now—to not be alone for too long, to not lock herself away, no matter the pull to do so. Alone was where pain was magnified by too much silence and too much time; alone for too long was where fear was bred. Gratefully even the work on her novel took her out of her own head, put her in the company of characters. Her favorite daydream was of the dedication she would someday write to Henry so that he would live on as a loved person in the first page of a book, maybe even live beyond her. And the idea of the acknowledgments at the back, to her friends, her first responders, to eternalize in print her gratitude for their lifelong rescue efforts.

Still she didn't want the girls to know just yet that she'd started working on her novel again. It might be a false start, another project she'd end up abandoning and then be ashamed about. It was still a fight every day, the rebuilding of a muscle that had atrophied—not just writing, but hope. She listened to the clatter and chatter of her friends as they headed to the car, let the noise sink into the background and finally disappear. Soon the ache for Henry retreated, or at least quieted to a dull pang. She opened the document and reread what she'd written. Then she stared at the blank page before her, put her hands on the keyboard and tried to trust that something would come.

★ ★ ★ ★ ★

ACKNOWLEDGMENTS

My amazing editor Emily Ohanjanians for understanding this book so well and helping me to shape it into what I wanted it to be. I feel so lucky to have you. My fierce agent, Catherine Drayton, for your support, critical eye and honesty. Everyone at MIRA who helped this book make its journey into the world.

Jeff Zentner for your unmatched wit, incredible mind, emotional attunement, beautiful books and best of all your friendship. You always show up.

Jennifer Niven, Angelo Surmelis and the rest of my LA friend-family who keep me in laughter, great conversation and lots of cake; Adriana Mather for your percipience and your chill; Nicola Yoon and Charlotte Huang, my original crew and favorite dinner companions; Jeff Giles, ever brilliant, funny and on call; and all the other wonderful, talented authors whom I have the great privilege to call my friends. You are the best thing in publishing and have brought so much joy and fellowship to my life.

Dr. Susan Nagin Thau for your empathy, wisdom and strength; Dr. David Neer, whose kindness makes my heart grow; Bob Maloney, a mentor, friend and a force of nature; Katie Cunningham Tashjian and Mary Cunningham, for your huge hearts and munificent spirits; the magnanimous and lovely Kelly Rutherford to whom I am indebted; Lori Barnett and Melinda Rennert Mizuno, who set me on this path; Alexa Jade, water child of my heart; Savannah Sullivan, the brightest light; the great Ryan Labay and his wonderful crew; Tammy Rayevich Leitch for all the summers; and all my friends near and far, old and new, who championed my first book with such unbelievable enthusiasm, generosity and kindness that I cannot even think about it without crying. To have your love and support has been the most humbling, beautiful, life-changing experience, and I'll never forget it.

For the readers, thank you for spending time in these worlds I imagine and letting me do what I love.

For the librarians, teachers, booksellers, reviewers and bloggers who spread their passion for books—we've never needed you more.

And finally, most important, David Zorn, love of my life, best person I've ever known, who should probably get cowriting credit on all my work for the endless (endless!) reads and smart, careful critiques of my many drafts. You are the king of patience, insight, comedy, kindness, compassion, integrity and good hugs. I don't know how I got so lucky with you but I'm grateful every single day.

Thank you.

EAST
COAST
GIRLS

KERRY KLETTER

Reader's Guide

mira

1. Hannah, Maya, Blue and Renee are all such distinct personalities. Which character did you most identify with and why? Did you empathize more with any one character than the others?

2. The four characters shared similar childhoods in that their mothers were absent or abusive. As a result they became one another's family. What are your thoughts on the subject of "chosen" versus "given" family?

3. The characters have all been deeply affected by the events of that terrible night twelve years ago. How did each of them internalize the incident, and how has that internalization played out in their life choices? How do their individual ways of coping now get in their way? What patterns do they each keep playing out?

4. What did you think of Blue and Renee's friendship? Did you agree with the reason Blue cut Renee out of her life after that terrible night? Did you want to see them restore their friendship during the story? What do you imagine you would have done in Renee's position?

5. How did you feel about Renee's character? Did you feel that you wanted to see scenes from her point of view or did you feel she didn't deserve one, given her role within the foursome?

6. How do you feel that the setting—Montauk, Nana's beach house—added to the story? What did it represent for the characters?

7. Lately there's been a lot of conversation about sexual harassment and the kinds of safety measures women are forced to take when they go out into the world. Men often seem surprised by the fact that many women stay silent and endure harassment, and yet, as in Maya's case, confrontation can carry its own risks. How do you feel about the bind women are put in, where they are forced to absorb street harassment and accept it as part of life or risk danger simply by defending themselves? What would you have done in Maya's position? What can we do as a society to put an end to the harassment of women?

8. How did the characters change throughout the story? How did your opinion of them change? Did any of the characters stay the same?

9. How did you feel about the ending? What did you like or not like about the way the story resolved?

10. Maya and Hannah have a yin-and-yang relationship. Sometimes Hannah takes comfort in Maya's practicality and the way she dismisses Hannah's fears. Other times she feels that Maya is insensitive—perceiving her anxiety as a weakness, hiding her Xanax, having strong, mostly unspoken opinions around the subject of Henry. Since Maya is largely a compassionate person, what do you imagine drives her insensitivity? Do you think it's simply

that she doesn't understand? Is she a product of a society that tends to see people struggling with mental illness in a diminishing way, particularly women? Or do you think Maya is acting out of her own trauma?

11. When Maya and Hannah go looking for the psychic, they grapple with the idea of fate. Do you believe in fate? Do you agree with Maya that, either way, it's better not to know the future, or are there things you'd like to know? If so, what are they?

12. If this was going to be made into a movie, who would you cast in the roles of the four women?

What inspired you to write this story?

I always start out with a question I'd like to find the answer to myself. In this case, I'd just sold my first book, my friends were so incredibly supportive and I was struck, as I often am, by how important and extraordinary it is to have good friends. At the same time, my best friend got very sick and, as happens, we were all suddenly confronted with the fragility of life. It was a very frightening time and I was keenly aware of just how hard and painful it is to love people when we have to live with the possibility of losing them. So I wanted to answer the question for myself, which is Hannah's question in the book: How does one live, really live—capital L—in such an uncertain, sometimes scary world where out of the blue something bad can happen? How do we let go of the reins and just accept what life brings us instead of wanting to run and hide and pull the covers over our head and never take a risk or love too much because what if something went wrong? And what are the ways in which those fears mute the experience of living and how can we step away from them— how can we hold the duality of joy and precariousness, love and loss? So I started from there and the book came out of that and then, happily, my friend got well and here we are.

Why did you decide to set the book in Montauk?

I grew up spending summers on the East End and surfing out in Montauk. It's such a beautiful place and has this interesting quality of being at once rugged and soft. There are these stark, ragged cliffs that hang out over gentle beaches and this odd combination of craggy fishermen and old-school surfers mixed with young hipsters and wealthy city people. I felt like it was a town that perfectly mirrored the past-present aspect of the story because of the transformations it's gone through over the years. Each summer I go back, the restaurants get a little fancier, the beaches more crowded, but just as one of the characters says in the book, "the bones of the place are the same." And that's exactly what old friends are like—they grow and change in ways that are both good and bad—but the essence of who they are remains steadfast and that's what keeps the bond intact.

Why did you choose characters who were all self-described orphans in one way or another?

We tend to say as a society that "family is everything" but not everyone has a loving family or one with whom they connect, so I wanted to write a story about the family we choose. These girls had far from perfect lives growing up, but what mattered was that their lives were perfect when they were together, especially when they had these idyllic times every July at the Montauk house. I loved the idea of these lonely, lost girls finding one another and having this cocoon of friendship where they raise one another and stand in for the families they each don't have. And of course, this gets more complicated as they get older because things happen, difficult experiences alter them and they start to bump up against each other. But still they recognize that they need one another, that they have agreed to be passengers on one another's life ride, through good and bad. So I wanted to write about how they traverse that and just in general about the saving grace of friendship. At the end of the day, this is my love letter to the friends in my life who have been my own chosen family.

The characters go through a traumatic experience together that changes them all in profound but different ways. Why did you decide to make that part of their history?

One thing I've been thinking about a lot lately is how by a certain age we've all been traumatized in one way or another, and the methods, largely unconscious, we each use to cope can interfere with our attachments and cause a lot of unintended pain. I made the characters experience the same traumatic event to illustrate how even when the pain is shared, we don't always see or recognize the wound that's driving someone else's behavior; how, for instance, someone turning away from us may be doing so because they feel shame and not because they don't love us. We're all interpreting other people through our own very limited and distorted lenses and it causes a lot of misunderstanding and strife. So part of this book, for me, was about exploring how that happens, how we can fail to see even those closest to us and then learning to find grace for our flawed humanity, our flawed methods of coping. At the end of the day, we're all just doing our best to get through an unpredictable world, and nobody gets it right even when there's love. I feel like that's an important thing to hold, especially in today's culture where people's humanity can be flattened to a single moment, and one mistake, even sometimes a small one, can define a life.

What was your favorite part of writing this book?

The girls having fun. I love the parts where the bond is really visible, whether in the past or present, and they're riffing on one another or simply happy to be together—all of that was a blast to write. It gave me the same warm, happy feeling that being with my real-life friends gives me.

And, too, I loved working with my editor. It's magical when someone sees exactly where your blind spots have been in the book, the parts you missed or didn't develop well enough, and as you're fixing it, you can feel the book coming to life in a new way. That was really exciting for me. Editing is always my favorite part but it's especially fun when that happens.

What did you find most challenging about writing this book?

It took me a long time to really understand Renee—in part because I wasn't writing her inner thoughts as with the others and also because I think she's the least like me. Draft after draft she kept eluding me until I finally realized she was eluding me by design—that she was unknowable to me because she was largely unknown to herself. She's been running from everything for so long, seeking herself in external things—her appearance, an engagement ring, the trappings of what society tells us is a desirable life—that her true self has atrophied to a certain extent by being denied air. Once I realized that—how Renee's entire personality is shaped around self-protection and trying to escape the one thing she can't, which is herself and her fear of being unlovable—I finally understood her and liked her and saw that glimmer of a person who wants connection and repair and realness and who could move toward it if she could find a way back into the group.

What kind of research went into writing this story?

One of my primary interests is the subject of trauma—how it affects our brains, behavior and attachments, so I'm always studying that and incorporating what I learn into my work. And of course, I researched Henry's condition but sadly was also able to draw on lived experience. Someone I knew was in a minimally conscious state for many years, and I watched someone I love, who was very close to that person, struggle with that very difficult reality.

Is there a character in the story that you identify with most? Or a favorite character among the four main women?

Oh, I think that would just depend on the day. Sometimes I can be anxious like Hannah—I'm definitely a bit of a germophobe and I really don't like uncertainty. My sense of humor and love of fun is pretty in line with Maya's. I have been known to cover hurt and vulnerability by shutting down at times like Blue, or even running away like Renee. So I see myself in all of them. As far as favorites, I think Maya edges the others out just a bit. I love her for being so unapologetically herself and I think she is always primarily motivated by love—not just the desire to be loved but to love other people, to share life with loved ones. She just wants everyone to be happy.

Can you describe your writing process?

So, as I said, I always start with a question I'm grappling with in my own life. Once I have the question, I simply start writing. At that point I have no idea what will pop up. If I just sit down and put my hands on the keyboard, a character with a problem inevitably appears. I let my subconscious rule until it runs out of steam—my hope is always that it will produce a fully formed book but, alas, the burst of creativity peters out by around chapter two. Then I have to stop and think about what I have and where it might lead and try to develop a loose outline of a story. The rest is just winging it until I have a draft. Then, because that first draft is terrible, I rewrite, replot over and over until finally it clicks and I hit a flow where I know what the story is, who the characters are and what I'm trying to say. I dream of the day I nail it on the first try—but until that miraculous day appears, I am very grateful to have early readers and an editor to help me out.

In writing as in life, we make mistakes, take wrong turns, and if we're lucky, we have people who gently, honestly set us back on track. I think it's what I love the most about it. It's a great reminder that you can always rewrite your story—if something's not working, you can make another choice. As the characters learn that in their lives, so, too, does the writer in her own.